SAVAGE SURRENDER

"I hate you," Katelyn cried.

"No, you don't hate me. You fear me but you don't hate me." Night Fox's voice was a mere whisper.

She met his haunting black eyes without flinching. "I hate you," she lied. "I hate you because you kidnapped me. I hate you because you made me your slave . . ." *I hate you because I can't despise you the way I should.*

Fox pulled her closer, savoring the warmth of her damp skin beneath his touch.

She trembled in his grasp, unable to tear her eyes from his. She remembered the taste of his mouth on hers and her tongue darted out to dampen her dry lips. "I hate you because you touch me . . ." she breathed.

Quivering, she let herself be drawn into his arms. No one had ever tried to comfort her before, no one had ever cared enough. Why did it have to be this man, she wondered, as he bent his head towards her. Why the enemy? She felt herself moving to meet his kiss, her arms easing around his neck to bring him nearer . . .

D1714648

Forbidden Caress

Colleen Faulkner

ZEBRA BOOKS
KENSINGTON PUBLISHING CORP.

ZEBRA BOOKS

are published by

Kensington Publishing Corp.
475 Park Avenue South
New York, NY 10016

First printing: May 1987

Printed in the United States of America

*To my mother, who taught me to read,
and inspired me to write.*

Prologue

The heavy library door swung open with a bang and the pale woman turned anxiously to face her father. Her slim hands were hidden beneath the folds of the full apron that covered her morning gown. Beneath the dust cap her russet hair was in slight disarray. She was embarrassed to be appearing before her father in such dishevelment but her young brother had insisted she come immediately. Father had just had two very important visitors and he wanted to speak to her at once.

"I have grand news, Katie. Your first proposal! We've waited so long for this! A Henry Artemis Bullman has requested your hand in marriage." The elderly Reverend Locke clutched his chubby hands in joy.

Katelyn's eyes widened, a slight smile crossing her lips. "So soon? I hadn't expected a proposal so soon!"

"Yes, the news traveled quickly. I knew it would. Every eligible man on the coast of Dover has known for some time now what a charitable wife you'd make, in the right circumstance."

Circumstances, Katelyn knew, meant dowry. No one had been willing to marry her before her father had inherited the three thousand pounds from a distant uncle.

"Tell me what this Henry Bullman is like, Father." Her voice grew husky with excitement.

The Reverend took a few steps closer to his daughter and grasped one hand. He knew Katelyn was a bit flustered by this sudden change in status. What unmarried girl of twenty-four wouldn't be? But, thank the Blessed Lord, his daughter wasn't going to be an old maid. No indeed! It seemed it was soon going to be her good fortune to be wedded and with child within appropriate time.

"Well, Katie, he's a grand young man."

Her honey-colored eyes dropped, the sparkle fading. She knew it had been too good to be true. "You didn't tell him how old I was, did you?"

"Now, now. I told him your precise age and it matters not." He beamed proudly, patting her hand.

Katelyn's eyelashes fluttered. "He . . . he knows?" She withdrew her hand from her father's sweaty palms. These unusual sparks of affection always made her uncomfortable. Who was deceiving whom? The Reverend Locke probably loved his daughter in his own way, but he never had a personal relationship with her or any other woman. After Katelyn's mother died he had remarried a much younger woman, hoping to father a son. Once Gaither was born, whatever time the Reverend didn't spend within his Parish, was spent with his son. He provided for his young wife and daughter but considered them merely tools the Lord had furnished him with to help carry God's word to the troubled men of England.

"So tell me, what is he like?"

"Naturally, I spoke mostly to the father, but the boy

seems rather intelligent. The elder Bullman is a Squire in the Maryland Colony, a very successful business-man as well as a farmer, he tells me."

"The Maryland Colony? They live in the wilderness of America?" Katelyn's pulse quickened. "You'd permit me to go to the Colonies?" She knew she must be dreaming. Things like this didn't happen to a Rever-end's daughter in Dover.

"We'll miss you dearly; a girl will have to be hired to take over your chores. But this is a fine opportunity. The father mentioned a wedding gift of some two thousand acres of prime farm land."

Her mind whirled. Up to this point in her life her days had been so orderly, so predictable, . . . so boring. Up until a month ago she had expected to live her days out imprisoned by her circumstances, in her father's dreary home. Because he was a clergyman, what little he owned would someday go to his son, leaving nothing for his daughter's dowry. Though she had been educated and reared as a lady should be, it had never been expected that she would have the chance to prove herself as a wife. Only because the fluke inheritance did Katelyn have a chance. But now the thought of leaving her father and little brother . . . her home . . . England . . . the thought was terrifying! But it was also exciting! Why, she'd never even been to London! Excitement was *not* part of Katelyn Locke's life.

"Yes." She nodded with stubborn determination.

"Yes, what?" The Reverend's eyes crinkled in confu-sion.

"Yes, I will marry this Colonial . . . Henry." She tasted the sound of his name on her tongue, suddenly more sure of this decision than of any she'd made in her life. Who was to say if there'd be any other proposals? She wasn't going to live the life of a spinster if she didn't have to! She was going to the Colonies!

"Wouldn't you like to meet the boy first? Talk to him? Perhaps your interests aren't similar." The pudgy man was bewildered by his daughter's abrupt decision. Granted, it would be easier once she was gone; her constant defiance of his rules had been a heavy cross to bear. But he didn't want her to think that she had to throw herself at the first man who ever paid her any regard.

"What interests should a woman have other than her good husband, abundant children, and God's laws?" Katelyn replied, a trace of sarcasm in her voice. "You've said so often enough. Besides," she added, a mischievous smile playing across her lips, "you've met him, Father. If you think he is suitable, than I'm in perfect agreement."

Chapter One

Katelyn sat in the rough wagon, her hands folded demurely on her lap. She took in great gulps of the fresh morning air, trying to absorb the sweet warmth of the sun just beginning to climb the cloudless, Dresden-blue sky. The seat swayed to and fro reminding her of the long journey from England.

The weeks aboard the *Cassandra* had not been easy ones, and she had spent most of the voyage below decks trying desperately not to be ill. No, she decided, she was by no means a sailor. But here she was, finally, the Maryland Colony. Katelyn had never imagined it could be so utterly beautiful, so . . . so untamed!

She smiled hesitantly at the man beside her as he slid his hand over hers and continued his conversation with the young blackamoor driving the team of horses.

She didn't know what was wrong with her. Henry was the perfect English gentleman—intelligent, cultured, and charming. He would make the perfect husband. He had rescued her from her father's home and brought her to the Colonies to be the wife of a wealthy tobacco farmer. So why was she so uneasy? Why didn't she trust him?

You should be honored he chose you, she told herself as she watched the way the breeze ruffled his flaxen hair, the way his clear blue eyes sparkled as he spoke. *You never expected to catch such a handsome husband. You never expected to catch a husband at all!*

Maybe it's you, a voice whispered inside her. *Why would he want to marry you?* Katelyn was no fool. She knew mud-brown eyes, pale skin, and hair of a nondescript color were not features a man looked for in a wife.

But what could be done now? She was betrothed to Henry Bullman, and they would be wed within the week. Only time would tell. She probably just had the jitters, like any woman about to be married to a man she didn't really know.

Her mind drifted to thoughts of the wedding . . . her wedding, the one of which she had dreamed. From what Henry had told her, the ceremony and party afterwards, as well as their trip to Williamsburg, were all just as if she'd planned them herself. She regretted that her father had not been able to marry them before they set sail. But, Henry's father had promised a wedding gift of two thousand acres of land, provided they were wed in America. Squire Bullman felt that it was only proper that they be married before their friends and relatives since Henry was the first generation of Bullmans born in the colonies.

The wagon hit a bump on the dirt road and jolted Katelyn out of her dreamy daze. Her eyes turned to the raw beauty of the surrounding forest as the wagon rolled on. The Maryland Colony was just as she had visualized, only the colors were brighter, and the scent of the wildflowers more intense. Father had been so wrong. He had warned her that the colonies were uncivilized, that wild animals roamed the woods and that heathen savages plundered the towns carrying off women and children. Mistress Plinkerton, the lady who had been her traveling companion, had been far closer in her description. This really was paradise!

Katelyn peered into the thick woods as the horses pulled the wagon down the path at an even clip-clopping pace. She wished Henry would offer her a lap robe as the dust was sure to ruin her blue brocade gown. The dress has been a going away gift from her stepmother who had said the brilliant color might brighten her sallow complexion. She knew she should put up her parasol before she began to freckle but she hated to block out the glorious sunshine. Had the sun ever shone this bright in England?

"Henry." Katelyn nudged him with a gloved hand.

"Yes, love, what is it?"

"What's that?" She pointed toward the deep woods. "That hut sort of thing."

"It's an Injun house, Mistress Katelyn." Jonathan reined in the horses so that she could get a better look.

"There's another one!"

"Redskins? Good Lord! Thought we'd driven them out of these parts months ago." Henry reached into his breast pocket and took out a gold snuff box.

Repulsed, Katelyn turned to study the odd Indian dwelling. That nasty stuff was the first thing that was going after they were married. She didn't care if it was all the rage. It was a disgusting habit that made her sick to her stomach!

"What say we have a look, love?" Henry sniffed through one nostril and then the other.

"Do you think we should?" she questioned, already standing to get out of the wagon.

Jonathan shook his head. "I doesn't know, Masta Henry. Big Masta Henry say I was to pick yous up at

13

the ha'bor in Nap'lis an' bring yous straight home. He di'n say nuffin' 'bout comin' this way an' he shore di'n say to be stoppin' an' lookin' at no Injun houses!"

"Nonsense. If you're afraid, sit here. We're going to have a look." He jumped down and reached to help her down.

"Are we in any danger?"

"From a few louse-ridden savages?" Henry laughed. "I hope we do see one. I'll make short work of him!"

"Big Masta gonna have my skin if'in anythin' happens to yous two." Jonathan tied the reins to the side of the buckboard and leaped off the other side.

"What could possibly happen? I'd just like to get a closer look, maybe find a trinket made by the red beasts. Wouldn't that be something to show our sons, love? Real redskin beads or maybe a tomahawk?"

"Anything you say, dear." Katelyn smiled, surprised by her bold use of such an endearment.

Together the three entered the forest, coming quickly to the clearing they had spotted from the road. Katelyn and Henry walked to the middle of the grassy knoll while Jonathan waited impatiently near the edge of the woods.

In the clearing were a dozen bark and grass huts in a circle, eleven round ones and one dome shaped hut with an arched roof. The huts were made of young saplings driven into the ground and then bent and tied with twisted reeds. There were smaller tree limbs threaded crosswise through the framework with shingles made of bark.

Katelyn stood with her mouth hanging open in a very unladylike manner. "It was a little town," she whispered in awe. "Look, there was the garden." She pointed to a raised bed of earth now overgrown with weeds. "Oh Henry, it's beautiful, isn't it?"

He turned to her, curling his lips cynically as he

14

spoke. "Are you daft, woman? Filthy savages lived here."

She took a step back, confused and hurt by his sharp remark.

Henry sauntered over to the oblong house, coming to stand in front of a mat on hinges, what was obviously a door. "Hey Jonathan, what are these spears doing here?" He pulled one from the ground.

The servant came running, his eyes wide with fright. "Masta Henry, I doesn't think you oughts to be touchin' that. Them there spears was put there for a reason. Them savages doesn't like people messin' with their things. I think we best be goin' 'fore we's in big trouble."

"Maybe he's right." Katelyn shivered despite the warm sunshine. Something wasn't right. She could sense it. "Your father is expecting us. Maybe we should go."

"Look, it will only take a minute. I just want to see if there's anything here worth taking." Henry leaned the spear against the hut and came to stand next to her, taking her hand. "Listen, Love, why don't you go into the next clearing and pick some flowers?" He pointed farther into the woods where yellow flowers bloomed.

"All right," she agreed against her better judgement. "But hurry."

Henry reached down to boldly brush his lips against her cheek but she stepped back, still angry with him.

"By your leave, sir! We're not wed yet!" Without another word she sashayed off, her head held high.

Reaching the next clearing, Katelyn dropped to the ground and began to gather the yellow buttercups that covered the ground. What was wrong with Henry? *What have I gotten myself into? Well, too late to worry now, only time will tell.* She smiled at herself as a old ballad Cook had taught her came to mind. Softly she sang, her bright hair swaying with the light breeze.

15

"Father, dear Father, you've done me
great wrong.
You've married me to boy who is
too young . . ."

The Lenni Lenape brave crouched amidst a thicket
of pokeberries watching the slim woman with hair of
the red fox wander closer to him. He crouched even
lower as she kneeled picking buttercups only steps from
him. She sang softly, entrancing him as soft wisps of
bright hair blew gently in the wind. Her eyes were the
color of a doe's, soft and gentle. The brave longed to
reach out and touch her pale skin, to run his fingers
through her magic colored hair. He wondered why she
was here as he began to move silently along the
hedgerow.

Tipaakke's hand slid to the stone knife in his belt and
his eyes narrowed as he spotted the white man dese-
crating the Big House in his deserted village. How dare
he disturb a gravesite!

Tipaakke pulled his lips taut, letting loose the cry of
the whippoorwill. His call was immediately answered
once, twice, three times as his hunting companions let
him know how close they were. The braves had been on
a hunting expedition when they had decided to pass by
the old village and leave an extra prayer for the passage
of their dead loved ones.

Henry pulled at the mat, finding it impossible to
untie the leather thongs that kept it shut. He didn't
know what the savages were keeping inside but it
certainly had to be worth something the way they had
the hut sealed. The door finally tore from the hinges
causing Henry to tumble back into the dirt.

Katelyn glanced in Henry's direction as he dusted off
his breeches. She shook her head and continued to pick

small flowers, wishing he would hurry.

"Damn, Jonathan! Nothing here but a few stinking bodies!" he shouted, sticking his head out of the door.

Jonathan retreated to the wagon and jumped onto the seat, reins in hand. "Lordy Masta Henry, say a prayer quick an' get you'self outa there! Mistress Katelyn, we goin' now," he shouted, obviously petrified.

Henry stepped into the hut, pulling a lace handkerchief from his pocket and holding it under his nose. Good God, he'd come this far, he decided he might as well have a look around. On both sides of the long hut were benches built from split logs, and on the benches were five bodies. Henry kicked over the bark buckets of water and meal lined neatly along the floor. He saw nothing of value. At the very end of the hut was the body of a young boy of five or six. He started to turn around when something caught his eye. Clutched in the rotting hand was a small axe with a wooden handle and a stone blade. The wood was painted red, with leather streamers and a fox tail hanging from it. Holding his handkerchief with one hand, Henry snatched the axe with the other.

Tipaakke let out a shrill, terrifying cry as he leaped over the hedge of pokeberries. The girl screamed shrilly. The Delaware brave wasted precious seconds turning to see a companion pinning her to the ground.

"Maata!" Tipaakke shouted, his voice threatening. *"Maata nahiila!"*

The brave leaped off the girl and sprinted towards the clearing.

Tipaakke swore softly under his breath as he spied the white man racing toward the wagon. The brave realized his concern for the girl had probably saved the dog's life. Irritated with himself, he set out after the man. What was this pale slip of a girl to him?

17

Henry leaped into the wagon, ripping the reins from Jonathan's hands and slapping the leather sharply against the horses' flesh.

"Masta Henry, Masta Henry! Mistress Katelyn! Where is Mistress Katelyn?" The servant held tightly to the buckboard as the horses bolted under the pain of the lash and took off.

Horrified, Henry looked back over his shoulder to see an Indian gaining on them. The redskin was running at an unbelievable pace. A war cry rattled Henry's bones, and he soaked his breeches with urine.

Jonathan grabbed for the reins Henry clutched in an inhuman grip. "Masta Henry! We cant's just leave Mistress Katelyn! What's wrong with you? Them savages will kill her for shore . . . or worse!"

Henry gave the blackamoor a swift kick. Jonathan lost his balance and tumbled out of the careening wagon. He screamed as he fell, his skull cracking like a rotten melon.

Katelyn lay in a ball in the tall grass too petrified to move. She knew she should be praying but no words came to mind. *My God! He's leaving me!* her mind screamed. She rolled over and forced herself to stand. *Run! Run!* Finally her limbs began to obey. She raced toward the road, her bonnet tumbling from her head, the bundle of wild flowers still clutched in her gloved hand.

"Henry!" she screamed. "Wait for me!" She leaped over a stump and forced her way through a hedgerow that stood between her and the road. The prickly ash briars tore at her gown, ripping the blue brocade to shreds; the tree limbs tore at her hair. She tripped, falling onto the dirt road. Pain shot up her right leg as she looked up to see Jonathan tumbling from the speeding wagon. The blood from his head spewed in a thousand directions as Katelyn dropped her face into

18

the dust, sobbing.

She wasn't sure how long she lay there in the dirt . . . maybe only a minute, maybe hours. As she lay there unable to reason, unable to comprehend, she felt something strike her. At first it was just one pebble, then another. Slowly she raised her head, squinting into the bright sunlight.

Standing before her, pelting small rocks, was Satan himself! She was sure of it. What other man could possibly be so magnificently wicked? Barely a breath taller than Katelyn, he seemed massive. Each muscle in his bronzed body was well defined, his shoulders square and broad. His hair, so black it seemed blue, was parted in the middle and hung to his shoulders. His eyes were two bits of black coal buried within a chiseled face. The only ornament the brave wore was one long, red fox tail dangling from his hair on the left side of his head.

Katelyn gasped. The savage was practically naked! He wore only a bit of animal hide tied around his waist like an apron with a small pouch belted around his midsection.

Tipaakke held out one copper hand. She grasped it, too frightened to do anything else. His strong grip pulled her to her feet.

"Please don't hurt me," she begged. Henry was forgotten . . . her father forgotten. The entire first twenty-four years of her life suddenly ceased to exist. Above all, she realized she wanted to live.

The redskin's top lip curled. "*Opeek hokkuaa*, where has your man gone? He's left you, the dog!" he snarled.

Katelyn began to shake violently. She didn't understand a word of the gibberish.

The Indian laughed deep in his throat. "I told you your man is a dog. He's worse than a dog. He's a coward. He is also a fool." His hand lifted to touch a lock of tangled hair. He had never felt hair so fine, so silky smooth. Catching himself he spat into the dirt. What was wrong with him? She was a white woman! "He was lucky he got away. He won't next time." His English was impeccable, though, he spoke in a sing-song manner, his words slightly accented.

Katelyn stared into the black eyes in confusion. "You speak English?"

"Are you touched, woman?" He tapped his temple with a finger. "Doesn't it sound like I speak English?" He hit her on the shoulder, practically knocking her over. *"Buumska!"* he shouted.

Katelyn hesitated, then ran as fast as she could, his harsh laughter echoing behind her.

Tipaakke was on her in an instant, shoving her to the ground and leaping on top of her. He held her hands down, forcing her to drop her buttercups. He leaned so close that Katelyn could feel his light breath on her cheek.

"Let me go! You savage!" she screeched, kicking and twisting.

"Listen to me," the Indian said in English. "I'll tell you once and only once. You do as I say and I'll not harm you. But cross me, and I'll kill you. You understand?"

Katelyn was mesmerized by the raven black eyes. *Yes, this is a man who could kill.* She nodded her head weakly, turning her head away. He had an odd smell, not at all unpleasant, but one she didn't recognize. She trembled licking her lips in response to his nearness.

Tipaakke hesitated before releasing the white girl. She smelled sweetly of wildflowers. The only white woman he'd encountered had been Quakers who had often reeked of uncleanliness. No, this feminine body beneath him was freshly bathed. He could feel her whisper-soft breasts beneath his chest heaving breathlessly. So soft, so inviting. He was tempted to bury his face in the rumpled tresses that framed her face and calm her beating heart with light kisses. What was it about this white girl that he found so desirable? Perhaps it was her magic-colored hair. A color he had never seen before. In the shade it was dark, brown, but in the sunlight, it exploded in fiery brilliance. Tipaakke suddenly jumped up, infuriated with himself. He was not a man who forced himself upon women. And certainly not white woman. This fox-haired beauty was going to be trouble!

Katelyn pulled herself up and stumbled behind the brave. She had come to the Colonies to make a new life. She wasn't ready to die, not yet at least.

Katelyn kneeled on the ground beside Jonathan, trying to pray for his soul. Tears streamed down her face, no words came to mind. The boy's skull was split across the forehead with bits of red and pink tumbling from within. She had never seen so much blood! With trembling fingers she pulled off one lace glove and then the other and used them to wipe Jonathan's bloody face. She used the gloves to push his eyelids shut.

She dropped onto the side of the road where the servant's body lay. The sun was climbing higher in the sky; the heat seemed unbearable. She watched the four Indian braves as they stood together in the clearing, speaking their strange, soft language. She knew there was no sense in running, not while they were all watching her so closely. But she had to have a plan. She had to stay alive until Henry returned for her.

Katelyn looked up in the direction of the Indians. They were all staring at her, their discussion heated. The tall brave with the spear shook his head and walked away. Something had been decided. The he-devil walked towards her, his stride long and fluid.

"Come. We go."

"No, please. Just leave me here. I won't tell where you've gone. Just let me stay."

"Woman! I said come!" He pulled her up by the arm.

"But . . . Jonathan. We can't just leave him like this." She pointed to the blackamoor's crumpled body.

"What is he to you?"

"Nothing," she spit. "He was my betrothed's servant. But he was a man. He must have a decent Christian burial."

"You desecrate a sacred burial house and then ask that I bury one of yours?" Tipaakke raised one dark eyebrow. "I knew white women were stupid, but you . . . you . . ."

"I didn't desecrate anything! I was picking flowers!" Katelyn took a step back, frightened by her own temerity. She was shouting at the redskin!

"No, but your man did." His voice was low.

"Tipaakke!" The tall brave shouted from within the hut Henry had entered.

Tipaakke left Katelyn where she stood and crossed the clearing. He returned in a minute in a rage.

"That fool has stolen a dead child's axe! I should kill you now!" He grabbed her by the sleeve, pulling her close. "No." He spoke softly under his breath. "You're of no importance to him. That's obvious. But he'll pay. Somehow he'll pay." He yanked at her sleeve, pulling her along with him.

"Please. Let me be," Katelyn pleaded.

"Silence!" Tipaakke shoved her ahead of him.

The three other braves joined them and silently they descended into the deep forest.

The five walked for twenty minutes at a grueling pace before the one called Tipaakke stopped to speak to a brave with a large seashell dangling from his neck on a leather thong. He spoke a few words in his own tongue, and then the brave ran off in the direction they had come.

"Where's he going?" Katelyn panted, trying desperately to keep up.

"I said silence, woman. You are my prisoner. Prisoners don't ask questions. They do as they're told. Now keep up."

She nodded, pulling her skirt up to keep from tripping. The beautiful blue brocade was in shreds. She wished she'd thought to pick up her hat from alongside the road. The sweat poured down her face in rivulets, pooling at her neckline. She pushed her sleeves up and ran to catch up with her captors. The trees shaded her from the direct sunlight, but the dense forest seemed like an oven.

Tipaakke turned to see Katelyn struggling to keep up. He stopped and pulled out his knife.

"Don't hurt me. I'll keep up," she entreated.

"Stop whining." He thrust the knife into her sleeve.

Katelyn cringed, faint with fear. She braced herself for the bite of the cold stone against her flesh. But to her relief, she only heard the sound of tearing cloth.

Cutting the sleeves off the dress, Tipaakke reached down to saw at the skirt. He cut the brocade off just above the knees, enabling her to walk more easily.

Katelyn breathed deeply as the first rush of cool air went up her skirt. It's the dress that's hot, not the woods, she thought as she pushed herself off the ground and fell in behind the Indians.

Tipaakke returned the knife to its place in his loin cloth and left the girl to trail behind them. He had her word, he knew she wouldn't try to escape. He smiled inwardly, thinking of how beautifully childlike she was. He was sure she was at least twenty summers, yet she seemed so innocent. She was unlike any English he'd ever encountered.

Katelyn walked, then ran, knowing she had to keep up. She had no idea how far they'd come, or in what direction. The towering trees all seemed alike; each stump and stream was like the next.

She turned back as she heard someone coming from behind. For one fleeting moment she thought it might be Henry. Instead, it was the brave with the seashell around his neck who said nothing but joined the group, giving Tipaakke a nod.

Finally, after what seemed an eternity, they stopped at a stream. The braves knelt to drink and Katelyn did the same. She had never been so exhausted in her life. The water was ice cold and refreshing; she'd never tasted anything so good. After taking her fill, she sat down on a fallen log to catch her breath.

The braves stood near the stream speaking quietly to one another, occasionally glancing at their captive.

What? They think I'm going to escape? Katelyn swatted a mosquito on her calf. *Are they crazy? Where do they think I'm going to go? I could never find my way out of these woods.* Her shoulders slumped in discouragement. *No, I'll never get away on my own. Besides, what if the attempt failed?* She shuddered. That he-devil would kill her. Better to wait for Henry, she decided. *He'll come for me. Or at least his father will. I've just got to keep myself alive until they come.*

She got up stiffly, pulled off her slippers and stepped into the stream. She attempted unsuccessfully to repin her hair. The long red-brown tresses had fallen from the neat knot and threatened to smother her in the humid heat.

Tipaakke stood entranced as he watched the white girl smooth her unruly hair. Such magical hair! They needed to return to the village as soon as possible, but he knew she was exhausted. He hoped the cold water and rest would revive her.

24

What is wrong with you? he asked himself, stepping into the water. *Why should you be concerned with her comfort?* "Come," he snapped. "Our village is not much farther. When we arrive you're to keep quiet and do exactly as I say . . . if you wish to remain alive." He paused, letting his words sink in. "Let's go. We've already wasted precious time!"

"Father!" Henry leaped from the wagon before it came to a stop. "We've been attacked by Indians!"

The elder Henry came running down the steps of brick farmhouse. "Indians? What are you talking about? Where's Katelyn? I sail two weeks before you, and you still manage to mess things up. Don't tell me she's changed her mind after all of this."

"Indians! They've taken her! And Jonathan, too! Oh dear God!" He fell to the ground whimpering as he clutched the older man's booted feet.

"What are you talking about? Get a hold of yourself and talk some sense!" He pulled his son up by the collar of his coat.

"We . . . we were riding along in the wagon . . . took a different path than usual. We were attacked! They knocked Jonathan out of the wagon and took Katelyn. I only escaped because I was strong enough to fight off the leader. Oh, she's gone. My Katelyn, she's gone!"

"You left her there? You fool!" Bullman wiped his brow. "Do you know where you were when you were attacked? We've got to get back there." He shook his son's sagging shoulders.

"Yes . . . I think so. But what's the sense in it? She's gone!" He leaned against his father, sobbing.

"Nonsense. We've at least got to retrieve the body. Now get in the house and change into riding clothes. I'll get some men together. Ye gads boy, you smell like you've pissed your pants!"

Henry stumbled up the white brick steps and into the house. He went straight to his bedchamber above the parlor and slammed the door behind him.

He saw no harm in changing the story a bit. Gads! By now the girl had been raped, tortured, and killed. And such a pity, she'd had such nice large breasts.

He stripped off his breeches and reached under the goose down tick of the bed. He needed a stiff belt. He could have been killed! He took a swallow of the cloudy liquid, savoring its taste as it burned a trail down his throat. A knock came at the door.

"Yes?" Henry answered weakly, shoving the bottle back under the tick.

"May I come in, son?"

"Just a minute." He reached into his coat pocket, pulled out the stolen axe and shoved it under the tick with the bottle. "Come in," he called as he reached for clean breeches in a drawer.

"I've sent Ryan over to White Oaks to get Glen Wright and some of his men. We'll be leaving shortly. Get moving. Every second counts if we're to try and save the girl."

"She's gone. You know she is. You'll have to write the Reverend. I just couldn't." He sniffed convincingly.

"How could you have let this happen? How could you have left her? Christ, she was the only girl in all of England who was willing to marry you!"

"The filthy savages! They carried her off! What was I suppose to do? Get myself killed too? I knew I had to get back to you. I knew you were the only one who could help."

"How many were there?"

"Eight . . . ten maybe. Hell, I don't know! It all happened so fast. I thought you said the Indians around here were peaceful. I should've stayed in

France where I was safe."

"The Delawares are peaceful. They were Delawares, weren't they?"

"They were Indians!"

"Maybe Iroquois. That's all I can think of. Up north they've got some mean Indians. Call themselves Mohawks." The stout man leaned against the bedpost. "Delawares just don't attack. Don't have it in them. Not at least without good cause, they don't. Are you sure you didn't do anything to rile them?"

"Of course not. Do you think me mad?" Henry pulled on a pair of heavy black boots and tucked his clean breeches into them.

"Let's get going." The older man arose, running a tanned hand through greying hair. He'd made himself a rich man but the life of a tobacco farmer was awfully hard. He was beginning to have his doubts now as to whether he'd ever make a farmer out of his son. He'd always known the boy's mother had had poor blood lines.

"I'm ready." Henry pulled a rough linen shirt over his head and stepped in front of an ornate mirror he'd carried from France.

"Stop preening yourself! That poor girl's probably dead and you're combing your hair. I swear, boy, I'm beginning to damned well doubt you could ever have sprung from my loins! Meet me outside in five minutes. Get something to eat from the kitchen and I'll get horses."

"That's quite an ordeal you've been through, boy. Most don't survive an Indian attack to tell about it. Had a cousin in New York. His wife and six little ones were scalped." Glen Wright shifted in his saddle.

"Guess I was lucky. Those red animals were wild. I'm not counting on finding Katelyn, not in one piece at least." He swung clumsily into the saddle and jerked

27

the reins from the bondsman's hands.

"All right, men," Squire Bullman called, leading his gelding from the barn. "Listen up."

They were eleven men in all. Glen Wright had brought his brother Hoss and three bond servants as well as Dwayne Carson who had been visiting from Chestertown. Bullman was taking three Scotsmen, all bonded. They were rough men — farmers who had made their way in the Colonies by sweat and blood.

"My guess is that we can make it back to the site before dusk. Let's hope they've left a good trail, or better yet, they're waiting for us. Let's go, men. Be sure your flintlocks are loaded. And let's pray they're alive and unhurt."

Before they came into the clearing, Katelyn knew they were near the camp. She heard the sounds of dogs barking and children laughing.

Tipaakke slowed down, allowing her to catch up. "Remember what I said, girl," he whispered in English.

She nodded, swallowing thickly. *Why is he warning me like this? Is this some cruel game? Is he protecting me now, only to torture me later?*

As they entered the village, all seemed to grow quiet. Even the small brown dogs ceased their yapping. Katelyn looked up to see dozens of pairs of coal black eyes staring at her.

There were more small huts, like the ones she'd seen in the clearing, than she could count. The women all seemed to be going about their afternoon chores, some cooking on open fires, others feeding small children. They were all dressed in deer hides scraped free of hair and rubbed soft. The women wore short skirts much like the men's with nothing covering their brown breasts. She tried to look away, ashamed by such a display, but no matter where she turned she saw bare flesh. Katelyn was even further shocked to see that most of the children were completely naked save for moccasins.

After a pause of silence, the Indians all began to chatter at once, drawing nearer to the newly arrived party of men. Katelyn tried to stay near Tipaakke, but was pushed aside by a young girl with braided hair, several years younger than herself.

"So, Tipaakke, what's this?" Her voice was honey smooth.

Katelyn eyed the girl cautiously. What were they saying about her?

"Leave her be, Tolaala. Where is Father and Mekollaan?" He wrapped one long, tanned arm around his captive, a strange feeling of protectiveness coming over him.

"In the family wigwam. What's happened? Why have you brought this white woman to our village?" she asked.

"Don't ask so many questions. Matshipoii, control your wife. She has a loose tongue."

Laughing, the tall brave wrapped his arms around the girl with the honey voice. "You know I would if I could, Tipaakke."

"*Buumska* . . . come." Tipaakke dropped back into English. "What's your name, girl? I suppose I must call you something."

"Katelyn." She spoke softly, all too aware of the heathen's touch.

"Follow me, Katelyn." His hand dropped from her shoulder as he reached down to snatch her skirt from the hands of a small boy. "Where are your manners?" he scolded, switching from English to Algonquian.

The child hung his head in shame.

"It's all right." Tipaakke tousled the small head,

29

ashamed that he had taken out his anger for the white men on the boy. "She's already frightened. Let us not make things worse."

The little boy beamed brightly in understanding.

Tipaakke took off across the grass, and Katelyn followed close behind, whispering a prayer as she went. If this was the end, she supposed, she was as ready to meet her maker as she'd ever be.

He led her into one of the larger huts and pushed her to her knees inside the doorway.

"Good afternoon, Father," he said in his own tongue to the old, grey-haired man. He spoke with great reverence, yet he was at ease with the chief of the tribe. He nodded to his older brother.

Katelyn stared at the two Indians who were sitting on a hide, scooping bits of meat and vegetables from sea shells and putting them in their mouths. The younger man wiped his hand on his loincloth and reached out to grasp her captor's hand. He was taller than Tipaakke and resembled him greatly, although he was not as handsome. He was dressed much the same as the other braves, but his head was plucked bald save for a small tuft of hair growing on top with black feathers fastened to it.

The old man smiled and continued to eat. Tipaakke squatted beside them and waited until his father had finished his meal. The chief ate noisily with great zeal, smacking his lips. His hair was snow white and hung much lower than his sons', but he was almost as muscular as they were. Finally he laid the eating shell aside and spoke to Tipaakke, ignoring her presence. The other man stared at her devilishly.

"So, my son, what is this you have brought to our village? Haven't I told you before not to bring home stray kits?" He spoke in Algonquian, as always, then grinned bearing even white teeth.

30

"We were out hunting and decided to pass by the old village. I wanted to pay my respects to the souls of our loved ones. But there was a white man there with a dark-skinned man and this girl. He . . ." Tipaakke clenched his fists, struggling to subdue his anger. ". . . this white man had broken into the big house, stolen Opossum's axe, and dumped the food baskets. It was the axe I gave him his fourth summer."

Kükuus, the chief, turned his head away so that his sons wouldn't see his tears. He didn't understand the white man's desire to steal and pillage. Wasn't it enough that his people had died of their small pox? Must they steal from a child in his final resting place? He turned back to his youngest son. "So what happened? Why the woman?"

"The white dog ran to his wagon and left her behind. He kicked the servant from the wagon. The boy fell against a rock and was killed. I would have killed the white man if I could have, but I meant no harm to the girl."

"Why do you bring her here? What are you going to do with her? English women are stupid. She could never be trained to be of any use. Most of them are mentally deficient. Interbreeding, I suppose."

"I don't know. I'm not even sure why I brought her here." *You know*, a voice whispered inside him. *She is beautiful, this fox-haired girl. She is yours. It is meant to be.*

"Well, Tipaakke, we'll talk of this later. You must return to the old village and repair the damage. Opossum must have a new axe to carry with him into the dream world." The Chief reached out to caress his cheek. "Take care, my son. I have already lost enough children."

Tipaakke lifted his hand to the old man's, and then dropped it. "I'll leave the white girl in my wigwam. She has given me her word she won't try to escape."

Mekollaan chuckled deep in his throat, startling Katelyn.

Tipaakke flashed a warning signal. *She's mine*, he threatened with his frown. He and his brother would never see eye to eye, but they kept their peace in the presence of their father.

"Take more men with you. The white man may return for his woman." He glanced for the first time at Katelyn. "Mekollaan will go, too. She is very pretty for a white woman. She has intelligent eyes, Tipaakke. We are not Iroquois. We are not stealers of women and children. This is not like you . . . there must be a reason. Only time will tell. I have faith that you'll do the right thing when Manito reveals to you His plans."

The brave nodded and reached down to pull Katelyn off the ground.

"Leave her to me, little brother. I'll care for her." Mekollaan smiled ominously, speaking their native tongue.

"*That* is why you are going with me." Tipaakke pushed Katelyn out of the wigwam and into another nearby. He closed the flap behind him and knelt beside a platform, digging through a bark basket. She spun around, terrified to be alone with her captor.

"Take off your clothes," he ordered in precise English.

"What?" she managed. *This is it. He's going to rape and kill me.*

"I said, take off your clothes."

"No!" Katelyn screamed.

"Shut up, girl. Don't make a fool of yourself. I have no intention of touching you. We don't rape women. It's bad medicine."

She stared in disbelief.

"Give me your clothes, Katelyn. You stink. Come now. I haven't got time for your foolishness. I told you I wouldn't hurt you as long as you did what I said, didn't I?"

She nodded, her arms wrapped tightly around her waist.

"My sister, Tolaala . . . Cedar, will bring you clothes and something to eat. Now do as I say."

Slowly, Katelyn turned around. *Must I be shamed like this?*

Tipaakke shook his head in disgust and ducked out of his wigwam. He would never understand why the white man was so ashamed of his body. It had been given by the Heavenly Father, Manito, hadn't it? "Throw your clothes out," he called from outside. "Stay here until I return. I'm trusting you, Katelyn. Don't disappoint me. I'll kill you if you do."

She stood trembling as she listened to the footsteps dying in the distance. Reaching behind her back, Katelyn pulled off what was left of the blue brocade gown. She knew it was best if she did what the Indian told her. So far, he'd kept his promise, he hadn't hurt her. She'd have to trust him. She had no other choice. She threw her clothes out through the flap and retreated to the other side of the wigwam, her back to the door. Against one wall was a low platform, obviously for sleeping. On it lay a rectangular piece of tanned deer hide. She snatched the hairless skin and wrapped around her naked body hastily as she heard the flap move.

Katelyn stiffened in horror as a large dark hand covered her mouth.

"Shhhhhhh . . ." the voice threatened.

She turned to find the black-feathered Indian's leering face above her.

He whispered in a gutteral tone as he turned her body around slowly, his hand still covering her mouth.

"Uiinguan Uatuhappe, Aluum," he murmured, forcing her against the wigwam's rough wall. He pinned her with his knee and rubbed his free hand across the deer hide covering her breasts.

Katelyn strained, squeezing her eyes shut. She was no match for the beast's strength.

Chapter Two

Her body went entirely limp as the redman tugged at the deerskin and dropped it onto the dirt floor. She tried to block out all feelings, all thoughts, as the dark hands fondled her roughly. *Is this any way to die*, she asked herself as her assailant forced his lips against hers.

No! If she was going to be raped and killed, it wasn't going to be without a fight!

"No!" she screamed. She bit down on the redskin's lip until she tasted blood. Startled, he pulled back, and she pummeled him with her fists. "Let me go, you filthy savage!"

Mekollaan chuckled, his voice frighteningly low. He spoke English. "You're a lively bit of meat. I've heard you white women are lusty. Come, let the Hawk smooth your feathers." He caught her wrists with his powerful hands and pressed seeking lips to her neck.

Frantically, Katelyn kicked, trying to knock him over. Instead, her knee caught in the Indian's groin. Her eyes flew open in surprise as he gasped and rolled to the floor. *Have I killed him?*

Mekollaan groaned gutterally and lay in a ball at her feet.

"Katelyn!" Tipaakke jerked the skin door aside and

rushed in. "Who are you . . ." His eyes fell to his brother's crumpled body and then settled on her lithe figure gleaming in the dim light of the wigwam. A smile crossed his full lips. He wasn't sure which sight was more pleasing—Mekollaan in great pain, or the fox-haired beauty standing naked before him.

"I thought you told me you didn't rape! That animal attacked me," she sputtered. As the initial shock wore off, she realized she was still naked and turned her back to the men.

Tipaakke tossed another skin from the platform, hitting her with it. He didn't trust himself to get any closer to her. The sight of her smooth back, rounded buttocks and long legs brought an ache to his loins. He watched silently as she retrieved the soft hide and wrapped it around her body.

"Thank you," she whispered, turning slowly to face her captor. Would she be tortured before they killed her? She knew that one was dying. No one could be in that much pain and not die.

"So Mekollaan, she's not the timid rabbit you thought . . . eh?" Tipaakke stuck out a hand to assist his brother. "You should know better than to force your attentions on someone. Especially a white woman. What's wrong with you? You become more like the white man every day." He spoke Algonquian so Katelyn wouldn't understand his words.

"So that's the way it is. She's yours."

"No, brother. I didn't say that. You know that's not why I brought her here."

"Maybe not. But now that she's here, she is a tasty morsel, isn't she?"

Tipaakke remained silent, warning Mekollaan with a single glance.

"Besides, I meant the girl no harm. I was only having a bit of fun." He knew when to back off. The girl wasn't worth riling his brother's anger over. "The shriveled old apple," he muttered, stumbling out of the wigwam.

Tipaakke turned to Katelyn, dropping into English. "My brother wouldn't have hurt you. He just has a poor sense of humor." He yearned to reach out and comfort her, to still her trembling lips with his.

She nodded, her soft eyes meeting his shadowy black ones. She had never seen such a magnificent man! The Indian's facial features were a chiseled work of fine art with high cheek bones and a square chin. His black hair was shiny and sleek, his skin smooth and as free of hair as her own. Her eyes trailed the sinewy neck to broad shoulders, to the wide expanse of his chest.

Tipaakke sensed her scrutiny and stood calmly. Like a frightened animal, she was surveying her new surroundings. It was always best to allow one of Manito's creatures to adjust in its own way. Finally, unable to resist her doe eyes, he took one long stride forward. Katelyn cringed as he reached with one hand, very slowly, and brushed a stray lock of tangled hair off her flushed cheek.

She held her breath. *Not him too?* No, she sensed somehow that he was different. He had given his word. As long as she did as he said, no harm would come to her by his hands.

"I am Tipaakke Oopus. Night Fox in your language." His thumb caressed her trembling lips. "Your eyes are the color of the autumn grass, your hair the color of the red fox." He paused, lost in his own thoughts for a moment. "Have you been sent to me by my god? Are you a gift?"

Katelyn wanted to break the invisible thread that held them so close. She wanted to shout, to run. She was no sacrificial lamb! She belonged to no man! Yet she was unable to move, unable to break the spell he had cast over her.

"So, you won't speak?" he asked tenderly. "That's all right. If I were in your position, I wouldn't speak either." He laid one hand gently on her bare shoulder. His touch was searing. "I must go now. I will return to my old village to repair the damage as soon as my brother has recovered." He laughed, his voice true and clear.

Katelyn became more frightened with each passing moment. Afraid of him, afraid of herself. This man was the enemy. Yet, near him, she felt strange, warm and cold at the same time. It was only a matter of time until she made a mistake or angered him. Then he would kill her. But she couldn't hate him . . .

"You'll be safe here," she heard him say. "If there's anything you need, tell my sister Tolaala. You must not leave my wigwam unless she is with you. My people are not vicious, but they have had enough of the white man and his ways."

Katelyn remained silent, staring boldly into his obsidian eyes. He was so calm and gentle for a man.

"You must promise me again that you will not try to escape. It is senseless. You could never find your way through the forest. There are Iroquois nearby. You wouldn't want to meet them. *They* are beasts."

She stuck her bottom lip out stubbornly. What was the difference between one Indian and the next? He was trying to scare her into submission.

He began to apply pressure to her shoulder with his hand. "Give me your word," he commanded.

"Yes," she whispered, but her eyes glinted defiantly.

"Yes, what?"

"Yes, you have my word. I'll not leave," she spit.

Tipaakke released her shoulder slowly, letting his hand glide down a slender arm and then he was gone.

Katelyn slumped to the ground in exhausted relief.

He was gone. Finally she would have some time to think without those eyes following her, reading her every thought. As much as she hated to admit it, he was right. She would never find her way back to a settlement. But she had to get away from him. *Henry! He's coming for me, he'll find me.* She lay her head on the dirt floor, not minding how hard it was against her cheek. She knew she would be more comfortable on the fur padded sleeping platform, but she wouldn't have slept in his bed if it was the last bed in the entire God-forsaken Colonies.

Tipaakke and six other braves including Mekollaan ran long and hard. The Delaware had a few ponies, but they were of little use in the dense thickets of the forest. They could make better time on foot. Trained from childhood, a Lenni Lenape brave could run all day and into the night, stopping only for water.

They ran at an unrelenting pace, coming to the old village just as the sun began to set in the western sky. Mekollaan cautioned his men to be silent and posted a guard at the edge of the forest. It had been decided by the chief that the old village would be burned to prevent any further desecration. The bodies wouldn't be buried—there wasn't time. Their souls would rise with the smoke. There was little chance of a forest fire; still, the Indians would wait until the blaze had died down.

Tipaakke entered the Big House, a prayer crossing his lips. He righted the turned over baskets and scooped the grain off the ground, returning it to its proper container. He considered making a trip to the stream but decided against it, knowing he must hurry. The white coward could come hunting for his woman. Besides, where his beloved friends were going, there would always be running streams.

Tipaakke stared at the bodies of the people he loved. They were all so close in the small village that each time a man or woman died, it was as if he'd lost a brother or a sister. He knew he shouldn't grieve for his loss, but these deaths were particularly hard for him because they had died from the same disease his wife and son had died from. Only a summer ago he had lost his family to small pox and he still grieved for them in his heart. After their deaths he had grown very close to little Opossum and now he was dead too. Sometimes it was very difficult to understand Manito's ways.

The brave kneeled, pushing Jonathan's body aside, and began to gather dry leaves and bits of bark from the floor. The servant's soul would be released to the heavens, too. He reached into the pouch around his middle and pulled out the fire stick. With a twirling motion he spun the stick against a piece of wood, faster and faster, until a spark leaped from the stick and began to lick at the dry leaves. Mekollaan made his fires with flint and steel he'd bought from the settlers, but Tipaakke still preferred his grandfather's method. Adding bits of bark, he stuck his head out the door, calling to his brother softly.

"Have the men bring sticks to light and we'll get these fires going. We'd better not stay long. This site is bad luck."

Mekollaan nodded, ignoring the fact that his younger brother was giving orders again. *Have no fear*, he told himself. *Soon I will be leader, and Tipaakke will mend his ways.*

Tipaakke stiffened. The hair on the back of his neck stood up with animal instinct as he heard the warning cry from the outlook.

Mekollaan signaled to his men to head back into the woods. He knew they were outnumbered by the sound

40

of pounding hooves—about a dozen men. To save lives they would retreat into the forest where the white men would be unable to follow them on horseback. Mekollaan was no coward, but it was his responsibility to lead his men home safely. He saw no need to fight the white men. They would keep the girl instead. Death was too honorable for men who left their women to be ravaged by the enemy.

"Good heavens, Father! Those filthy redskins have set fire to the woods!" Henry reined in his horse, his hands trembling. If there was any chance those savages were still there, he didn't intend to come face to face with them. Having escaped once, he knew the odds would be against him if he tempted fate again.

The grey-haired Bullman spurred his animal forward, rushing into the clearing. The other men followed close behind, shouting and firing their weapons as they spotted the Delaware braves. Despite Bullman's instructions, the attack disintegrated into utter chaos. The men rode in circles through the smoke and flames, shooting in every direction as fast as they could reload their flintlocks and muskets.

As the first shot rang out, Tipaakke spotted an unlit wigwam. He grabbed a dry branch, lit it on a blazing bark roof, and rushed to set it on fire. He had no intention of allowing these men to do his people any further dishonor.

Mekollaan signaled his men to go on without him as a musket ball rang out above his head. When he realized Tipaakke was missing, he knew he had to go back. He wouldn't leave his brother behind.

The heavy acrid smoke irritated Tipaakke's lungs and blurred his vision as he started back from the clearing, the thundering of hooves behind him.

"Come back here, you louse-ridden Injun!" A white man on horseback appeared through the smoke.

Tipaakke didn't hear the shot. He didn't feel the leaden ball enter his skull. He saw only the ground suddenly leaping toward him and heard the leaves crumble and crack as his body fell.

At the instant the white man pulled the trigger, Mekollaan's arrow pierced his heart. The man tumbled from his horse, blood spewing from his mouth as the Indian leaped over the hedge. He reached Tipaakke in a split second and dropped his head to his chest. Through the sound of pounding hooves, shooting men and ricocheting musket shots, the red man heard the faint flutter of his brother's heart. He lifted him to his shoulder with ease and trotted off, his stride long and determined.

In the confusion of thick smoke and unorganized men, it was several minutes before Squire Bullman realized the Indians had disappeared into the darkening forest. When he spotted the dead bondsman, he glanced about frantically, fearing for his son's life.

"Henry! Where are you, boy?" Bullman tied a handkerchief around his nose and mouth to filter out some of the choking, blinding smoke. He spun his horse around and made his way out of the clearing and back up onto the dirt road. "They're gone! They've gotten away! Has anyone seen Henry?"

As the men began to emerge from the clearing, Bullman continued to shout for his son. He pressed his horse beside the other men. "Glen, have you seen Henry! Has anyone seen my boy?"

Glen shook his head, wiping the sooty sweat from his forehead with his sleeve. "Haven't seen him, but the smoke's so thick that I didn't see much of anything. Nothing but those savages leaping over bushes and heading into the woods. I think we'd be foolish to follow them. The damned forest is so dense."

The Squire nodded and turned his horse around, heading back to the burning village. He had to find Henry.

Glen dismounted when he spotted his brother and called to him. "Christ! Did you see what happened to poor Clyde? An arrow, right through his heart!" He beat his chest with a fist, throwing his head back and gasping as if he'd been hit and then straightened up, laughing.

Hoss let out a loud cackle and reached into his saddle bag, withdrawing a bottle of amber-colored liquid. "How about a bit of refreshment?"

"Why not?" He waited until Hoss had taken a sip, and then he tipped the bottle, pouring the fiery liquid down his parched throat.

Hoss leaned against his saddle, waiting for another swig of the brandy. "Just as soon as the smoke clears some, we'll strap him to his horse and haul him home."

Dwayne Dawson came limping through the smoke, leading his horse behind. "Which one of you sons of a bitch shot me in the leg?"

Hoss laughed, handing him the bottle. "You're only grazed, quit complaining."

"Grazed, hell! I've got lead in my leg!" He dropped onto the ground, gritting his teeth at the searing pain ripping through his leg.

Bullman came back out of the cloud of smoke, coughing and spitting. "No sign of Henry anywhere. Ryan, get down and see to Dawson. A man can die from loss of blood awful quick out here." He took control of the group, pushing his concern for Henry aside.

The red-haired Scot slid off his saddle slowly and kneeled to examine the injured man's leg.

"All right, men," Bullman continued with authority.

"The smoke is beginning to clear now that the wind's picked up. Let's get down there and see if we can find any signs of the girl . . . or of Henry." He shook his head in disbelief. "I can't imagine where he could have disappeared to. His horse is gone too."

"You know, Henry, I don't recall seeing your boy down there. Saw everyone else." Hoss swung into his saddle and tucked the brandy back into the saddle bag.

The men entered the clearing and dismounted, their voices hushed. They didn't think the Indians would be back, but who could tell what a savage might do? The men were ready to get this over with and get back home to a hot meal. No one was genuinely concerned about the girl except Bullman. They all knew she was long dead.

"Let's take a look around, men. Then we'll be on our way. Get something to poke through the ashes." Bullman dropped the reins of his horse and left him, knowing he wouldn't wander.

"Hey, look what I found, Master Bullman!" The bond servant came running, a woman's bonnet in his hand.

Bullman fingered the wide ribbon on the bonnet. There was no doubt about it. She'd been here. "Put it in my saddle bag."

"Henry!" Glen stood near the blackened pile that had been the Big House. "Better get over here. I knew something smelled putrid. Those heathens were burning people!" He stepped back in disgust, hoping he wasn't going to be sick.

Bullman joined the other men who stood in a semicircle studying a charred, human leg bone. He took a stick and began to poke through the smoldering pile, the bile rising in his throat. What a horrifying way to die. He prayed they'd killed them first.

Suddenly a fresh flame shot up and soon the remains

of the wigwam were engulfed again.

"God . . . they did this intentionally. Dried pine . . .
they meant to build a hot fire." Bullman threw the stick
in a rage, watching it sail until it disappeared into the
semidarkness. "Must be them. There's a couple of
bodies here. I just can't figure out why they burned
them. The Delawares don't burn." He took a deep
breath, suddenly weary. He was getting too old for
colony life. "Let's go. There's no more to be done here.
There's no sign of Henry."

Hoss leaned to whisper in Glen's ear as Bullman
mounted. "More than likely the coward's taken off," he
mumbled, a grin creeping across his broad face.

Glen winked and swung into his saddle, digging his
heels into the bay. It was time to get home.

Katelyn's eyes flew open in terror as a hand in the
dark shook her awake. It was the sister. She tugged at
Katelyn's arm, pulling her to her feet.

"Come." She said in English that was almost as clear
as her brother's. "Tipaakke said you were to have a
bath. He doesn't want you stinking up his home."

Katelyn swallowed hard. She was almost as afraid of
this young girl as she was of her brothers.

"Come, girl." Tolaala held the door flap open, waiting for her to step through.

"Please, can I have something to wear? I can't go out
like this." She clutched the deerskin wrapped tightly
around her body.

"You don't put clean clothes on a dirty body. You
whites have the strangest ideas." Tolaala shook her
head, bemused by her brother's prisoner. "Let's go."

Katelyn kept her eyes on the grass beneath her feet
as she followed close behind. As they passed through
the village, the sound of laughing children and the low

hum of contented voices surrounded them. This time no one came near; in fact, no one paid any attention to her at all. The smell of roasting meat and fresh baked corn cakes tantalized her senses, reminding her that she hadn't eaten since dawn aboard ship.

She followed Tolaala out of the village and through a line of ancient trees to a running stream.

"There." The girl pointed. "That's where it's deep."

"I can't swim," Katelyn stated, staring at the beautiful dark-skinned girl. "No one ever taught me."

"It's not that deep!" She laughed. "Who ever heard of a grown woman who couldn't swim." Tolaala plopped herself down on the bank and dropped her feet into the water. She knew she shouldn't be mean to the girl, her upbringing was certainly no fault of her own. Her voice softened. "You'll have to hurry. My little girl will be awake soon."

Katelyn dropped the skin to the ground with resolution and waded into the stream. Before this day she couldn't recall ever being totally naked in front of anyone. This girl made the third today.

"Over there," Tolaala called in her sing-song voice. "That's the best spot for bathing."

The water was frigid! But as Katelyn waded deeper into the pool, her body numbed and grew used to the chill. She crouched in the moving stream and rubbed her body briskly, wiping the dust and grime from her pale skin. She splashed her arms, noticing in the light of the rising moon the streaks of dried blood on her forearm.

Jonathan's blood . . . She watched in a dream-like state as the blood again ran bright and wet as it mixed with the water. *Don't think about him. There's nothing you could have done. You've got to start worrying about yourself. You must keep yourself alive until help comes. It will come, Kate. Henry will come. He will take you away from that savage.*

46

He'll marry you and you'll live in a big house and have lots of children. She glanced back at Tolaala sitting at the edge of the water tossing pebbles and watching the ripples they produced. *The sister has done you no harm, nor has . . .* She didn't dare speak his name, not even to herself.

"Hurry. My daughter will be awake and screaming to eat."

Katelyn dipped her head in the water again and then waded towards the bank. *You're going to be all right,* she told herself as she squeezed the water from her tangled tresses.

"Here. My brother said to give this to you. It's a winter dress, but he said you wouldn't be comfortable unless your *tuulke* were covered."

She reached for the dress and thanked her, appalled to think that the brave and this girl had been discussing her private parts.

The dress Tolaala gave her was made of animal skin, though, she couldn't recognize what kind of animal it had come from because it had been scraped clean. It was simple with a round neckline and no sleeves, reaching just above her knees. She pulled the dress over her head and smoothed it over her body. She was a little larger than Tolaala so the dress was tight, but she was so glad to have something to cover her nakedness that she would have worn just about anything.

I don't suppose I'd better ask for underdrawers, she thought, grabbing the skin she'd used for a wrap and trotting to catch up with the Indian girl.

Mekollaan kneeled near a running brook and laid his little brother gently in the soft moss. His eyes were closed, his breathing shallow. Mekollaan whispered a prayer to Manito as he plucked grass and dipped it into the cool water. He passed the wad of dripping grass across Tipaakke's forehead.

My brother must live! He must! Mekollaan knew he wasn't ready to rule alone as chief of his people should the time come. No, his brother could sometimes see and understand what Mekollaan feared he himself might not ever understand. There had been talk between he and his father about dual leadership. Tipaakke hadn't been told, yet.

The brave dipped the grass into the cold water again and replaced it. He knew he couldn't allow Tipaakke to sleep like this for too long. The longer he slept, the father Fox's soul wandered. After a certain point, he wouldn't be able to return to his body if he wanted to.

"Listen to me, Tipaakke. You must come back. I need you, little brother. Come back to me and one day we will rule side by side, something never done before in the history of our great people." Mekollaan wished desperately now that he hadn't ordered the other men to return to the village. Now he would have to carry his brother all the way home himself.

He bathed his brother's head one last time, washing the blood encrusted hair where the leaden ball had entered his skull. He then kneeled again and swung him up onto his shoulder.

Home, he told himself. *Take him home. The Shaman will know how to care for him. He will use his power with the great spirits to bring my brother back.*

48

Chapter Three

Slowly, Katelyn still dazed with sleep, raised her head. For two days she had kept her vigil over Fox, forcing broths down his throat, mopping his sweat-drenched body, and praying.

The ancient, wizened medicine man had come three times. Each time he lit an odd smelling stick and sang and danced until its flame burned out. In the back of her mind Katelyn could still see the old man's long white braids swinging as his feet created intricate patterns on the dusty floor, his body moving to the silent music of his ancestors. The old man had come to be a comfort to Katelyn, for they both worked toward the same goal. Fox's survival.

He must live! He must! For if he died, so would she!

When Hawk carried his brother in his arms into the wigwam, his words had been brief. "Do you see what you have done, white woman? You have killed my brother."

"He's dead?"

"No. Not yet. His soul hovers above his body. But if you don't do something for him, he'll soon be gone."

"Me? What can I do for him. I don't even know what's wrong with him!"

"Can't you see the blood!" he snarled, his lips curling

49

at the corners. "He's been shot in the head by a white man. One of your white men!"

"Henry! You've seen Henry! He came back for me?"

"I wouldn't concern myself with your man right now. I have sent for the medicine man. But *you* must make him live!"

"How? I know nothing of medicine. He needs a doctor."

"I don't know what you're going to do for him. But you will care for him. Do you know why?"

Katelyn shook her head as a tremor of ominous fear surged through her body.

"Because if he dies, you will be mine. And you will not live to see another sunrise."

Katelyn rubbed her aching eyes, pushing thoughts of Hawk's threats aside. She ran her fingers through tangled hair and attempted to straighten her stiff legs. She'd fallen asleep on the dirt floor again, her head resting on the platform where Fox's body lay.

What had woken her? It was still dark outside; a cool night breeze tugged at the door flap. Had there been a sound? Had someone spoken? Was she just dreaming? Katelyn's eyes adjusted to the dim light. Movement? Had the Indian just moved his hand?

She got to her knees and peered anxiously into the quiescent, tanned face. Suddenly his eyes flickered open.

"Fox!" she gasped. "Heavenly Father, bless you!" She grabbed the brave's hand and it tightened. "Can you hear me, Fox?"

As he slowly drifted back to earth, leaving behind the souls of his wife and son, Tipaakke became aware of the faint scent of femininity. He could feel someone leaning over him; hair, thick and sweet smelling, tickled his face. He struggled within his mind to clear

50

the smoke from his thoughts as he listened to the soft, reassuring voice.

A woman was calling him. *Who? Who is calling you, Tipaakke? Think!* Slowly he struggled from the depths of the drugged-like state. *The voice . . . the white girl with the fox hair.* But something wasn't right . . . *Name . . . what is her name? Something's wrong . . . something's very wrong.*

"Katelyn . . ."

The deep voice startled her. "Yes. Yes, I'm here, Fox. You're all right. You're safe here in your . . ." Her mind searched for the right word. ". . . wigwam. I must get your father and brother. I promised." She stood up, but Fox groped for her hand.

"No. Stay with me. I can't see. I'm blind."

Katelyn dropped to her knees, clutching his hand. Thoughts of her own safety vanished from her mind. Tears trickled unchecked down her pale cheeks. She squeezed his hand tighter, not knowing what to say. *How does one comfort an Indian? How does one comfort any man who has learned that he's blind?*

"What's happened to me. Can't remember. Tell me girl."

"You . . ." Her heart quickened. "You were shot by one of my bethrothed's people. He had come to rescue me." Her shoulders slumped. With these words, she knew she had condemned herself to die.

"I remember going back to light one of the wigwams." He pulled his hand from her's and swung his feet to the floor. "Take me to my father's wigwam."

"No. I can't. Your brother told me not to let you up. Let me get them." Trembling, she pushed a strand of knotty hair behind one ear.

Tipaakke pulled himself to his feet then fell back onto the platform, sweat beading across his forehead.

51

"Just sit, I'll be right back." She lifted the flap and flew across the compound to the chief's wigwam.

Katelyn hesitated in the shadowy moonlight. Should she knock? *Don't be silly, Katie! Where are you going to knock?* She lifted the hide flap and stepped in. On one platform she spotted the old man curled in a ball, sleeping contentedly. Across from him lay Hawk who was stretched out with one arm flung across his forehead.

Whom should I wake? She had no desire to get close enough to Hawk to wake him, but it would be senseless to wake the chief. He didn't speak English. Katelyn took a step closer to Hawk and then another, eyeing him closely.

Suddenly an arm shot out and grabbed her, holding her prisoner with an iron grip. A faint squeak escaped from her lips as Hawk drew her between his knees.

"Come looking for the Hawk, did you?" He smiled wolfishly. "You should be watching over my brother. But I suppose it can't be helped. I too, sometimes get the urge in the middle of the night."

"Take your hands off me!" Katelyn shouted, waking the Chief. "I've come to tell you about your brother, swine!"

"What of him? Tell me!" He shook her until her teeth rattled.

"He's awake and speaking." *Coward . . . you couldn't tell him the rest, could you?*

Hawk leaped from his platform, the sleeping skin sliding from his body.

Katelyn spun around making a quick exit. These heathens had no shame! Imagine! Sleeping without a stitch on! It was no wonder they had such vile thoughts! She grabbed the water skin and ducked into Fox's wigwam. He still sat where she left him, his head

52

resting in his hands on his lap.

"Who's there?" Tipaakke's head snapped in her direction.

"Me. Katelyn. Your father and brother are coming." Hesitantly, she took a few steps. "I brought you water." She wrapped his hands around the skin.

He took a long pull and then another before handing it back to her. "Retie the thong. I cannot."

She did as ordered and hung the bag on an inside beam where other baskets and bags hung. "Are you hungry?"

"There's no need to shout, woman! I'm blind, not deaf! Yes. I will eat."

Katelyn searched through the small bark baskets on the floor and found the leftover corncakes Cedar had given her. She unwrapped them from the leaves and laid two on a small board. She was dumping some berries into a large clam shell when Hawk and the father entered the wigwam.

"Tipaakke, you are well. You scared me." Mekollaan's voice caught in his throat as he stared into his brother's sightless, ebony eyes.

"No. As you can see, I am not," he answered quietly in the Delaware tongue.

Kukuus squatted in front of his son for a moment, then got up, returning shortly with a blazing stick. He passed it back and forth in front of Tipaakke's face.

"I smell. I feel. But I do not see. Not even light, Father."

Kukuus stroked his chin thoughtfully, gazing into his son's glassy eyes. "You shouldn't have lived, my son. Our Shaman tells me the musket ball is still lodged in your skull. It's sad that you are sightless, but you have cheated death. So you are a lucky man."

"I should have died."

53

"No. Don't say that. Manito puts you on this earth for a reason. And you must stay here until He decides it is time for you to go."

Katelyn watched Tipaakke slide back into his platform and close his eyes. She wished she could understand what they were saying; not knowing made her uneasy. And worse yet, Hawk stood silently at the door glaring in her direction. They're going to kill me anyway, she thought, pulling herself into a tighter ball on the corn-husk mat.

Kukuus stroked his son's bandaged head. "Go back to sleep, Fox of mine. The Shaman will return in the morning." He got himself to his feet, pushing away the hand that Hawk offered. It was funny how his body had grown brittle with the years, yet in his mind he was still a young man. "Mekollaan, we will leave your brother. Come."

As the chief ducked out of the wigwam, Mekollaan turned to Katelyn. "Do you see what you have done to him?" His upper lip curled slightly at one corner. "He will never see again and you are to blame!"

"Mekollaan!" Tipaakke called, his eyes still shut, one arm flung across his forehead. "You will keep silent and leave her alone." He spoke through clenched teeth in the Delaware tongue.

They were going to kill her. Katelyn feared the worst. It was only a matter of time before they thought of an inventive way to torture her before doing it.

Mekollaan left the wigwam without another word. He knew Tipaakke was still ill from the fever that had raged within him. Once his head cleared, his opinion of the girl would change.

"Will you eat now?" Katelyn whispered. The moon shone a faint light through the hole in the roof, casting a shadow over her deathly pale face.

"No! Go to sleep, girl!" Tipaakke rolled over, presenting his back to Katelyn, leaving her to spend another night dreaming of her impending death.

"Wake up, girl!" Tipaakke shook her roughly. "I said get up!"

Katelyn's eyes flew open; she bolted upright. "It wasn't my fault," she murmured in sleepy confusion.

"Wake up. I haven't accused you of anything, except laziness. Take me to the edge of the woods."

"The woods? This early? What are you going to do in the woods?"

"The same thing you do in the woods, girl."

Katelyn's eyes widened. Her mouth formed an 'O'. *You* want *me* to . . . I couldn't!"

"I only need you to take me to the woods. I can do the rest myself."

"Get someone else." She rubbed her eyes, hoping she was still dreaming.

"No. I said you'll do it. Take me now." The Indian sat determinedly, waiting.

Katelyn covered her face with her hands, shaking her head. She couldn't believe she was doing this! "All right. I'll take you." She stood up slowly and took the tanned hand that groped for hers. "Which way?"

"Straight out of the village. Hurry."

Katelyn dragged him through the village, hurrying to get back before the others began to rise for the day.

"Slow down. You're going to make me trip and . . . Ow!" Tipaakke stopped and lifted his foot to massage his big toe. "I can see I should have worn my moccasins. Into the woods!"

She passed the last wigwam, then stepped into a denser part of the forest. Though the village was in the woods, she realized the Indians had spent a great deal of time clearing the compound of brush and small trees. The actual woods surrounding the village was practically impassable. Katelyn pulled at Tipaakke's hand as they floundered through the undergrowth, barely warning him in time to miss a low branch. When they were well out of sight of the village, she stopped and dropped his hand.

"There. That's as far as I'm taking you."

"Do you always come out this far? Now I know why it takes you so long."

Katelyn gritted her teeth and stalked off. How dare that heathen speak of such delicate matters in front of her!

"Don't leave. I won't be long," Tipaakke called as he heard her trudge off.

"If you think I'm going to stand there while you . . . well you can just forget it! Kill me, I don't care," she shouted over her shoulder. "But I'm not going to do it!"

Tipaakke grinned to himself. She was no meek rabbit. When he was ready for her he called out her name.

"Are you done?" she shouted from a distance.

"Yes. Now come and get me!" He scratched his head irritably. It seemed rather silly that she thought it necessary to go so far. Whites had the strangest ideas about their bodies!

"Take me to my father. I'll have my morning meal with him and my brother. Can you find your way back?"

She didn't catch his slight smile. "Of course I can!" She reached for his hand, but Tipaakke slid hers up around his arm. "I think I'll fare better this way." His heart skipped a beat as her light fingers curled around his arm. Her touch was warm and reassuring.

She nodded, then felt foolish. *He can't see you nod!* As they started off, her hand gripped the bronzed arm, and she absently fingered the muscular hardness. She had never seen a man with such muscles — and certainly never touched one! It amazed her that each muscle, each tendon, was so well defined. So pleasurable to touch. *Better keep your mind off such things.*

"May I ask you a question?" Katelyn blurted out.

"You may ask, but I don't promise I will give you an answer." The soft caress of her fingers eased his impatience with her.

"How is it that you speak my language so well?"

"I wondered why you have not asked anyone that before. From the Quakers north of here in Penn's Colony. My people travel often to avoid the white man and rival tribes. When I was a boy, we lived near a settlement of Quakers. My brother and I learned to speak their language. Most of my people speak some English. It's very helpful in trade. My father is the only one who hasn't learned anything of your people. Not their language, not their customs. He says he is too old."

Katelyn was so engrossed in what Tipaakke was saying that she didn't think to warn him of a tangle of brush at his feet. His bare foot caught sharply on a vine, and he tumbled to the ground pulling her with him.

"Oh no! You fool!"

"I'm sorry. I'm sorry! I wasn't thinking. Let me help you up." Katelyn struggled to rise but Tipaakke had her pinned. She pulled desperately at the doeskin dress wrapped around her waist. *Why didn't they at least let me keep my underthings?* Here she was with her bare bottom stuck in the air for anyone to see and that savage had one hand on her thigh!

"I can't believe you've done this! I can't believe I let you!"

"It won't happen again. Now get off me so I can get up!"

"Too late," Tipaakke growled, sitting up.

"What are you talking about?" Katelyn slid out from under him.

"This . . ." He held a clump of bright green leaves in his hand, shaking his head in disbelief.

"What? They're leaves. So . . ."

"Three leaves in a clump, right?"

"Yes."

"They feel oily don't they?"

Katelyn reached out to touch a leaf. "Yes, I suppose so."

"This is what the English call ivy. Poisoning ivy."

"Oh . . ."

"Do you know what's going to happen to us now that we've practically bathed in it?"

"No. I don't," she replied tartly. "I've never seen it before. I didn't spend much time in the woods!"

Tipaakke pulled himself slowly to his feet. "Just wait, girl. You'll see."

Katelyn scratched furiously at her arm and then dug at her bare leg. She'd never been in such infuriating pain in her life. The burning itch was more than she could tolerate. She'd been in the stream eight times since she'd broken out yesterday. And Tipaakke had fared no better. She glanced inside the wigwam. He was lying on his sleeping platform scratching his elbow. He'd sent for someone to bring a balm to help soothe the pain and swelling.

Katelyn reached up under her doeskin gown and

58

scratched her thigh. She didn't care if anyone saw her or not. They were just Indians. Besides with all of these naked bodies walking around, no one was likely to notice her bare thigh. The itch was maddening. She wished someone would hurry and bring the balm. The Indians weren't going to have to kill her; she was going to scratch herself to death. She glanced back at her captor.

He spent most of his time lying there morosely, his eyes open, seeing nothing. He left her well enough alone, speaking only when he needed something. Nothing more had been said about what was going to be done with her. She had been too fearful to ask. Time seemed to stretch out endlessly as she sat scratching, wondering if Henry would rescue her in time.

Katelyn's eyes fell upon a pair of large feet in front of her and traveled slowly up the body. A man's feet . . . long muscular legs . . . a woman's deer-hide dress! A bare chest . . . broad and flat . . . a man's grinning face . . . a woman's braids tied with beaded leather thongs.

Katelyn blinked, getting to her feet.

"They're right. Your hair is very beautiful," a deep, but feminine voice stated as she . . . he reached out to touch a shiny red lock. "I'm Won. Tipaakee sent for me." The English was heavily accented and spoken slowly, but Katelyn was able to understand every word.

"Come in." She motioned for Won to enter the wigwam and followed behind.

Tipaakke opened his eyes at the sound of footsteps. "Katelyn?"

"Yes. Won is here."

"I know. I heard her." He swung his feet over the sleeping platform, planting them firmly on the ground. "I hope you brought the healing salve. I'm in great

59

need." He spoke in his own language, just as he always did when another Indian was present.

Won nodded. "I heard what happened. Don't be too angry with her, Tipaakke. She didn't know."

"I did not ask for your opinion, Won," he snapped.

Won knelt in front of him and placed a small clay bowl in his hands. "I have faith in you," the soft voice teased. "You'll do the right thing. You always do. That's why we all have such respect for you. But then you already know that, don't you? I'm envious of her fire hair."

"Don't you think I have more things to concern myself with right now than that white woman? I've captured her, and she will be my servant until I decide otherwise."

"Of course." Won shrugged her shoulders, smiling. "No one has said otherwise. She is a beautiful slave, nothing more."

Tipaakke growled an inaudible comment as he smoothed the cream from the pot along the irritated skin of his left arm.

"You should give her a little, too. There is plenty and it would be a shame to mar that soft skin."

"Perhaps I should make her suffer for what she's done to me."

"Perhaps. But you won't." Won stood up, taking the container that Tipaakke handed her after a moment of indecision. "I hope this will ease your pain," she said in English to Katelyn.

Katelyn whispered a thank you and took the pot from her hand. Was that the faint scent of wildflowers she smelled?

Won spoke to Tipaakke for a few moments and then bid him farewell. She ducked low as she left the wigwam, taking care not to strike her head.

She was the tallest Indian Katelyn had seen since she'd entered the village a week ago. Why was she wearing woman's clothes but had no breasts? Katelyn was thoroughly confused.

"Well, go ahead. Ask." Tipaakke's tone was rough. He continued to spread the balm from the palm of his hand on his legs.

"What?"

"Won. You think her odd, don't you?"

So she is a girl. "Well, yes. She talks like a woman, wears the clothes of your woman, yet she's tall and has no . . ." Katelyn's face went crimson. What was wrong with her? She'd only been with these heathens a week and she was already acting uncivilized!

"No *tuulke* . . . no breasts. That is your English word, isn't it?" He couldn't help smiling at her embarrassment.

"Yes." She dropped her head, unable to believe she was discussing someone's private parts with this half-naked savage.

"Won is a woman who was born in a man's body."

"How can that be?"

"I don't know! I'm not the Creator. I only know what I see . . . or should I say hear? Won is a woman in her heart, so she is a woman to her people."

"Your name is Fox in my language. What is hers?" She scooped a bit of the balm from the pot and smoothed it over the welted rash on her arm, savoring the coolness.

"Her name is Bud . . . something Bud. A flower, red or yellow that climbs in sunny places. I don't know your word."

Roses! That's what she smelled! "Her name is Rosebud?"

"Yes. I think that's it. Won . . . Rosebud. The

English word is pretty, isn't it?" he finished thoughtfully.

Katelyn was taken aback. This was the first time he had spoken to her without menace in his voice, the first time he had appeared to be anything but a devilish savage. Henry would never have thought Rosebud was a pretty word. Henry . . . What was wrong with her? Had she gone daft? Comparing a gentleman like Henry Bullman to a heathen . . . a heathen that intended to kill her.

Tipaakke broke the silence with his calm, soothing voice. "When you finish with the balm, come put some on my back."

She came slowly, knowing she had to do as he said for self-preservation's sake but also knowing that touching him could be very dangerous. Dangerous because she knew what her reactions had been before at even the slightest physical contact. She sat down beside him, closer than she'd been since the day they'd fallen in the ivy. She dipped her hand into the pot, then hesitated, her hand in the air.

"Come. I'll not harm you." That same kind voice . . .

Katelyn took a deep breath and touched his broad back. He was warm, so warm. She'd never touched a man's back before, never felt the muscles ripple beneath her touch. God had created a wonderful thing when He created a man's back!

Tipaakke felt the spark leap between them as her hand first made contact with his skin. She was his prisoner, his slave. Her people had blinded him. What was it about her that brought this tightening in his loins? Was Manito playing games? Punishing him for something he had done? Or was he being compensated for his losses?

Katelyn ran her hand slowly across his shoulders,

62

rubbing the ointment into his raw flesh. She saw now that he had fared far worse than she. His entire body was covered with a welting rash, where only her arms and legs had been affected. She wondered how he had such willpower to keep from scratching. He hadn't dug at his skin like she had.

"That eases the pain, doesn't it, Katelyn?" Tipaakee closed his eyes, deciding to take what Manito handed him. What was wrong with a little pleasure of the flesh, slave or not? The white girl's hands were gentle but thorough. Her touch was nothing like his wife's had been, yet was equally arousing.

The muscles beneath her hands uncoiled. She continued to work in the salve, fingers and palms gliding over his abraded skin. *I should be ashamed to touch a man this way, a man who is not my husband. Have I fallen so far?* "There, I've finished." Her hands withdrew as if stung. She gasped when one was caught by a firm grip. "How did you do that? You said you can't see," she whispered, caught in his spell. She didn't attempt to pull away.

"I don't know how I did it. I felt your hand near me, I wanted to take it." He was as amazed as she. "You have a very soft touch, Katelyn. You have the hands of a healer. Did you care for the sick in your land across the oceans?"

"No. My father thought it indecent for a woman to touch others' bodies." She was mesmerized by his voice, so soft and liquidy, enchanted by the feel of his strong hand clasping hers.

"What do you think?" His voice came in the same breathy whisper as hers.

"I don't know." She felt her pulse quicken.

"Did you like touching me? Be truthful."

"Yes."

"Yes, what. Tell me. There is no one here to hear you."

"Yes." Her voice caught in her throat. "I liked touching you."

"There is nothing wrong with that, Katelyn. That is why men and women were made. I like you touching me." He paused, letting her absorb his words. "I don't know what is passing between us, but time will tell. I'm a patient man." Tipaakke brushed his lips across the back of her hand, sending a shiver of delight through her already trembling body. "Now go the stream and get water. Won will be back soon. I have asked her to teach you some of the duties that will be expected of you." He released her hand reluctantly.

"Yes," she returned breathlessly. She got to her feet. "I'll get the water."

The salve had done wonders for Katelyn's itching by the time Won reappeared, a small boy in tow.

"Katelyn, this is my son, Ameen." She wrapped one large arm around the boy and swung him into the air, forcing a string of giggles from him. "He is a good boy. Aren't you, my little bird who flys?" She dropped him to his feet, and the boy ducked into Tipaakke's wigwam.

Katelyn swirled her bare foot in the dust, unsure of what to say. But, Won continued to chatter, seemingly unaware of Katelyn's discomfort.

"It is a good thing for my boy to spend time with Tipaakke. He helps to bridge the loneliness. Tipaakke had a fine son. It is sad that he is gone." Won seated herself in front of the wigwam on a patch of grass and patted the earth beside her. "Sit. I am here to teach you a Lenni Lenape woman's duties. Tipaakke says you

64

must learn to cook and gather food so that you can care for him. What a lucky woman!" she added, giggling. "Such a fine man!"

Katelyn ignored her last comments and sat down to watch Won remove woven bags from around her shoulder and neck. She reached into one of the bags and, to Katelyn's horror, removed two wiggling fish.

"Just caught them. I will show how to clean and cook them. Also, we will make cakes of ground corn."

Katelyn wrinkled her nose. "They're still alive!"

"Yes, they are," she answered, wacking one and then the other on the back of the head with a rock. "But now they are not."

Katelyn swallowed hard. *Don't be a child. You've seen a dead man. What is a dead fish, but a meal?* "I've never cleaned one before. We ate them rarely in our house. My father was a mutton man."

"Mut-ton? What is this mut-ton?" Won's eyes flashed brightly.

"It's lamb. Sheep."

"Sheep? This word, I don't know."

"No. I don't guess there would be sheep out here. The meat is strong, very fatty. It was Father's favorite; always served on Tuesdays, Thursdays, Saturdays and alternating Sundays."

"Fatty? This mut-ton might be good for tanning hides, but not for eating. It is not good for the skin to eat the fat of animals. I eat many berries, fish and birds. It keeps my skin smooth. Did you like this fat mut-ton?" She removed a thin stone from one of her baskets.

"It didn't matter if I like it. It was what the Lord provided."

"Pro-vided?"

"Gave."

"I think it is what your father gave. Humph! If I did not like this mut-ton, I would not eat it. I would tan my hides with it. Now watch me."

Katelyn leaned over Won, who had retrieved a large, flat stone from near the wigwam. She resigned herself to the fact that she must learn to clean this smelly thing if Fox wanted her to. She had to. Her life lay in the palm of his hand.

"This rock is for cleaning and fixing the meal. Is there a flat piece of tree in the wigwam? This big." She opened her arms in demonstration.

"I don't know."

"Get up and look!" Won shook her head. Maybe Mekollaan was right. Maybe the girl *was* touched.

Katelyn scrambled up and ducked into the wigwam. The boy was sitting in front of Tipaakke on the floor, giggling as they played some sort of game patting hands. Tipaakke didn't play well, only hitting the child's hands by accident, but that made Ameen all the happier.

"Fox." His name tasted tingly on her tongue. "Is there a flat board here? Won says there's one to clean fish."

"Yes. Where the baskets and pots lay on the floor. It was my wife's." He returned to the game as Ameen pulled his large hands up to meet small ones.

"Here. I found it. It was his wife's." Katelyn returned to Won's side. "Do you think it's all right? To use her board, I mean?"

"Yes, why not? She would want someone to care for her man. Now watch me."

She nodded, leaning closer. If it was necessary to clean fish to stay alive, then clean fish she would.

"To clean the flesh of animals, you place the board on your rock. It is better that the cutting stone hits

66

wood. It doesn't dull so fast." Won crossed her legs, pulling her skirt down delicately. "I make the best fish of anyone in the village, so watch me. It is the secret flowers I grind and sprinkle on them as they cook." She laid one fish on the board and began to scrape the scales with great efficiency.

"Why do you scrape the skin?"

"To take off the . . . I don't know the word. Here, feel." She grabbed her hand and ran it against the scales. "There are some fish that you peel the skin off, ones that swim in the great water. But these we scrape." She flipped the fish over and continued. "You have not asked me why I have a son when I have a man's body."

Katelyn's eyes grew wide. Everyone here was so blunt. "I did wonder," Katelyn stammered, "but, I was afraid to ask. I didn't want to be rude."

"Yes. Sometimes it is not right to ask questions that don't concern you or your family. But I don't mind questions. I know I'm different."

"Why do you have a child, then?" Katelyn kept one eye on the fish Won was scaling.

"His mother drowned in the great water, his father was killed in a Mohawk raid. He had no grandparents so I asked the chief if I could take Ameen for my son. Our chief is a very wise man. He gave me my wish. I am a good mother to my boy, and the men in the village are his fathers. Watch me."

The bile arose in Katelyn's throat as she watched Won split the fish's belly open and pull out long strings of goo.

"You clean the insides out. Save them, we'll use them later. You can cut the head and tail off, if you want. I like to leave them on; the fish looks so nice, baking that way. Do as you wish." She pushed the fish aside and opened Katelyn's hand, sliding the slimey stone knife into it. "Now is your chance. Show me what a smart girl you are."

Katelyn gripped the knife in her hand, whispering a quick prayer. She wondered what her father would think if he knew she was asking God to help her clean a fish. "Well, here goes," she mumbled. *If I can survive an Indian raid, I can certainly clean a fish!* She began to scrape at the skin, but the fish kept sliding across the board.

"Here, slide your hand in here. It will give you a better grip." Won pushed her fingers into the fish's gills. "Isn't that better?"

She could only nod and continue to scrape. *Now what? The other side.* When she finished scraping the scales, she glanced up at Won, who gave an encouraging nod. This was the test. If she could open the fish's belly without getting sick, she would be done.

"Go ahead." Won smiled reassuringly.

Katelyn slid the tip of the knife in at the tail end, amazed at how sharp the stone knife was. It was far sharper than the metal knives in her father's home!

"Good. You learn well." Won was delighted with her pupil's progress. "Remove the insides and you're done." She clasped her hands in excitement.

Katelyn squirmed when her hand touched the still warm, squishy strings, but she persevered until the flesh was clean.

"You've done it right! And your first time. I've won the bet!"

"What bet? I'm not finished yet." She caught her tongue between her teeth and sliced at the fish's head with the knife. She wasn't cooking any fish with the head still attached!

"It was nothing. Mekollaan heard that I was coming to teach you how to clean fish and he bet me that you couldn't do it. He said that you would make such a mess of it that no one would be able to eat it but the dogs. But you did it, and now that she-hen owes me a new necklace."

Katelyn smiled at Won's mirth. "Then I'm glad I helped you win. I don't like Hawk; he is an evil man."

"No. He isn't evil. He has his own ideas and it is not easy to sway him. Behave and work well. His mind will be changed."

"I don't care what he thinks! He's a horrible man. He attacked me the first night I was here."

"I heard. But you should forget that. He meant no harm. We hear stories of what the whites are like. They are not always true. Hawk was just testing to see what you'd allow. What man doesn't with a pretty young girl?"

"I am not pretty, and I'm not that young. Tell me how to make these corn cakes. I'll show Hawk and his brother. They both think me daft just because I wasn't brought up the way they were."

"Not young! Of course you are. What are you, twenty-two summers?"

"Twenty-four."

"You do not look like my people, but in your land I am sure that many men offered your father many horses and blankets to get you in their wigwam."

"Certainly not! It is not our way to sell women!" Katelyn's eyes dropped. *Not our way? Then why did no man come to call on me all those years? Why did I sit in the window watching others go to parties? Because I had no dowry. And why did Henry appear so quickly after her father's inheritance came through?* She had been sold to the only bidder . . .

"I see that you are one of those woman who doesn't know her worth. I've been told that whites don't have respect for their women like we do." Won stood up.

69

"Where is your washing bowl?"

"There." Katelyn pointed to the large pottery bowl that she had been instructed to keep full so that Tipaakke would always have clean water to wash with.

Won dipped her hands into the water. "In our village, a woman is a precious thing. Here, we are the heads of our households. The children are ours, the wigwam is ours, and everything in it. If a woman wishes her husband to be her husband no more, she places his tools and weapons outside her door and announces that he is not her husband." She shook her hands to dry them. "When a man marries, it is into this wife's family. It is he who must deal with another mother. I like being a woman among the Lenni Lenape. Men do nothing but hunt, war, and give us children." She laughed. "I like being a woman because I like the power." She raised a clenched fist.

Katelyn rinsed her hands, too. Women with power? *Here I would have the right to make my own decisions. No, you've forgotten, Kate. You're not one of them; you'll never be. You're a prisoner. Take things one day at a time. You may not be here tomorrow.*

"Now I will show you how to make corn cakes, and then we'll cook them. Stir up the fire so that it will be ready." She pointed to the smouldering ashes near the wigwam. "Tolaala and I have been tending Tipaakke's fire, but now you will care for it. In the summer we keep our cooking fire outside, but in the winter it is in the wigwam."

"That's what the hole in the roof is for!"

"That's right. You're not dumb. You must keep the fire going at all times. During the day you can cover it with damp leaves, it will smoke some, but will not go out."

Katelyn took a seat beside Won, determined to learn

70

all she could from her. It didn't matter that Won was different. If she had the patience to teach her, she was going to learn. Each day that she learned and carried out more tasks properly, the more use she would be to Tipaakke. If he needed her, he wouldn't kill her. This would all be something she and Henry would sit around the fire in the parlor and laugh about someday.

Katelyn concentrated as Won taught her to mix the ground *huskuiim* with water and a bit of fat and to fry the flat, little *apoon* cakes on a heated rock. They then wrapped the fish in damp, green leaves, after sprinkling herbs from a bag of them, and buried the bundle in the hot coals.

"There. You have learned well today." Won patted Katelyn on the back. "Ameen, *buumska!*"

The dark-haired boy appeared from the wigwam, bringing Tipaakke in tow.

"I told your son that I can't take him hunting, but he won't listen. He says he will spot the animals, and I will shoot in the direction he tells me!" Tipaakke laughed, tousling Ameen's hair.

Katelyn suddenly realized he was speaking in English. It had to be for her benefit, but why? He'd never spoken to another Indian in English before.

"How has she done, Won?"

Won began tucking her cooking utensils into the reed baskets, a smile crossing her wide face. "Wait, you will see. I like her, this white girl. I have her to thank for a new necklace." She glanced back at Katelyn, giving her a wink.

Katelyn giggled, happy to be in on the joke.

"You must have had a good day. She is giggling like a maiden with her first man." His voice was light and playful.

"I'll be back tomorrow. Enjoy your meal, Tipaakke.

71

I'm glad to see that my herb balm has improved your mood. Where is that boy? He's as slippery as an eel!"

"There he goes, Won." Katelyn pointed across the village. "There, petting the dog."

Won swung the two bags over her shoulder and headed in the direction of her son.

When the fish was baked, Katelyn led Tipaakke back outside the wigwam and sat him down. She unwrapped the fragrant meat carefully and divided it, placing the larger portion on a small square board and pushing it into Tipaakke's hands.

"Smells good."

Katelyn lifted the corn cakes from the hot stone and dropped them onto his board and hers, licking her burnt fingertips.

"Here are your corn cakes . . . *huskuiim apoon*."

Tipaakke nodded, taking note that she had spoken her first Lenni Lenape words. "They're good." He nodded his head. "Sit. Eat."

Katelyn dropped onto the ground and pulled her wooden plate onto her lap. All of the work and concentration had made her hungry. "I've never cooked anything like this before. The food we ate in England was quite different."

"I heard you speaking to Won. I have eaten mutton. I wouldn't feed it to my father's dogs. Help me with this fish. I can't pick the bones."

She got up obediently and sat down beside him, surprising them both. "Give me your plate."

"Plate? Oh. Yes, you're right, girl. These are our plates. I hadn't thought of them that way. We eat mostly from shells, but I find it much easier to eat from this board."

Katelyn picked his fish carefully, piling the clean meat on one side. "Here." She pushed the board onto his lap again. "The clean meat is here." Without thinking, she grabbed his hand and guided it to the meat.

Lightning . . . Lightning passed between them. Neither could deny it.

Katelyn stared into the sightless dark eyes. Those eyes haunted her when she tried to sleep at night. They were the eyes that she found herself searching for in the crowd of so many dark eyes.

"I think I like this kind of help," Tipaakke teased softly.

"Fox . . ."

"Hush, girl. Enjoy the moment. Isn't it a wonder that a person can gain such pleasure from touching another's hand? Savor the moment, Katelyn. It doesn't happen often in a lifetime." He turned his hand so that it held hers.

Katelyn could feel his breath on her cheek, he was so near. Yet, she didn't pull away, perhaps out of fear, perhaps because she knew she liked his touch.

Tipaakke raised his other hands to caress her soft cheek. "I think I'll kiss you," he whispered, her warm lips guiding him near. "Sight is not always a necessary thing."

"Please . . ." Katelyn caught her breath as his lips met hers, softly, briefly . . . teasingly.

"Sins of flesh . . ." her father whispered across the ocean. "Filthy heathens!" Henry echoed.

She pulled away, shaken. She had *let* him kiss her. "Eat. It will grow cold." Her heart pounded.

Tipaakke nodded. He didn't know what had possessed him to kiss her, but he was glad he did. There was no denying his desire for the white girl. He just didn't understand it. "This is good, too." He spoke lightly, trying to calm her. "You've done a good job.

From now on you'll cook all of the meals. Won will teach you more. I like fish, but I couldn't eat it every day."

When they had finished the meal, Katelyn scraped the boards clean and rinsed them with fresh water. After stoking the fire, she stepped into the wigwam and retrieved the spare dress Tolaala had brought her the morning before.

"Where are you going?" Tipaakke sat just outside the wigwam door.

"To take a bath." What right did he have to ask her? He'd promised she could come and go as she pleased. "You said I could go to the stream as often as I wished." She spoke slowly, her lips tight with anger.

"Yes, go ahead. You wouldn't be foolish enough to wander off." He stood up, groping for the door. "Let me get a clean loin cloth. I'll go, too. You can help me with my bath."

"Help?" Katelyn choked. "Help you bathe? I think that ball in your head has made you crazy. If you think I'm going to . . ."

Tipaakke ducked into the wigwam before she could finish, smiling mischievously.

Chapter Four

"If I were the captive, I'd hold my tongue, girl."

Katelyn's eyes narrowed. Was he joking? She couldn't be sure. Was there a hint of a smile? "But if you were my prisoner, I wouldn't ask you to give me a bath," she dared.

Tipaakke laughed, enjoying her wit. Not many could find humor in her situation. "Perhaps the enemy and his prisoner could bargain . . . if the enemy wished." He leaned against the frame of the wigwam.

"Perhaps."

"Ameen can take me to the woods. But you—" he pointed. "You will take me to the stream. A path leads to the water. As long as you keep to the path I should be safe."

He knows I have no choice. She nodded. "All right."

"Good. Now, come." He extended a hand. "Take the poor blind man to bathe."

Katelyn hesitated. Each time she touched him, she felt herself slipping further. He's cast a spell over here. She wanted to touch him again and again. Henry must rescue her in time, not only from the Indian, but from herself. Looping her arm in his, they set out across the village.

"Why were you in that wagon with the coward?"

75

Tipaakke's voice was softly inquisitive.

Katelyn's eyes drifted from the giant maples and oaks that towered above them. "Why do you care?"

"I don't. I am curious. You don't have to tell me."

"I know I don't."

"I've warned you. Watch your sharp tongue. You are still my prisoner. Your life is mine to do with as I wish."

She stopped abruptly, turning to study the chiseled bronze face. "I'm not likely to forget that, am I!" She inhaled sharply. "Come on." She tugged on his arm. "How dare you call Henry a coward. We were to be married . . ." Mentally, she counted the days that had passed since her capture. ". . . in four days."

"Where were you going in the wagon? That is not a path traveled often by the white man."

"We were coming from Annapolis where the ship docked." Katelyn held a branch until he'd passed. "Henry decided to take that road to his father's plantation."

"You love this Henry?"

No matter what she said, it would be wrong.

"No need to answer. I don't remember the eyes of a woman in love. That dog! He doesn't love you."

"That's not true. Step over the log. He went to get help. He had no choice. He couldn't have fought you and the others off with no weapon."

"What lies did he tell his people? . . . A man who comes home without his woman."

"You're cruel, do you know that? Henry was right. You're nothing but filthy, ignorant savages!" Katelyn jerked away. "Just wait. He'll be back for me and he won't be alone. Then you'll be . . ."

Instinctively, Tipaakke caught her arm, jolting her. "Listen to me, girl. He's not coming back. Not ever. The man is a worthless coward. You are better off without him. He was not even among the men who

76

attacked us at the village."

"What do you mean? Of course he was. He went to get them. He was there, he was looking for me. You just didn't see him!" Katelyn struggled, dropping her spare dress and beating him with her fists. "He's coming for me! I tell you, he's coming!"

Tipaakke pinned her against him. "Shhhh." He whispered in Algonquian. "It is not your fault he left you. He was a fool to leave a woman so beautiful. Hush, my dove. You deserve better. He was not the man for you. It was not meant to be."

Halfheartedly, Katelyn tried to break free. How could she be so stupid? He could have knocked her senseless. "I'm all right now. Let go of me," she ordered through clenched teeth.

"If you behave," he said in English. "But you must learn to control yourself! You make a fool out of us in front of my people. You think they can't hear?" Slowly, he released her.

"There's the water."

"I know, I can hear it. I can smell the rocks, too."

"No one can smell rocks!"

"I can. I smell moss growing on the rocks."

Katelyn planted her hands firmly on her hips. "Well, if you can hear and smell so well, why do you need me to lead you around like a child!"

Tipaakke winced. "Because, girl, I can't smell fallen logs!"

"Stop calling me girl!" Grabbing her dress, she stormed off.

Why was this happening to her? She was supposed to marry a wealthy tobacco farmer and move into a big house with servants. She wasn't supposed to be in the wilderness with a crazy blind Indian! She should have died with Jonathan. It would have made things easier. And where was Henry? It had been more than a week.

He should have found her by now.

"Don't go too far," Tipaakke called.

Katelyn turned to shout, then spun back in horror. He was naked! She'd just seen a man's naked buttocks! Fox's naked . . . She plunged into the frigid water. Nothing would save her from burning in hell now.

Tipaakke waded into the stream, feeling along the dirt bottom with his toes until he found the pool his people had dug out when they'd settled in this spot. He leaned forward, dipping his hair in and then swinging it back so that the water splashed in all directions.

"Take care, brother. That's cold!" Mekollaan shielded his body with his hands.

"Don't do that unless you wish to lose your life."

"Do what, little brother?" He raised his eyebrows innocently.

"Sneak like a rat."

"I didn't mean to startle you. I wasn't really sneaking."

"Don't lie, foolish one. I know why you were sneaking, hiding in the bushes. Forget it. She swims with her dress on. She takes it off only to bathe and that is behind brush."

"You accuse me of such young-buck games?"

"I accuse, but not falsely. I think you should go hunting for a few days. You are like a caged cat."

"It's only because I worry over you." Mekollaan slipped off the bank with a splash. "Do you still intend to go through with this foolish notion?"

"Don't you understand?" Tipaakke clenched his fists. "I am blind. My life has been taken from me, yet I remain here. I cannot hunt. I can never provide for a family. There is nothing else for me here."

"But how will you live through the winter? When I return in the spring I will find nothing but bones." Mekollaan floated on his back, his hands propelling him in circles.

"She will care for me," he replied, half to himself.

"How? The woman can't care for herself. She is helpless. And how will you defend yourselves? You know the Mohawks raid that area."

"She is not as helpless as you think. She is very intelligent. Won has taught her much already. I will teach her to snare, maybe hunt. She will learn to handle a weapon."

"Hunt. You are joking. If the Mohawks or trappers don't kill you, you'll starve." He cupped the water in his hand, splashing Tipaakke in the face.

"Then I will starve."

"She will starve, too," he taunted.

"That is enough. I will decide how to live. It is only for the winter. I need time to think away from my people . . . away from you and our father."

"And *with* her?"

"*Her* name is Katelyn. Why do you concern yourself with my prisoner?" Tipaakke waded slowly to the shore.

"Because she's trouble. Kill her or take her back to them." He followed behind, flinching when Tipaakke tripped, almost going under.

"She is mine. That coward does not deserve her." He pushed his long, sleek hair off his shoulders.

"She could never be one of us you know. She hates us. She hates you."

"Did I say I wanted her to become one of us? I don't care what she thinks. She doesn't know what is best for her."

"I just don't know what it is you want her for. Any of the young ones could be your servant. You haven't even made use of her body."

"This conversation has come to an end, brother." He spoke through clenched teeth, his voice deathly low.

79

Mekollaan shook his head, running his hand along his scalplock. "I just hope you know what you're doing." He retied his loincloth and walked silently away.

When Katelyn returned she found Tipaakke sitting in the moss, leaning against a tree. He turned his head, recognizing her footsteps, then returned to his sightless staring.

"I heard you arguing with him. He wants to kill me, doesn't he?"

"You don't know our language. You don't know what we said. Where do you get your silly ideas?"

"I'm silly? You think I'm silly because I don't want to die?"

"I told you. You won't die as long as you do as I say."

"Maybe I'd be better off dead." Her eyes narrowed speculatively.

"Maybe I would, too." Tipaakke nodded solemnly. "But we are not, so we must deal with life. Let us go."

After a morning meal of fresh berries, Katelyn went into the wigwam to get some baskets. She was to meet Won at the garden for her lesson. Tipaakke lay on his platform staring at the roof, seeing nothing. Katelyn ignored him.

They hadn't spoken since the night before at the stream. She hated him. Only the fact that Henry was coming kept her sane.

She snatched up two woven baskets and stalked out stiffly. She'd show that high and mighty savage. Just wait until Henry and his father got here; then he wouldn't be so smug. She expected them any time now. They had to be near, maybe even watching them this minute. She would only have to play this game a little longer and then she'd be free of all of them.

She ambled through the village toward the raised garden, taking in the busy excitement of morning. Children ran laughing while women gathered cookware and clothes to be washed. They would take their things down stream from the bathing area and wash the cooking utensils and then the clothes. They would hang the clothing on branches stripped of leaves, and sit and gossip while their belongings dried.

"There you are. I thought maybe you not coming." Won grinned, her braids swinging. "I thought maybe you think I work you too hard."

"No, you're good to me, Won. You're my one friend." Katelyn dropped her baskets to the ground beside Won's.

"What is the matter with you so pucker faced? I can't believe that handsome brave treats you bad."

"Yes, he treats me badly! I'm a prisoner, aren't I?" She ground her teeth.

"Yes. But if you were here of your own will, wouldn't this be a good life?" She picked up a basket and started down a row of squash.

"I wouldn't be here! No. This is not the kind of life I would lead. I'm going to have a big house. My betrothed is very rich. I will have dresses, money, jewelry even."

"And for that you sell yourself . . .?" Won shook her head, stooping to pick the crooknecks.

"No! What has he been telling you? Don't believe what he says, he twists my words."

"But does he twist your thoughts? A man who leaves his woman to fend for herself is not a man. A woman who leaves her man in the hands of the enemy is not a woman. You don't need this man, this Henry Coward. Better to marry Fox and have many kits."

"Marry him? You're as crazy as he is! I hate him. Besides, I won't be here much . . . I don't want to talk about this anymore. Tell me what we're doing."

"This is a squash. It is good boiled. It is good sliced, rolled in cornmeal and fried. We will dry much of it for winter. When the wind blows and the snow falls we will be glad to have it."

"How do I know if they're ripe?" Katelyn kneeled between the cultivated rows behind Won.

"Do you see how the stems have shriveled and turned brown? This is ready." She tapped another yellow squash hidden among the vines. "This one, another day or two."

"You have become a good slave woman, Kate-lyn."

Katelyn looked up to see Mekollaan towering above her. She turned her back on him, hoping he would just go away.

"I tried to get my brother to sell you to me but he was asking too much. I have no wife. I could use a woman to cook for me, give me baths . . ." he taunted, kicking idly at a basket on the ground. "Couldn't find an Indian woman to do all that."

"Do you want something?" Katelyn turned venomous eyes on Mekollaan. He was wearing a deerskin loincloth and a large white-linen shirt.

"You. But I guess you won't be around much longer."

"Mekollaan, you walk where you're not wanted. Leave her be. Your brother will be angry." Won shook a squash angrily at him.

He stroked his scalplock, enjoying himself immensely.

"What are you talking about. You're right, you're not going to have me, but neither is he." She threw another squash into the basket and got to her feet. "I'm not going to be here because my betrothed is coming with his men and he's going to kill the both of you!"

"That is foolish, girl. You know he's not coming. We live less than a day's ride from your brave man. He's not coming for you, not ever."

"I'm not going to argue with you. Just leave me alone, you filthy . . ."

Mekollaan caught her arm as she swung at him. "But if he is coming, he'd better hurry. In another moon you and Tipaakke will be on your way."

"On our way? On our way where? What is he ranting about, Won?"

Won got up and pulled Katelyn's arm from Mekollaan's iron grip. "He wanted to tell her himself. Sometimes you are a foolish man." She walked away, pulling Katelyn behind her.

"You and my brother will be spending the winter in a cabin," Mekollaan called after them. "Alone . . ." He laughed deep in his throat.

"Stop, Won. What is he talking about? I can't go. Henry won't be able to find me." She struggled frantically.

Won dragged her along, ignoring her protests. She wanted to get Katelyn back to the wigwam before she caused another scene. She pushed her through Tipaakke's door, sending her sprawling.

"Tell me what he's talking about. Tell me!" Katelyn scrambled up and stood before Tipaakke.

He leaped to his feet. "What is she talking about, Won?" Tipaakke grabbed Katelyn's hands.

"The Hawk has swooped again. He told her about the cabin. I tried to stop him. I don't like to see her hurting." Won spoke softly in the Delaware tongue.

"I know. It's all right, it wasn't your fault. You can go." He nodded to dismiss her.

"Will you please speak English! You are the coward! You! You don't tell me I'm going somewhere when everyone else knows. Then you stand in front of me and talk that gibberish as if I don't exist! Let go of my hands!" Katelyn's body shook with anger.

"Calm down and I will let you go. I will make you understand."

"You can't take me away. He won't be able to find

83

me." Her voice had reached the point of desperation.

Tipaakke longed to reach out and comfort her, to protect her from the pain, but he knew he must be strong. It was for her good. It was the only way.

"I have decided to make a journey. I must spend time away from my people. I must have time to think."

"Just let me stay here . . . with Won. Please."

"Katelyn, you must face the fact. He is not coming."

"He is!"

"No. He is not. If he was coming, he would have been here days ago. If you had been my woman, I would not have slept until you were back in my arms. You have no one but me now. I need you to care for me. We will go to a cabin a few days from here. We will winter there. Mekollaan will take us there and come back for us in the spring."

"Why are you doing this to me?" Katelyn pleaded desperately. "Why do you hurt me like this? Just let me go." She stared at the stone face only inches from hers, tears forming in the corners of her eyes. If she didn't hate him so much, she would have thought he was handsome with his sleek, dark hair and haunting eyes.

"I do not do it to hurt you. But I don't question the stars. You are meant to be here with me. He was never for you. He was only Manito's way of getting you here. Don't you see?" Tipaakke pleaded softly. Though he had no sight, he could see her in his mind. He could feel her fiery hair. He could hear her pain. He could taste her tears.

"Why me, Fox?" she whispered. "Tell me why." His touch sent a strange shiver down her spine.

"I don't know. Just give it time. Nothing happens without a reason." He reached out to touch a bright lock bouncing on her shoulder and she jerked back as if his fingers were flames. "I won't hurt you," he murmured reaching for her again.

This time Katelyn allowed him to grasp the long strand, and watched, mesmerized, as he wrapped it around and around his finger.

"Never have I seen hair this color," he breathed, his voice wafting to caress her ears.

When Tipaakke moved his hand to brush her cheek, she stood perfectly still, her eyes searching his. She had never felt so odd in her life. Every time he touched her, she trembled, her stomach grew fluttery and her heart palpitated wildly. What was this feeling deep in the pit of her stomach that made her yearn for her enemy's touch? She closed her eyes, enchanted by the feel of his hot breath on her face.

"That's right," he soothed in Algonquian, running his fingers over her quivering lips. "No need to fear me. You have no one but me, let me care for you. Let me heal your wounds of life. Heal mine. I can promise you nothing. But that is no less than you have now." He pressed his lips to her dewy eyelids, first one, then the other. Her skin was as soft as the down of a newly hatched eaglet.

Katelyn trembled as he guided her hands over his bare chest and coiled them around his neck, but she didn't pull away. His skin seared her hands, but she felt no pain, only an odd tingle of pleasure.

"I can make you feel very good," he tempted as he lowered his mouth to brush against her lips.

Shame flooded Katelyn, staining her cheeks crimson, but she offered no resistance. As much as she hated to admit it, she liked the feel of his lips on hers. She saw no logic in it, the man held her against her will, but she couldn't help swaying against him as his kiss became more insistent. When his tongue slipped from his mouth to touch her lips, she stiffened. What was it about this savage that made her do what she would never have dared before? Slowly, she parted

85

trembling lips, allowing his to penetrate her mouth.

Tipaakke tightened his grip around Katelyn's waist as he explored the cool, moist lining of her mouth. Never had he tasted anything so sweet, so arousing. Molding his body to hers, he ran his fingers through her thick hair, breathing deeply. Her soft, alluring scent enveloped him setting his loins on fire. "Ah, my sweet vixen," he murmured.

Overcome by the flames of her awakening desires, Katelyn moaned softly, astonished by the mixed emotions that washed over her. She was so confused. She wanted to run, but she wanted to stay. She wanted him to stop his intimate caressing, but a small part of her wanted to touch him in return.

Tipaakke heard the sharp snap of leather. Only one person would be so rude as to enter a wigwam when the door was closed. "Mekollaan, has blindness overtaken you as well?" His voice was brittle. His brother would destroy all he had just accomplished!

Katelyn shrank back at the sound of the moving leather and Tipaakke's harsh voice. Jerking her hands off his shoulders, she spun around, mortified by her actions. Had she lost her mind? She'd actually let that heathen kiss her . . . no, she kissed him.

"Well, well, what do I see here?" Mekollaan spoke in English for Katelyn's benefit.

Katelyn sank down on Tipaakke's sleeping platform, dropping her head in her hands. She had to clear her mind. This was more than she could stand.

"Mekollaan . . ." Tipaakke threatened, standing his ground.

"Forgive me. I didn't realize you two were . . . busy. I will come back later. I know better than to bother a man and woman when they are . . ."

"Mekollaan, unless you want a knife in your throat you will leave!" Tipaakke commanded in Algonquian.

"Now!"

Katelyn looked up to see Hawk grinning. When he caught her eye he raised one eyebrow questioningly . . . accusingly.

With each passing second, she became more furious. If she had a gun right now, she could blow his leering face off. She hated him. She hated all of them!

Afraid she would be unable to suppress her anger any longer, she ran past both men and ducked out of the wigwam. She couldn't stay here! If Henry wasn't coming for her, she would just have to find him. Better to be eaten by wolves in the forest than to be devoured by men like these.

When Katelyn returned to the wigwam at nightfall, she went straight to her mat on the floor. She had sent Ameen with Tipaakke's dinner so she wouldn't have to face him. She had spent the rest of the day with Won and her son, refusing to return to Tipaakke's wigwam until it was time to sleep.

She pulled a deerskin over her body, snuggling down in the soft fur that covered her mat. Her mind was made up. She was leaving tonight. She had only to wait until the entire village retired. Tipaakke was already asleep on his platform, his back to her. When he woke in the morning, she'd be gone. He wouldn't be able to look for her and no one else would care enough to. She would follow the stream, then cut inland, walking into the sun when it rose. She would find Henry and her new life or die trying. Her mind was made up. Fox couldn't stop her.

Katelyn rolled over on her side and gazed through the darkness at Tipaakke's sleeping form. A deerskin was flung carelessly across his middle; his legs and back were bare. She watched as his side rose and fell with each breath. His back was lithe and muscular. She yearned to reach out and stroke those well-formed muscles, to run her finger along his spine, to knead his massive shoulders. She had never seen such beautiful hair on a man, so black, so sleek. She could almost smell the clean, woodsy scent that clung to it.

She rolled over. She had to get away from him before it was too late. What was wrong with her? Only a brazen hussy would think such indecent thoughts. Besides, he was the enemy. He had taken her from her betrothed and forced her into slavery. He was holding her against her will!

Slowly the moon rose until Katelyn could see its full roundness through the hole in the wigwam roof. Still lying on her back, she reached out feeling for the corncakes she'd hoarded. She stuffed them into a woven basket she'd left purposely near her mat. Very slowly, she got up and swung the basket over her shoulder. Grabbing the fur skin from the sleeping mat, she slipped silently out the door. Tipaakke slept soundly.

Katelyn crouched in the shadow of the wigwam, checking to be sure no one was about. She wrapped the hide around her shoulders and made her way to the outside ring of wigwams. She knew she would have less of a chance of being seen if she kept behind the wigwams until she reached the path to the stream. She walked slowly, taking care to stay on the grass. *Fox thinks he's so smart. Just wait until he wakes and finds me gone!* She smiled in the semidarkness.

The full moon lit her way to the path, and she was soon at the bank of the stream. She debated for a moment and then decided to leave her moccasins on. They would protect her feet from sharp stones on the bottom, and she could dry them out in the morning. She stepped into the water, silencing the urge to cry out. The water was so cold! It was hard to believe winter would soon be upon them. In a matter of days it would be September. Won said the snow would be falling by October.

She walked far enough from the bank so as not to bump into the grass. She knew from Won's stories that the Indians were excellent trackers. But if she kept to the water for a mile or two, she thought she'd be safe. Without any signs, no one would look too long.

Soon the excitement of her escape wore off, and she began to tire. Katelyn pulled the deerskin cloak closer, wishing she'd chosen one with leather ties. It was difficult to keep her balance in the knee deep water when she was carrying the basket and holding the cloak.

Her legs grew numb, and she trudged on, trying to ignore the hooting and calling of the strange animals in the forest. She wasn't easily spooked, but the moon gave off such eerie shadows that, more than once, the bear she spotted turned out to be a tall bush or a fallen log.

After what seemed an eternity, Katelyn decided she'd come far enough by water. She had to rest. The moon had moved far enough in the sky that she knew two or three hours had passed. She waded to the bank and climbed out, using a young sapling for support. She fell into the grass and pulled the damp skin cloak over her. How could it be so cool already? Then she remembered Won mentioning that summer had come so early this year that winter was sure to arrive early, too.

Realizing she'd probably get warm more quickly without the damp animal hide, she shrugged it off her shoulders and got to her feet. Once the sun came up she'd make good time. Heading east, she'd be bound to find a plantation by dusk. Pacing back and forth, Katelyn suddenly realized her basket was gone. She laid it by that tree, she was sure of it. She glanced around frantically. Was she losing her mind? She started around the massive trunk of the tree. Maybe she'd knocked the basket over and it had rolled.

Practically running into Mekollaan, she screamed. "What are you doing?" Her hand went to her pounding heart. "You scared me to death!"

Mekollaan gave her one of his half-lipped smiles, swinging her basket on one long finger. "You didn't give up as soon as I thought you would."

"Why are you sneaking up on me? I know you hate me. Just let me go. Tell him you couldn't find me." She snatched the basket from his hand.

"Couldn't find you? Tipaakke could have found you on his own! Your tracks were all over the riverbed." He laughed coarsely. "I do not hate you. But you do not belong with us."

"So let me go." She stood her ground. She wasn't going to be bullied by him anymore.

"If I had my way, I would. You could probably find your way back to your white man. But my brother wants you, so he will have you."

"No! Not ever!" She turned to yank the skin off the ground and stalked off.

Mekollaan took two quick steps forward and grabbed her arm. "I don't like this any better than you, but my brother has some strange idea that you are a gift from our god. He says you are his. So you must go back."

"You can't make me go. You can kill me but you can't make me go!" Her brown eyes went steely.

He felt a flicker of admiration as he leaned over to swing her onto his shoulder. The girl had spirit.

"Let me go! Just kill me! I'd rather be dead than go back to him!" She kicked furiously pulling at his muslin shirt.

Mekollaan swung her over his back, letting her

dangle from the waist down and started off.

Katelyn kicked and swung until she didn't have an ounce of strength left in her and finally she grew still.

"Has the child finished?" Mekollaan swung her to the ground.

Katelyn slumped to the grass.

"Now you will walk, Kate-lyn?"

She spoke softly under her breath in the Algonquian manner. "You will carry me every step of the way . . ."

Mekollaan rolled his eyes and leaned over to pick her up. *Women!* he swung her over his shoulder, refusing to make things easy for her.

Katelyn hung over his back the rest of the way to the village, refusing each time he stopped to walk herself. It made her dizzy and nauseated to hang upside down like this but she didn't care. He'd leave her, kill her, or carry her, those were his choices. Those were the choices *she* gave him.

They entered the village just before dawn. Mekollaan gave her one more chance to walk to Tipaakke's wigwam to save face, but she refused. Mekollaan ducked into the wigwam and dumped her unceremoniously on the ground.

Tipaakke turned from where he stood, his face grim. "You found her." He spoke English.

"Yes, he found me," Katelyn snapped, pulling herself to her feet.

"I would have been back sooner but she refused to walk. I had to carry her." Mekollaan added good-naturedly in his own tongue. "You have quite a woman here, I hope you can handle her."

"Thank you, brother. You are good to me." Tipaakke reached out and touched Mekollaan's arm.

Mekollaan made a quick exit, closing the leather flap behind him.

Tipaakke turned to face Katelyn, almost as if he

91

could see her. He *could* see her . . . in his mind. He could see her bright, wind-strewn hair, her long legs, the determined look on her face. And he could smell her anger.

"So what is to be done here, Katelyn? You promised you wouldn't try to escape. I trusted you. I heard you leave but I hoped you would return on your own. Mekollaan followed you out of the village. I asked him to stay close enough to keep you safe but to give you a chance to change your mind."

"I didn't change my mind; I still hate you." The tip of her pink tongue darted out to dampen her dry lips. She was scared.

"No, you don't hate me. You fear me but you don't hate me." His voice was a mere whisper.

"I would rather be dead than be here with you," she flung back. She didn't know how to deal with his calm, even-tempered manner.

"You are ready to die?" His words fell like stones between them.

Katelyn gazed at the serene bronzed face. She couldn't lie to him. "No, not yet. And you know it." She met his haunting black eyes without flinching. Though he had lost his earthly sight, he seemed now to be able to see into her very soul.

He reached out, grasping her arm. "You don't hate me. Tell me you don't hate me." The scent of her soft femininity enveloped him.

Katelyn strained, but didn't pull away. "I hate you," she lied. *I do, don't I?* "I hate you because you kidnapped me."

"You hate Henry because he left you. . . ."

"I hate you because you made me your slave. . . ." *I hate you because I like gathering your water . . ., because I like baking your fish. I hate you because I can't despise you the way I should.*

92

Tipaakke pulled her closer, savoring the warmth of her damp skin beneath his touch.

She trembled in his grasp, unable to tear her eyes from his. She remembered the taste of his mouth on hers and her tongue darted out to dampen her dry lips. "I hate you because you touch me . . ." she breathed.

"You hate the coward Henry because he never touched you, never like this." Tipaakke stroked her cheek, drawing her into his arms.

Quivering, she let herself be drawn into his arms. No one had ever tried to comfort her before, no one had ever cared enough. Why did it have to be this man, she wondered, as his face loomed over hers. Why the enemy? She felt herself raising her chin to meet his lips; her arms snaked around his neck as if by their own accord. She knew this was wrong, but she couldn't help herself.

"You have never been kissed," Tipaakke murmured, his lips brushing hers ever so softly, like the wings of a butterfly.

"I have," she protested, savoring his taste.

"Not the way a woman was meant to be kissed." He plucked at her bottom lip, then the top, nibbling until tiny shivers rippled through her body. His assault on her senses was deliciously slow.

"So soft, so sweet," he whispered. "Let me taste your honey." He tightened his hands around her waist, pressing his lips to hers, this time with burning urgency.

Overcome by some unknown dire need, Katelyn parted her lips, molding her body to his. She feared Fox. She knew she should turn and run, but somewhere, deep within herself, she wanted this man to kiss her. She wanted to feel his hard, lean body against her soft curves. Just for a moment, she told herself, as she allowed him to explore her mouth with his flickering tongue. Just for another moment and then I'll break away. Then I'll run.

When Tipaakke withdrew his mouth from hers, Katelyn was breathless. Her heart was pounding; her legs were weak. Run! Run! an inner voice warned . . . before it's too late! But all she could do was moan softly, rolling her head to and fro as he tugged at the soft flesh of her neck with his teeth. She had never imagined anyone could feel this good.

Tipaakke took his time, tasting, exploring her lips, her neck, her ears. She was completely innocent of a man's body, even of her own body; yet, she moved instinctively against him until he throbbed with the pain of desire. A soft gasp of astonishment escaped her lips as he stroked one rounded breast. He whispered sweet foolish words of love, words he had not uttered in years. His blood was rising, his heart pumping faster; he could feel the familiar stiffening in his loins. He could never recall wanting a maiden so badly.

The blood in Katelyn's ears pounded as Tipaakke continued his brutally tantalizing assault. She had no resistance. She could only cling to Fox, writhing against him, trying to ease the unfamiliar throbbing deep within. From the day they had met she had been drawn to him by some invisible desire, by something greater than herself. Was this as he said? Was this meant to be?

Slowly, Tipaakke led Katelyn to his sleeping platform, caressing her neck and shoulders as they walked. "Please," he begged huskily, "let me take off your dress. Let me see you."

"No," she shook her head. "I couldn't." She raised her lips to his, drugged by the sensations he caused.

"You can. There is nothing to be ashamed of," he urged planting soft, fleeting kisses across the bridge of her nose.

94

"No," she murmured over and over again, yet slowly, she raised her hands over her head. Never had she been in such turmoil. She knew this was wrong, but how could it be? How could it be wrong to feel so good?

Easing Katelyn onto the platform, Tipaakke slipped in beside her, running a hand over her glorious flesh. She cried out in surprised ecstasy as his hand swept over her damp, shimmering skin. Burying her face in his sweet smelling hair, she tried to suppress the sounds that escaped her lips. When he moved to mold his body to hers, she arched her hips, welcoming the pressure.

Katelyn's eye flew open at the first touch of his wet tongue against the hardening bud of her breast. "No," she cried, pushing his head aside. But her body betrayed her and she arched her back inviting him to suckle at her breast again. With one hand, Tipaakke stroked her abdomen in a circular motion as he sucked and nipped at a ripe nipple.

"I have waited too long for you," Tipaakke murmured huskily in the language of his ancestors. "Now and for always you are mine." His hand trailed down her silky thighs, lingering at the patch of downy hair, then stroking and pleasing elsewhere.

Katelyn didn't care that she couldn't understand a word that he said. It didn't matter. His hot breath in her ear and the tender sound of his voice was enough. For now, there was no one in the world but the two of them. No hands but his. Each time that his hand brushed against her triangular patch of bright hair, she called out, raising her hips to meet his hand. Each kiss, every caress, fanned the flames of a fire of unknown origin within her.

When Tipaakke rested his hand between her thighs, probing gently, she bolted halfway up. "No," she protested, swallowing hard. Her eyes fluttered open. "Please . . ."

"I won't if you don't want me to." He pressed his mouth to the valley between her breasts. "But you know I would not hurt you. I want only to give you pleasure."

Katelyn ran her fingers through his soft, sleek hair, forcing her breath to come more easily. "I'm afraid," she squeaked. "This is wrong."

"No, it is not wrong. It is what a man and woman were made for." His voice caressed her senses, making her feel as if she floated on a cloud. "I have pleased you haven't I?"

She laughed, dropping her head back. "Yes, yes you've pleased me."

"Then let me show you the ways of love." He picked up her hand, kissing her palm.

She relaxed with resignation, running her hand over his bare back. "Yes," she whispered, her voice barely audible. "Show me."

Kissing her face and neck, Tipaakke parted the folds of her womanhood. When she cried out with the intense pleasure of her awakening desires, he covered her mouth with his, muffling her voice. He stroked her damp flesh until she quivered, her hips moving to the rhythm of his hand.

"Please, please," she called out, not knowing what she begged for.

Removing his loincloth, Tipaakke moved astride her. She raked his back with her fingernails as he eased his body down until he lay flat on top of her. Their lips met fiercely as he probed. Instinctively, she parted her thighs. "I might hurt you," he warned in her ear, "but only for a moment, and then it will feel very good."

Katelyn nodded, hearing his words as if far from a distance. She gasped with pleasure as he entered her, arching her hips to his.

Slowly, Tipaakke began to move in the ancient

rhythm of loving, diving deeper and deeper. Katelyn cried out once and he stopped the movement, letting the pain subside, covering her face with feathery kisses. Then he continued. . . . His senses spun as he thrust faster, no longer able to control his movement. Higher and higher he climbed until he reached the moon and stars and came tumbling down.

Katelyn's heart finally slowed its pace and her breath came more regularly as the rivers of pleasure subsided. There was still a dull ache in her loins, but that, too, soon eased.

Tipaakke rolled off her onto his side and lay his head on her stomach, his hand caressing one thigh. For a long time he said nothing, then his voice pierced the silence. "Next time it will be better for you."

Katelyn laughed uneasily, her voice still shaky. "Better?" She ran her hands through his dark hair. "No one has ever made me feel this good."

Tipaakke slid his hand under her back and rested his head on her breast. "Wait," he teased warmly. "The Fox knows many things."

Chapter Five

Katelyn woke slowly, content to let her mind drift. Once completely awake, she knew she would have to deal with what had taken place only hours before. She would have to face the truth. She loved Fox. She was in love with a savage.

Her eyes opened cautiously and she peered at him through a veil of dark lashes. He was not a handsome man by the white man's standards . . . but he was handsome to her. She watched as his bare chest rose and fell with each breath. A silly smile crossed Katelyn's lips. She remembered how smooth and rippling his chest felt beneath her touch and she longed to reach out and finger the male nipples again, maybe even taste them. But she didn't want to wake him, not yet. She wasn't ready to face those obsidian eyes.

Katelyn moved slightly, trying to escape the platform, but his hands were entwined in her hair. So she settled herself, her head still resting on his broad shoulder, his breath light on her cheek. Her eyes drifted shut again and she snuggled close, savoring the comforting heat of his body.

What had she done? She'd let him make love to her,

that's what she'd done! No . . . she'd made love *with* Fox. And she had enjoyed every touch, every whisper, every fierce kiss.

But nothing had changed. He was still the enemy; he still held her captive. He kept her from marrying Henry. Henry . . . that was something else to deal with. How could she ever go back to him now? How could she become his wife when she'd made love with another man? A real man . . . a man who didn't have to prove his masculinity by boosting or impressing with daring feats. Even blind, Fox was twice the man Henry Coward would ever be. Katelyn giggled, remembering the name Won had dubbed him with.

"Is it me or my loving that you find funny?"

Katelyn's eyes flew open and her heart fluttered. She stared at the bronze face. "It was nothing. Something Won said." Her voice was hesitant.

Tipaakke's hand came to rest on the edge of the deerskin that covered her breasts. His fingers brushed lightly to and fro as he shifted positions, his arm still around her. "So what is to be done now, my beautiful slave?"

"Done?" Katelyn stared at the ceiling of the wigwam, counting the seams.

"You know what I mean. You care for me. You cannot deny it. Do you still want to return to your people?"

"I don't know what I want to do, Fox." She chewed her bottom lip nervously.

"I don't know if I would let you go if you wanted to."

"I know . . ."

Silence stretched between them as they both introspected on their own situations. Finally, Fox broke the awkward spell.

"Nothing has to be decided yet. There is the winter. We will go to the cabin before the snow falls. In the spring, we will decide. I need you now." He ran his fingers through her tangled hair, wishing he could see its brilliance in the late morning sun.

Katelyn nodded, swallowing hard. He wasn't going to make things easy for her. The thought of spending the winter with him excited as much as frightened her. She could imagine quiet evenings in front of a fire wrapped in Fox's arms. But she could also see the snow flying and the creeks freezing. Would they be able to survive a winter in the isolated cabin? How would they eat? Would she be able to care for him? What if someone got sick? Katelyn shuddered inwardly. It would be better if they just spent the winter here. With Hawk bringing game and Won helping with the cooking they'd be fine. But she knew there was no sense in thinking about it. Fox had made up his mind. She was leaving, willing or otherwise.

As the autumn leaves draped the land in fiery brilliance, Katelyn and Tipaakke prepared for their journey. Though they would hunt and trap for meat, their staples had to be packed along with the necessary cooking utensils and hunting implements. Katelyn spent most of her time with Won, packing Fox's belongings in bags and baskets, and trying to absorb all Won told her. Katelyn was constantly amazed by the advanced methods the Indians used to dry and preserve food. If the trapping went well, she and Fox would have enough food to last even the harshest of winters.

When the cool evenings came Katelyn and Tipaakke retired to their own world on their sleeping platform. Many nights she just lay in his arms savoring his strength, trying to come to terms with her feelings. She wasn't an Indian, she didn't belong here. But where did she belong? Certainly not with Henry.

Other nights, Katelyn crawled into Tipaakke's arms,

wanting him to make love to her. She didn't understand her desire for him, nor did she quite accept it. Each morning she would rise, telling herself she must flee. She must escape from him before it was too late. But each night she could put up no resistance. She reached out to him like a child reaches for a forbidden sweet. For the first time in her life someone wanted her, someone needed her. How could she deny herself that pleasure?

If only Fox would say he loved her, then she could have accepted her love for him. But no words of love passed his lips. Desire and need should have been enough for her. But they weren't. Like a child, she was greedy. She wanted to be loved by him, too.

As the days passed, Katelyn found herself almost eager to leave the Indian camp. She needed time to think. Though the Indians were kind, making no judgement upon her, her face burned with shame. Everyone knew that they weren't married, yet they shared a sleeping mat. And *she* knew it was wrong, even if they didn't.

On the morning that they were to begin their journey, Katelyn rose early, stretching catlike as she slipped from beneath the bedfurs into the chilly morning air. She pulled a soft leather dress over her naked body and sat on the edge of the sleeping platform to slide on her knee length moccasins. They were a gift from Won. Katelyn fingered the beaded seams. A great deal of time and caring had gone into making these moccasins. Won had been so good to her from the beginning. It would be hard leaving her and Ameen, especially when she couldn't honestly say if she'd ever be back. These Indians were the first people who had ever cared about her. Was she foolish to consider leaving them? She snapped the leather thongs, lacing them awkwardly. A firm hand reached from beneath the covers to fondle the small of her back.

"You're up early." Tipaakke stroked the soft leather absently, imagining the pale skin beneath it.

"I still have things to do. We're out of drinking water and I've got to borrow Won's mush pot. I packed ours." Ours . . . the word tasted funny on her tongue. She'd never had anyone to share anything with before Fox.

"There is time. We will leave when you're ready."

Katelyn stood up, not wanting to feel his caress. "I know, but we might as well get started as soon as possible. Ameen said the Shaman says the snow will fall in a matter of days."

Tipaakke rolled onto his back, tucking his hands behind his head. "You've done well making things ready to go, . . . just as any good Lenni Lenape woman would have done." He grinned waiting for the sparks to fly.

"I'm not an Indian and I have no intention of becoming one! You think you're so funny! Well, you're not! She pulled a porcupine-tail brush from a basket and began to jerk it through her hair, parting it to braid.

"No? Deerskin dress, proper moccasins . . . and I think I heard the swish of braided hair last night when you prepared our meal."

Katelyn threw the brush through the air knocking him soundly in the head. "You just wait, Fox," she threatened. "One of these days I'm going to lead you into the woods and I'm going to leave you. And I'm never coming back."

"I'll follow you," he teased.

"Not if I take your moccasins, you won't!" She strutted out of the wigwam without another word.

Tipaakke laughed. Won must have told her the Indian tradition of removing children's moccasins to keep them from wandering into the woods. Whether she knew it or not, she was thinking more like a Delaware everyday. He smiled, getting up. The winter was certainly going to be interesting. Between her temper and her passion he had no need to worry about the cold.

Tipaakke's laughter rang in her ears as she made her way across the compound. She hated him! He made fun of her, he teased her, he baited her. She should just keep walking, never turn back. They would never be able to get along. So why did she love him?

Katelyn eyed the short-legged pony suspiciously. Here they were, finally ready to go when Hawk had come leading this black-and-white-spotted pony. She tugged on Tipaakke's arm. "I thought you said we were walking . . ."

"*We* are. But Father has given *Uiil Tahuun* to you as a gift. Get on. Father doesn't give gifts."

Katelyn stole a glance at the old chief who stood in front of his wigwam. Why did he want to give *her* a gift? And if he had to, why a horse? She and these four-legged creatures had never gotten along. "I'd rather walk."

"Katelyn, get on her. It is a great honor to receive a gift from a chief."

"I thought you said he doesn't give gifts."

"He never has before. You must show your respect by accepting." Tipaakke's voice was urgent. "Get on *now*, Katelyn. This is not the time to cross me."

She released his arm and walked hesitantly towards the beast. It certainly wasn't very big. The pony was covered with a blanket of sewn rabbit skins and wore a bitless bridle.

Mekollaan stepped forward to assist her. "Come, Katelyn." He grinned, enjoying her discomposure. "We are ready to go. Everyone waits."

She turned to look at the Indians who had come to say goodbye. Everyone in the village was there, young and old. Kukuus, the chief, had left the wigwam and was walking slowly in their direction.

"My father is coming. Get on, girl." Mekollaan gripped her arm, lifting her onto the hedging pony.

Katelyn gripped her steed's long mane, wrapping her fingers around and around the black and white strands. She had no intention of falling off right in front of the whole village.

Mekollaan caught the pack pony's bridle in his hand and clicked between his teeth, moving the pale-grey nag ahead.

Katelyn's pony stood where Mekollaan had left it. She waited for Fox, watching as Kukuus approached his younger son and threw his arms around him. She couldn't resist a smile. Never in her life had she seen her own father hug his son.

Tipaakke patted his father on the back, speaking in low tones. Together they made their way to Katelyn.

"My father is pleased that you have accepted his gift. He wishes us good will in the coming winter and say he will see us when the creeks thaw."

The grey-haired man spoke again, flashing even white teeth and patting Tipaakke on the back.

"He says he likes you. You are a brave woman to live so well among his people." Tipaakke paused, debating whether or not to repeat the rest of the message. His voice was halting. "He says he hopes you return in the spring. He thinks your magic hair would bring good spirits to his family's home." He did not tell her that Kukuus had said she would make a fine wife for his son.

Kukuus reached out to touch her hand, speaking again.

104

"He says you will do the right thing. You will know what is right."

Katelyn couldn't take her eyes off the kind man. She had never seen a face so wrinkled with time yet so bright with life. "Tell your father that I thank him for his gift and I will treasure it always." She gave him a soft smile.

Tipaakke repeated what she had said and Kukuus nodded, stepping back.

Tipaakke grasped Katelyn's foot, turned to nod to his father once more, and clicked to the horse, giving her a jab in her side with his knee. Together he and Katelyn left the village, following Mekollaan who led the pack horse.

Katelyn turned back only once, and that was to catch a last glimpse of Won. Tears were running down the Indian's broad cheeks. "Goodbye," Katelyn mouthed wordlessly, then turned back.

Once out of the village, Tipaakke took his place beside his brother, leaving Katelyn to trail behind on the short-legged pony. After a mile or so she grew used to the beast's stride and settled down to enjoy the beauty of the forest.

The woods sparkled magically as the morning frost thawed and ran in tiny rivers down the tall blades of grass. The fallen brown and orange leaves crunched beneath the pony's hooves as they headed northwest. As they traveled on, the sun on their backs, the forest became less dense. She knew that by morning they would reach the mountains.

Katelyn shivered, drawing her rabbit-skin cloak closer. Was she mad to be traveling into the wilderness with two Indians? She was certainly mad to intend to winter with one. Where had her sense of decency gone? Fox was not her husband and never would be. Henry had, at least, been willing to marry her. But was

105

she meant to be the wife of a wealthy plantation worker, a prisoner in her own society? Or was she meant to be the prisoner of this soft spoken man, the first man who had ever showed her any true kindness? There was no love in either situation but at least she had a chance with Fox. Was Henry the kind of man to ever love anyone?

Tipaakke released his brother's arm and waited for Katelyn's pony to catch up. "You are quiet." He rested his hand on her knee and walked beside her.

"So are you."

He nodded, and together they walked on, both respecting the other's need to think.

Tipaakke fingered her leggings absentmindedly, wishing instead that it was her soft skin he stroked. He didn't know what was wrong with him. He was obsessed with her. He had only seen her for a few short hours, yet even in his sleep, he saw her fiery hair tumbling about her heart-shaped face. He couldn't eat, he couldn't sleep without thought of her. He listened for her footsteps, the sound of her sweet voice.

What was Manito doing to him? His sight had been taken from him, but he had been given Katelyn. Still, she *was* just a white woman; she was just a slave. She would be better off with her own kind. But how could he send her back to that coward? He knew enough of the white man's ways to know what her life would be like with him. Women to the white men were treated no better than their dogs. She would be brushed and combed for appearance sake, but behind doors she would be kicked and cajoled. She would give birth to child after child until it killed her and then Henry Coward would marry again and start all over.

Was this what he wanted for his Katelyn? Wouldn't she be better off with him? But how could a blind man care properly for a wife. He couldn't hunt, how would he feed a family? Besides, she could never love him. She hated him. The differences in their society's were too great.

A family . . . children . . . Tipaakke groaned inwardly. He had completely forgotten. Won was supposed to give him the powders that would keep Katelyn from growing with child. They had been giving them to her since the first week she had arrived, even before they had made love. But he had forgotten and Won had too. Was this planned by the Heavenly Manito, too? If his seed became planted within her, he could not give her up. It would not matter if she wanted to return to her people or not. She would have no choice. But was he really going to give her that choice in the spring? He didn't know.

Katelyn looked down at her brave. His face was pensive. She liked Fox's winter dress. He wore short leather walking moccasins, she herself had sewn extra soles into, and long leather leggings that went from his ankles to his upper thighs. He wore a white man's muslin shirt and a beautiful cloak of joined fox skins. Like herself, he wore his cloak over one shoulder and pinned beneath the other arm. In his hair he wore a fox tail, tiny shell earrings in his ears, and a necklace of smooth stones around his neck. He made a stirring picture in her mind with his long dark hair fanned over the brilliant rust of the fox coat. He was magnificent.

Without thinking, she reached down to run her hand over his sleek head. His hair was always so sweet smelling and freshly washed. Her stepmother could have used a lesson from him in personal cleanliness.

Tipaakke turned to her, his sightless eyes unblinking. "Have you grown bold now that we have left my people?"

"I think I was pretty bold in your wigwam last night . . ." Her heart fluttered as an air of sexual tension clung to them.

"Last night!" He laughed, his voice ringing in the crisp morning air. "And this morning too. You will wear me out, girl!"

"Hush. Your brother will hear you. Why is it that you only raise your voice when I don't want you to?"

"You think he doesn't know what we do in our wigwam?" He brushed the inside of her thigh lightly with his fingertips.

Katelyn rolled her eyes in exasperation, shifting on the pony. His fingertips were stirring a tiny fire deep within her. "I know he knows, but have you no decency? You don't talk about such things."

"You don't talk about what is good in our lives?" He shrugged his shoulders. "We do what all other Indians do in their wigwams at night."

"Fox, that's enough."

"I would even think that white men do the same thing in their . . ."

"Fox! Why do you embarrass me like this?" A blush stained her cheeks crimson. He's looking; you know he can hear us."

"She is wrong, Tipaakke. I can't hear a word you say," Mekollaan quipped in perfect sing-song English.

Katelyn began to giggle, then laugh, Tipaakke joining in. She didn't know what had gotten into her. She should have been deathly embarrassed . . . ashamed. But all she could do was laugh.

Mekollaan slowed the pack animal down, waiting for them. "I think your woman is possessed by some spirit, brother." His voice, for once, was without malice towards her.

"I think you are right."

Katelyn just laughed harder, tears trickling down her cheeks.

"Could it be that the spirit of the fox has entered

her?" Mekollaan pretended to be serious.

"A blind fox . . ." Tipaakke added, tugging a strand of Katelyn's hair playfully.

Mekollaan chirped to his pony and moved ahead of them once again, chuckling to himself. Perhaps he'd judged the girl too harshly. She had a good sense of humor. He liked a person who could laugh at himself.

The rest of the morning passed leisurely. They continued at a steady pace, Tipaakke spending equal time walking with Katelyn and his brother. The three laughed together, enjoying the warmth of the bright sunshine and the companionship of each other. Katelyn joined in the brothers' conversations hesitantly, surprised by their depth of knowledge of so many things.

"Hey, you two," Katelyn called. "I don't know about you, but I'm hungry." She slid off the pony carefully, catching the reins in her hands and walked along beside her.

"You want to stop? How can you be tired? You have done nothing but ride. With you dressed like that, I forget you aren't an Indian." Mekollaan slowed down to let her catch up.

Katelyn started to answer him in the usual biting tone she used with Hawk, then realized he was just teasing. "Tell your brother that if he doesn't shut his mouth, I'll stuff something in it." Her voice was playful.

Fox began to repeat her message in a falsely effeminate voice. "The lady says . . ."

"I heard her!" Mekollaan whistled to his grey pony which came to a halt. "I'll stop because I need water, and the ponies need some, too. I do not stop because the white woman commands me."

Katelyn pulled back on her pony's bridle to stop her, but she walked on. "Hey! How do I stop this thing?"

The pony walked around Tipaakke and Mekollaan

109

and continued down the deer trail, ignoring Katelyn's protests. The men watched with amusement.

"Help me!" She pulled fiercely on the reins, running to keep up.

The two brothers began to laugh as Katelyn and the pony disappeared behind a huge pine.

"Tipaakke, I think your woman has decided to go on without us." Mekollaan dropped the reins on the pack pony and followed Katelyn.

"Tipaakke didn't tell you her name?" Mekollaan whistled, tugging on the pony's mane.

"Not in English." She planted her hands on her hips angrily.

"My father calls her Wooden Head." He whistled again, this time changing pitch.

Katelyn followed him down the deer path shouting. "He gave me a pony with wood for brains!"

"She will listen. But sometimes she has a mind of her own." He pulled on the pony until she turned and started back in the direction they'd come. "Our ponies are trained by voice command. Tipaakke will teach you."

Katelyn stormed past him. "Another joke, Fox? You knew I wouldn't be able to make her stop. Making fun of me has become quite a pastime, hasn't it?" She yanked a bag off the pack pony and went to sit under a tree.

Tipaakke followed her slowly, guided by her movement. "I'm sorry. I didn't mean to . . . what is your word? Embarrass . . . I did not mean to embarrass you, Katelyn. It's just that I didn't think." He reached out to touch her.

Katelyn ducked, coming to her feet. "Here." She pushed a piece of venison jerky into his hand and strutted off. "There's water in the skin. Get it yourself!"

Tipaakke let out an exasperated sigh as he handed

his brother a piece of his jerky. "She is hard to understand," he said half to himself, in Algonquian. "She is laughing with us one moment, the next she cannot stand my touch."

Mekollaan nodded thoughtfully. "Give her time. It's hard for her. She was raised much differently."

Tipaakke squatted on the ground, chewing the tough jerky, and sipping from the water skin Mekollaan had handed him. He was right. She needed time. And they would have plenty of it once winter settled in.

The rest of the afternoon passed without event. Katelyn kept to herself, riding, sometimes walking, while the brothers wiled away the afternoon talking of their childhood in their own language. Both of them tried bringing Katelyn into the conversation but finally gave up, leaving her to herself. By the time the sun had begun to set, Mekollaan had found a suitable place to spend the night. He would have preferred to go further but Tipaakke had said Katelyn had gone far enough in one day.

"We will camp here tonight, Tipaakke called over his shoulder. He let go of Mekollaan's arm and caught Katelyn's pony, whistling at it. After two tries Wooden Head finally came to a halt.

Katelyn slid off her, glad to be rid of the beast.

Mekollaan unloaded the pack pony and left her to graze. "I'll bring back our meal," he called to no one in particular as he disappeared into the woods.

Katelyn dug through a reed bag until she came up with her flint and steel and a knife with a jagged edge. She'd be here all night if she tried to start a fire the way Fox did it. She gathered small twigs and sat down to clear a spot for the fire. Brushing the dry leaves on the ground into a pile, she lit the fire, blowing until the leaves were ablaze with flickering flames. Adding a few sticks, she set out to find a young sapling that would

111

make a good spit. Spotting one near the creek, she cut it down with her knife. Bringing the sapling back to the fire, she removed a hairless hide from a pack and unrolled it, taking a seat on the smooth leather.

After Tipaakke had removed the animals' bridles and blankets, he came to sit down beside Katelyn.

He listened to her struggle to cut the right seams in the sapling. What was he doing to her? Was he causing her more harm than good? Could she ever become one of them? He yearned to reach out and stroke her cheek, to brush away her frown. Though he couldn't see her, he could picture in his mind the piercing stare of her eyes, the hardened lines of her face. He knew enough to leave her alone for now, giving her time to work her anger out herself. Tipaakke leaned back, tucking his hands behind his head and closing his eyes. For now he would have to be content to have her beside him.

Shortly, Mekollaan returned, a squirrel slung over his shoulder. He dropped it beside Katelyn and went to dig for his own bag among the many on the ground.

"Squirrel?" Katelyn wrinkled her nose distastefully. She didn't like squirrel.

"Looks like it," Mekollaan replied coldly, tired of her childishness.

She let out a sigh. No longer mad at Fox or Hawk, she was angry with herself. What had ever made her think she could be one of them? She couldn't. That was obvious, wasn't it? She would never learn their ways. She stood up, grasping the squirrel by the back legs and going to gather the things she would need to clean it.

Katelyn skinned and gutted the furry animal and soon had it roasting over the fire. She placed leaves on the skin side of the pelt and rolled it to be cured later. "Never waste anything," Won had told her. The pelt, once clean, would make a good pouch for small tools. Tucking it into a bag, she returned to the fire to wait on the meal.

After scorching her fingers several times, Katelyn finally deemed the meat roasted well enough to eat. Tearing a juicy leg from the body, she sat on the hide to eat, leaving the brothers to get their own. When she finished she went to the stream to wash and returned shortly, ready to turn in. Unrolling another mat, she lay down within the shadow of the fire.

"No, Katelyn." Tipaakke loomed over her.

"No, what?" She pulled her cloak over her body.

"This is not something to start." He leaned over, tugging at her cloak. "Get up."

"I'm trying to sleep, Fox. Leave me alone." Her voice quivered. She knew he would win; still, she didn't give up easily.

"I don't care if you are mad at me. At the end of the day we sleep together. Always." He pulled the cloak off.

Katelyn sat up. "Fox . . ." She took a deep breath. Shouting got her nowhere with him. "Please . . . I just want to be alone."

"No. You are my prisoner. I don't want to force you, but you will sleep with me. So, come. I'm tired, too." He turned, walking to the other side of the fire, shuffling his feet slightly.

Katelyn groaned, coming to her feet and yanking the hide mat off the ground. There was no use. No one would get any sleep until she'd done what he said. Coming to stand beside him, she flung the mat on the ground. "Here?"

"Yes." He removed his fox cloak and sat down on the mat. "Lay down." He patted the ground.

Mekollaan stood watching from the shadows. The girl had spirit.

Katelyn dropped onto the mat and lay on her back,

her cloak covering her body.

"No." Tipaakke was losing patience.

"What now? I'm here. Now let me sleep." She rolled over on her side, her back to him.

Laying down, he reached out to wrap his arms around her waist, drawing her close to him.

Katelyn struggled. "Don't you understand? I don't want you near me." His hands were warm around her middle.

"But I want you," he returned softly, pulling the fox fur cloak over them. "Just let me hold you." He could feel her body relaxing. "I told you I was sorry about the pony. I don't understand why you're so upset about the pony. No harm came to you."

"I don't know why I am either . . ." She breathed deeply, enveloped by his nearness.

"Look at me."

Slowly Katelyn rolled over to face him, an unwelcome tear sliding down her cheek. "I'm afraid," she whispered.

"I am afraid, too. Can we be afraid together?"

Katelyn drew her arms up around his neck, holding him tight, her face pressed against his neck.

"Shhhh," he hushed, running his hands through her hair, smoothing the loose strands. "All will be right, my love," he murmured in Algonquian. "When two people love each other, it is said the Heavenly Father guides them. Love me, Katelyn, and he will help us."

Katelyn snuggled closer listening to his soothing voice. Though she recognized only her own name, it didn't matter. It was almost better when he spoke his own tongue. Then she could imagine he was telling her that he loved her. Listening to the crackling fire and Fox's steady breathing, she drifted off to sleep, safe in his arms.

Katelyn breathed sharply. "Fox, it's so beautiful!" Her eyes widened with awe as she scanned the horizon. The majestic mountains stretched out before them, mapped by dark greens and frosty whites.

Tipaakke squeezed her leg lovingly. "I smell them." He took a deep breath, exhaling puffs of smokey white. "I hear them, but tell me what they look like, Katie girl."

She slipped off the pony, her hand on Tipaakke's shoulders. "I don't know that I can. I'm no good with words."

"Tell me, please."

She sighed, still mesmerized by the breathtaking vista. "Well, the mountains are like great lumps of mud Ameen and his friends pile on the creek bank, only these are green and brown with white tops. They are many sizes. Some are just hills, but others are very steep. They're so beautiful. The cliffs of Dover are beautiful but these mountains are beautiful in a different way."

Tipaakke snaked his arm around her waist, pressing his body to hers. The crisp mountain air made his blood race. "It has been a long time since I made the journey here. It was one of my favorite places as a boy. My grandfather brought me here many times. He and a white man built the cabin together."

"Are you two going to stand there all winter or are you coming?" Mekollaan leaned against the pack pony a hundred yards away. "We'll reach the mountains by the time the sun is high if you will start walking."

"Have you no respect for the beauty Manito has created?"

"The mountains' or hers?" He moved his head in Katelyn's direction and turned to start off.

Tipaakke started forward, too, his arm still around

Katelyn. "Walk with me. The pony will follow."

She walked beside him, overcome by the magnificence of the land and the love she felt for Fox. If time would suddenly come to a standstill, this is how she would want to end her life. She would want to be at the foot of these mountains, walking with Fox. For a single moment there were no conflicts, no pain, no decisions to make, only the two of them together beneath God's hand.

"Look at you two." Mekollaan shook his head. "Like a young buck and his first doe."

"You are jealous, my low flying hawk. It has been too long since you have felt the stirrings of love," Tipaakke returned in his own tongue.

Katelyn grasped his hand, swinging it playfully. "You know I hate it when you speak your language. I can't understand a word you say."

"No, you can't . . ." Mekollaan turned to smile, raising an eyebrow.

Katelyn stuck her tongue out at him, refusing to let him dampen her spirits. What did she care if he liked her or not? She certainly didn't like him.

"Then you must learn to speak our language." Tipaakke brushed a stray lock of hair off his forehead.

"You would teach me?" She released his hand, walking backwards in front of him.

"I will teach you." He smiled, pleased to hear gaiety in her voice. He liked the sound of her moccasins dancing on the hardened ground.

"When can we start?"

"Better to start now, Tipaakke, as slow as the whites are said to learn."

"That's not so. Won says I'm smart. I already know a couple of words." She placed her hands on her hips indignantly.

"Oh. What are they?" Mekollaan pulled a long pipe

116

from his cloak.

"I know *hukuiim apoon*," she stumbled, "and, and . . ." she rattled her brain trying to come up with another word. ". . .and *tuulke*!" Her face colored in embarrassment realizing what she'd said. Why couldn't she have come up with a better word than breasts?

Mekollaan laughed heartily, finding a bit of flint and steel. "Good start." He chuckled, shaking his head.

Tipaakke smiled good-naturedly. "Come, my fox-haired beauty." He reached out with one bronzed hand. "Lead a helpless blind man through the valley."

"Maybe blind, but never helpless," Katelyn sang, reaching out to clasp his hand.

The rest of the morning was spent on Katelyn's Lenni Lenape lessons. Making a game of it, all three enjoyed passing the time while they grew closer to the mountains ahead. Katelyn pointed out objects, and one of the brothers told her the Algonquian word. She learned quickly, much to everyone's surprise.

"I'll be speaking Lenni Lenape in no time," Katelyn said, tasting the proper pronunciation.

Mekollaan whistled to stop the ponies. "You will have to walk now, Kate-lyn. The land is growing steeper."

She dismounted, surveying the surroundings. "How long now?" The mountains seemed so steep.

"We must go over this ridge and then the next. If you keep up, we will make the cabin just after dark." Mekollaan passed the water skin to Tipaakke.

"She will keep up," he answered, taking a long pull on the skin.

When the ponies moved again, Katelyn fell in behind the men, thankful for the walking stick Hawk had cut for her. She would make it to the cabin if it killed her.

But Katelyn soon found that the terrain was more

difficult to cross than she'd anticipated. Each step was an effort as they climbed higher, the air growing noticeably cooler. Her legs ached fiercely as the hours passed and the sun began to set, but she trudged on, making no complaint. Thankfully, the ache soon dulled to a numbness, giving her some relief.

"We'll be there soon, girl," Tipaakke murmured in her ear, supporting her sagging body.

She nodded, too exhausted to reply.

The downside of the ridge gave her a chance to rest, enabling her to start up the next steep incline.

"You're doing well. I'm proud of you. He has not slowed his pace for you," Katelyn heard Tipaakke whisper, just before she felt herself slumping to the ground. A peaceful darkness overtook her.

When Katelyn came to, she could feel motion beneath her. Her face was buried in soft fur. She raised her head slowly, clinging to the spotted pony.

"You all right?" Tipaakke ran his palm across her cheek.

"I'm sorry." She bit her bottom lip, willing her legs to move. She attempted lamely to dismount.

"Stay there." He pushed her back up. "The pony can carry you the rest of the way. The cabin isn't far." He held onto her leg, his fingers caressing her thigh through leather.

Katelyn stared into the darkened sky. "The sun's gone down."

Tipaakke laughed, the rumble tickling her ears. "You've been asleep a while, my dove. Tell me, are the stars bright tonight?"

"Mmmm, so bright, like dots of white sugar on a molasses cookie."

"You must be hungry," he replied, amused.

"And cold, too." She pulled the cloak over her shoulders tighter, noticing it was rust in color. Fox now wore her cloak of rabbit skins.

"Tonight the dew will freeze." He slid his hand under her dress, letting it rest high on her bare thigh.

Katelyn nodded, falling silent. His hand sent shivers of warmth through her chilled body.

The pony trudged on, starting up a new incline, this time following a narrow path.

"We are following a trail used by the *aatu* for many years."

"Deer?"

"Yes, good. The cabin is through the next thicket. We are coming from behind."

"How do you know?"

Tipaakke's voice grew faint with thought. "My moccasins have traveled this path many times with my grandfather."

"You loved him very much?"

"Very much. He was good to me. He taught me many things."

"I had a grandfather who lived with us when I was very small. My father said he was senile. He lived in the room above mine. When I could sneak away from my chores, I would creep up the back stairs and slip into his room. He used to hold me on his knee and rock me. He told me many stories."

"It is good that you have memories of him. As long as we have memories, those we love are still alive in our hearts.

"Fox . . ." Katelyn's throat tightened. She had to ask. "Do you still have memories of your wife?"

"So many memories." Tipaakke turned to her, his hand sliding from beneath her dress to touch hers. "Her voice was like a bell, clear and sharp. When she laughed, everyone around her laughed, too." He squeezed Katelyn's hand tightly. "But she is gone. We had a good life together. We lived as man and wife many summers. A man cannot ask for more."

She turned away, tears brimming. She didn't know if she cried for Fox and his loss or for herself. He could never love her, not when he had been married to such a perfect woman.

"You know, girl," Tipaakke murmured tenderly. "I do not ask you to replace her. I wouldn't ask that of anyone. That part of my life is over. Maybe we can make a new life." Giving her hand another squeeze, he quickened his pace, catching up with Mekollaan.

Katelyn rode in silence, her head bobbing sleepily. Did he mean what he said about a life together? What kind of life did he mean? He hadn't said he loved her. He hadn't asked her to marry him. Is that what she needed to be happy? Maybe there were degrees of happiness. Maybe she was expecting too much. Could she learn to live without love? Would she miss what she had never had? If she stayed with Fox, she would always have food and a roof over her head. With a friend like Won and those nights in the wigwam with Fox, maybe she could be content.

Within a short period of time, the ponies halted and Tipaakke came to Katelyn. "We are here, dove," he whispered, shaking her gently.

Far in the distance she could hear Fox's voice.

"Wake up, Katie girl. You must walk to the cabin. I can't carry you."

But Katelyn only snuggled deeper into the fox cloak. She was dreaming. Far in the distance she could see Fox running. They were in a meadow. He was coming for her! His raven hair blew in the breeze as he neared her, his muscles giving and taking with each stride. He reached her, picking her up and swinging her in his arms . . .

"Katelyn, please." Tipaakke shook his head. He was getting nowhere with her and he was tired, too. He could hear Mekollaan unloading the bags onto the ground.

"Having trouble, brother?" Mekollaan smiled good-naturedly.

"She's off in the dream world. I can't wake her." He stroked the soft hair at her temple.

"Well, I'm certainly not going to carry her. Once was enough for me." Mekollaan turned the pack pony around and headed toward the lean-to they used for a barn. "I'll be back for *Uiil Tahuun* in a moment. The door is seven, maybe eight steps from her head."

Tipaakke listened to his brother's footsteps on the hardening ground. "Katelyn." He tried once more. "You must get up." Realizing his attempts were futile, he walked in the direction of the door, his steps slow and measured. Finding the door he pushed it open and made his way back to her. He reached up, sliding her into his arms and lifting her off the pony. "Shhhh," he murmured, burying his face in her sweet smelling hair.

Katelyn snuggled closer, aware only of Fox's closeness. She was still dreaming. She could smell his masculine scent that clung to him. She could feel his hairless cheek on hers.

Slowly, Tipaakke made his way back to the door, stepping up into the cabin. Once he was inside, he knew exactly where everything was. He turned and took six steps, his moccasinned toe hitting the rope bed. "Here we are, love." He laid her down gently, wrapping the fox cloak closer. "I will start a fire and then you'll be warm."

Mekollaan stood in the darkened door watching as Tipaakke tried again and again to light the bundle of dry sticks on the hearth. "Want help?"

"No." Fox shook his head. "I must learn. I want to care for her just as she cares for me."

Mekollaan nodded and started to bring in the bags

and bundles he'd left outside the door.

Finally, as if Manito had smiled upon it, the pile of leaves and twigs ignited. Tipaakke sat back, proud of himself. Next time it would be easier.

Bringing a rolled mat to the hearth, Mekollaan made himself a place to sleep. "Climb in beside your woman, Tipaakke. It is late. I must leave in the morning. I want to be back in time for the hunt."

Tipaakke made his way across the floor, having no trouble finding where he had left Katelyn. Memories of the days he had spent with his Grandfather in the cabin would be forever etched in his mind. He knew every inch of the small room. He could almost see the table and benches, the shelves that lined the wall. He slid in beside Katelyn, drawing her close. "Goodnight, my Katie girl," he whispered, his eyes drifting shut.

Katelyn woke slowly, the sound of the crackling fire bringing her back to reality. She opened her eyes to see Tipaakke sitting on benches at a table. She sat up, dropping the fox cloak. They were in cabin! It had a fire place, even a small window.

"You are awake." Tipaakke turned toward her.

"Yes. I'll make something to eat." She slid out of the bed. A bed too!

"You have laid in bed so late that we have made our own." Mekollaan raised a bowl of hot mush.

"You should have awakened me." Katelyn dropped onto the bench beside Tipaakke.

"We have made mush many mornings on our own." He patted her leg under the table.

Mekollaan spooned the last bite of hot meal into his mouth and got up. "I must go. I will see you in the spring, brother. Take care." He wrapped his arms around Tipaakke, giving him a quick hug. "I hope you find what you are looking for here," he added in Algonquian.

Katelyn walked with Tipaakke and Mekollaan to the door.

"Goodbye." Mekollaan stepped out of the cabin and started around the back.

"Goodbye." Katelyn caught Tipaakke's hand in hers. Mekollaan raised his hand to her in reply and disappeared behind the cabin.

Tipaakke swung the door shut, still holding Katelyn's hand. Wrapping his arms around her waist, he whispered in Algonquian in her ear.

"Fox!"

"You do not even know what I said." He nipped at her neck playfully.

"I don't have to. It's the same in any language."

"Come. I have been like a stag, rubbing my antlers for two days." He pressed his lips to hers, sliding one hand beneath her dress to massage her bare buttocks.

"It's barely sun up!" Katelyn protested, welcoming his searching lips on hers.

"Mmmmmm, but it is what we do best in the early morning."

"What if Hawk comes back?" She ran her fingers lightly over a patch of bare chest.

"He knows better. He will not be back until spring." Lifting her up in his arms, he walked to the bed. "Pick up the cloak."

She did so, and he carried her to the hearth.

"I'm getting good at this." He laughed, setting her on her feet.

"I wondered how I got in last night." She watched as he laid the cloak down, fur side up.

He stretched out a hand. "You're lucky I didn't leave you on the pony last night."

She came to him. "You wouldn't have done that to me, would you?"

Tipaakke knelt, pulling her down in front of him.

123

"You'll never know, will you?" he teased, stroking the nape of her neck as he leaned forward to plant a kiss on the end of her nose.

"Never know," she whispered leaning to press her lips to his.

Chapter Six

"Tell me my *dah-quel-e-mah* . . ." Tipaakke paused in midsentence. *Coward*, he told himself. *You call yourself a man, yet you don't have the courage to call her your love in her own language*.

Katelyn looked up, her eyes resting on his broad, bronze face. "Tell you what?"

He reached out with one hand to caress her flushed cheek. "Tell me why you come to the Fox now when two moons ago you would have slit my throat if I had touched you." He pulled her onto his lap, cradling her like a child.

"Don't ask me these things . . . please?" Her doe eyes pleaded.

"We must talk. I don't want to hurt you. I don't want you to hurt yourself. You must admit to yourself what you feel." He rested his cheek on the top of her head, breathing in the sweet smell of her hair. He could almost smell its fire.

"I come to you because I have no choice. I am still your prisoner." Her body stiffened with each word. "You said I must do what you say or you'll kill me."

"But I never said you must make love with me," he answered evenly.

"What do you want me to say, Fox? Do you want me to say that I find you attractive, that I want you? Well, I do. There, I've said it. Now are you happy?"

"I know those things. I just want you to admit them to yourself." He planted soft fleeting kisses on her neck. "There is no wrong in wanting a man, any man, red or white. That is why man and woman were put here by Manito. To love and be loved." He drew her closer, wrapping his arms around her until her breasts pressed tightly against his bare chest.

To make love is not to be loved, she thought. But she couldn't bring herself to speak. What she had right now with Fox was more than she had ever had with anyone. She wasn't ready to jeopardize that . . . not yet at least. "No more talk, Fox," she whispered, "not now." She reached to pull his head down until his lips met hers. He was right. She had to accept what was given to them. If this was all she was ever meant to have then she must accept it gratefully. She mustn't be greedy. What she shared with Fox was more than her father and stepmother had ever shared.

"You're a vixen, Kate," Tipaakke murmured, welcoming her advances. "And for shame . . . in the light of the morning!"

She laughed deep in her throat as his tongue slipped out to trace the corners of her upturned mouth.

"You are as sweet as the honey of clover," he told her in Algonquian. Tenderly he kissed her mouth, parting her trembling lips. His tongue darted out to explore the inner sweetness of her mouth, tongue meeting tongue in a dance of love.

Katelyn's breath caught low in her throat, a soft moan escaping from her moist lips. His hot breath in her ear ignited a fire deep within her, and she felt the

126

heat rising with each fiery kiss. She reached up to run her hands through his thick, black, silky hair, one hand coming to rest on the nape of his neck. Her tongue darted out to meet his in midair as he lay her gently on the soft mat of rabbit.

Slipping the doeskin dress from her shoulders, he pressed his mouth to her soft, fragrant skin. He planted kisses along the line of the dress, dropping it further and further until her bare breasts sprung forth.

"*Uitiissa*, so beautiful," he breathed as his black lashes lowered, heady with her magic. "I could never be without you, not now, not when I have tasted such loveliness."

Tipaakke's voice caressed Katelyn's mind as she whirled faster beneath his touch. It didn't matter to her that she didn't understand what he said, the sound of his voice was enough.

His hand stroked one full, silken breast, his thumb teasing, tantalizing, until the tiny bud stood rigid, ripe for the picking. Unable to resist any longer, he leaned to taste what he knew so well, yet never tired of. Ripples of pleasure coursed through Katelyn's veins as she pressed her body to his male hardness, eager for more.

Sitting up, Tipaakke tugged at the soft hide dress, slowly, tantalizingly, revealing more of the snow-white flesh, flesh he had only once caught a glimpse of. "So beautiful . . ." he told her in English.

Slowly, she opened her eyes, staring through heavy, veiled lashes. "How do you know, you can't see me?" Her voice was soft, with an edge of vulnerability.

"I feel beauty" he sighed, running his hands along her slim, bare legs as he crawled along her body. "I smell it." His head lowered, guided by some unknown force, to press against a downy triangle of fiery curls.

Katelyn called out with unexpected pleasure, pushing back a long lock of hair feverishly.

"And I taste . . ." His tongue darted out to sample her nectar. ". . . beauty."

She arched her back, entangling her long fingers in his silken tresses. "Fox . . . don't . . ." She smiled. "Not yet . . ."

Tipaakke laid his head down for a moment, giving her time to slow her pounding heart. Breathing in her heady, arousing scent, a smile crossed his lips. She had never said anything before when they made love. He liked this new found brazeness. She was learning the art of love well.

Still smiling, he climbed astride her, pressing her hands to her sides and kissing her eyelids gently.

Her eyes fluttered open. "Why are you smiling?" She reached up to caress a broad cheek. His skin was moist and velvety beneath her touch. She still found it amazing that, though he was thirty years old, he had the beard growth of a spindly boy.

"I like to hear your voice when we love." Dropping a kiss on the end of her nose, he stood up. "Roll over."

"What?" Her eyes crinkled questioningly.

"Roll over. Where is the bag with the strap of marsh reeds?"

"I'll get it."

"No. Lie there. I'll get it."

"Beside the bed. The foot board."

Retrieving the bag, Tipaakke came to kneel beside her digging into it. "Roll over, Kate."

"What are you doing?"

"Trust me . . ." As she rolled over, he pulled a small glass bottle of scented oil from the bag. Uncorking it, he poured a little into his palm and rubbed briskly with the other.

"What is that for?" Katelyn pushed up on one elbow.

"You have never had your back rubbed with oils? It

128

is a wonderful thing." He sat astride her again, sitting at her waist.

"Who would I ever have had to rub my back?" She laughed at his foolishness, resting her head on the soft rabbit hide, savoring the warmth of the burning fire in the fireplace. Only moments ago it had been far too hot in the small cabin, but now they welcomed the heat.

"That is true." He nodded, laughing with her. Laying his hands on her back he began to massage the muscles, his oily hands sliding easily over her flesh.

"Mmmmmm, nice."

"There is an art to this I am told. Some medicine men use body rubbing to heal. He continued to knead her muscles leaving nothing untouched, her neck, her back, her buttocks, her legs. Always applying equal pressure, he rubbed until she cried out with pleasure.

"This is wonderful, Fox. You must teach me how to do the same."

"I would like that," he whispered, kissing a soft spot behind her ear.

Unable to stand the delightful torture any longer, Katelyn rolled over beneath his body and reached up to draw his head to hers. This time it was she who explored his mouth, savoring his taste as she ran her fingers over his rounded shoulders. Pushing with one foot, she started to roll him over.

"Where are we going?" He smiled lazily, pleased by her initiative.

"Over . . ." She giggled, seating herself on his flat muscle taut stomach.

Tipaakke leaned back, relaxing as her mouth lowered to catch one male nipple.

Murmuring words of pleasure in his own tongue, he wrapped his fingers in the cascading mass of burnt-red tresses.

129

The low rumble of his voice spurred her on as she mimicked his actions, swirl for swirl, nibble for nibble. She was amazed to find that his reactions were much like her own. And each sigh that escaped from his lips sent her body spiraling higher and higher, hot waves of pleasure washing over her.

"Come, I can take this no longer," Tipaakke murmured huskily.

Katelyn laughed, starting to roll off him but he caught her around the waist with his broad hands.

"No. Stay there."

She swallowed thickly. "I can't . . ."

"You can. You'll like it." Pulling her forward, he slid her slowly onto his manhood, both shuddering at the first intimate contact. "That's right, love."

Trembling, Katelyn took the hand he offered her.

"Slowly," he murmured, as she began to move instinctively.

She moaned, biting her lip as her eyes drifted shut of their own accord. She had never known a man and woman could make such pleasure together!

"Good. That's right, dove." His voice was almost inaudible, slipping between English and Algonquian as his breath came quicker.

Caught up in the rhythm of his breathing, Katelyn began to move faster, striving for a mountain peak far in the distance. Closer they moved as one, higher . . . faster. Her breath came in short gasps as she saw the peak just ahead.

"It's all right," she heard him whisper through the fog of pleasure. "We go together."

Reaching to pull her down, he aided in the last thrusts, and together they stood on that mountain peak for one glorious moment before they drifted slowly to earth.

"I love you," he whispered in his own tongue as he

pressed a kiss on her damp forehead. "I will love you always."

Katelyn lifted her heavy eyelids to gaze at the dark eyes. "Why do you always speak your language when we make love? I don't know what you're saying." She rested her head on his broad shoulder.

"I think Lenni Lenape. I make love like a Lenni Lenape."

"Are you going to get up, lazy?" Katelyn pulled her doeskin dress over her head.

Tipaakke tucked his hands behind his head, imagining what it would be like to watch the soft hide slide over her lithe body. "Come back. Where are you going?"

She turned to see him sprawled naked in all of his splendor across the rabbit-hide pelt. Just a glance of his sinewy body sent chills of desire through her body. How could she still want him? Her skin was still moist from making love. Had she no shame? No . . . she was not ashamed.

"Come back and lie with me a little longer." He put out one hand invitingly.

"If I do, we won't be up until noonday. We have things to do, Fox. Now get up." She retreated safely to the bed, retrieving her moccasins.

"Listen to you. You sound like a calling crow. Only a wife has a right to talk to a man like that." He sat up, feeling for his leggings and shirt.

"Well, I'm not your wife, but you've still got to get up. We've got a lot to do, Fox, and I don't think the snow is going to let up any time soon." Tying her moccasins, she went to hand him his.

Accepting them, he set himself to the task of putting them on and lacing them up. After three tries the first

131

one was tied. The second moccasin only had to be retied once. Coming to his feet, he reached out. "Come, my beautiful slave. We go to the stream. We will get water and set a snare for our meal. Get your short knife with the jagged edge."

"My knife?"

"Yes. You must always carry it with you. It may save your life someday."

Katelyn kneeled to search for the knife among the bags. She felt like someone had just thrown a bucket of cold water in her face. *Save my life?* The thought was sobering. This was no jaunt in a carriage. She was somewhere in the mountains of the Maryland or Virginia Colonies with a blind man. They would have no human contact until spring. If someone grew sick or was injured, there would be no way to get help. They must care for each other and find their own food. If they didn't, they would die.

Sensing Katelyn's thoughts, Tipaakke rested his hand on her shoulder. "We'll be fine. Do not fear. We can trap, even do a little hunting. There will be plenty to eat. No harm will come to us."

Unconvinced, she took his arm and together they stepped out of the cabin and into the frosty morning.

"Which way, Fox?"

"Listen and then tell me."

Katelyn stood quietly for a moment. "I don't hear anything."

"Shhh. Listen," he commanded in Algonquian.

She let out an exasperated sigh but did as she was told. At first she heard nothing, then slowly the forest became alive with sound. First she heard breathing, Fox's then hers. Then the sound of branches swaying and brushing one another in the wind. They turned to catch a glance of two squirrels chattering as they scurried up an oak. She smiled. A distant gurgling caught her attention. "This way!" She tugged at Fox's arm and took off through the woods, forging a path through the snow.

"Do you know what you just did?"

"What? I think it's this way." She went around a tall pine, bearing to the left.

"I spoke to you in Algonquian. You understood me."

Katelyn turned to him. "I did? I didn't realize . . ."

"And this is not the first time. You are learning." He stroked her arm through the rabbit cloak.

"Well, keep doing it. I want to learn. Come on, it's not far, is it?"

He shrugged. "How would I know? I can't see where we're going."

"You know." She punched his arm playfully.

Tipaakke just laughed.

Only a short distance through the trees, Katelyn found the bubbling creek. "Told you I could find it." *So beautiful*, she thought, looking around her. *If only Fox could see it, too.*

Standing on the rocky bank, she could see that the stream was shallow but the flow was strong. Though ice clung to the rocks along the edges of the shore, the center of the stream ran clear and swift. The giant pines and occasional oaks formed a roof over their heads, their branches laden heavy with snow. It was a winter paradise, with no one but them and the wild animals of the forest to share it with.

Tipaakke knelt to fill the water bags he carried on his shoulder, steadying himself so that his moccasins wouldn't touch the icy water. Katelyn watched him as he filled each bag meticulously, his fingers guiding him when his eyes could not. He was as at home with the stream and snowy brilliance as any of God's wild creatures. Somehow, Katelyn suddenly felt like an intruder.

Finishing with the water bags, Tipaakke laid them in the snow. "Now we will catch our evening meal. Listen and you will learn. Mekollaan said there were many rabbit tracks just around the bend in the stream, near a birch."

"We're going to catch a rabbit?" Katelyn furrowed her brow doubtfully.

"It's very simple. A child could do it. But first you must cut three sticks. Two this long." He spread his hands apart. "The last one this long." His hands moved closer together.

She nodded. "That's easy." Stepping into the brush, she reappeared minutes later, carrying three sticks. Proudly, she handed them to Tipaakke.

He ran his long tanned fingers up and down the sticks swiftly. "These are a little long, but we can snap them. Now lead me around the bend. You must search for the tracks. There will be a trail where rabbits come from the forest to the creek to drink."

Leading him only a short distance, Katelyn spotted tracks in the snow. "Yes, you're right. I see them!"

"Where?"

"Right here." She moved him forward a few steps.

Tipaakke squatted, handing the three sticks back to her. "You must learn to do this yourself. If something happened to me, you would have to remain here alone until my brother returned."

Something snapped inside her. "If something happened? What do you mean? I couldn't stay here by myself." Her lip quivered. "We don't have enough dried food to last, I would starve to death."

The muscles in Tipaakke's jaw tightened with impatience. "You would *not* starve because you would know how to snare rabbits. Do as I say and stop being childish. Nothing is going to happen to me, anyway." His tone was biting. "Cut a notch in the two longer sticks high enough so that once the sticks are in the ground, the notches will be above the rabbit's head. Remember," he added sarcastically, "you are trying to catch one, not provide a jump."

Katelyn chipped at the sticks angrily. Why had he brought her here? What was wrong with him? She could never learn to trap or hunt. If something happened to him, she wouldn't have a chance. "There."

"Give them to me."

Katelyn slapped them into his hand and tucked her own hands back under her cloak. Her fingers were numb from the cold.

"That will work." He nodded, running his fingers over the notches she cut in the branches. "Now look for a sapling close to the tracks, one that can be bent. It will act as the spring for the noose." He withdrew a length of woven string from under his fox cloak.

Muttering under her breath, Katelyn set out in search of the right sapling. "Like this?" She grasped a bare stick no taller than herself.

Coming to touch the sapling, he shook his head. "No. It must bend. This is too thick. I said it must bend," he finished sharply.

Her eyes narrowed dangerously. "Maybe you should find one yourself," she said through clenched teeth.

"No. You must do it. You must learn. Hurry, now. It's cold and we're not dressed properly. Find the sapling and we'll set the trap."

"Here, how's this one?" She snapped it in front of his face, almost smacking him in the nose.

Tipaakke snatched it from her and squatted on the rabbit trail. "Come here beside me." Fingering the sapling, he nodded. "This will do."

"Good, because I'm not finding another."

Ignoring her, he went on. "Now place the tall sticks across the rabbits' path and balance the shorter be-

135

tween them in the notches."

Katelyn pushed the sticks into the ground slowly, drilling through the frozen earth, and balanced the other between them. "Now what?" she snapped.

"Bend the sapling over, tie this noose on the end and let it fall over the crossbar."

She did as she was instructed, only once knocking the crossbar from its supports. "There." She threw up her hands. "I hope it's right because I'm not doing it again."

Tipaakke reached out to run his fingers lightly over the propped sticks. "The notches are high, but I think it will work," he said, coming to his feet. "The rabbit will come running down the path, knock the crossbar with its chest and the sapling will snap up, tightening the noose around its neck."

"You've done this before?" Katelyn questioned doubtfully.

"Many times, I told you. We have even caught deer in this manner, my brother and I."

"Well, I'm going back to the cabin." She walked back to where the water bags laid and scooped them up. "It's too cold for me out here."

Tipaakke followed her up the path they'd made to the door. "Put another log on the fire," he ordered. "I'm going to get my traps from the lean-to. Tomorrow you will take me along the creek to set them, then I will check them each day."

"You'll check them? How are you going to do that?" she challenged.

"I will count the steps, girl." His voice was equally sharp. "How else do you think I get from place to place?"

Katelyn slammed the heavy hand-hewn door behind her in response.

Tipaakke shook his head, feeling for the wall and

following it around to the back. *Perhaps this was a mistake. Maybe I should have stayed in the village.* He reached the back wall and took the allotted steps to the lean-to where the pony was stabled.

Tipaakke reached out to stroke the pony's velvety nose, crooning. "What do you think? Is Fox a fool, Uiil Tahuun?"

The pony nickered softly.

Tipaakke walked slowly to the far wall and reached for his traps. When his fingers met cold metal, he smiled. They were just where Mekollaan said he would leave them. Maybe his father was right. Maybe his fingers could become his eyes. Maybe there was hope. He wanted so much to believe that he and Katelyn could make it through the winter safely. He wanted to keep her warm and safe so that in the spring she would decide to stay with him always. Then he wouldn't have to make the decision himself.

Katelyn dropped the water bags on the table and threw her cloak on the bed. She was fooling herself to think this was ever going to work. Catching rabbits with pieces of string! But how else were they going to get meat? She hadn't really thought about it before. She had assumed Fox would take care of that. It hadn't occurred to her that he would expect *her* to catch the game.

Throwing a log on the fire, she slumped into one of the simple hand-hewn chairs. Resting her head in her arms on the table she held back the tears that threatened to spill over.

Why had all of these terrible things happened to her? Why couldn't she have just married Henry and become the wealthy mistress of a tobacco plantation. Why was she out here in the wilderness with a crazy, blind Indian?

They were probably going to starve to death. Mekollaan was right. When he returned in the spring he would find nothing but bones. But what could she do? She couldn't run . . . she had no idea where she was. And worse yet, she didn't know if she could leave Fox up here alone if she wanted to . . . *So this is what I've gotten myself into with my silly ideas of romantic love.* Fool! Fool! The words echoed in her mind.

At the sound of the door latch, Katelyn pushed herself up and out of the chair.

Tipaakke entered, the traps slung over his shoulder, and settled himself on the floor at the hearth. He said nothing.

Ignoring him, Katelyn set out to do the cleaning necessary before she could unpack.

For most of the afternoon they worked in silence, both caught up in their own doubts. When most of the baskets and bags were unpacked with the items on clean shelves, Katelyn went to put on her rabbit cloak.

"Where are you going?"

His voice startled her. "To . . . to check the snare. It's time I started a stew."

He nodded, going back to oiling his traps.

Katelyn stepped back into the cabin, closing the door with a thump and a rattle. She leaned against it heavily, her face an ashen white. "You said it would work. You said it was simple. You said a child could do it . . ." Her voice grew higher in pitch with each word.

Tipaakke came to his feet, brushing long, dark locks aside. "What are you talking about?"

"The trap, Fox. The snare. You said it would work but there wasn't a rabbit. It had sprung but there was nothing there." She clasped her hands, blowing on them to warm them.

"So we didn't catch one." He shrugged his shoulders.

138

"Tomorrow we will get one."

"Tomorrow? What if we don't? We're going to starve aren't we?" she asked desperately.

Tipaakke laughed merrily. "Starve? When there are so many of Manito's creatures out there?" He laughed again, thoroughly amused.

"It's not funny. Why are you laughing at me? I can't catch anything. I told you I couldn't. There's not enough dried food for the winter; you said so yourself." She reached out pleadingly.

Tipaakke's eyes narrowed. From the sound in her voice, he knew she was serious. "Katelyn, you are being childish. People do not starve in the mountains where game is so abundant. We are Lenni Lenape." He hit his chest with his fist soundly. "Manito provides for us." He was growing impatient.

"No, I'm not Lenni Lenape. I'm no Indian." She went to him, grabbing his linen shirt. She stared into the sightless ebony eyes. "I cannot live like this. You cannot live like this. We'll never make it."

"Listen to me." He grabbed her shoulders, shaking her soundly. "You will stop this foolishness now. I *told* you we'd be fine. There will be plenty to eat. We will not starve." His voice was jagged with anger.

"But you can't even catch one stinking rabbit!"

"Me? I told you the notches were a little high." He released her but didn't move, his face remaining only inches from hers.

"I hate you. You know I hate you," she whispered through clenched teeth. "I hate you for doing this to me. Why didn't you just kill me when you captured me? Why have you dragged me across half of this colony to let me starve to death in this cabin?"

"Listen to yourself, Katelyn. Do you really think I would . . ." he stopped in midsentence. *She is a hysterical child*, he told himself. *There is no reasoning with a hysterical child.*

Without another word he walked to the bed, flung his cloak over his shoulders and walked out the door.

"Coward! Where are you going? Just kill me now!" Katelyn shouted as the door swung shut with a silencing thud.

When Tipaakke returned from caring for Uiil Tahuun he found Katelyn preparing a stew over the fire in an old metal pot that hung on a bar at the hearth. He stood for a moment just inside the door knowing he must say something. He had let her get the best of him. She'd provoked him and he'd lost control. He had to make her understand that he would never let any harm come to her. He had to remember that no one had ever loved her. She didn't understand what it was to love and be loved. He would have to teach her.

"Katelyn." He spoke quietly, his voice seeming to echo in the small room.

"I made stew. Should I make corn cakes or should I save the meal?" She continued to stir with the barkless cooking stick.

"We will be all right. I know you're afraid but you must trust me."

"Why did you leave? Why can't you stand here and fight with me?" She swung around to face him, thick gravy dripping from the stick onto the floor.

"It's not my way."

"Well, it *is* my way! You've asked me to change in so many ways and you've made no effort to change at all. We're so different, Fox. This will never work."

Tipaakke walked slowly to the table. "You are right. I have asked much of you." He ran his hand over his sleek head thoughtfully. "But know this. I would never let any harm come to you. I wouldn't have brought you here if I had thought you were in danger."

"Not long ago you threatened to kill me if I didn't do

as you said," she challenged.

"Yes. But things were different then."

"Would you?"

"Not now, no. Then?" he paused. "Maybe."

"I believed you. The only reason I didn't try to get away again was because I thought you would kill me." She planted one hand on her hip disbelievingly.

"I know." He slipped into a chair, a wide grin on his handsome face. "That's why I didn't tell you."

Katelyn turned to the stew, then back to Fox. "I didn't mean what I said about hating you . . . , but I could learn to, you know."

"Hate is sometimes very close to love, my song bird."

Tipaakke listened from the bed as Katelyn moved about the cabin, preparing to retire. In his mind he could see her long, fiery braids swinging as she walked. He could see the slight curve of her smile, the sparkle of her dark brown eyes. He noted how her footsteps had changed since she'd come to him. No longer did she walk like a white man, ambling without purpose, but rather she walked lightly with unspoken determination. Her movements were becoming more fluid-like, more graceful. Whether Katelyn Locke was willing to admit it or not, she was becoming more like Lenni Lenape each day.

"Come to bed, my busy bee. I hunger for honey." Tipaakke stretched.

"It's early yet." She leaned against the table, wiping it down with a bit of precious cotton. "I'm not tired."

"Winter is the season for laziness." He propped himself up on one elbow. "Besides, who said anything about sleep."

Playing the game, Katelyn ignored him, taking the wet pewter plates to the hearth to dry.

Hearing the clink of pewter, Tipaakke sat up. "Do you like it here? I thought it would make things easier for you. Grandfather liked to come here and pretend he was white, I think. He built all of this, he and a trapper. The tables and chairs, the bed. If you look at the leg of one of those chairs you will find where a young boy gnawed at the wood with his axe. I don't know how the chair has stood all of these years."

Katelyn smiled, thinking of a young Fox working to please the grandfather he loved so dearly. "I meant to ask you about one of these chairs. It's so rickety, I thought I'd use it for kindling when we run out."

"When we run out you'll take my axe and chop kindling." He laughed, joining in on her joke. "Now come . . ." He reached out with one bronze hand.

Katelyn turned to him, wiping her wet hands on her doeskin dress. She watched as the firelight danced across his taut, tanned chest, and she felt a stirring in her loins. He was as perfect as any of the wild creatures his god or hers had put on this earth. She walked to him slowly, pulling the leather ties from her hair so that she could loosen her braids. "Why do you do this to me," she questioned softly. "You know I'm weak."

"It's not weakness, it's love," he replied in Algonquian.

"You must teach me more of your language," she told him, coming to sit on the edge of the bed. "I want to know what you say in that low voice."

Tipaakke ran his hand along her spine, his fingers kneading. "I tell you how beautiful you are. I tell you how much this man needs you." He pressed her to the bed, cradling her fall with one long sinewy arm.

Her eyes fluttered shut of their own accord as his mouth met hers. "What else?" she murmured against his lips. "Tell me what else you say."

"I tell you that when you touch me, I soar like an

eagle in the sky." He reached up to brush her tender lips with his fingertips.

Katelyn tightened her arms around his shoulders breathing in his heady scent. Her tongue flickered out to touch his fingers. "What else do you say?" She licked one of his long fingers, taking it in her mouth to suckle.

"I say . . ." He caught his breath as her hand brushed against his thigh boldly. ". . . I say your laughter is a bubbling brook, your smile is the first bloom of spring." His head dropped to her breast as his hand explored beneath the doeskin dress.

She brushed a long lock of sweet smelling hair from his cheek. "Your hair is so beautiful," she whispered, fingering it lightly. "I never thought a man's hair could be beautiful."

"Beauty is where we see it. There is beauty in everything." He nibbled at the smooth leather that covered her breasts. "Can we take this off? I prefer your taste to the doe's."

Sitting up, Katelyn pulled the dress over her head, squirming as Tipaakke wrestled her to the bed again. "Fox, my moccasins!" She giggled, running her hands through his hair as she guided his mouth to one rose-tipped breast.

"Keep them, it's not your feet I'm interested in."

"Fox! Get up! Look what we've got! I got one! Katelyn raced across the floor to the bed, leaving the cabin door wide open. "I really got one!"

Fox bolted upright, reaching instinctively for his stone knife beneath the sleeping pelts. But once he realized it was Katelyn's voice he heard, he relaxed, releasing the knife. "Katelyn!" He dropped back onto the bed. "The door!"

"Sorry." She ran to shut it and was back in an instant.

"Look what I got, a rabbit." She dropped the stiff body on his chest.

He laughed, running his fingers through the soft fur. "You're right, it's a rabbit."

"Fox . . . we caught it in the snare. I can't believe I caught one." She perched herself on the edge of the simple framed bed.

"I'm glad you're so happy, but must I sleep with it?"

Katelyn stuck her tongue out at him and scooped the rabbit off the bed, dropping it on the table.

Tipaakke slid out from under a layer of soft pelts and reached for his shirt on the floor beside the bed. "It's still early isn't it?" He fingered the linen material, looking for the armholes.

"I woke up early so I went to fill the water bags. When I got to the stream, I found the rabbit." She grinned, still pleased with herself, as she went to throw another log on the fire. "I set the snare again."

"Don't be greedy. We can't eat more than a rabbit a day." He pulled his leggings on and tied them slowly.

"I thought I would tan the hides and make a real dress with sleeves. It would be warmer. Won gave me two metal needles. Someone got them in a trade."

"That's a good idea. It will give you something to do while I'm out checking my trap lines."

She poured some meal into a bowl, adding water slowly to make gruel. "I thought I'd try making you a pair of breeches, too." She waited for his reply.

Tipaakke raised one eyebrow. "Breeches?"

"Yes. Breeches would be warmer than your leggings." She sprinkled a few dried berries over the hot meal.

"But my people have always worn leggings." He turned to her. "Are you trying to turn me into a white man?"

She looked up from the bowl to glance at his overly

144

serious face. Such a handsome man, she thought. No matter what happened or where she went she would never forget those haunting black eyes. "No, of course not, Fox," she assured him quietly. "They've not been very good to me, have they?"

Chapter Seven

"The holly and the ivy,
Now both are full well grown,
Of all the trees within the wood,
The holly bears the crown."

Katelyn's voice lifted skyward as she busied herself sweeping the hearth, brushing the dust and bits of bark into the fire. Her hips swayed to and fro in a seductive dance as she followed the twig-broom partner across the dance floor. Her feet tapped softly, rhythmically, as she hummed words long forgotten.

Tipaakke looked up from where he sat beside the bed, mending a torn leather pouch. His finger went instinctively to his lips when a sharp sting brought blood. She's too distracting, he thought. He listened to his captive's sweet haunting voice, her words echoing in his mind as he drew a picture deep within himself, imagining how her body swayed as her feet tapped lightly on the cabin floor.

Life had not been easy for her since they had arrived at the cabin more than two moons ago. Tipaakke smiled wryly. Life hadn't been easy for him either. She was a temptress. She was the vicious enemy. She would sit by the fire tanning hides and speaking broken Algonquian of days to come when he would take her to the great water to fish and gather clams. At these times

146

she would be so convincing that even *he* thought she was Lenni Lenape.

Tipaakke's head dropped and he concentrated on the hide pouch again. *Then*, he thought, *then* she would wake up one morning as if an unhealthy spirit possessed her. She would rant and rave, ordering that she be returned to Henry Bullman at once. She would say she wanted no part of the Lenni Lenape and their cruel ways. Tipaakke ran his fingers along the finished seam. They told him he'd done a good job.

He turned in Katelyn's direction, listening as she stacked the chairs on the table to sweep beneath it. He had never known anyone like her, red or white. There were days when she would laugh and tease, taunting until they were rolling naked on the furs at the hearth. She could be the seductress or the seduced, playing both parts well. Then there were times when she wanted no part of him, cursing and throwing pewter plates. Tipaakke's dark eyes sparkled with amusement. No, life certainly hadn't been dull.

Katelyn replaced the chairs on the floor and set the twig broom in the corner to rest. Her eyes went to the wall where dozens of pelts hung. She wouldn't have believed it if she hadn't seen it with her own eyes. She brushed the back of her hand across a soft grey fox hide. There was more to her Indian brave than she'd first realized. The fact that he was blind seemed to make no difference to him. He cut and hauled wood for the fire, he trapped, he cared for her pony. In the close quarters of the cabin, he seemed to have sight. He walked without shuffling, knowing exactly where everything lay. It was eerie to watch him. He *looked* like he could see. His eyes met hers when he spoke, following her when she crossed the room. A stranger would never know he was blind.

Katelyn tossed another log onto the fire and added

some water to a pan for tea. Fox was so good to her at times, surprising her with tea leaves he'd brought or fetching water for her so she wouldn't have to venture out into the bitter, cold. But there were other times when he could be unmerciful. He drilled her constantly on survival techniques forcing her to repeat what he'd taught her over and over again. He made her practice shooting a bow he'd fashioned for her until her fingers were frozen beyond feeling. He would bring game home for days and then for days he would refuse to help at all, forcing her to use what she'd learned to hunt or snare their meals.

Katelyn sighed, dumping a few precious tea leaves from a small bag into a pewter mug. There were days when she hated Fox. Days when she wished with all her heart that she was safe in Maryland with Henry Bullman. But then there were days when she thanked the Lord for having such a thoughtful, caring man. The more she thought about spring and the decision she must make, the more confused she became.

"Katelyn . . ."

She blinked, looking up. "You said something? I'm sorry. I didn't hear you. Tea?"

"No. You were walking in the dream world again. I said sing the song again. It's very pretty." Tipaakke came to his feet, tucking the needles into the sewing bag.

"No. It's silly. Those days are long gone." She sat on a chair, breathing in the tangy bitter tea. She wrapped her fingers around the mug, savoring its heat.

"Then tell me about the Yuletide again."

"Not again." Katelyn threw up a hand in his direction. "You've heard it twice in the last three days."

"I know, but I like to hear you speak of happy times. I was a happy child. I like to think you were, too." He crossed the room and returned the sewing pouch to its proper place on the wooden shelf above the fireplace.

Katelyn watched as he glided across the floor. He moved as smoothly and as confidently as a wild animal in the forest. "Well, you know father never approved of any gaiety, and certainly not at the Yuletide. It was a time to contemplate Christ's birth and our sins like all good Protestants. But, Aunt Patricia, she married a Catholic!" Katelyn's eyes grew round with excitement. "It was a great scandal. For a while we couldn't see Aunt Pitty, but then Father came around and let me spend Christmastide with her one year." She took a sip of her steaming brew.

Tipaakke slid a chair from under the table and sat down beside Katelyn. "Get the brush and my leathers. Do my hair while you tell me the story. I still must check my traps today."

"Please?" She arched her eyebrows, a slight smile playing across her face.

Tipaakke turned to her confusingly. "Please what?"

"You're supposed to ask me to braid your hair, remember?" She crossed her arms, pleased with herself.

"Please," he spoke through tightly compressed lips, "would you be so kind as to braid my hair, Mistress Katelyn?" He jumped out of the chair and bowed formally.

She got to her feet and curtsied low. "I would love to, Sir Tipaakke Oopus." She laughed spinning around to retrieve the brush and leather ties.

Tipaakke settled himself in the chair again. "Now, tell me the rest of the story."

Katelyn ran the porcupine tail brush through his long hair, smoothing it with a hand. "Well, Aunt Pitty came to get me in the carriage, and we sang songs all the way back to her house. Oh, and Fox, the house was so beautiful with candles twinkling in all of the windows and boughs of holly piled high on the mantles." She stopped brushing for a moment and rested her cheek on the back of his head. She loved the feel of his sleek hair against her skin.

Tipaakke reached behind his head to caress her cheek. "Go on . . ." His hand slid back to his lap.

"Where was I? Oh, the house." She started to run the brush rhythmically through his hair again, parting it in the center. "I remember it being so warm in there. She must have had every fireplace in the house lit. Father never allowed us to waste precious wood like that."

"Ouch, that hurt!" Tipaakke rubbed his head. "You're pulling the hair from my head."

"I am not. You asked me to do this. You know my braids are tighter than yours." She took half of his hair and began to form a long smooth braid. "Now do you want to hear the story or not?"

"Yes. Go on." Tipaakke slid his hand along the table until it touched the warm pewter cup and raised it to his mouth.

"We had a wonderful meal of boar's head, breads, jellies, and puddings and then we went into the Great Room for gifts. My aunt and uncle gave me a beautiful music box that played when I opened the lid." She gave the braid a final tug and tied the end tightly with a leather strap.

"And the log?" Tipaakke prompted, enchanted by the sound of her happy voice.

"The servants brought in a huge green log decorated with pine and holly, and they threw it into the fireplace. They said it would burn until Twelfth Night!" She tied the second braid.

"It must be almost that time of year by now." He snaked his hand around her waist and pulled her onto his lap.

"The Yuletide began on December twenty-fourth. I

150

know it's December by now, but I don't know when." She peered into his ebony eyes thoughtfully.

"It is late in the month." Dropping a kiss on the end of her nose, he stood up, sliding her to her feet. "I must tend my line now."

Katelyn watched as he gathered his necessary belongings. At first it had worried her that he packed so many things when he would only be gone a few hours. But now she had accepted that a man must always be prepared when he left home.

"Fill my bag . . . please." Tipaakke handed it to her and sat on the edge of the bed to remove his leggings. He had laughed about the trousers Katelyn had made for him of rabbit skins but he never set out to check his traps without them. Though they were bulky with the fur sewn inside, they were the warmest leg coverings he'd ever worn.

Katelyn waited patiently while he shrugged on his cloak. He had complained when she first added a few seams to his prized fox cloak, but he soon realized she was right about that, too. It was much warmer when she was through making her alterations.

"I will be back as soon as I can. Don't worry if I'm gone longer than usual. The snow is deep further down the mountain, near the beaver dam. I must take care there so I don't lose my direction."

Katelyn bit her lip. Each time he left, she feared he wouldn't come back. There were so many things that could happen; he could fall in the stream and freeze to death; he could be killed by a pack of wolves. Yet, she knew he must go. Though, he didn't really need the money the pelts would bring in the spring, he needed to feel useful, and he needed to keep busy. "Good luck." She put on her best smile. *"Nihiila oopus ia nac."*

Tipaakke looked up, smiling. She always said the same thing. She knew a red fox in a trap would be a good omen. He reached out to rest a hand on her shoulder. "Uiil Tahuun will need more dry grass. Go down by the bank and dig some from the snow."

Katelyn nodded. *"Kihiila."* Between hunting for food, caring for the pony, cutting wood for the fire and preparing the hides, she always kept busy while Tipaakke was gone. If she has a spare moment, she would even practice with her bow. She hadn't shot an animal with it yet, but she was getting better. "I hope you get a duck. I'm so tired of rabbit."

"A what?" He slid his knife into the sheath strapped to his leg.

"A duck." She looked up questioningly. "Oh." She paused for a moment, thinking. Their language was so different from her own. *"Nihiila kuikuiingus ia nac."*

"I will see what Manito leaves me." Pulling his raccoon cap over his head, he started for the door. "Take care. Keep your ears open and your knife at your side."

Katelyn rolled her eyes. "Yes, yes I know. You're too serious sometimes, you know that." She pressed her hand to his back. "Now get going. If you don't hurry it's going to be dark before you get back."

Tipaakke snorted, shaking his head. "It already is dark, girl!"

Puzzled, she paused, her hand still resting on the small of his back.

"You are always a drum beat behind, Katie-girl. Dark . . . it's always dark to me." He dropped a kiss on her laughing mouth. "See you when I get back."

Katelyn waved, not caring that he couldn't see as she watched him disappear around the bend.

Slamming the heavy door behind her, she added another log to the fire. *What to do now*, she asked herself, dumping her now cold cup of tea back into a metal pan to reheat. When they first arrived at the cabin, she had looked forward to the times when Tipaakke would leave to tend his traps. But lately, even when she kept herself occupied, she found herself counting the hours until he returned.

She stared into the fireplace watching the hot flames leap and lick the charring logs. She just didn't understand herself. Why couldn't she just accept her situation and be content with it? She was happier in this cabin with Fox than she had ever been in her father's home. No one had ever cared about her like Fox did. And she knew he *did* care. So why was she being so greedy? Why did she want love, too? How could she even be *considering* returning to that Henry Coward? She pored her heated tea into the pewter cup and leaned against the mantle to sip it.

What kind of life could I ever have with Henry? Would he even take me back after being captured by wild savages? She laughed. Wild savages . . . the sad truth was that the only real savage she'd met in this new world *was* Henry. Even Hawk was a better man. At least he was honorable. He would never have left his woman in the hands of the enemy. *How could Henry have left me?* She'd asked herself that a million times and still she had no answer.

Katelyn dropped her mug on the mantle with a thud and crossed the room to get her sewing. She couldn't keep going over and over this in her mind. It was going to drive her crazy. Sitting cross-legged on the floor in front of the fire, she pushed all thoughts from her mind and concentrated on the rabbit hide in her lap. Once cut properly and sewn, she'd have a bag to keep her own collection of stone knives and hide scrapers.

Engrossed in the tedious task, Katelyn lost all track of time. Only when the dimming light filtering through the tiny windows made it difficult to see, did she realize it was near dusk.

"Poor Uiil Tahuun," she murmured to the empty

room. "He must be starving by now." Coming to her feet, Katelyn dropped the almost completed bag on the table and went to get her cloak from the peg near the door. Shrugging it over her shoulders, she wrapped a grey fox pelt over her head and around her neck and stepped out into the frosty air.

"Brrrr, it's going to be a cold one tonight." She shivered, pulling the cloak closer and tying a dangling strip of leather hide around her waist. Rubbing her hands briskly, she walked around the back of the cabin to the lean-to where her pony was stabled.

"Hey there, Wooden Head. How's my girl?" She paused to scratch her behind her ears. "Hungry, girl? I bet you are. Well, just hang in there and I'll be right back." Giving her shaggy neck a pat, Katelyn yanked the feed bag of its post and headed off in the snow.

Down near the creek she kneeled in the snow and began to dig with a stick, searching for the tufts of dry grass she knew were there. Once she'd cleared a small area of snow and warmed her hands inside her cloak, she began to pull grass as fast as she could. It was so cold!

Katelyn paused for a minute, breathing deeply, the frigid air burning her throat and lungs. Something didn't seem right, but she didn't know what it was. Stuffing a few more handfuls of grass in the bag, she got to her feet and started back up the path to the cabin.

The forest seems awfully quiet, she thought as she hurried along. *Too quiet. I'd better feed Wooden Head and get back to the cabin.*

Reaching the lean-to, she walked around the windbreak wall and went into the pony's stall. "Told you I'd be back, girl. I brought you some grass." Dumping the bag of grass on the dirt floor, Katelyn ran her frozen fingers over the black and white mane. "You're so warm!" Moving closer, she wrapped her arms around the pony's plump stomach and rested her head on her back. "If it gets any colder out here, we're going to have to bring you in the cabin." Katelyn nuzzled the soft coat, savoring the heat that slowly seeped from the pony's body through hers. "I hope I brought enough grass because I'm not digging any more tonight."

Wooden Head made no response but continued to munch on the pile of grass at her feet, making no attempt to move away.

Suddenly, Katelyn picked her head up. "What was that?" She listened for a moment but heard nothing but the pony's grinding teeth.

Something was wrong. Ducking under the pony's neck, she began to creep towards the outer wall so that she could peek out. Slowly, her hand went for her knife in her cloak. "No, God, no," she whispered. It wasn't there. She'd been in such a hurry to feed Wooden Head before it got dark that she'd forgotten her knife. A person only made a mistake like this once and didn't live to tell about it.

There it was again. Katelyn pressed her body to the wall. A low growl, then another. There was no need to look over the wall, she knew what was out there. Wolves . . .

Tipaakke had taken her far from the cabin one afternoon to show her a pack of wolves devouring a deer. It had been a frightening sight for her but Tipaakke had accomplished what he'd set out to. He'd given Katelyn the proper respect, but also the fear of The Maker's deadly creatures.

Katelyn slid slowly to the ground as her mind whirled in terror. *How many?* First she had to determine how many. She might be able to distract one long enough to get to the cabin or up a tree, but if it was a pack, she didn't have a chance.

Sensing danger, Wooden Head's ears perked, and she looked up, leaving the grass at her feet.

"Shhhh," Katelyn crooned, coming to her feet to stroke the pony's neck. "It's all right, girl. I'll think of something."

Wooden Head nickered, snorting as she started to move back and forth in the small stall.

Walking around the pony, Katelyn slowly edged toward the opening of the lean-to. If she was a true Lenni Lenape, she would have been able to tell how many there were from the sounds they made. But she wasn't. She had to see them. Stiffly, she put one leg in front of the other. She was petrified but she couldn't stand to just wait until they came for her. She had to do something.

Reaching the edge of the windbreak wall, she took a deep breath and leaned to look out. She no longer felt the ice-cold air, she no longer heard the frightened pony hedging nervously in the stall. All she could hear was her own heartbeat and the low rumble of growling.

"One . . . two . . . three." She took another deep breath, shuddering as she released it. There were three more creeping from the edge of the woods.

Katelyn's doe eyes made contact with glowing gold. Her breath caught in her throat as she stood frozen. "Heavenly Father," she breathed. The closest one had to be the leader. She was a female, older . . . the deadliest kind. In the dim twilight Katelyn could make out scarred flesh and missing hair from the mangy grey hide. The she-wolf was huge and she was a fighter. Bravely, Katelyn's eyes darted to the others in the pack. Slowly they moved closer to her, circling faster, driven by hunger and the instinct to kill. *Two males, two younger females, and a young male in the rear.*

Katelyn pulled her head back behind the wall. She listened to the padding of paws in the snow as they circled closer and closer to warm flesh. Tipaakke said *tumme* were habitual creatures. Their pattern was always the same. First they seek out their victim, study him, surround him . . . then they attack. She clutched her hands together, forcing the wheels of her mind to turn. She dug deep within herself, recalling all Fox had taught her about the instinct of survival. The wolves killed to survive. If she wanted to live, *her* instincts must be stronger.

I am Lenni Lenape, she told herself, as her breath came more evenly. *Think.* Her eyes narrowed as she withdrew within herself. A white girl couldn't escape a pack of hungry wolves, but a Lenni Lenape *equiwa* could!

Katelyn's heart skipped a beat. Was that . . . ? Yes! It was! It was Tipaakke, she was sure of it! The sound of a whippoorwill pierced the night air again. Katelyn clutched her hands to her breasts in thanks. Then she suddenly realized that this meant that Fox was out there with *them*. Trembling, but without hesitation, she started forward again and peered from behind the wall. In the rising moonlight, she spotted Tipaakke's shadow just inside the line of the woods.

"Tipaakke!" Katelyn shouted before she thought.

The she-wolf shifted on her haunches, her glowing eyes on Katelyn as the others slinked in the shadows. The low growling penetrated Katelyn's very soul, sending waves of fear coursing through her veins.

Tipaakke shook his head, signaling Katelyn to stay back and keep silent. Then he lowered his body until he crouched near a leaning pine.

Katelyn could see he was thinking, weighing the odds. She watched as the grey wolves circled round and round until their circles encompassed Tipaakke, too. Still, he sat silent.

Finally, she could stand it no longer. An eternity had

passed and he had done nothing but sit and watch the restless predators. "Tipaakke . . ." Her voice split the frigid air. Again the wolves reacted to the human voice.

"Hush . . ." His voice came through the darkness as if from nowhere. "Listen, girl." He spoke half in English, half in Algonquian, yet she knew every word. "They will circle closer to me. I am a threat. When I give the signal, you will run for the cabin. Your feet must not touch the snow. Let the wind carry you."

"*Maata!* No! I won't leave you."

"This is not the time to argue." Tipaakke remained perfectly still.

"I won't do it. You would never leave me . . ." Katelyn bit her lip hard.

"You have no choice. Do as I say." He stood slowly, unsheathing his knife in one fluid-like motion.

The she-wolf snarled, turning slowly in the direction of the moving human being. She bared her teeth, raising her head to release a long terrifying howl. The others answered, each with the same eerie, piercing moan.

"Fox, there's got to be a way." Her voice reached out to him pleadingly. "Rip the bellies of the muskrat you've caught and throw them to them. All they want is food. They'll go away." Her voice trembled as she spoke, not believing what she said but wanting desperately to.

"No. They would only be back."

"What . . . and you don't think they'll be back if they have you for their evening meal?" She took a step forward.

"I have my knife. Maybe I can . . ."

"There are six of them. They won't let you live." Her voice whipped out across the snow bitterly.

"There are seven, Katie-girl. The leader moves closer. She's getting restless, I can hear how her paws move in the snow. Watch the one that circles the farthest out. He moves like a young one but they're just as deadly." His voice was hardly a whisper.

"Tipaakke, please . . ." She took another step forward and her moccasins hit the snow.

"Now!" Fox's voice thundered.

Katelyn screamed as one of the males leaped through the air knocking Tipaakke into the snow.

She ran, as fast as the wind would carry her. She had to do something. Around the corner and to the door she ran. He couldn't die. He couldn't leave her.

She raced across the floor and grabbed the twig broom from its corner where it rested. Pushing the bristles into the fireplace, she watched as it caught fire. Out the door she leaped, almost falling in the snow. Her cloak fell from her shoulders as she rounded the corner.

The sound of barking, snarling wolves filled her head. Katelyn jumped over the still body of the young male and ducked under a branch, thrusting the burning broom in a face of glowing eyes. One wolf backed off yelping as it turned to run, then the next. Katelyn could hear Tipaakke wrestling in the snow as she backed the next wolf further into the brush. She had to get to him. She had to help.

Frightened of the blaze, the wolves turned to run one by one. Reaching Tipaakke, Katelyn beat the wolf on top of him with the flaming torch. The animals howled unmercifully and leaped into the air. The stench of burning hair and flesh filled Katelyn's nostrils. She let out a piercing Algonquian war cry as she sprinted into the woods following the wolf pack.

She didn't turn around until the wolves were well ahead of her and then she spun around racing back towards Tipaakke, the fiery broom still in her hand. Her lungs burned and her legs ached, but she ran until she saw his still body lying in a dark puddle in the snow.

"Tipaakke!" The broom fell to the ground, sizzling as it was extinguished. "Please be all right, please . . ." *So much blood*, she thought. Leaning over him, she gazed at his calm face. His eyes were half open, his lips parted. His fox cloak was covered with blood, yet by some miracle his chest still rose and fell jaggedly. Tenderly, Katelyn reached out to wipe the blood from his cheek. "Tipaakke?"

Slowly, he opened his eyes and that lazy smile crossed his face. "Where has that wild woman gone?" His teasing voice was hardly audible.

Katelyn's brow furrowed in confusion. He must be delirious, she thought. Sitting in the snow, she pulled his upper body into her lap, cradling his head.

"That beautiful Lenni Lenape maiden. You are only *manake equiwa*, white woman. Where is that brave woman who defends her man running screaming into the woods?" His breath came in short gasps as he recovered from the struggle.

"You must be all right," she laughed, still shaken. A blush creeped across her cheeks. "You are teasing me. I should leave you here in the snow. There's hot tea in the cabin." Her soft brown eyes caressed his blood spackled face. She hadn't realized how important he was to her until she'd almost lost him. He was all she had . . . and she loved him.

Tipaakke blinked as her tears fell, hitting his face. "It's all right love," he murmured against her hair. "Just let me rest a moment. Then we'll go." His hand slid to his side.

Katelyn's hand followed his. Through a tear in the fox cloak she could feel warm, wet blood oozing from a wound. "We've got to get inside, Fox. We'll freeze to death."

160

He nodded, wincing as he forced his legs to move.

"Can you walk?" She stooped low, looping his hand over her neck before she straightened up. Grasping his wrist, she wrapped her other arm securely around his waist.

Leaning heavily against her, he took a step. "You see, I can walk. I'm no girl-child. You don't think I'd give my life to skinny wolves?" He limped forward slowly, thankful for her support.

"I wouldn't be that lucky. Do you want to stop and rest?"

"No, I don't." He took a deep breath and started forward again. "You're going to have to try a little harder if you want to get rid of me."

"Maybe I could send you for a walk off the side of the mountain. We're at the door now. You'll have to step up." Katelyn ducked, releasing her grip on him. "Let me get in the doorway and I'll help you up." Pushing the door open, she turned around. "Give me your hands."

He raised his hands to hers and lifted his injured leg. Sweat beaded on his forehead as he shifted his weight and stepped up into the cabin.

"Just a little further, Fox." Katelyn led him to the bed, half carrying him.

"No . . ." His breath came in short gasps.

"No what?" Her eyes fell to the blood spattering the floor. She had to stop the bleeding.

"Take me to the fireplace. I want to lay on the skins." He smiled wearily. "I never got used to your beds."

Knowing better than to argue with him, Katelyn led him to the hearth. "I have to get your cloak off."

Tipaakke reached up to tug at the corner of the fox cloak but she brushed his hands away.

"Unless you want to challenge another she-wolf today, you'd better let me do it." She slipped his arms from the cloak gingerly. His cloak and shirt were stuck to the wound where the blood was congealing. *Good sign*, she thought. *He looks worse than he is.* Easing the cloak from the wound, she dropped it to the floor.

"Take care with that." He grasped her arm for balance. Was he hallucinating? Another streak of light flashed within his brain. *My mind is playing tricks on me*, he told himself.

"Your cloak will be fine. A few stitches and it will be as good . . ." She glanced up at him. "Are you all right?"

Tipaakke pressed his hand to his forehead. "Yes. Just need to lay down."

Guiding him to the furs on the floor, Katelyn pushed a rolled skin under his head. "Now lay back. That's good. I need to see the wound. Can you roll over a bit?"

Patiently, he rolled over and allowed her to remove the stained muslin shirt.

Katelyn winced as she pulled the shirt from where it stuck to the oozing gash. She was relieved to see that it was long but shallow. Properly cared for the wound would scar, but he would live. After removing the shirt she could see that most of the blood must have been the young wolf's. Other than the bite on his side and a few scratches, he was unharmed. "Now the breeches, Fox."

He chuckled deep in his throat, letting her pull the rabbit skin breeches from his legs. "Tell me the truth girl, this is all you wanted." He gave her that lazy smile she knew so well.

Katelyn looked down at his naked body, her eyes caressing the long sinewy legs, the broad chest. "Very funny. I can have you any time. Now lay back and hush." She got to her feet, averting her eyes. There was no escaping him. She was lost. Even weak and injured he sent warm waves of desire through her body.

Busying herself, she found her cotton dishcloth and ripped it in half, returning to kneel beside him.

Heating water over the fire, she dipped the rags in the scalding water. "This is going to be hot but it will cleanse the wound. Bites must be tended carefully. I've heard of people who have gone mad and died of animal bites." She dropped one of the steaming rags on the wound.

Tipaakke's eyelids fluttered but he didn't move. "I know of the sickness. I will not get it. It comes only from animals possessed by the spirit of madness."

Katelyn nodded, retrieving the other bit of cotton from the bowl and began to wipe his blood-stained face.

"I am very proud of you, Katie-girl." Tipaakke reached out to rest his hand on her knee.

"Fox . . ."

His eyes flew open. "Let me speak for once." Closing his eyes again, he continued. "You were not only brave, but you were smart. I wouldn't have thought to make a torch." He laughed, half to himself. "And certainly not from a broom."

Katelyn dabbed at his lips, embarrassed by his words of praise.

He grabbed her hand. "You acted as a true Lenni Lenape woman would have. This will not be forgotten. And for your reward, I will skin the dead wolf, and you will wear it as a headdress."

"I don't want any reward." She dropped the rag into the pot with a splash. Brushing back a wisp of fallen hair, she stared at the calm bronze face. "The wolf is yours. You killed it."

"But you deserve it. It is my gift, so you will wear it proudly." He opened his eyes, staring her face so near to his.

Katelyn lowered her lips to kiss him softly. "When

163

you look at me like that," she whispered, "I could swear you can see me."

"I see with my heart." He tapped his breast lightly. "And if I was not wiser, I would think you cared for me."

"Well, I'm glad you're wise enough to know better." She shifted uneasily.

"You could have let me die. You were safe in the cabin. You came back for me. A man does not save his enemy from wolves."

Katelyn turned her head to stare at the wall lined with pelts. "It's been a long time since you and I have been enemies, Fox." Her voice seemed to come from far in the distance.

Tipaakke stroked her arm through the folds of doeskin. "Don't leave me, Katie-girl. Come home with me in the spring. We will make many songs together."

She turned back to him. "You're foolish, Fox, if you think we could ever have a life like that. Those were just stories your grandfather told you . . . songs of love and happiness. You live in a child's dream world. Our life could never be one of your Indian songs . . ."

Tipaakke sat up, looping his arm around her waist. "Now you're being too serious. You didn't think we could come this far. Dare to dream a child's dream. Sometimes they come true."

Katelyn sighed, staring at the burning embers in the fireplace. "Let me get some of those herbs Won gave me and make a paste. Once the wound is cleaned and treated, you must rest. I'll make tea."

Tipaakke nodded, lying down again. "You're doing it again . . ."

"Doing what?" She rose to her feet with the pot of water.

"Just like a wife . . ." He shook his head, clicking between his teeth.

"I don't think that's funny, Fox." She spoke icily as she crossed the floor to throw the foul water out the door. She didn't like it when he toyed with her feelings like this.

"I'm just teasing you, Katie-girl. You're very good to me." He added thoughtfully, "You could be, you know."

"Could be what?" She banged the pan down on the table and reached high on the shelf for the small bag of healing herbs.

His voice drifted across the cabin ". . . be my wife."

Katelyn's breath caught in her throat. Fingering the leather pouch, she turned slowly to face him. Was he teasing still? She didn't think so. "Don't say what isn't true." Her voice quavered. "It could never be." She stood staring at him stretched before her, his bronze skin shimmering in the firelight.

Tipaakke spoke evenly. "It could be true. I can marry anyone I want to."

Katelyn shook her head, pulling Tipaakke's spare muslin shirt from a peg. "They'd never accept me." She shook her head again.

"Who wouldn't? If I married you, you would be one of us." He shrugged his shoulders.

She took a knife from the table and started a hole in the shirt, ripping it into strips. "Are you asking?"

Tipaakke sat up slowly. "Do you think that's so odd? Why shouldn't we marry? You've adjusted well to my life. We like each other. Our life is good on the sleeping platform. It's time I had a wife. Once we return to the village, I must go back to my life as a brave of the Lenni Lenape."

Katelyn sighed, walking slowly to Fox, the bandages in her hand. She laughed silently to herself. This was the second proposal in a year, yet no one had spoken of love to her. She knelt, lost in her own thoughts as she mixed the herbs with boiled water and packed the

165

wound.

Tipaakke remained silent, sensing Katelyn's need to think. He lay back to wait for her to speak.

Katelyn applied the herb poltice carefully and reached for the strips of muslin. She didn't want Fox to say he loved her if he didn't. But why couldn't he love her? She bit her lip, suppressing the urge to cry out in pain. It would make things so much easier if only he could say he honestly loved her.

"Katelyn . . ." His voice reached out to comfort her. "You don't have to decide now. We have time. We would have to be married by my father, but we could be married by minister if you wish. I know of a Quaker who would do it for us. You know it makes no difference to me what name we give the creator. He is the same by any name."

Katelyn looked up, her eyes caressing the broad cheek bones of the man she loved. She smiled sadly. He was the only man who had ever been kind to her. How could she think of asking for more? He would always protect her and keep her fed and clothed. He would never be brutal and never expect her to do something he wouldn't do himself. She reached out to brush a long dark strand of hair from his bare shoulder, and he caught her hand.

"Think, Katelyn. I told you you would have until spring. I won't go back on my word. It's just something to think about." He brought her hand to his lips and kissed it softly.

"Spring," Katelyn whispered as she leaned forward to meet his lips. ". . . plenty of time . . ."

Chapter Eight

"Wake up, Katie-girl." Tipaakke shook her bare shoulder. "Get up, lazy squaw. Your man has already gathered water and stoked the fire."

Katelyn's eyes fluttered open, focusing slowly. She pulled the fur wrap over her shoulder and snuggled deeper in the warm bed. "Brrr, it's cold in here."

"It will warm soon. Now get up, I have something for you."

She smiled lazily, watching as he crossed the room in one fluid-like motion. "Something for me? Why?" She kept her eye on him as she sat up, touching her toes to the cold floor. He seemed breathtakingly handsome this morning as he moved about the cabin dressed in a rabbit-hide jerkin and knee high moccasins. His wound had healed quickly and was already turning into a long, pink scar. The day after the wolf attack he rose early as usual and set out to tend his traps. He never made mention again of the wolves, but worked evenings on the hide of the young male he was preparing for her.

"It's a surprise. It's Christmas, isn't it?" Tipaakke

poured fresh water from the skin into the pot over the fire.

Katelyn blinked in confusion. "Christmas? I think it's come and gone." She slid out of bed and reached for her doeskin dress.

"I say it's today. Now come and sit down." He patted a wooden chair, as eager as a child on Christmas morn. "I made you tea. You get the sugar."

"Sugar?" Katelyn's eyes grew wide with excitement. "I wondered what you were saving that little bit for. I love sugar in my tea. We always had it on Sundays."

"Sit down." He poured the steaming water into two pewter cups. "This summer we'll collect honey. I'll get English tea in my trading and then you can have sweet tea whenever you like."

Katelyn threw a short rabbit wrap over her shoulders and went to search for the tiny brown packet of sugar. "Why didn't you tell me we were going to have Christmas? I don't have a gift for you." She sat down, laying the package of sugar on the table.

Tipaakke slid the steaming cups across the table and opened the sugar slowly, taking care not to spill a pinch. "I don't need a gift. This is for you. Now, close your eyes."

She squeezed her eyes shut, squirming in her chair.

He crossed the room and stepped out the door. "Keep your eyes shut," he called, carrying in a huge log.

"Now? Can I open them now?" Katelyn got to her feet, listening as he grew closer.

"All right. Now you can open them."

Katelyn's eyes flew open, and her mouth dropped. "A Yule log! Oh, Fox, it's beautiful." She reached out to touch the decorated log.

"It's heavy, too." He walked to the fireplace and rolled it onto the smouldering embers.

Katelyn clasped her hands, watching as the flames

licked at the holly and standing pine wrapped so carefully around the log. "It's far more beautiful than the one Aunt Pitty had . . ." She looped her arm in Tipaakke's. "It's perfect. Thank you." She leaned to kiss his smooth cheek.

"I'm glad you like it, Katie-girl. Now for your other present."

"Fox, this is perfect." She squeezed his arm gently. "I don't want anything else."

"What have I told you about gifts? They must be accepted. It's a dishonor not to accept. I'll be right back." He patted her on the backside and picked up his cloak on the way outside the door.

Katelyn slid to the floor and sat cross-legged staring into the fire. The Yule log snapped and cracked as the greenery and bark caught fire.

It's so beautiful, she thought. *He's so good to me. He's right. I should marry him. I should go back to the village in the spring and become his wife. There's no life for me with my own people . . . with Henry. They'll never take me back. Besides, Henry would make a lousy husband.* She drew her legs up and rested her arms on her knees. *Maybe, in time, Fox will come to love me. He likes me. He wants to marry me.* She watched as a bit of holly caught fire, the flames licking, consuming, until the leaf was gone. People can learn to love, she told herself.

Tipaakke rounded the cabin wall and started for the pony's stall, knowing the way step by step. Suddenly he stopped. It was happening again. He raised his face to the sky, turning to the heat of the morning sun. *I see it*, he thought. *I'm not imagining it. The sun! That ball of bright light in the darkness is the sun!*

He whispered a prayer of thanks and started towards the lean-to again. First he had seen only streaks of light flashing in the dark. But now shadows were coming and going. He would go days seeing nothing but the inky blackness he had grown used to. But then, only for a moment, there was light. *I'll wait a little longer before I tell her*, he thought as he gathered his gift from beneath a pile of dead grass. *I don't want to give her hope only to find that this means nothing. We will be returning to the village before the moon has passed three times. I'll wait and see what the Shaman says. If my sight is meant to be returned, it will. I have heard of men injured far more seriously who have regained sight, even movement. The Shaman says no mortal man can understand the mind and injuries to it. Yes, it's in The Creator's hands*, he told himself as he walked back through the snow, back to the cabin. He looked up again before going in. There it was, the sun . . . forcing its way through his darkness. He smiled. This was a good omen. Things would be better now.

Katelyn jumped up when Tipaakke came in the door, running to meet him. "What have you got behind your back, my cunning Fox? Let me see!" She swayed to and fro, trying to catch a peek.

"Close your eyes," he commanded, keeping his hands behind his back.

"Fox . . ." She gave an impatient stamp of her foot.

"Close your eyes or you'll get nothing."

"All right." She let out an exasperated sigh but did as he said, squeezing her eyes shut.

Tipaakke grinned, pleased with himself. "Now put out your hands." She complied, and he pushed a soft bundle into her waiting arms.

Katelyn opened her eyes to find a pile of beaver hide items. "What have you made? A hat! Oh, and mittens! They're beautiful. Mittens!" She pulled the beaver hat over her head and slipped the mittens on. "I can't believe you made these for me." She looked up at him.

"You're always complaining that your hands are cold when you gather wood. Now they won't be."

"But when did you get time to make them?" She

170

brushed a mitten across her cheek, then blew the fur, watching it ripple.

"In the lean-to." He reached out with both hands to feel the hat on her head. "What did you think I was doing out there for so long?"

"It must have taken you hours to sew all of these seams." She buried her face in the huge, fluffy mittens.

"Now that you've seen how pretty they are, turn them inside out. They will be warmer." He brushed the hat lightly with his knuckles.

"No! I've been cold this long. I won't know what I'm missing." She took a step closer, allowing him to draw her into his arms. "They're too beautiful to wear inside out."

He planted a kiss on the end of her nose. "I thought you'd say that."

"Take off your cloak, it's warm in here," she told him in her silkiest voice.

He smiled as she lowered the cloak and let it fall to the floor. "It is warm in here," he murmured against her smooth neck.

"And getting warmer," Katelyn teased as she pressed her hips to his.

"Let's sit in front of the fire and drink our tea." He dropped light, feathery kisses here and there on her upturned face.

"Tea? I thought you might be interested in something else," she purred.

"That, too." He pressed his lips to hers, sampling what was yet to come. "You taste of honey . . . wild honey. Not honey of the clover, but honey of the fire weed," he murmured huskily. "Come, lay with me near the fire." He scooped his cloak off the floor and led her to the hearth, still wearing her beaver hat and mittens.

"This is the best Christmas I've ever had, Fox." Katelyn watched as he spread out his cloak and sat down.

Tipaakke reached out to take her mittened hands and bring her to sit on his lap. "I like to hear your voice when you're happy." He rested his cheek on her head, breathing deeply. Her hair always smelled so fresh, so bright. It smelled like sunlight on a hot summer day.

"You are very special, Fox of mine. You've shown me kindness when I didn't deserve it." She pulled her mittens off and layed them on the floor.

"Everyone deserves some kindness." He brushed the hair back from her shoulder, running his hands through the magical tresses.

"You know what I mean. I've not always been very nice to you." She traced his long straight nose with a finger.

"No." He shook his head. "You haven't. But fear makes us do strange things."

"I've really been thinking about what you said . . . about you and I . . . getting married, I mean," she finished softly.

"And . . ."

She looked him squarely in the face. "I don't know. I can't tell you, yet. This is so hard for me. But I *have* been thinking." She stared, mesmerized by his haunting ebony eyes.

"That's all I ask. We have plenty of time." He ran his searching fingers over her jaw, catching her chin with his hand and drew her mouth to his. "Let me taste you. I can't wait another moment." He kissed her deeply, molding his chest to her soft inviting breasts.

Katelyn withdrew her mouth from his, giving him another light kiss before pushing herself off his lap, onto her knees.

"Where are you going?" he asked huskily.

"Your jerkin," she breathed, tugging at the leather shirt.

Tipaakke rose to his knees, allowing her to pull the soft jerkin over his head.

". . . and the moccasins . . . and now mine . . ." She slipped her moccasins off and tossed them carelessly, reaching behind her neck to loosen the ties on her dress.

He listened as she pulled the doeskin over her head, imagining what it would be like to watch as she slowly revealed the soft, shimmering flesh beneath the simple dress. "You're so lovely," he told her, his tongue darting out to moisten his dry lips.

"How do you know? I might be an ugly witch!" She tossed the dress aside, straightening the beaver hat, still perched on her head.

"No. You don't think Fox would take an ugly witch for his woman do you? Don't you remember the first day I brought you to the village? There in my wigwam I saw you, only for a brief moment, but I saw beauty I could never forget. These eyes missed nothing." He tapped his temple lightly.

"Well, my Fox," she took his hand, "you will have to see this with your hands . . ." She pressed his hand to her bare breast, catching her breath as his thumb found her budding nipple.

Easing her onto her back, his hand brushed against the hat still on her head. He laughed deep in his throat. "Why are you still wearing this?"

Katelyn stretched out like a lazy kitten, her hands high above her head. "Don't you like it?"

Without a word he snatched the beaver hat off her head and sent it sailing through the air.

She laughed with him, pulling his head down until his lips met hers. Stretching out beside her, Tipaakke began to run his fingers lightly over her silky flesh. "So soft . . . so fresh . . ." He told her in his own tongue, leaning to nip at a peaked breast.

173

Katelyn arched her back, running her hands through his long silky hair. No one would ever be able to make her feel like he did. She would always be his slave. A slave to his touch. She moaned, alternately relaxing and tensing her muscles as he explored her yearning body until she was breathless. Her mind and body whirled with desire until nothing existed but the two of them.

"Where are your mittens?" she heard Tipaakke ask through a fog of intense pleasure.

"My mittens?" She struggled to think clearly.

"Yes. I want a mitten." He kissed her damp cheek.

Her eyes fluttered open and she fumbled with one hand until it touched soft fur. "Here. What do you want with it?"

"Shhhh . . . lie back," he breathed in her ear as he slipped his hand into the mitten and began to stroke again.

"Mmmmmm . . . that feels so nice . . ." Katelyn told him, her words coming in short gasps. Her body began to tingle . . . then grow warmer as he brushed the soft tantalizing fur over her willing flesh. Her loins quickened, aching with heat as he brushed her thighs teasingly, careful not to touch the soft fiery bed of curls.

"Fox . . . please . . . I can't stand this anymore . . ."

He laughed as he swung his leg over her, and pressed his naked body to hers.

She pulled the mitten from his hand and tossed it. "You're a tease." She twisted her fingers in his satiny hair, and pulled his mouth to hers, kissing him deeply, fiercely.

Tipaakke's eyes drifted shut as he felt her hands stroking down his back to his buttocks, kneading them, pressing his swollen manhood against her thrusting hips.

"Now Tipaakke, please," she called in Algonquian. "Love me now. I need you."

He smiled, pleased with himself as he kissed one eyelid and then the other. This was the first time she had ever called him by his true name. "I will love you now, Katie," he whispered in the same tongue. "But I have already loved you a long time."

Lost in the heat of sweet, aching passion, Katelyn did not hear his words. She heard only the pounding of his heart and her own, as they strove to become one.

"Get up, Katie-girl." Tipaakke pushed her over onto her back, and leaned to tie his moccasion.

Katelyn opened one eye and then squeezed it shut, settling deeper in the fur bed covers. "It's still dark out," she mumbled sleepily. "Why are we getting up so early? Why are we getting up at all?"

Prodding her again, Tipaakke moved to the fire to pour hot herbal tea. "Your tea is made, now get up. We've many miles to cover if we're to get there by nightfall."

She sat up, scratching her head. "Get where? Where're we going?" She ran a palm over her face. "You didn't say anything about going anywhere."

"No." He shook his head. "Didn't decide until I got up."

She swung her legs over the side of the bed. "Didn't decide what?" she asked with exasperation. "You're doing it to me again. Don't your people ever come right out and say anything?"

Tipaakke laughed. "We're going visiting; now get dressed while I pack our bags."

"Visiting?" Katelyn's voice perked. "Visiting where? You mean we're going to see someone?" She crossed the room hastily, a skin wrapped around her naked

175

body. "Who are we going to visit?" She reached for the steaming mug on the mantel.

"An old friend, Cooking Joe. He's a trapper. He lives a day's walk from here." He pulled a bag off a peg and began to fill it with necessary items.

She took a sip of the scalding brew. "You never told me anyone lived anywhere near here. I thought we were the only ones for days in any direction."

He shrugged. "If I had told you there was anyone nearby, you would have tried to leave me." He looked up. "I wanted you here with me. This has been our time together. I didn't want to share you."

"But what if you'd been killed? I could have sat here until I died of starvation when there was help a day away." She slammed down the pewter tankard. If he cared so much for her welfare, why didn't tell her where she could get help if she needed it?

"I see Joe often. I told him in the fall that if he ever went half a moon without seeing sign of me, he was to come here and take you back to your people." Tipaakke continued to stuff the bags, dividing food and water between the two equally.

For a moment, Katelyn was stunned, then she was touched. Once again he'd had the foresight to make plans to keep her safe. And he was right not to tell her, as much as she hated to admit it. She would have tried to escape earlier, and probably would have died trying.

Tipaakke stood waiting in silence, then spoke quietly. "Do you want to go? Joe has a wife. I thought you would enjoy her friendship. She's a good woman, his Lena." He stood with one hand balanced on his hip.

Katelyn nodded, breaking into a grin. "Of course I want to go! I'd do anything to speak to another human being." She ran to the side of the bed where her dress lay and dropped her wrap to the floor.

Tipaakke stared with a bemused twinkle in his eye.

"And what am I? You said you like to hear me talk. You said you liked my stories."

"Of course I do," she exclaimed excitedly, pulling the dress over her head, "but it's been months since I've talked to anyone but you and Wooden Head." She leaned over to get her moccasins. "Besides, half the time I don't understand what you're saying."

Tipaakke reached for his white man's breeches. "I thought we should go now, before the river thaws. We'll stay a night or two and then return."

"We can stay!" She leaped in the air like a young child. "Thank you! I can't believe it!" She ran to throw her arms around him.

Tipaakke welcomed her embrace with amusement. "I didn't know such a thing would make you so happy. You don't even know my friends." He pressed a kiss to her forehead.

"I don't care; I'm so lonely I'd even go visit that rotten brother of yours." She released him, dancing away. "I can't wait to get out of here. Can we take Wooden Head?"

He ignored her comment concerning his brother. In time they would learn to respect each other. "No. We leave her here. We will travel down the frozen river that leads west. She's too heavy to walk on the ice; she would break through. Get your mittens and hat, the sun is breaking."

Katelyn pulled her hat over her head and began to shrug on the layers of furs she'd devised to keep warm. Reaching for a bag, she threw it over her shoulder. "Why's this so heavy? Why can't you carry it?" She pulled the gift mittens over her hands.

Tightening the ties of his cloak, Tipaakke glanced back at the extinguished fire and held open the door. "You must carry your own supplies. I carry mine. If we are separated, you must have your own food, your own water, your own dry leaves and sticks to make a fire."

She stooped in the doorway. "If we get separated? I hope you're not planning on leaving me somewhere." She arched one eyebrow.

"You are being silly again, now go. We have many miles to cover if we're to arrive by nightfall."

Katelyn stepped into the brilliant white of the dawning day, shading her eyes until they adjusted to the glaring sun. She waited until Tipaakke closed the door and swung his bag on his back, and then they started forward.

"What about Wooden Head? Did you feed her?" She walked just in front of Fox, treading backwards. The icy cold nipped at her nose and cheeks, bringing a healthy tingle to them.

"She is fed and warm. My grandfather built the lean-to in a good place. The pony is as warm as we are inside with the fire."

Together, the two made their way down the mountain and then turned west. Shortly, they came upon the river and climbed down its slippery bank. Katelyn and Tipaakke laughed, dancing across the ice as they made their way toward the friend's cabin. For once, there was no unrest between them. She was ecstatic about the adventure and he was well pleased that such a simple thing made her so happy. When the sun rose high in the sky, they stopped to eat and rest briefly and then continued on. Tipaakke surmised that at the rate they were walking, they would be in Cooking Joe's cabin by mealtime.

As the day passed and the shadows began to lengthen, Katelyn finally began to tire and slowed her pace. "It's so beautiful out here, Fox." She kicked at the snow. "How much further?"

Tipaakke pointed ahead. "See the bend to the left and then the sharp right?"

She squinted, nodding. "Yes, I see it, where the log's fallen."

"Yes. There after the right, we cross the bank and Joe lives not more than half a mile from the grandfather oak off the bank." He reached to drape an arm over her shoulder. "You've moved swiftly and with care today." He smiled. "Soon you will track and hunt with the best of our braves."

"Oh, no, not me." She pushed at him playfully. "I want no part of that. It's wonderful to get out and get some air, but I like the cabin. I want to be near the fire with a cup of your tea in one hand a corn cake in the other." She stepped ahead, picking up a broken twig to toss.

"That's fine. Not all of us were meant to be chiefs. I think I've grown used to the fire, too." He winked. "Especially when you're near."

Katelyn smiled. He didn't speak his affection for her often, but when he did, he made her tingle with pleasure. "Just wait, soon you'll grow lazy and fat just . . ."

"Shhhh!" Tipaakke held up a hand, freezing in his steps. "Do not move," he commanded. "Listen."

Her heart beat pounded with terror at the sound of his voice. What was wrong? What was he talking about? A few months ago she would have voiced her thoughts, but now she listened intently.

At first she heard nothing, but then a terrifying noise filled her eardrums, a great booming resounding through the trees. The ice . . . it was moving.

"Listen, move quietly to the bank," Tipaakke instructed, sliding his feet slowly to the left. "Do not speak. The ice is giving way."

Carefully, the two made their way to the bank, listening to the moaning ice, watching as crack after crack appeared.

At the instant that Katelyn thought she was safe, the earth beneath her gave way with one great splintering swoosh. Instinctively, she grabbed for the overhanging branches above, managing to gain a hold as her feet hit the icy water.

Tipaakke reacted without thinking, throwing his body at hers, forcing her onto the bank. Katelyn screamed as she watched him fall behind her, his head striking the ice as he went down.

For a moment, she didn't breath. If she had, she knew he would have slipped into the frigid darkness forever. But then, as the creaking ceased, she pulled herself the rest of the way onto the bank, ignoring the cold, wet pain that seeped at her legs.

She stared down at Fox. He lay motionless, his body half in the water, half out. His head rested in a spreading puddle of congealing blood, but his chest still rose and fell.

What am I going to do, her mind screamed. *How am I going to get him up here? If I try to get down to him, the ice is liable to give in and we'll both drown.* Frantically she looked around. She had to find a way to get him up to her. His body lay close to the bank's edge. Maybe she could pull him up.

First, Katelyn eased herself down the bank again, but she soon realized she didn't have the strength to hold on to her support branch and pulled him up the bank. She'd never be able to budge him that way.

Back on solid ground, she stared down at Tipaakke's still body. There had to be a way! He told her there was always a way when you wanted something badly enough. Hopping up and down to bring the circulation back to her feet, Katelyn's mind raced. She had to think of something fast. Did she risk the chance and run to Joe for help? No, if the wound didn't kill him, he would freeze to death before they got back. No, she

180

had to save him and she had to do it alone.

Then something caught her eye. Still on Tipaakke's arm was his bag. Of course! There had to be something in there she could use to tie around him and pull him up! Dumping her own bag onto the frozen ground, she threw the packages of sugar and tea aside. There at the bottom was a snare string!

Anxiously, Katelyn got to her feet, untying the knots in the string. It was short and thin; it might cut into his flesh, but it would do. Now she had to find the strength to pull him up.

Jumping up and down a few more times to ward off the numbing cold of her wet feet, she lowered herself down the bank again. Balancing carefully, she reached for his arm. On the third swing she caught it and tied the string around it. Tying the other end around her waist, Katelyn began to pull herself up by the hanging branches. Slowly, with tugging and sweat, she made her way up with Tipaakke's body sliding behind her. As she reached the top and began to pull him up the slight bank, she blessed him over and over again for being a small man. If he'd been much taller than she, she'd never have been able to get him up. Still, it was an effort every inch of the way to move his dead weight. She called to him again and again, saying his name, talking to him, but he never flinched.

Finally, Katelyn flung herself onto the ground, her breath coming in short pants. Once she began to breath more easily, she got up again, knowing she had to keep moving if she was going to keep herself from freezing. Calmly, she walked into the woods and pulled her knife from its sheath. Sawing at a small limb, she worked on it until it came down. Though she had only about a mile to walk, she couldn't pull by his arms that far. But if she could cradle him in the branches and pull the limb, his weight would be dispersed and easier to move.

Methodically, Katelyn worked, stopping only to jump up and down long enough to restore the circulation to her deadening limbs. When she got his body rolled onto the branch and positioned correctly, she tied him on with the snare string. She could have used his string as well, but his bag had been lost in the water.

When he was situated, she grabbed the limb and started off in the direction of Joe's cabin. The going was slow over the snow because she had to go around stumps and fallen trees, but she made her way, further and further from the place in the river where they fell in.

When Katelyn felt like she couldn't walk another step, she took two more and then she stopped to rest. Again and again she pulled for a few minutes and then rested, then pulled again. Once or twice a groan escaped from Tipaakke's lips, but other than that he said nothing and never attempted to move.

When it became almost too dark to see, Katelyn realized she could pull Tipaakke no further. She was too tired and too numb with cold. Her mind was beginning to work more slowly, her eyes playing tricks on her. Pulling Tipaakke under a tree for protection, she yanked off a layer of semidry skins and covered him up. Then she started out in the direction of the smell of smoke. She knew Joe's cabin couldn't be far.

When Katelyn reached the small lean-to, she was barely coherent. Leaning against the crude door, she banged with a fist.

"Who is it?" a gruff voice called from within.

"Joe? Joe, help. Tipaakke's fallen in the river, his . . ."

The door swung open and a small man appeared. "Fox has what? Where is he?" Grabbing her arm, he pulled her into the warmth of the cabin.

Katelyn pointed out the door. "Not far back, I can show you. Fell in the river." Her head rolled with exhaustion.

"No. You stay here. My Lena'll take care of you." The dark-haired man reached for a heavy woolen cloak near the door.

"Come, poor girl," a soft voice plied. "Come near the fire, you're half frozen."

Through her eyelashes Katelyn saw the dim outline of a dark-faced woman with a bright cloth tied around her head. The room was so warm, she wanted to just melt in its dim light. But, she had to get back to Tipaakke; she had to help Joe.

"No, stay here. My Joe'll find him. Follow your tracks in the snow." She spoke in a strange way, her words oddly accented.

In a dream-like state, Katelyn moved to the bright fire, allowing the strange dark woman to pull the layers of skins from her shoulders.

"Hush, baby-child," the woman murmured. "Ol' Lena's here now, she'll take care of you."

Without much insistence, Katelyn lay down on the dry mat the woman offered in front of the fireplace. After that, she drifted into a heavy, dreamless sleep.

Sometime in the middle of the night, Katelyn woke. For a moment she didn't know where she was, but then memories of the ice and Tipaakke's fall flooded her muddled mind. Bolting upright, she glanced around the tiny cabin. With relief, she spotted Tipaakke only a few paces from her. Getting on her knees, she crawled to where he lay and peered down at his face.

He lay flat on his back, his head bandaged with a strip of clean white cloth. His chest rose and fell evenly. For a moment Katelyn debated whether or not she would try and wake him. Was he still unconscious?

How long had she slept? She peered across the fire-lit room at the two figures sleeping in the narrow built-in bed. Cooking Joe and Lena wouldn't have gone to sleep if he hadn't been all right, would they? She looked back at Tipaakke's calm face. The light of the fire highlighted his high cheekbones and bronze skin. She reached out to brush his cheek with the palm of her hand. Tomorrow will be soon enough to know his fate, she decided, laying her head on his chest. Tonight he's in Manito's hands.

Tipaakke's brain stirred as he felt a wave of consciousness flow through his veins. His mind flickered with pictures of the river bed he and Katelyn had walked on, the deafening sound of the cracking ice. As he forced his head to clear, he realized an image was forming. It was orange, red, and brown all at once and its scent enveloped him. Then he realized his eyes were open. He was seeing something! Slowly the image came into focus as he lay quietly giving it time. His head pounded until it echoed and the bright light of the room pierced him from all sides; but, he forced his eyelids to remain open. He raised a hand slowly to run it through Katelyn's hair. It was hair! The hair he saw!

Tipaakke smiled at his blessed luck, keeping his eyes fixed on her magical hair. It was even more beautiful than he'd remembered with its autumn browns and golds and brilliant streaks of light and dark. He wound a bright strand round and round his finger in disbelief. Was this really happening? Had his sight returned, or was he walking in the dream world? He recalled his fall on the ice and the great crack that had sounded in his head before darkness overtook him. Maybe he was not alive at all. . . .

No, this was life; he knew it! The air smelled of life. It tasted like life! Slowly he dared to move his eyes. Laying in his arms was Katelyn. Her face rested on his

184

bare chest, her pale body curled at his side. Had her skin always been of such a luminescent ivory hue? He reached to stroke a bare hip tentatively. Her flesh was smooth and warm beneath his touch. It was the flesh he had come to know and worship but had never seen more than a glimpse of. Heavenly Father she was sweet!

Katelyn stirred at Tipaakke's touch, then her eyes flew open and she sat up. "Fox." She stared into his silky, dark eyes. A smile played on his familiar lips. For a moment she was confused. He looked the same, yet different. Then her jaw dropped. "You can see! You can see!"

Tipaakke nodded, the smile forming into a grin. "I see, my dove."

Katelyn stared, still in shock. "How? Why?" Words tumbled from her mouth, but she gave him no chance to reply. "The knock on the head . . . it must have . . . you must have . . ." She leaned to press kisses to his face. "Why didn't you wake me?"

He ran his finger along her bare shoulder. "I was busy looking at you." He ran the finger over her lips.

"Does your head hurt?" She layed her head on the blood-stained bandage.

"It hurts. My eyes hurt; but, I see." His voice filled the air with a soft hum. "All of my sight has returned except for a few shadows on this eye." He pointed to the left.

Katelyn dropped her head back on his chest, squeezing him tight with her arms. "I can't believe it! I can't believe you can see. I thought the Shaman said you would never see again."

"He didn't know. An injury to the head is a strange thing. The white man's bullet is still in my head. It must have moved."

"I don't care," she cried joyfully. You can see." She

looked up to see Lena and Joe rising. "He can see!"

Lena broke into a grin. "This is good. I make us our morning meal, and our friend will see his cakes and honey."

Cooking Joe heaved up the suspenders on his woolen breeches and came to them. "So my friend, Fox, sees again. I knew you would."

Katelyn shrank beneath the wool blanket she was wrapped in, trying to conceal her nakedness. "Could I have clothes, Lena?"

Lena handed her the doeskin dress Katelyn had worn the day before. "It was damp, but Lena dry it and make it soft again." She turned to Joe. "You get out of here and let this Kate-lyn get her dress on. You get water and more wood." The small, dark woman gave her husband a shove on the back. "That Joe," she shook her head, "he got no sense sometimes." Shaking her head, she went to her pantry shelves and began banging pots and moving jars of flour and honey onto the table.

Pulling her dress over her head, Katelyn got to her feet. "So are you going to get up and have some of Lena's cakes and honey or are you going to lay there all day?" She prodded Tipaakke's arm playfully with her bare foot.

He grabbed her foot with a quick sweep of his hand, forcing her to balance on the other. "Take care, Katie-girl. We'll have no more of your silly games now. The Fox's sight has returned. Now he will teach you how to be the proper squaw." Still holding her foot, he propped himself up on one elbow. "You must learn from Lena. She knows how to care for her man, and she knows her place."

Lena laughed, throwing up a dark hand covered in flour. "Our men, they talk so much," she shook a finger, "but they know who honeys their bread."

186

Katelyn stared down at Tipaakke with sparkling brown eyes. "Are you going to let me go or am I going to stand on one foot all day?" She knew by the look on his face that he was amazed that she had kept her balance so long. He had taught her to control her body, and control it well.

"I think I will let you go." He released her foot, tucking his hands behind his head. "But only because I wish to, not because my squaw tells me."

Katelyn looked down at his striking bronze face. This was a game they'd played all winter. He did things for her because she asked, but always made it a point of telling her he did it because he chose to, not because she wished it. These redmen were a strange lot, Katelyn decided, going over to Lena. "I haven't thanked you for helping us," she told the black woman, leaning over to stare into the bowl.

"No need to thank. You did it all. My Joé, he didn't have to bring our friend far. You are a smart girl." She dripped melted fat into the mixing bowl. "Those fancy breeches saved him from freezing. If he had only worn moccasins as he used to, my Joe says he would have lost toes, maybe flesh." She stirred the mixture with a hand-carved spoon, then lifted it to shake in Tipaakke's direction. "You are a lucky man, Tipaakke Oopus to have this smart girl. She save your life."

Tipaakke pulled on the woolen breeches left for him by Joe and came to stand with the women. "I am lucky. I know this," he spoke huskily, reaching to tuck a tendril of hair behind her ear. "And when we sit down to your meal of honey and cakes, she will tell us just how she saved the Fox."

For three nights Tipaakke and Katelyn remained with Cooking Joe and Lena, enjoying their hospitality. Together the four ate and drank their fill, remaining in the cabin where they sat around the fire telling stories

187

and talking about their pasts. Seeing Tipaakke among friends and listening to him tell tales of his childhood gave Katelyn great insight as to what kind of man he was and she left the cabin with a new respect for him. She was beginning to realize that she really was happy with him. She needed him and she loved him. He needed her. Maybe he would learn to love her.

Hand in hand Katelyn and Tipaakke left Joe and Lena on the fourth day and with light hearts they returned to their own cabin, traveling by land. The temperature was beginning to climb, and they knew spring would soon be upon them.

Chapter Nine

"Don't say that!" Katelyn flung. She took another step back, moving like a caged animal. Her world crumbling again. "Leave me alone! Don't touch me! I don't want to talk to you; I don't want to look at you!"

Tipaakke held his ground, reaching out impatiently with one hand. "What's wrong with you? You knew it would happen." He dropped his hand in exasperation.

She pushed back a lock of wildly tangled hair, narrowing her eyes. "It can't be . . ." A sob escaped her tightly compressed lips. "I can't be with child . . ."

"Katelyn." Tipaakke tried reasoning with her. "We've shared a mat for many moons. How long has it been since your last woman's time?"

She blushed a deep crimson. "How dare you ask me such a thing," she spit.

"How can you be so childish? I was a married man for many years. You think I don't know a woman's body?" He clenched his fist tightly, trying to control his anger. Everytime he thought things were going well between them, she went crazy again, and he was tired of it. Things between them had gone so well since his sight had returned that he was beginning to believe they really could live together in peace. And now there was this!

"It doesn't matter, a man shouldn't ask a woman a question like that." She took another step back.

Tipaakke swung around, banging his fist on the wooden table. "I have had enough of this, Katelyn Locke!" He spun back around. "Do you know what's wrong with you? You're a child. You want to be treated like a woman, you want the pleasures of a woman, but you act like a babe on her mother's board."

"This is all your fault," she snapped. "Don't talk to me about being childish, because I don't want to hear about it. I wouldn't be in this mess if it weren't for you!"

Tipaakke curled his fingers until his fist was a ball and began to stalk her. "Yes, I took you from the coward who left you to die. Yes, I brought you here to care for me, but I *never* made you lie with me. Never." His voice had become deathly low.

Suddenly, Katelyn was frightened. Fox had never shouted at her like that. He never lost his temper. No matter how hard she pushed, he'd never let anger get the best of him. He had never been cruel like this.

"Tell me," Tipaakke threatened, moving closer. "Tell me how long it has been. I have had enough of your foolish games. The Fox does not play games."

"I can't be having a baby," she shook her head wildly, "only married women have children."

"Don't be daft, woman!" He grabbed her arm, yanking her closer. "Now tell me before I strike you."

Katelyn's face hardened, her mouth grew taunt with spite. "I hate you. You're nothing but an ignorant savage. You've ruined my life!" She raised a hand to hit him in the face, but Tipaakke's hand flew up to stop her.

"I do not believe in hitting women. I have never struck anyone in anger, but you tempt me." He spoke in the low, calm voice that infuriated her. "Don't you ever raise your hand to me again, do you understand?"

He tightened his grip on her hand until she threatened to cry out.

"Let go of me," Katelyn warned. "I can't stand your touch."

"You want that Henry Coward to touch you? I've ruined your life you say. That man left you in the hands of the enemy. You would like that man who is no man to touch you?"

"Liar!" Katelyn spat.

"You want that murderer to run his hands over your breasts?"

"What do you mean? Henry is no murderer. What are you talking about?" Tears threatened to spill from her dark eyes.

"He killed the servant boy the day he left you. He kicked him from the wagon to save his own skin. The boy wanted to go back for you."

"Liar! Liar!" she screamed, sinking to the floor.

Tipaakke released her arm, letting her slump to the floor. Turning, he began to pace the floor. What was wrong with him? Why had he gotten so angry with her? Why had he let her goad him to the point of making threats? This was so unlike him. Only this women could make him so irrational. He listened to her sob, crouched on the floor near the bed. He had never heard her weep like this. Was the thought of caring his child so unbearable? He thought she loved him. He thought she was going to surprise him with the news of the child. Among his own people, the coming of a child meant great rejoicing. The Delawares had very small families so each child was a precious gift from the Heavenly Father. "Katelyn," Tipaakke called quietly. "Katelyn."

"I feel so stupid! You make me feel so stupid!" She sniffed, trying to hold back the tears. She was so embarrassed. Why did she act like this with him? Why

191

did he make her so crazy?

"I do not mean to make you feel that way." He came to her hesitantly. "I do not think you're stupid."

"I never thought about it." She raised a hand and let it drop. "I never honestly thought about it." She wiped her running nose with her sleeve. "I guess I didn't want to think about it." She bowed her head. She couldn't look at him.

"Sometimes we push from our minds the things we fear most." *Why*, he asked himself, *why does she not want my child*? There was a dull ache in his throat. He had been so happy since he'd realized she carried his child. He missed his own son dearly and rejoiced at the thought of a new babe in his arms.

"I can't have a baby," Katelyn murmured into her hands. "I just can't."

"Why not? Women have babies everyday. Having a baby is good in our village. Our women do not suffer like your white women. We have herbs to kill the pain. It is a time of happiness in the wigwam when a babe comes into our world."

"It's a sin." She looked up at him. "I'm not married." She shook her head. "I'd be better dead."

Tipaakke got down on his knees. "Don't say what you do not wish. Manito may hear you and bring your wish true." He brushed damp hair off her forehead. "I can marry you if that's what you wish. My father will marry us and I will even take you to my friends up north. The Quakers can marry us in your way." He waited for an answer. Would she refuse him?

Her eyes widened. "You would do that?" She choked back another sob.

He nodded having a seat on the floor in front of her. "Give me your hands," he told her.

Cautiously, she held out her hands. Her anger had passed and now she felt afraid and alone. He was willing to marry her. That surprised and pleased her. But it hurt that he still didn't love her.

Holding her clammy hands in his, Tipaakke peered into her face. Her golden brown eyes were sad ones. If only he could wipe that sadness away. "We can marry and live in the village with my family. They will treat you well; you've earned that right by staying with me here. Now that my sight has been returned to me, I can care for you and our child. It would be a good life." He stroked her palms. "Your people, they would not accept you now."

Katelyn laughed a funny little laugh. "No, you're right, they wouldn't. I have no choice, do I?" A sad smile formed on her lips.

"Yes, you do have a choice. You do not have to marry me. It makes no difference to me," he lied.

"It's not that I don't want to marry you." Her dark eyes pleaded with his. "It's just that two married people should . . . if only you would . . ." her voice trailed into nothingness.

Tipaakke stared at her intently with confusion. What was the girl talking about now. "If I would what?" He got up, pulling her with him.

Katelyn shifted her weight from one foot to the other. "Never mind, it's not important." She shook her head, avoiding eye contact with him.

"It is important. What do you speak of?"

"I can't say it. It's not something you ask someone to say, Fox." She walked slowly to the door.

He followed on her heels. "What? You have to tell me. I'm no Shaman. I have no magical powers. I cannot read the mind of another." He reached out imploringly. "Tell me."

"No." She shook her head, pulling her beaver hat over her head and tucking her braids beneath. "It really doesn't matter." She slipped her rabbit cloak off the peg and swung it over her shoulders. "I will marry you and I will have your baby." There was no joy in her voice, only resignation. Up until this moment she had still thought there was hope. She had still prayed he would come to love her.

"You say that as if I sent you to your death." He followed her. "Where are you going? Don't run away from me, Katelyn."

"I need to go for a walk—alone, please." She looked back at him. "Don't you understand how difficult this is for me?" Without another word, she turned to the door.

Tipaakke listened to Katelyn close the door softly behind her. *I should have gone*, he thought. He picked up his bag of tools from the table and went to sit at the hearth where a small fire burned. Work always helped when he had thinking to do. He dumped the instruments out on the floor and picked up the half-completed axehead. With the chipping stone, he began the long and tedious process.

Now what do I do, he asked himself, chipping with even strokes. *She carries my child. I can't let her go. She's mine. It was meant to be.* He ran his fingers over the axehead, feeling the tiny nicks. *I don't want to force her to marry me, but maybe marriage is best. Maybe she will come to love me after the child is born. Where have I failed*, he asked himself. *I've given her gifts. I've been respectful of the white man's way of life. I love her; I'm good to her. I listen to her ranting and raving; I ignore her mistakes. I certainly please her on the sleeping mat.* He stared at the burning embers. Never would he understand the mind of the female creature.

Katelyn hurried along the path, her arms crossed and pressed tightly against her stomach. "I can't believe it," she muttered over and over again. "I can't believe

I'm going to have a baby." She continued along the path until she came to mud and then stepped off into the grass. This was the second time this week that it had snowed at night but melted during the day. The spring that she had thought was so far away was almost upon her. It was time to make a decision.

Her mind churned as she rounded the bend near the stream. *Fox is right, I can't go back to Henry. He would never take me if I wanted him to. So, I either have to go far away from here and start a new life with my child, or I can stay with Fox and accept what happiness I have.*

Staring at her reflection in the stream, Katelyn couldn't resist a smile. Who would ever recognize her now? She laughed at the woman who laughed back, dressed in furs, tanned by the winter sun. The Katelyn Locke she'd once known was gone. This was not the woman who left England. This woman spoke in halting Lenni Lenape, wrestled with her brave on his mat, and thought like a Lenni Lenape *esquawa*.

She turned from the stream and and continued along the deer path, noting fresh tracks. Just let the Lenni Lenape in you do the thinking, she told herself. That hysterical woman in the cabin was the old Katelyn. *Start thinking like a Delaware squaw and you'll know what's right*, an inner voice commanded.

"I will marry him," she whispered with an even nod. "I will marry him," she repeated a little louder. *I will marry him and have his child and I will not give up hope. Someday he might still come to love me. I must leave it in the hands of the creator.* She stepped off the path and into the forest, heading in the direction of the beaver dam. Suddenly, her feet felt lighter.

I will give Fox a son he can be proud of, she told herself, *or maybe a daughter.* She remembered that Won had said the Lenni Lenape treasured their girls as much as their boys. They were both gifts from heaven. Katelyn knew she would never have to cower like her mother when she had admitted to her husband that she'd given birth to a worthless girl child. Now lighthearted, Katelyn leaped over a rock and started to run, spotting the dam just ahead.

Chester Rummond released the reins on his mule and ducked beneath a leaning scrub pine. Grinning, he reached beneath his hide cloak and pulled out a hunk of tobacco. Taking a bite, he tucked it beneath the hide again. He chuckled as he worked up the spit in his mouth to get the full flavor of the fresh chew. "What do ya think we got here?" He turned to his two partners behind him.

Morgy tugged at his bottom lip speculatively. "Think we got us a fresh bit of Injun girl, that's what I think." He ran his fingers through his long greasy hair, smacking his lips soundly. "Real fresh."

The third partner, Kaiser, just stared longingly through the bushes. No one expected Kaiser to answer. He never said anything.

Chester leaned on his musket, flicking his tongue out to catch a long drool of tobacco spittle. "What's say we have a look-see, gen'leman." He tugged on the leather reins, giving his mule a vicious kick when she didn't move fast enough.

The trapper led the mule along the woodsline of the meadow, his partners close behind. Twice they stopped to watch the squaw who'd almost reached the running stream. Tying the jenny's reins to a fallen log, Chester left her behind, signaling the others to follow. Together, the three skirted the meadow until they reached the stream just beyond the beaver dam. Crouching low, Chester pointed to the Indian woman who'd perched herself on the steep bank of the stream. "What ya think she'd be doin' out here, brother?" He eyed Morgy thoughtfully.

"Don't really make much matter, do it?" Morgy grinned bearing blackened teeth. "We won't be needin' her long." He elbowed Kaiser kiddingly, sending the man into a fit of snickers.

"Hush!" Chester warned. "Ya know these Injun's, she'll be off like a willer wist, disappearin' inta the air."

"Can't see her face," Morgy chimmed in, leaning through the bushes. "Wish she'd turn around so's we could get a look-see."

"Fartin' beans, Morgy! What do you care? I seen you bed women uglier than horses's arse's! Don't be tellin' me you got any particulars."

Kaiser fell into another fit of snickers, his whole chest heaving up and down.

Chester leaned to knock him on the head. "I told you to keep your trap shut. Ya scare her off and ya'll not get a taste of a woman's thighs 'til early summer. Ya understandin' what I'm tellin' ya, Kaiser?"

Kaiser bobbed his head up and down, throwing up a hand to promise he'd be quiet. The wide smirk on his face told the men he was as anxious for a bit of sport as they were.

Chester scratched his hairy chin, watching the girl toss pebbles into the churning water. "Come to think of it, gen'leman, we might just tie her onto that old jenny-mule and carry her with us a few days. That way, we'd get us our fill." He hawked up a good gob of spit and let it fly. Rubbing his sweaty palms together, he slipped off his cloak and let it slip to the ground. Giving the other two directions, he waited until they slipped offf, then dropped down on all fours, crawling towards the squaw. *Damnation!* he thought. *What a man don't have to go through these days to cool his boiling blood!*

Tipaakke ran his fingers over the axehead and sent it

197

hurling through the air. He'd worked two weeks on it and now he'd just taken a big chip out of it. It was worthless to him. He'd have to start all over again with a fresh stone. He got to his feet and began to pace the floor.

What was wrong with Katelyn? What was wrong with him? Why couldn't she love him? She just wasn't being sensible about this. He pounded his fist in the palm of his hand. He wanted her, and he would have her. She'd given him a joy in his life he hadn't known since his wife and son had died. Tipaakke walked to the far wall and jerked his fox cloak off the peg. It was time this was settled; he couldn't stand the unrest. He loved her and she was going to marry him and have his child. Maybe in time she would come to love him. He would just have to take that chance.

Slamming the cabin door, Tipaakke started down the path. Shading his eyes, he stared up at the breathtakingly blue sky. Never again would he take for granted those pale blues and fluffy whites. He smiled to himself. The Creator had been very good to him. He had returned his sight. Now Tipaakke knew it was time he took control of his own life; it was time he made amends with the woman he loved.

Tipaakke quickened his pace, keeping his moccasinned feet on the hardened dirt path. Running faster, he threw back his head, letting the wind whip through his hair. He took a deep breath, inhaling the fresh near-spring air. It had been a long time since he'd felt like running.

Katelyn rested her chin on her knees, tossing small, round pebbles into the water below. Now that she'd made her decision, she felt so much better. She would make the best of the life she'd been handed and she'd try to make Tipaakke happy. She ran her palm over her slightly rounded stomach; in a few moons, she would

198

have two people to call her own. She hoped Hawk returned soon. She wanted to get back to the village with them and be married as soon as possible. She wanted to get on with the new life she'd just chosen.

Abruptly, Katelyn froze, the hair on the back of her neck bristling. She took a deep, unsteady breath. Someone was behind her and it wasn't Fox. She knew his movements, his earthy scent by heart. No, this was an intruder. Her blood turned to ice as it raced to pump her heart faster. Steadying herself on the steep bank, she slid her hand down her leg until it touched the hilt of her stone knife. She whispered a silent prayer as her fingers closed over the lethal weapon.

Concentrating, Katelyn made her assessment of the situation. A man . . . a man crawling. She caught his scent in the breeze. It was a white man, an unbathed white man who reeked of horseflesh, rotting food, and body odor. Sliding the knife from its leather sheath, she made a decision. Surprise was an element she needed on her side.

Letting out a high-pitched shriek, Katelyn leaped into the air, spinning to face the man before her feet touched the muddy bank. In horror, she caught sight of a second and third man coming at her as well.

Chester gave a startled yelp and sprang to his feet. His hand slid to the flintlock on his belt and he eased it out. He signaled to the others to stay back. "Hey there, Missy. No need to fear me." He grinned, baring tobacco-stained teeth. "I'm yur friend. I ain't gonna hurt ya." He slid a foot forward.

Katelyn crouched in the attack position just as Tipaakke had taught her. Her mind raced half in English, half in Algonquian as her primal instincts kicked in full force. Narrowing her eyes, Katelyn shifted her weight, checking to be sure she was balanced. Her life lay before her and she wanted it. She

199

wanted her child. She wanted a life with Tipaakke.

"Come on, Missy." Chester reached out to beckon her with one dry, cracked hand. "You understand English?"

She growled deep in her throat.

"Feisty wench, ain't ya?" He straightened up. "Me and the boys, we like 'em feisty." She was half his size. The way he figured it, he could overpower her himself, and that way he'd get the first bite. Spitting a long stream of brown juice, he took another step closer. "Tell ya what squaw, you throw down that there knife and come see Uncle Chester, and I'll give you something pretty. You like bangles, don't ya?"

Katelyn's mind was in a turmoil. Even if she managed to kill the big one, how would she defend herself against the others? *Take one at a time, then worry about the next,* the Algonquian in her instructed.

Chester slid his flintlock into his belt and untied a filthy pouch. "See the pretties, girlie?" He pulled a necklace of shiny stones from the rotting pouch. "Wanna touch 'em?" He extended his hand, smiling.

Katelyn struggled to breath. The stench from the man was almost unbearable. If he took another step, she'd vomit in sheer disgust. But slowly, she lowered her knife, smiling back at him. She could see the other men hedging out of the corner of her eye. *Just play the stupid Indian,* she told herself. *Give them what they expect. Then give them the unexpected!*

"That's a good, girlie. Come see Uncle Chester." He threw a grin over his shoulder at his partners. "I'm gonna show you something else real nice, too." He patted the bulge between his legs. "It's something yer gonna like real well. All the ladies do." He drew the necklace back a bit. "Come on . . . that's right. Just a little further, squaw."

Katelyn took another step forward. *He still doesn't*

200

realize I'm white, she thought. *No matter. It would make no difference to them at this point.* She took another step, reaching for the necklace, keeping the smile pasted on her face.

The trapper reached out his other hand. He could feel his breeches straining in anticipation. *Boy, I'm gonna have her and have her good*, he thought as he caught scent of her freshly bathed skin. *Might even have a second go-round after the others have finished.* In an instant, his hand jerked out to catch her around the waist, but Katelyn was ready.

Screeching at the top of her lungs, she lunged forward with the knife, catching him in the cheek, and laying him open.

"Little bitch," Chester snarled, knocking her to the ground with a balled fist. "Ya want it rough, do you?" He ran his palm across his cheek, smearing blood. "Well, me and the boys, we're gonna give it to ya rough."

Katelyn scrambled to get up from the ground, but the trapper was too fast. In an instant he was on her, pounding her wrist. "Let go of the knife," he warned, his reeking breath hot on her cheek. From behind, she could hear the voices of others, cheering their friend on.

Katelyn gritted her teeth against the mind-numbing pain. *In another moment, he'll break my arm,* she thought. *He's too big to fight like this, I'll have to outsmart him. Then I'll deal with the others.*

Suddenly, the struggling squaw beneath Chester went limp. "That's it, girlie," he crooned, yanking the knife from her fingers and tossing it into the grass. "We're glad yer gonna see it our way." He sat up to get a better look at his captive, Kaiser and Morgy gathering around anxiously. "Just right for the pickin'," he muttered, running a finger along her cheek bone.

"Purty thing, ain't she?" Morgy peered over Chester's shoulder. "Got spirit, too, ain't she?" He elbowed Kaiser. "That's the way I like 'em." He tapped Chester on the shoulder. "Would ya be willin' to sell your first rights to her, old partner? Damn! If I'd known she was this fetchin', I'd have wrestled her down myself!"

Chester shook his head. "No, indeed. I caught her. I'm gonna have her first." He leaned to touch her lips with his fingers and then snapped his body around. "Look, if'in you two can't stand back and give me a little room, I'll take 'er elsewheres and then you'll miss the show." He watched as the two men backed up reluctantly. "That's better," he murmured with a nod of his chin.

The pressure of the huge man's weight on Katelyn's body was stiffling, but she forced herself to remain still, listening to the men's banter. She didn't know how she was going to get out of this, but she'd not be raped. She'd kill herself first with her own blade. When the stinking giant touched her again, her eyes flew open and she stared coldly at him. He was disgusting with his long hair and beard, tangled and matted until you couldn't tell which was which.

"Hey, wait a minute." Chester's eyes narrowed distrustfully. "You ain't no Injun!" He yanked the beaverskin hat from her head and watched with amazement as the long fiery braids tumbled to the ground. "A white girl! Well, I'll be damned and sent straight to hell! We caught us a white girl." He leaned to one side to let his partners get a look. "This sure is our lucky day, ain't it?" He chuckled to himself. "Tell me something. What ya doin' out here by yerself all dressed up like a savage, girlie? Yer brains addled?" He ran a filthy exploring hand beneath her cloak.

Katelyn swallowed hard as he fumbled with her breast. She could hear the others calling words of encouragement as they jeered the giant on. "Dog," she accused evenly in Algonquian. "Stinking, man-eating dog . . ." She forced herself to stare at the shaggy face. "I'm not one of you," she added softly in English. "Never."

Chester chuckled deep in his throat, pressing his hot, wet lips to her bare neck. "Got me a crazy white girl who thinks she's a squaw." He clamped his teeth down hard on her tender flesh.

Katelyn jerked in pain, straining to release her arm from where he held it pinned to her side. If she could just get free with one hand, she could hit the oaf with something.

The man yanked open her rabbit-skin cloak and ran his hand roughly over her breasts. "Nice . . ." he told her, reaching down to tug at her doeskin dress. "Nice tits, now show Uncle Chester what else ya got. Ya show me yers and I'll show ya mine." He shot a grin at Kaiser over his shoulder. "You want to see too, Kaiser?"

The moment he turned his head, Katelyn swung her freed hand, punching him square in the nose.

"Ow! Damnation, girlie!" He cuffed her in the side of the head, sending her mind reeling. "Now ya best be behavin' yerself and stop showin' off for my friends." He pinned her arms again, wiping his bloody nose on his shoulder. "That girl can really heave a punch," he called over his shoulder.

Katelyn squeezed her eyes shut as the man ripped at her dress above the waist. *Please don't let this be happening,* she thought. *Why didn't I stay with Fox where I was safe? He's warned me time and time again of the dangers in the woods.* She lay limp beneath her would-be-rapist, conserving her strength. If she was going to get away from these men, she couldn't waste an ounce of energy. *There has to be a way out of this,* her inner voice screamed. Where was Fox? Maybe he would come for her! No, he

203

was a man who respected other's privacy. She had asked him to leave her alone, he'd not be coming this way. She couldn't believe her fate! After being captured by Indians, she was going to be raped and killed by white men!

Taking her lack of movement as a sign of surrender, Chester sat up to loosen his breeches. He couldn't wait another minute! "Now yer gettin' the idea. Ya be nice to Uncle Chester and his friends and maybe he won't kill ya." He moved his hips, trying to get his breeches down. "You be real nice, and we'll take ya with us a few days." His laughter mingled with the other's. "Ya can be the entertainment!"

Katelyn's eyes flew open as she heard his breeches slide down. "Nooo," she screamed, wretching her hand free. Before Chester could catch her, she pulled his pistol from his belt and knocked him in the forehead with it.

Chester rolled backwards, dazed, grabbing his head. "Catch the bitch," he shouted, rolling onto his side.

At the sound of Katelyn's voice, Tipaakke froze. She was in trouble. Where was she? Which way had the sound of her voice come from? The beaver dam! That had to be where she was. She always went there to think. Tipaakke flew down the path, his moccasins barely touching the hardened dirt. *Why did I let her go alone? Why did I let my anger have the best of me? Please, Heavely Father, protect her.* Keep her safe and I will care for her the rest of her life, he vowed.

Backing up slowly, Katelyn aimed the flintlock at the two trappers. Her attacker still lay on the ground. Her fingers ached to pull the trigger. If she killed just one, it would be easier to die. When her attacker moved, she dropped her aim to his form on the ground.

Chester looked up slowly from where he lay, his breeches still caught around his knees. "Let me take care of this," he commanded. "She's mine." Then he turned back to Katelyn. "Go ahead, girlie. Shoot," he challenged. "But ya better kill me on the first try, cause ya don't get a second. And then I'm going to kill ya."

She stared at the man at her feet. He seemed to want her the most. If she killed him, she might have a chance at escape. The others didn't seem willing to risk their life for her. They were just going along for the sport of it. Besides, even if they did come after her, she could lose them in the forest. They didn't seem bright enough to track her too far. *So, why can't I pull the trigger,* she thought.

Chester staggered to his feet, blood streaming from his forehead. He heaved up his breeches with both hands, ignoring his partners' snickers.

"Need some help there, Chester?" Morgy questioned with amusement. "Just let us know when she wears you out."

"Shut up, Morgy," Chester commanded, "before yer dead meat." He stared straight at Katelyn again. "Go ahead. Ya ain't no Injun . . . ya might think ya are, but ya ain't. An Injun would've blowed my head off."

A wide grin crossed Katelyn's face as she watched the trapper's smugness disappear.

"No," he shook his head, taking a step back as he watched the gun barrel be lowered. "That ain't even funny."

Unhurried, she lowered the flintlock until it was aimed at the man's groin. Chester dropped his hands to protect himself and the other men stepped back, horrified. With a smile, she squeezed the trigger.

When the pistol only clicked in response, Katelyn's blood turned to shards of ice.

"Damnation! Saints in hell!" Chester shouted jovially, leaping in the air. "Told you this was my lucky day, boys." He knocked the pistol from Katelyn's hands, tackling her as she turned to run. "Powder got wet again," he told her, "now where was I?" He clamped his damp, bloody mouth on hers, squeezing her buttocks viciously with one hand.

When Tipaakke caught the sound of a man's voice, he slowed to a walk, stepping into the edge of the woodsline. He heard Katelyn whimper and his breath caught in his throat. *She's alive!* he thought as he followed the woodsline until he spotted the two men standing near the stream. *She's still alive!* Moving behind the trees, he saw her pinned beneath the trapper. "Whippoorwill . . . whippoorwill," he sounded.

Katelyn's heart leaped beneath her breast. He was here! He'd come for her! Her brave wasn't going to let her die! She opened her eyes, ignoring the trapper who ran his slimey lips over her face, fumbling with her breasts as he held her flattened to the ground. Where was he? Where was Tipaakke? Protect him, she prayed to his God.

Chester reached down to run his hand under Katelyn's doeskin dress. She couldn't stand this vile man touching her while the others watched another moment! "Tipaakke!" She shouted. "Here I am! Help me," she sobbed.

"What the hell?" Chester turned to look in the direction the girl was staring. Jerking her up by one braid, he sat up. Watching Tipaakke move through the trees, he swore under his breath. "So ya got yerself an Injun brave, do ya?" He snapped her head violently. "That's why yer all dressed up in skins and jabberin' like a stinkin' savage."

Katelyn curled her upper lip. "You pig, he is twice the man you will ever be."

Chester ignored her insult, getting to his feet and dragging her with him. Hoisting up his breeches, he nodded to Morgy. "Where's your gun?"

Morgy shifted his weight nervously, pointing into the trees. "In there on jenny," he nodded, "but she's with the Injun." He wiped his chin. "Let's just go, whilst we still can. Leave the girl. Me and Kaiser, we don't like fightin' them Indians."

Chester growled under his breath, keeping a tight hold on Katelyn. "Ya two afraid of one lousy Injun?" He eyed Kaiser.

"No, we ain't afraid, but we ain't crazy either. We got one pistol between the three of us and the girl to tangle with." He kept looking into the woods, watching the savage move slowly.

"You'd better run," Katelyn dared, "because my Fox will rip out your gizzards and hang them from the trees," she lied. She knew Tipaakke was an honorable man; he didn't desecrate bodies, not even those of his enemies. But the trappers didn't know that. She watched with great pleasure as the men's eyes lit up with terror.

"Shut up!" Chester ordered, shaking her until her teeth rattled. "Don't just stand there, Kaiser, reload the pistol." He pushed it with a foot in his direction. "What's that savage doin'?" he wondered aloud as Tipaakke stepped into the meadow.

Katelyn could see the fierce sparkle in her man's eyes from where she stood. These men would not see the dawn again, she surmised.

"Chester, me and Kaiser, we don't have no powder and balls, left them on the jenny." He started to edge his way toward the stream, Kaiser following. "We ain't fightin' no mean savage with no gun."

Realizing he'd get no help from his partners, Chester turned to face the Indian coming the short distance

207

through the meadow. He released Katelyn, shoving her to the ground.

Taking his steel-honed knife in hand, Tipaakke parted his lips, baring his teeth. A low, rumbling growl escaped from his throat sending a shiver of primeval terror through Chester's body.

The grin fell from the trapper's face as he fumbled for his knife. "Might need a little help here," he hollered over his shoulder. "He's only got a knife. It's three to one. We can beat him together. Damn! Damn, where's my knife?" he muttered to himself shakily as the Indian brave circled him like a predator. Chester was suddenly more frightened than he'd ever been in his life. He'd never seen such a wild-looking Indian. He was dressed much like they all were, but something about those black, piercing eyes made him shudder with fear.

Katelyn got to her feet, but stood back out of Tipaakke's way, keeping an eye on the cowardly partners. If they made a move, she figured she could keep them distracted until Tipaakke could deal with them.

Around and around Tipaakke circled, moving closer to Katelyn's attacker. His patience, his cold glaring eyes, and his determination would be enough to overpower the white man. They always were.

Rivulets of sweat ran down the side of Chester's face as he turned around and around, watching the brave move closer. The sound of the Indian growling like some wild animal was beginning to wear on him. He wished he would make his move, he couldn't take much more of this. Staring at the red man's bared white teeth, Chester suddenly lunged forward, unable to keep still another moment.

Tipaakke dodged the trapper's knife with an easy step to the left. It felt good to fight again. When Chester lunged again, Tipaakke threw himself forward, knocking Chester off his feet.

Morgy moved forward to pull the Indian off his friend's back, but Katelyn ran at him from the side, kicking him low in the groin. Morgy fell to the ground moaning. Kaiser started to make his way slowly to Morgy.

Wrestling, arm locked in arm, Tipaakke and Chester rolled toward the creek bank. *What will I do if the trapper kills him*, Katelyn thought, balancing her attention between them and the other two trappers. *I can't live without him. He's my world.*

When Morgy got to his feet and started after Chester and Tipaakke, Katelyn was ready for him. Picking up a rock from the bank, she heaved it in his direction, knocking him squarely in the head. Just as Morgy went down, Tipaakke and Chester went rolling over the bank.

Peering over the side of the bank, Katelyn bit her lip hard to keep from crying out. She couldn't break Tipaakke's concentration, not for a moment. Chester's knife fell to the ground and then only Fox held his. She watched as the men wrestled, one with brute strength, the other with flexibility and cunning.

Then, it was over. The trapper grabbed a hunk of sleek black hair, trying to wrench the knife free from the red man's hands and Tipaakke lunged forward, burying the knife to the hilt in the man's chest.

Chester's eyes grew round with surprise as he stared down as the knife sunk in his chest. He watched glassy-eyed as the Indian pulled the knife from his flesh and crimson blood bubbled from the wound. Taking one deep rasping breath, the trapper shuddered and fell still, his sightless eyes staring heavenward.

Tipaakke slid off the dead man and leaned to wipe the bloody knife on his stained coat before he got to his feet. Leaping up onto the bank, he ran past Katelyn to where Kaiser was pulling his friend Morgy across the grass.

Kaiser shook with terror, but didn't release his friend's arms. He waited to see the savage raise the knife to him.

Tipaakke stood glaring coldly, the knife in his hand at his side. But he made no attempt to move closer as he watched the one white man drag off the other. Those two had done no real harm. He saw no reason to take their lives.

Katelyn watched with pride as Fox allowed the man to make his retreat to his mule, pulling the partner along. What other man could have been so gallant? She watched as the light breeze blew his long blue-black hair off his shoulders, emphasizing his chiseled face. Her eyes ran over his high bronze cheek bones, the familiar curve of his lips. Mesmerized by his haunting black eyes, she trembled. She'd almost lost him. She'd almost lost the only person she'd ever loved. They'd almost lost each other.

Before Katelyn could think, she was running into Tipaakke's arms, tears threatening to spill over. "Forgive me," she begged, feverishly pressing kisses to his face. "I have no life without you Tipaakke Oopus. I will marry you. I'll marry you and have your child, and I'll make you love me."

Tipaakke wrapped his arms around her tightly, dropping his head onto her shoulder. "Make me love you?" he murmured in her ear. "What do you mean. I've always loved you. I've loved you since the day I found you picking buttercups."

Katelyn pushed his head off her shoulder and peered into his face. "You love me?" she asked, stunned by his words. "But you never said you loved me." She shook her head, her eyes wide with confusion. "Why didn't you ever tell me that before? You could have saved me a lot of heartache!"

Tipaakke tipped back his head to laugh. "Are you telling me you love me?"

"Of course I love you. How could I not? You rescued me from a life of unhappiness." She stroked his handsome cheek, wiping away a smudge of creek mud.

"But I captured you. I've held you against your will. And now you carry my child and will never be the lady of one of your Tidewater plantations," he teased.

"No. I won't." Katelyn lowered her voice. "But I will be the lady of a very brave and handsome man's wigwam."

Tipaakke pressed a soft kiss to her lips. "I can't believe we've been so foolish, Katie-girl. Why didn't you tell me that you loved me?"

"I wasn't in a position to tell you such a thing. I was your prisoner. Not many moons ago, you were threatening to kill me, Fox." Her brow furrowed with serious thought. "Why didn't *you* tell me that you loved me?"

Tipaakke thought for a moment, reaching out to brush a damp, stray tendril from her face. "I was afraid to tell you. I was afraid you didn't love me. I kept telling myself that you weren't ready to hear those words, but the truth, my dove, is that I was afraid."

Katelyn couldn't believe what he was saying. After all she'd gone through, he'd loved her all along. "And now I will have your child," she whispered.

He took her hand, kissing one finger and then the next. "Yes, you will have my child, and we will grow old together, Katelyn Locke."

Katelyn kissed him softly on the lips and then looked over his shoulder. "Do you think they're gone?"

"The men and their mule? They are far gone from here by now." He chuckled to himself. "They will probably run for days."

"I was afraid you weren't going to come." She looped her arm and his and together they went back to the

211

creek bank. "I was afraid they would carry me off and I'd never see you again. They said they were going to kill me." She was amazed at how calmly she spoke.

"It would not have happened. Manito meant us to have a life together. It was not your time to go. It was his." He pointed at the trapper's dead body.

"Can you do something with the body?" She wrinkled his nose. "I'll not have him stinking up the creek."

Tipaakke laughed. "You want me to drag that man somewhere? He'll break the Fox's back." But already he was down the bank, tugging on the man's arms.

When Tipaakke returned from the woods where he'd dragged the trapper's body, he was pleasantly surprised to find Katelyn standing on the bank, stripping off her clothes.

"What are you doing?" he asked with a twinkle of amusement in his eye. With this woman, he would never grow bored.

"Taking a bath." She shivered involuntarily as the first wave of cold air hit her. "That stinking man ran his hands all over me. I feel fithly." She made no attempt to suppress the venomous anger in her voice. She looked straight at Tipaakke as she dropped her dress to the ground. "He was disgusting. I would have rather died at my own hand than let him do more. I would have killed him if I could have."

Tipaakke nodded, only half hearing what she said. His mouth was dry, his palms damp. No matter how many times she stood naked before him, she still made his heart thump painfully at the sight of her. "Isn't it too cold for you." He pointed at her full, rounded breasts, her nipples puckered from the cool air.

Her eyes snapped and crackled with life. "And who's always telling me great tales of how in the winter they break ice to bathe?" She dropped a hand on her hip seductively. "If I'm to be one of the Lenni Lenape, I'll

212

have to grow used to it, won't I?" With that, she turned to walk gracefully down the bank. "But you can come with me and keep me warm . . ."

Tipaakke grinned, following her down the bank. She was a vixen, this one. Pulling his shirt over his head, he dropped his loin cloth. It was as if his body had a mind of its own. He had to follow her, he had to touch her pale skin. He was lost in her spell.

Katelyn laughed gaily, reaching to the bottom of the stream to retrieve handfuls of sand. Watching Tipaakke's every move, she began to rub the sand over her body, scrubbing away the foul man's touch.

Mesmerized, Tipaakke ignored the shock of the icy water. The closer he grew to her, the less he felt it. Now he felt only the heat of his rising passion. Taking a hand of the clean sand, he began to rub it over her. First a slim arm, then her back, then her softly rounded bottom.

Katelyn lowered her eyelids as the pleasure of his touch washed over her. She had always enjoyed the feel of his skin touching hers, but now it was different. Now she knew that he loved her. Now she knew it was all right to love him. Tipping back her head, she moaned softly. He no longer rubbed sand on her body, now it was only his strong hand caressing her supple flesh.

"You take a man's senses from him," Fox murmured as he felt her touch burning his skin. Lightly she ran her hands over his back, over his sinewy shoulders.

"Tell me you love me," she whispered hotly, nipping at his neck and chest.

"I love you," he responded, taking her mouth in his.

Parting her lips, she welcomed his sweet searching tongue. The deeper he probed, teasing, taunting the warm lining of her mouth, the warmer her skin felt beneath his roaming hands. Pulling away breathlessly, she rested her head on his chest, pressing his buttocks until their two bodies molded as one. "Tell me again, and then again. I could never tire of those words." She stared up at him through feathery lashes.

"I love you, I love you," he repeated over and over again as he reached to swing her in his arms.

Resting her head on his shoulders, she let him carry her to the bank where he lay her in the soft new blades of grass. "Cold?" he asked, stroking her boldly.

She shook her head. "Hot!" She laughed, her voice bubbling with joy, hoarse with passion. "Touch me, Fox, touch me like you do."

Fox lowered his body onto hers, taking a damp, taut nipple in his mouth as he lowered his hand to the triangle of bright curls he knew so well. "You are like honey," he crooned, stroking in a circular motion. "So sweet."

Katelyn moved her hips to the rhythm of his hand, running her hands over his back, pressing his body to hers. "You know me so well," she whispered when she could take the torturous pleasure no longer. "Now let me show you how well I know you."

Chuckling deep in his throat, Tipaakke moved off her, molding his body to her side. Giggling, Katelyn pushed him onto his back. Their legs tangled as she marveled at the sensitivity of his hardening male nipples. Flicking at his broad chest and flat stomach with her tongue, she slid her leg seductively between his, rubbing, twisting, turning until she could feel the evidence of his love, pressed against her damp flesh. Smiling, she reached down to stroke his swollen manhood, moaning with him.

"Love me," Katelyn begged when she could no longer stand the way his hard, lean body tempted her. Guiding his body onto hers, she strained, writhing until she felt his welcomed thrusts.

At first both were eased by the ancient rhythm of

give and take, but then the embers brightened. The clear sky above spun faster. Their hearts beat harder. "Please," Katelyn urged, unaware of the sounds that escaped her lips. Thrust for thrust she rose to meet Tipaakke, drowning in sensation. *He loves me!* she thought shakily as she climbed higher and higher. *He loves me!*

And then in a heartbeat it was over. Katelyn arched her back, straining to control the last shuddering waves of pleasure and then she sighed, loosening her hold around Tipaakke's shoulders. She waited until his breath came easier, pressing kisses to his damp forehead, running her hands over his back. Then he looked up, his dark eyes searching hers. "Tell me," he murmured, his words breathy.

"I love you." She tightened her arms around him, rejoicing in his love.

Chapter Ten

"Tipaakke! Wait," Katelyn panted, gasping for breath. "You're going too fast!" She slowed to a walk. "I can't run any further. Will you *stop* and wait for me?"

"Come on, lazy squaw. You're weak!" Fox slowed down, turning to run backwards so he could face her.

Katelyn laughed at his antics, starting to run again. "You're going to fall and break your neck."

"Not Tipaakke Oopus, brave Lenni Lenape warrior!" He beat his broad chest with his fist. "Now come. You'll never make a hunter at that turtle pace."

Katelyn threw back her head, letting the wind whip through her long, unbound tresses. "I don't want to be a hunter. You be the hunter. I want to sit in your wigwam, make babies with you, and grow fat on fried corn cakes."

"I thought you white women wanted the world?"

She shook her head, panting. "I have seen the world. You may have it, thank you."

Tipaakke laughed, shaking his head. "With my people, you can do what . . ."

"Fox! Watch out for the . . ." Katelyn's hand flew to

her mouth as she watched him trip over the branch and go sailing into the grass. Unable to contain herself, she ran laughing to help him. "I told you you would fall, you strutting buck!"

Tipaakke reached out with both hands for her. "Come here, vixen. Come to your man and take your punishment. You must be punished for your most serious crime."

"Punished? Me? Why?" She flopped down on top of him, still giggling. "I've committed no crime."

"You dare to laugh at this brave warrior?" he asked her indignantly. "That is a crime of nature."

"That's because this brave warrior," she poked his chest with one finger, "is a foolish warrior to run backwards!"

Tipaakke wrapped his arms around Katelyn, rolling over until he was on top of her. "You're getting round," he told her huskily, running a hand over her belly.

She nodded, looking up at him. "Does that please you?"

"Yes," he answered softly. "Does it please you?" He brushed his hand across her flushed cheek.

"Yes, it pleases me, now that I know you love me." She took his hand and planted a kiss on it. "So what's to be my punishment for loving a foolish brave?" She grinned.

Tipaakke propped himself up on one elbow to relieve her of his weight. In the days that had passed since they'd declared their love for each other, life had been wonderful. He tugged at his bottom lip, his face set in a serious scowl. "Let me see . . . I could take your fingernails one at a time . . ?"

"Fox!" She knocked him in the side of the head playfully.

"I could brand you, or maybe take a bit of scalp for my belt." He ran a hand over bright green grass, just beginning to sprout.

"Oh, that's horrible. Don't even say such a thing!" Her brown eyes grew wide with insistence.

"Our Iroquois friends think nothing of such things. Torture is a game to them." He shrugged his shoulders.

"But you are not an Iroquois." She bit down lightly on his finger. "Now tell me, what kind of punishment would a Lenni Lenape brave dole out to a naughty squaw?"

"*That* punishment," he shook a finger at her, "that punishment is very terrible, very painful." He smiled that smile she knew so well. "It is the worst kind of torture." He leaned to tug at her bottom lip with his teeth, placing hand on her round, full breast.

"I think I might like this torture," Katelyn purred, running her hands through his silky hair. "Do I have any choice?"

"No," he murmured in Algonquian, taking her mouth in his.

Her arms tightened around his neck as she surrendered to his fierce kiss. Her body strained against his, as a fire was kindled deep within her.

Tipaakke tugged at the leather thongs that laced the vee at her neck. "Untie these," he whispered, "or I will cut them." He dropped feather-light kisses across her face as she fumbled with the ties.

"Cut them," she replied in Algonquian, her voice rough with desire.

He unsheathed his knife and slit the thongs without hesitation. Katelyn sighed as she slipped his warm hand beneath the doeskin to caress her swelling breasts.

"You are so beautiful, my dove," he murmured, taking her mouth in his again.

She ran her hands over the flexing muscles of his back, her tongue meeting his in a sweet dance of yearning. "Your shirt," she whispered. "I want to touch you. I want to feel your skin against mine."

Tipaakke sat up to pull the linen shirt off his back.

"This too," Katelyn told him, giving his leather loin cloth a tug. "I want to feel all of you." She leaned back, stretching cat-like as she watched him strip to bare bronze skin in the brilliant afternoon sunlight.

"And you." He pulled her into a sitting position and slid the doeskin dress over her head. He ran his fingers over her silken flesh, marveling at her heated response. He ran his hands slowly over her, enchanted by her rounding curves. "My child has given you such a woman's body," he told her as his lips captured hers again. "I can't get enough of your sweetness. Tell me you'll never leave me, Katie-girl. You are my star in the heavens."

"I could never leave you, Tipaakke. Never. I'm yours. I'll love you forever." She ran her hands over his buttocks, kneading the taunt muscles. "Love me," she begged.

"I have always loved you. Our spirits were meant to be one," he answered softly, stroking the tender flesh of her inner thighs.

Again their mouths met fiercely and soon they were engulfed in the fires of love. Both reached out to fan the other's flame, neither wanting to unite until the other could stand it no longer.

Finally Tipaakke spoke out, his voice barely audible. "Please," he told her, his breath coming in short gasps. "I think you are torturing *me*. Come ride with me, Katie-girl."

Welcoming him, Katelyn rode the final bit of familiar path with him, moving faster and faster in a ritual of love until they both broke away and raced to become one again.

Tipaakke rested his head on Katelyn's shoulder for a

moment, waiting until her breath came evenly again. Finally, he lifted his head.

She opened her heavy lashes to stare at the face curtained by ebony locks. Unable to resist, she ran her fingers through the dark hair. "So this is the usual punishment for a Lenni Lenape squaw?" She grinned devilishly.

Tipaakke ran a finger over her love-bruised lips. He would never tire of her smile. "Yes. It's the usual punishment. In my village, when a wife is not behaving as she should, it is the husband who we blame. We say he isn't doing his duty on her mat and that's why she is acting that way."

"Brrr, it's cold down here." She shivered, the spring's damp ground beginning to seep through her. She pushed Tipaakke's arm, trying to sit up.

"You didn't notice the cold a few moments ago . .. " He raised one eyebrow.

"Oh, you! Now let me up! I want my dress." She pushed him onto his back and got to her feet.

Tipaakke rolled onto his back and stared straight into the brilliant sunlight. He listened to Katelyn dress. "The sun is getting warmer each day. My brother will return soon."

She pulled the doeskin over her head. "Will you be glad when he gets here?"

"I want to go back to my village so I can marry you. And I want my friends to know you." His eyes drifted shut as he bathed naked in the warm sunshine. "But I'll be sad to leave this place. I have been very happy here alone with you. I wish I didn't have to share you with anyone."

Katelyn smiled, pleased with his reply. "How soon do you think he'll be here?" She tugged at the cut thongs at her neck and tossed them to the ground. "I'm ready to leave now."

"I told you before. We wait for Mekollaan. I will not risk the life of our child, stumbling through the forest." He tucked his hands behind his head.

"Please Tipaakke, we could surprise them!" She sat down in the grass beside him and ran a palm over his smooth, bare chest. "You could find your way. You know you could."

"No. Mekollaan will be here in a few days. We wait. We have waited this long to marry. We can wait a little longer. I told my brother we would be here when he returned. So, we will be here." He rolled to his side, propping himself up with an elbow.

Katelyn stuck out her lip stubbornly. "I don't know why you think we need him. We've gotten along fine all winter without him." She dropped her hands in her lap. "I don't like him very much, Fox."

Tipaakke sat up. "You must listen to me. Mekollaan is my brother. Our souls are bound together just as yours and mine are. You must accept Hawk. He will soon be your brother, too. Then he will be your friend."

"Friend? Ha! He doesn't like me anymore than I like him." She picked at a blade of new grass.

"He acted as he did in the village because he cares for me. He didn't want me to be hurt by a white woman. He knew that I was in love with you."

"Why would a white woman hurt you anymore than an Indian woman? Why doesn't he like my people? What have I done to him?"

Tipaakke stood up and began to pick up his clothes off the ground. "Many years ago when we were still young bucks, my brother fell in love with a white woman, a Quaker. She said she loved him. But when Mekollaan asked for her to become his wife, she laughed. She said she would never marry a red man." He pulled his shirt over his head and began to tie the thongs on his loin cloth. "She married a white man

221

days later."

Katelyn got to her feet and went to stand in front of him. "Not all white women are like that. I love you. I wouldn't care if you were blue." She wrapped her arms around his neck, hugging him tight. "You have been better to me than any white man. I love you and I will not leave you. Not ever. My home is with you, Tipaakke Oopus, brave of the Lenni Lenape."

Tipaakke held Katelyn tight, breathing in the fresh sweet scent of tumbling tresses. "I love you, too, Katelyn Locke. Now, come. We must go back. We have much to do before the hawk flys near."

"Race you!" Katelyn dared, releasing him and starting off down the path.

Tipaakke laughed, running to catch up, his strong voice echoing in the trees.

Katelyn stared at the wall lined with pelts as she placed her cooking utensils in a leather bag, one at a time. "You've done well, haven't you, Tipaakke?"

He shrugged his shoulders and continued to remove the beaver hides from the west wall. "Better than some winters. Not as good as others."

"Where will you trade them?" She went to the shelf on the wall and ran her palm across the board to be sure she hadn't left anything behind.

"There is a man my brother and I trade with. He's a good man. We'll give the pelts to him and tell him what we want . . . material, tobacco, sugar . . ." He turned to grin at her. "Maybe English tea."

Katelyn returned the smile unable to resist. He knew she would give anything for more tea. "I think you've done better than you tell me, Fox. Just how much will this buy?"

Tipaakke turned back to his work. "A lot of tea,

many pipes of tobacco. I don't know. Maybe enough so that I can sell to my people when they need something. Those who sell to us are not always as honest as my friend. I will wait and see what the hides bring in Annapolis."

Katelyn spun around. "You'll be going there?"

"We go once a year to do our trading. I won't be gone long." He ran his fingers over the pile of hides, counting before he tied them into a bundle.

"But someone might recognize you." Her face grew severe with concern. "One of Henry's men."

He laughed, shaking his head. "No one would recognize me. White people think we all look alike."

Katelyn rested her hands on the table, leaning against it. "After all that's happened to us, haven't you had enough of them?"

"Them?" He went down on one knee to tie the bundle of hides with a leather thong. "*You* are one of *them*, Katie-girl. You, my reason for living."

She shook her head. "Not any more. If I had my way I'd never lay eyes on another white man as long as I lived. Those trappers were proof of what they're like."

Tipaakke picked up the bundle and dropped it on the bed with two others. "There are good and bad people of all races. You will meet bad Lenni Lenape. I have met one or two good Iroquois. Katelyn, you may speak the language, wear the clothes, but there will always be a small part of you that will be white."

"I wish I weren't. I wish I'd been born Lenni Lenape, grown up in your village, and met you a long time ago." She pushed her bag of tools aside and started to sort the packets of herbs.

"You have not seen the bad things about being an Indian yet. You haven't seen how measles can kill half of a village. You haven't seen a village burned to the ground." He went to stand beside her. "You know, if you had been born one of us, we might never have loved each other."

"But you said it was in the stars, our lives were preplanned." She dropped a packet onto the table and turned to face him.

"Maybe. Maybe not. We will never know. Maybe this is the Creator's way of blending our peoples. We must learn to live among each other. What better way then to become the other?" He dropped a hand on her shoulder and fingered a heavy braid. "Our child will be of both of us. Of two worlds."

"Maybe he will have a better life than either of us," she answered thoughtfully. "Maybe our child will not experience the pain we've experienced."

Tipaakke wrapped his arm around her waist. "Now, mother of my child, go get some water. It's time we both ate."

She looked at him. "Why don't you go get the water . . ." she poked him playfully, ". . . and while you're at it, take the fishing line down and see if you can catch something. Fried fish would be nice. I don't think I could eat another piece of rabbit if I tried."

He laughed. "I'll get the water and try with the line. But I promise nothing. Fishing is woman's work. You always do better than I do." Planting a kiss on her head, he retrieved the water bag and line and left the cabin.

After he'd gone, Katelyn went to search for the last of the sugar among the piles of bags and bundles on the table. Mixing flour, sugar and water, she searched for a brown spice. The flat sweet bread would be a real treat after months of doling out supplies so carefully. Placing a metal rack over stoked coals, she put the metal pan of bread on the rack and went to open the door. It was getting too warm for a fire during the day.

Filling the water bag, Tipaakke swung it over his

head and under one arm and went to perch himself on his favorite rock. Plucking a piece of grass, he wrapped it around a sharpened metal hook and dropped it into the water. Resting his arms on his knees, he jiggled the line, knowing it would look just like a grasshopper caught in the stream. Tilting his head back, he absorbed the sunshine's sweet rays. Visions of Katelyn and his child wafted through his mind as he leaned back to relax.

Hypnotized by the hot sun and thoughts of his life with the fiery-haired white girl, it was several seconds before Tipaakke realized the woods were becoming strangely silent. The birds ceased to call one by one, the squirrels stopped their busy chattering . . . even the insects quieted.

Pulling his line in, Tipaakke dropped on all fours behind the rock and listened. At first he heard only silence and an occasional frenzied cry of a grackel. Something had disturbed the delicate balance of the surrounding forest. The brave's heart beat faster and his palms grew damp as he listened, watching for a sign. Something was definitely awry. He could smell it in the air.

Then he heard movement . . . men's voices . . . laughing, calling out in play. They were moving upstream at an easy pace . . . straight for the cabin.

Tipaakke was off in an instant, his moccasinned feet beating the familiar path toward the cabin . . . and Katelyn. Reaching the open door, he slipped in and pulled it quietly behind him.

"Fox . . ." Katelyn turned from the fireplace where she was checking the cake. She stared at his stricken face. "What's wrong?" Crossing the floor, she tugged at his arm. "Where's the fish?"

He pulled the water bag from over his head and dropped it over hers. "Get your cloak and your knife."

His voice was razor edged.

For once, she moved without question. She had never heard fear in his voice like that before. Something terrible was happening; he was afraid for their lives.

Tipaakke strapped his spare hunting knife to his leg and pulled a sleeveless leather vest over his head. "Put out the fire," he commanded.

Katelyn ran to douse the fire with water from the bag around her neck.

"No. Don't waste water. Use a pelt." He spoke in halting English, his sentences laced with Lenni Lenape.

Smothering the fire, Katelyn ran to the table to stuff a bag with anything she could reach on the table . . . dried meal . . . herbs . . . it didn't matter. She knew they were leaving in a hurry. "Tell me, Fox." Her voice was as brittle as his.

"Men moving upstream. Iroquois war party . . . Mohawks." He pushed a handful of arrows into the neckline of the vest behind his head and turned to face her. "Come to me." He stretched out one hand.

Katelyn accepted his hand, squeezing it tight. Unable to speak, she waited for the instructions she knew were coming.

"You must wait until they are well gone. Nightfall, if you have to. Then you must leave. Follow the stream to the bottom of the mountain. Keep the morning sun here." He tapped her right arm. "Mekollaan will come upon you, but if he doesn't go on in that direction. Remember all I have taught you and you will find my village."

"But where are you going?" She clung to him, trying to remember each word he spoke, every movement he made. Somehow she knew she would never see him again. "Don't leave me, Fox. I'll die without you." She threw her arms around him.

He pushed her arms down firmly. "They will probably kill me. But maybe not. Maybe they will take me prisoner." He grabbed her arm and started to drag her towards the fireplace. "Tell Mekollaan what has happened when you reach the village. If I'm still alive, he will find me." He pressed his lips to hers. "I love you, Katie-girl," he murmured tenderly. "Now go."

"Go? Go where?" She stared at him in confusion.

"Up." He pointed at the fireplace. "You'll be safe. Don't stick your head out the top." He pushed her hard. "Now. Your life and our child's depends on it."

She remained absolutely still for a moment, transfixed by his haunting eyes and then she nodded slowly. He was right. She knew he was right. As she turned to the fireplace, something caught her eye. She was across the room in an instant pulling the wolf headdress from the wall. It had been his gift to her . . . proof of her bravery. She tugged the hollowed skull over her head and ran back to the fireplace. "Now I go." Taking one last look at Tipaakke's bronze face, she crouched low to stare up into the chimney. It would be a tight fit. She looked back. "Tipaakke . . ."

"Go," he told her, all tenderness gone from his voice. "If we don't meet again in this world, we will walk together in the dream world." His eyes drifted shut as he listened to her turn and kneel. He couldn't bear to watch her disappear from his life.

Getting down on her hands and knees, she crawled beyond the hearth and stood up inside the chimney. Coughing from the lingering smoke, she stretched and ran her fingers over the stones, feeling for a hand hold. When she found a shallow niche she stepped up, catching her toe on a tiny ledge, and disappeared up inside the chimney. "I love you," she called out.

Tipaakke forced himself to turn away. They both

couldn't hide. The Mohawks would know someone was living in the cabin. They would lay in wait for them. And he and Katelyn could never outrun them. The Mohawks were human wolves, only more deadly, more insiduous than a pack of wolves. Once the scent of human prey filled their nostrils, the Man-eaters would be unrelenting. A Mohawk brave could run from the great mountains of the Adirondacks to the Smokies in five days. Without Katelyn, Tipaakke could have taken on the soul of his totem, the fox, and disappeared in the depths of the forest he called home. But she would never have a chance. They would devour her like wolves.

Tipaakke slid his knife from its sheath, savoring the sound the cool metal made as it brushed against the hardened leather. His only regret at the thought of making his death walk today was that he would never live to feel Katelyn's skin beneath his touch, leathery with age. He would never sit before a fire with his child and sing the songs of his people's ancient past to him. But only through his death would Katelyn and his child have a chance to live. He smiled sadly. *What better way to die*, he asked himself, *than to die at the hands of one's fiercest enemy?*

As he gripped the hilt of the knife in his hand, Tipaakke prayed that he would have the courage to die quietly with dignity beneath the torturous hands of the Mohawks. He must remember that pain could be turned off, just as a man could stop water from flowing out of a clay pot. If he could remain silent, no matter what ingenious form of torture they thought of, they would soon grow tired of the game and kill him.

Tipaakke's eyes narrowed and his breathing became more shallow as he prepared to challenge the hungry wolves. His bronze skin began to glisten with tiny pinpricks of perspiration as he flexed his muscles.

Years from now, the women of his enemies would sing songs telling of the courage of the great Lenni Lenape warrior, Tipaakke Oopus.

A brief hint of a smile appeared on Tipaakke's face as he reached to lift the latch on the door. *Today is a good day to die*, he thought, as he stepped out into the brilliant sunshine to meet his enemies.

Katelyn caught her breath and stretched to reach another crevice in the stones. She felt as if the four mud-mortared walls were slowly closing in on her, squeezing the last bit of breath from her. But she had to climb higher. She couldn't take the chance of slipping. She must find a place to wedge herself in. The scent of the freshly baked bread seeped through her nostrils and she rested her head against the warm stones. *Why is this happening to us? I love him! Why can't I be with him to live or die?* The pain that tore at her heart made her oblivious to the pain of her bleeding fingers.

Katelyn took a deep breath and began to claw her way up again. Fox was right, she had to do this for their child. For him. Reaching behind her head, she tugged at the wolf headdress that threatened to slide from her head and fall to the hearth to give her away. Above her a patch of blue sky beckoned her. *At least I will see what happens to him.*

Spurred on by that thought, she inched her way up, higher and higher until her raw fingers caught the lip of the chimney. Turning slightly, she propped a leg on the opposite wall and stood straddled. Taking a moment to find her courage, she peered out.

Katelyn's heart leaped beneath her breast, pounding so hard she could hear it. Tipaakke stood only a few feet from the cabin. He had her bow slung over one shoulder and his hunting knife clutched securely in his left hand. The light breeze blew his hair off his shoulders revealing the silhouette of his bronze face.

229

Movement in the trees caught Katelyn's attention and she turned to catch a glimpse of bright green moving through the trees. She bit her lower lip until she tasted the salt of her own blood. *I must not cry out. No matter what I see.*

She watched from her tower on the roof as the band of blackhearted warriors descended on her brave. One by one, the Mohawks appeared, each more fiendish than the last. Katelyn had never known true terror until she laid eyes on the first red man that stepped out of the brush.

The flash of green became a waist coat as a warrior raced from the woodsline bellowing a high-pitched war cry, only to stop a few steps from Tipaakke's feet.

Tipaakke leaped into the air, throwing up his hands to protect himself. The Mohawk just threw back his head and laughed. He made no move to attack, just stood there, staring with lifeless black eyes.

Katelyn's blood chilled as she stared at the man in the waistcoat. She recognized the look of murder in the Indian's eyes. He was the most terrifying man she'd ever seen in her life. The right half of his face and head were painted a deep black-green and his bare chest a blood red. On the right side of his head he wore his ebony hair long and flowing. A white stick pierced one ear.

The warrior barked something at Tipaakke, but the words were a meaningless jumble to Katelyn. Tipaakke answered, but spoke too softly for her to hear.

The Mohawk did not like Tipaakke's reply. He growled bearing his teeth like a dog and turned to speak to his companions. Katelyn wondered why they didn't make a move. Why didn't they attack?

Each of the Mohawk warriors was painted in some fashion and wore odd bits of white man's clothing and animal skins. They carried assorted guns and knives on leather belts, and some toted long-barreled flint-locks. There were seven in all. One wore a pocketwatch around his neck on a piece of red ribbon and carried a woman's hog-butchering knife. Katelyn shivered. What fate had the owners met? Remembering well the tales of torture and death by Mohawks, she hoped they had died quickly and with honor.

Slowly the Mohawks closed in on Tipaakke, making a vicious game of it. They tried to aggravate him, force him to fight. A warrior wearing men's breeches picked up a stick and hurled it at Tipaakke's head. When the Fox threw up his hand to catch the stick and dropped it to the ground, the men began to laugh and reached for rocks and sticks to join in the sport.

Tipaakke lowered his head to keep from being hit in the face, but he stood his ground. If he fought back, the Mohawks would surely descend upon him and kill him, but if he played their foolish games, his life would be spared, at least until they grew bored with him. As the rocks flew, he dodged and ducked, surveying the band of warriors, spotting the strongest, the weakest, the most intelligent. A man had to know his enemy to beat him. Tipaakke knew his chances would have been good to get away, killing several, had he been alone. But with Katelyn hiding in the cabin, he would have to kill every man in the raiding party. And he couldn't take that risk.

Katelyn watched, horrified, as the stones were thrown and sticks tossed. When a well aimed rock flew, striking Tipaakke in the cheek and leaving a bright red gash, she almost threw herself out of the chimney.

She wanted to protect her man. She wanted to hurl herself from her haven calling the war cry. She wanted to kill the dogs that threatened to leave her unborn child fatherless. But the lessons Tipaakke had taught her ran deep. The Lenni Lenape in Katelyn knew she must remain still. The logic of the red man told her that if someone must die today, it must be Fox. And she knew at that moment that sometimes it was harder to live than to die.

The leader in the bright coat stepped forward and shouted at Tipaakke. When he made no reply, he turned to nod to his men. In an instant, the Indian wearing the pocketwatch lunged forward with a steel tomahawk.

Metal flashed in the bright sunlight as Tipaakke's knife sliced through the air. The man with the watch howled with pain and leaped back, surprised at the Delaware's fierce defense after standing for such humiliation.

Tipaakke turned to protect himself from a man on the left, but a man on the right knocked his legs out from under him with the barrel of a flintlock and sent him tumbling to the ground. The Fox had forgotten that the Mohawks fought without honor. Having no pride or morals, all was fair. There were no unwritten laws guiding a fight as there were with the Lenni Lenape. Rolling forward, Tipaakke came to his feet, his knife still clutched in his hand. These men were not going to kill him, not yet at least, he could feel it in the air. There was no smell of upcoming death. *"Bakkuunda . . . Nahiila-Oopus* . . . Come, strike . . . kill the Fox . . . if you can,"* he taunted. Lowering his center of balance, he crouched, waving his knife to and fro, baring his teeth to growl. The Mohawks liked a man with fierce words.

Katelyn watched as Tipaakke defended himself bravely with skill and ingenuity. He moved with the grace of a swan, and the craftiness of his totem as he waged battle on his enemies. But he did not fight to kill, she could see that in his movements. Why wasn't he killing when he got the chance? She hoped his plan was a good one.

Slowly, Tipaakke tired. It was very difficult to take on so many men and only be on the defensive. As the strength was sapped from his blood, he wondered if he had fought well enough to be kept alive and taken home to their village in the far north. He had heard tell of the Mohawks capturing superior braves to take them home and force them to fight for their entertainment. If they decided to transport him, he would have plenty of time to escape, once he knew Katelyn was safe and far away.

Unabashed tears ran down Katelyn's sooty cheeks as she watched Tipaakke hauled to the ground and kicked and beaten like a scullery dog. She lowered her head to rest it on the rough stone chimney. Swallowing a lump in her throat, she forced herself to look up again. She couldn't abandon Fox, not now. If she couldn't be with him in the flesh, at least she could remain with him in spirit. Why had he given in so easily? Surely he knew they were going to kill him! Slowly, agonizingly, she raised her head, praying his death would be swift and merciful, knowing it wouldn't.

Then, unexpectedly, the leader in the waistcoat began shouting at his men. One by one the Mohawks rose from the ground to leave Tipaakke lying deathly still on the fresh spring grass. The man with the watch gave him a vicious kick as he got to his feet. Tipaakke groaned and his body went limp.

Was he dead? Katelyn wondered. She saw no mortal wounds, only cuts and pulpy bruises. She couldn't believe he could die so easily, but she wished he had.

The man in the breeches and another disappeared into the woods and returned with a straight sapling as thick as a man's wrist. Pulling Tipaakke's limp body into a kneeling position, they began to lace his wrist together behind his back with a length of leather strap.

Once his wrists were securely tied, they ran the sapling through his looped arms and shoved him face first back to the ground.

Katelyn's heart twisted beneath her breast as she watched the men lace his feet together in the same manner. Then, she suddenly realized he meant to take him with them. That was how they tied prisoners. They mean to keep him alive! . . . At least for the time being. But if they took him as a prisoner, he would have a chance. If she could get to Hawk in time, he would find his brother. He would find Tipaakke and bring him back to her! If only the Mohawks would spare him long enough for her to get to Hawk.

Katelyn shifted her weight to steady herself as a tiny spark of hope was kindled. The Mohawks were beginning to ransack the cabin now. If she could remain undetected until they left, she'd soon be on her way to find Hawk. She didn't know how far she would have to walk to find him. It didn't matter to her if she had to go all the way to the village. There was hope now! Maybe Tipaakke would live! Maybe their child would have a father!

As she clung to the rough stones, listening to the bang and clatter of the men below, Katelyn considered making her escape now. If she hung over the side of the roof and dropped to the ground, she could sneak around the back of the cabin and start out for the village. It was a long drop to the ground, but she knew she could do it. She bit her lip in indecisiveness, her eyes returning to rest on Tipaakke's body lying in the grass.

She knew he had told her to stay in the chimney until the Mohawks were gone. But he had thought they would kill him! He didn't know they were going to take him prisoner.

The Mohawks are busy with their looting, Katelyn

234

told herself. They had gone in and out of the cabin several times dumping piles of Tipaakke's precious hides on the ground. She could see the leader in the coat strapping bundles to her pony now. No one would ever see her if she went now.

Then Katelyn smelled smoke. Where was it coming from? She peered over the side, counting the braves. All five were standing near Tipaakke's limp body dividing up their loot. One of the warriors grabbed Katelyn's beaver hat from another and pulled it over his head.

The smell was becoming stronger, the air heavier. Katelyn took a step down to be sure her head wasn't visible from the ground. What did they set on fire, she thought frantically. The acrid smell clung to her nostrils. She saw no smoke.

The cabin! It wasn't enough that they'd taken a prisoner and stolen everything they could find, they'd set the cabin on fire! She clutched the edge of the chimney, her knuckles turning white. What could she do now? If she climbed out, the raiding party would surely spot her!

Smoke began to seep up through the chimney, enveloping Katelyn as she tried to keep from panicking. The fire was spreading fast. She could hear the roar of the flames as she imagined them consuming the interior walls of the cabin. Smoke billowed from below as the Mohawks began to load Tipaakke's precious red fox pelts onto their backs.

Gasping for breath, Katelyn climbed up, sticking her head out above the chimney. She had to have fresh air before she suffocated! Choking, she hoisted herself a little higher. If she didn't make a move soon, the roof would begin to collapse.

Making her decision, Katelyn took one last glimpse of Tipaakke. He was beginning to move now. He was alive! She could see him through the clouds of smoke being pulled to his feet.

Standing Snake, leader of the Mohawk raiding party, shouted a harsh order to his men. Green Briar should not have set fire to the cabin. There was evidence that another had lived here with the Delaware. Since they had not found him, Standing Snake thought it best that they start moving north as soon as possible. This was not their territory, he didn't want his men becoming entangled with the white men on unfamiliar ground. He turned to look at the Delaware brave being hauled to his feet by his men. He was an excellent warrior; he would let him live. At least for the time being. That would be quite a feat to capture a Lenni Lenape and take him home, still alive. As far as he could recall, no one had done it in years.

Signaling for Green Briar to move the prisoner forward, Standing Snake glanced over his shoulder at the burning cabin. Movement on the roof caught his eye. Turning, he squinted, brushing the back of his hand across his eyes. Through the smoke, he saw something moving over the roof. A wolf? He blinked several times in confusion watching the silhouette of a walking wolf disappear over the edge of the burning roof. Calling for a man, he raced for the back of the cabin. Standing Snake turned the corner just in time to see the wolf shedding its skin. The green-coated Mohawk came to a halt, throwing a hand out to stop his companion. The Mohawks stared unbelievingly as they watched the wolf transform itself into a woman . . . a white woman with hair the color of fire!

What game is this the gods play with me, Standing Snake thought, his eyes narrowing suspiciously. He hesitated for a moment, watching the she-wolf turn to face him. Was this creature sent to protect the Delaware? Was it a wolf, or a mortal? What ever it was, it was frightened

. . . he could see it in its honey-colored eyes.

Katelyn eased the breath from her body, sure it would be her last. She stared at the two Mohawk braves standing only a few paces from her. 'Never let the enemy see your fear', Tipaakke's voice echoed in her mind. Katelyn dropped her lids slightly and continued to stare through the slits. Slowly, evenly, she reached out to pull her wolf-skin headdress from where it had caught on the roof's edge. Why hadn't the two Indians made a move? Why were they eyeing her so intently . . . almost in amazement?

The other Mohawks in the raiding party appeared from behind the cabin. They had seen the walking wolf, too.

The leader in the green coat expelled a string of jumbled words and hand signals, telling his fellow warriors what he'd seen.

As he spoke, Katelyn spied Tipaakke coming around the corner, his hands and feet tied together, the sapling thrust through his arms. The brave with the watch moved him along, giving him a shove when he didn't walk fast enough or tripped with his bound feet.

Tipaakke forced his face to remain frozen as he listened to the leader's words. Not knowing the language of the Mohawks well, it was difficult for him to comprehend. They had caught Katelyn . . . He sifted through the man's recognizable words. *They think she is a wolf-woman? They saw her shed her skin?* He tipped his head ever so slightly in Katelyn's direction. He could hear her breathing like a frightened animal. This must have something to do with her headdress, he surmised.

A gust of wind came up, feeding the fire and the group of Mohawk warriors stepped back from the intense heat and shooting flames of the cabin.

Katelyn remained absolutely still, as she tried to figure out what was going on. *Why were they staring at her like that? Why hadn't they attacked?* She knew she must have been a sight with her hair flying wild and tangled and her face and clothing sooty black with ashes. But it wasn't her appearance that frightened them enough to hold them back. She'd *done something* to make them behave like this.

As Katelyn's back became hotter and hotter as the seconds past, she realized she would have to move before her dress burst into flames. Would they attack if she moved? She'd have to take that chance. Slowly she took a single step forward . . . the Mohawks took a step back. She stared in confusion at them for a moment and then took another step forward. The Mohawks took another step back.

Tipaakke watched carefully as Katelyn moved and the Mohawks reacted. His chest ached and his mind was swimming in circles. He stretched his head back, relieving the tension in the back of his neck. *How can I make them set her free*, he asked himself. He tugged his bound wrists. No, they had tied him securely. There was no chance of escape now. But there had to be a way to use this mistaken identity to her advantage. The Mohawks were very religious people. Maybe if they thought she was some spirit sent by the gods . . .

Tipaakke heard himself speak in the unfamiliar tongue. "She wolf-woman. Crazy in head." He shook his head wildly. "No touch her . . . she crazy . . . work bad magic . . . no look in eyes . . . make man blind . . ."

The Mohawks all turned their heads away from her. The leader's eyes dropped to the ground. He turned to face the prisoner. "What is this you tell me? Do you speak the truth?" He wasn't sure if he believed the Delaware or not.

Tipaakke's heart began to beat a little faster. He searched for the right words. "I tell truth. She come

238

from woods, dark night. Do evil magic. I look her eyes. She make me blind many days. I just see now few days. She bad, she evil. Back! Listen Lenni Lenape brave, Tipaakke Oopus."

Standing Snake shifted his weight from one foot to the other. He looked back at the wolf-woman, careful not to let her eyes meet his. The story sounded a bit far fetched to him, but he had heard of stranger tales.

Apprehensively, Tipaakke waited as the Mohawk leader considered his words. The Mohawks were very superstitious people. Maybe they would believe . . . or be afraid not to. Then, seeing the look of confusion on Katelyn's face, he realized he'd better warn her of what was taking place. Speaking quickly, the English words rushed from his mouth. "They think you're a crazy wolf-woman. Go along with anything I say. They think you've been sent by the gods. Half woman, half wolf. Act crazy. It may save your life."

The man with the watch swung his club in the air, knocking Tipaakke in the head. "No speak. No English," he ordered half in Iroquois, half in Algonquian. "No English!"

Shaking his head to clear his mind, Tipaakke struggled to remain on his feet. Good, they must not know English, he thought. In his hurry to make Katelyn understand their situation, it hadn't even occured to him that one of them might know the white man's tongue.

Standing Snake scratched his chin, thinking of what should he do with this wolf-woman. Better not to kill her, he decided. Just in case she is what the Lenni Lenape says she is. He looked at the woman standing with her chin held high, a certain glint in her eyes. Yes, better to take her, he thought. He looked up at his men who were waiting for his decision. "Take her," he ordered. "She is harmless. We'll sell her to the captain

239

at Fort Richardson," he told them in Iroquois. "He is giving four muskets for each woman we bring him." Standing Snake laughed as the Mohawks descended on Katelyn. It will be a good joke, he thought to himself. Selling the captain a crazy wolf-woman!

Chapter Eleven

Katelyn studied the Mohawk who wore her beaver skin hat as he reached out to grab her arm. She smiled, baring her teeth, as she had seen Tipaakke do, and Beaver Hat loosened his grip on her wrist.

I don't know why I have to be the one to tie the wolf-woman, the warrior thought as he reached beneath his jerkin and pulled out a length of sinew. He didn't like the idea of bringing her along. As he saw it, nothing but trouble could come from it. For all he knew the woman could turn herself back into a wolf at any moment and rip them to pieces.

Katelyn lifted her other arm and presented it wrist up so the Mohawk could bind her hands. The haunting grin remained on her lips as she tried to get him to look her directly in her face. Tipaakke had explained to her just moments ago why the Mohawks were afraid to look her in the eye, so she intended to use it for all it was worth. She knew how superstitious they were. They were very cautious of anyone who they thought might be touched by the spirits — good or evil.

Beaver Hat cast a quick glance at the prisoner's face. Why had she offered her hands to be bound like that? He didn't like it. He didn't like it at all. A woman with hair that color couldn't possibly be of this world. If he was leader, he would have left the both of them behind. He saw no reason to risk the wrath of the gods over a few white man's thunder sticks. But then maybe that was why Standing Snake had been appointed leader of the raiding party and not him. Giving the leather strap a good tug, he released the wolf-woman's hands. He didn't even like touching her. "Tie the feet?" he asked Standing Snake, who had come up beside him.

The leader cast a quick look at the wolf-woman. "No need. Look at her. She is willing to go," he answered in the tongue of the five Iroquois nations. He glanced at her suspiciously, wondering if he'd made the right decision. He didn't like the way she looked at him. He rested his hand on the war axe at his belt, vowing to keep an eye on his back.

Katelyn threw back her head and gave a little laugh deep in her throat. She chuckled to herself as Green Coat walked away, obviously unnerved. He shouted a command to his men and started down the path, putting as much distance as he could between himself and the fire-haired wolf-woman.

Beaver Hat grabbed Katelyn's hands again and looped a lead line through the binding. Dropping her hands, he tied the other end around his waist and gave a tug.

Katelyn tugged back in response and the Mohawk's eyes widened. She nodded her head in the direction of the wolf-hide headdress that lay on the grass near her feet.

Beaver Hat shook his head. "No. Come." He turned to go. He wasn't picking her skin up.

Katelyn held back, refusing to budge. She needed the headdress to remind them of what they had seen. "My skin," she commanded in Algonquian. "I must have my skin." She flung back her head letting the breeze rifle through her tangled hair.

The Mohawk glanced up to see the other men beginning to move out of the clearing. The wolf-woman waited for his response. Finally, he reached in his belt and pulled out a pistol. Catching the head of the wolf hide with the barrel of his pistol, he raised it in the air and dropped it over her looped arms.

Katelyn smiled and nodded and then started forward to follow the other men.

Beaver Hat shook his head and moved forward. Whom did she think was leading whom? He walked by her, giving her a hard nudge with his elbow as he passed by. Wolf-woman or not, she was still his prisoner and she would have to respect that.

As the raiding party left the burning cabin and entered the woods, Katelyn and Beaver Hat fell into place in the rear. Tipaakke walked just ahead of the warrior wearing the pocket watch. Tipaakke didn't look back as they started to move, so Katelyn made no attempt to speak to him. She knew that if they were going to play this charade, they must play it carefully. The Mohawks were superstitious, but they weren't stupid. If they recognized any attachment between their prisoners, they would know Tipaakke had deceived them and they would probably kill both of them without hesitation. So until Katelyn could speak alone with Tipaakke and make plans for an escape, she would bide her time. Both of them walked a very fine line between life and death. For now, she would have to be content to watch Tipaakke walk ahead of her and be thankful he still lived.

As the flaming orange sun began to sink in the pale western sky, the raiding party turned and moved east, picking up its pace.

Katelyn mentally thanked Tipaakke again for increasing her walking endurance as she stepped over a fallen log and ducked beneath a low-lying elm branch.

The trees seemed to hang lower as the forest darkened and Katelyn quickened her pace to keep up with her captor, ignoring the dark shadows, the branches, and hanging vines cast across her path. She breathed deeply, absorbing the life's breath of the dense forest surrounding her. Tipaakke had said that to survive in the forest, one must become part of it. One must hear the dew settling in at the end of the day; one must feel the rich sap of the trees flowing through one's veins. Allowing the sights and sounds of the retiring forest to revitalize her, Katelyn moved ahead to walk beside Beaver Hat. She had to keep them apprehensive. She had to make them wary of her. She had to do the unexpected.

Although her hands were tied, and the Mohawks moved at a grueling pace, Katelyn had had no trouble keeping up. But her heart went out to Tipaakke. The most difficult part of the journey was watching him stumble along, bound so tightly, knowing she couldn't risk reaching out to help him. He and Pocket Watch had fallen back until they walked just ahead of Katelyn and her captor. Shortly after they left the cabin behind, Pocket Watch cut the lashings at Tipaakke's feet, realizing they would never be able to move fast enough with the Delaware falling every few paces. Still, the walking was hard on Tipaakke as they crossed unfamiliar ground, often stepping off the deer paths and cutting through underbrush to another path. The sapling thrust through his hands made it difficult for him to maneuver because the ends constantly hit tree trunks and caught in brush. But, that was what it was intended for. It was meant to make it impossible to run through the dense forest.

Katelyn stared up at the streaky pinks and oranges of the sky, estimating how long it would be before darkness settled in. She was so thirsty. Though she carried the water bag around her neck, with her hands tied and the heavy headdress in her arms, she'd been unable to guide the bag to her mouth. She would have asked her captor to raise the bag to her lips, but since she had seen no Mohawk drink, she refused to show them any weakness. Besides, she didn't know if she could have brought herself to take a drink as long as Tipaakke went without.

As the raiding party turned and headed north again, Katelyn realized they were moving toward a specific destination, probably a base camp. As the inky blackness began to settle in, she knew they would have to stop soon. Though the Mohawks could have easily walked through the night, she doubted they would try it with prisoners — especially with a wolf-woman.

Katelyn chuckled to herself at the thought and her captor gave her a sideways glance, checking, she was sure, to be certain his prisoner hadn't transformed into a wolf.

Long before they entered the camp among the scrub pines, Katelyn caught scent of a burning fire and roasting meat. Her mouth watered at the thought of roasted squirrel and she wondered if the Mohawks would feed them anything. She had a few strips of dried venison and a handful or two of dried berries in one of the bags around her neck, so at least she and Tipaakke would have *something* to eat. If Beaver Hat would untie her hands so she could get to it, that was.

As the raiding party stepped into the clearing, several other Mohawks moved to greet the arrivals. To Katelyn's distress, she spotted two white women and a middle-aged white man tied to a tree just beyond the light of the campfire. One of the women was half sitting, slumped over, her once yellow-blonde hair sheared close to her head, and her face a mass of purple bruises. Her green work dress was torn beyond

245

repair and blackened from days of travel. The man and other woman seemed to have faired better, but they had probably been captured more recently

Beaver Hat led Katelyn past the fire where rabbit and squirrel were roasting and tied her lead line to a tree only a few paces from the other prisoners. Katelyn sank to the ground and opened her arms to let the wolf-headdress fall into her lap. She leaned her head on the tree, thankful for the rest as her captor cut the knot on the leather that bound her wrists and retied one wrist so her hands were free. Katelyn looked up at Beaver Hat nodding her thanks and giving him that same grin that made him so uneasy.

Beaver Hat just shook his head and made his way to the fire, wishing he'd never made this trip to begin with. He was relieved when Standing Snake had told him they would be starting north at dawn. All he wanted to do now was get home to his wife and her mat and get as far away from the wolf-woman as possible.

Pocket Watch shoved Tipaakke unceremoniously to the ground and the Delaware brave recoiled at the feel of his leg against hers. "No," he protested in the Iroquois tongue. "No wolf-woman. Other tree. Wolf-woman kill Lenni Lenape brave. Night Fox suffer enough from hand of wild woman." He leaned as far from her as he could without toppling over.

Pocket Watch laughed, clapping his hands in amusement. "Coward," he teased as he reached down to secure the prisoner to the tree. "Great Lenni Lenape brave fears a white woman!" He shook his head, still laughing as he removed the sapling from Tipaakke's looped arms and leaned it against the tree. "I think you stay. Maybe you will learn courage." He threw up one hand. "And maybe she will eat you and we will find nothing but your bones in the morning." He walked off in the direction of the others, his round face still marked with amusement.

Katelyn waited until the Mohawk was well out of earshot and then reached out with her free hand to touch Tipaakke's arm. "Are you all right?" she questioned in Lenni Lenape. His skin felt damp and slightly feverish beneath her touch.

"Speak only in English," he told her quietly. "They know some of my people's language."

She nodded, withdrawing her hand before anyone noticed. "Are you hurt?"

"Broken ribs. But I am fine. You?" He listened to her sweet voice, savoring each word. He had never expected to hear her, to touch her again.

"Tired. Scared. But not hurt." She glanced at the other prisoners, squinting to see them in the dark. "Did you see the others, Fox?"

"Others?" He kept his head turned from her so that no one would know they were talking. "No, I was watching you."

Katelyn reached out to poke Tipaakke, trying to appear to the Mohawks like she was harassing him. Pocket Watch nudged Beaver Hat and both laughed, turning back to face the fire.

Katelyn spoke quietly, intermingling her words with an occasional loud taunt. "There are other prisoners. Two women, and a man. One of the women looks bad. It looks like they've had her a while. I'm not even sure if she's alive." She laughed loud and hard, her voice echoing in the trees above.

Beaver Hat turned and shouted at her. She was sure he was telling her to be quiet.

"You play the game well," Tipaakke whispered, his voice rich with pride, but laced with amusement. "Can you tell if the woman is still breathing?" He rested his back against the rough trunk of the tree, giving his sore muscles release. "I can't see from here."

"No. It's too dark. I can barely see them. I'm glad we're outside the light of the fire. The Mohawks can't see us very well."

Tipaakke smiled. "You know why we are tied out here, don't you? Wolves. If they come near, they will attack us first, giving them time to be ready."

Katelyn's body trembled slightly at that thought and she turned to whisper through the darkness. "Are you all right?" she asked the other prisoners.

"You speak English?" the man answered faintly.

"I'm English . . . was. Is that woman dead?"

"We pray she is," the haggard voice replied. "This one hasn't spoken or heard a word since they took her." He indicated the dark haired woman tied beside him. "Have you water? We haven't had any since last night."

Katelyn's hand went instinctively to the water bag at her waist. The precious water she carried might be enough to keep her and Tipaakke alive. If she shared it, there wouldn't be enough for anyone. It all depended on whether or not their captors intended to feed them and give them water. "Yes . . ." she replied hesitantly. "But I'm not sure that I can get it to you. My line is pretty short." She pulled the bag slowly over her head and untied the strap that kept it closed.

"Bless you child. There must be a way. We only need a sip." The man's voice was hopeful.

Katelyn checked to be sure no one was looking and quickly pressed the bag to Tipaakke's lips.

"You are a good woman," Tipaakke told her as he pulled back savoring the cool water as it slid down his throat. "You will be rewarded in the next life if not in this one."

Katelyn took a small swallow and then another. She was so thirsty she could have drank it all. But after the second sip she retied the leather mouth and stared through the darkness again. "Sir, how are you tied?"

248

"My hands are lashed together, but they're in front of me. If you can get the bag to my hands I can get a drink and give this woman one. I don't think I can reach the other," he finished weakly.

"All right. Listen. The Indians think I am crazy. I'm touched. They think I'm half wolf, half woman. Go along with what I say."

"A wolf-woman?"

"No time to explain, sir." Katelyn got slowly to her feet. "Just trust me." She glanced at the men who were beginning to sit around the fire and break off bits of the roasted meat to eat. The sight of food made Katelyn faint with hunger. Slowly, she took the few steps to the man and woman tied to the tree. When she reached the end of her lead-line she stretched out her arms.

The man scrambled to his feet and stretched until his fingertips barely touched the leather bag. "Bless you child," he murmured, pulling it eagerly to his mouth.

Beaver Hat came up behind Katelyn, startling her. "Why you give water to prisoners?" he asked in Algonquian.

Katelyn's mind whirled. Then she smiled, narrowing her eyes. "He's plump. Would be good meal. I don't want him to die. A wolf likes to stalk its prey." She reached out a hand to run it along the Mohawks muscular arm. "Would you like a drink, too?"

Beaver Hat took a step back. Was she playing games with him? He stared through the darkness at her. He had known men thirsty for human blood, but somehow this woman was different. She was driven by a passion he didn't recognize. And that frightened him.

The seconds ticked on endlessly as Katelyn waited. Did Beaver Hat believe her story? She reached out to take the water bag from the man tied to the tree. Then she spoke. "You bring me squirrel." She pointed to the inner circle of light where meat still roasted on wooden spits. "I feed these prisoners. Make them plump." She laid her hand on his arm again.

Beaver Hat shoved Katelyn's hand aside and ran his hand over the place on his arm that she had touched. "Food for woman prisoners. Must keep alive for Fort captain. Sell women. Men . . ." he shrugged his shoulders, turning to go.

"Men eat mine," Katelyn called after him, returning to her tree.

Beaver Hat shrugged his shoulders again, stepping back into the light of the fire. "You eat, you not eat. This brave no care. I give."

"I don't have to have mine cooked. Have any raw?" She slid her back down the trunk of the tree and seated herself on the damp moss.

Beaver Hat pretended not to hear his last words and moved to the other side of the fire, crouching next to Green Briar. "I don't like this, brother." He spoke beneath his breath.

"What?" Green Briar wiped his greasy fingers on his leather jerkin and reached for his water bag.

"The wolf-woman. She is trouble. Maybe dangerous."

He looked up to see where Standing Snake was. "I question our leader's decision."

Green Briar looked up at his friend. "I don't believe she's a wolf-woman. It's a story. Look at her." He pointed into the shadows. "She's just a white woman. The Captain will pay us well for her. We need the guns."

"You aren't with her. I don't see you offering to have her tied to your waist." He stared into the flames of the fire. "There is something about her eyes that I don't like. She has such a look of . . ." He searched for the right word. ". . . determination. You don't see that in the eyes of many women. And certainly not white

250

women. She's dangerous, I tell you."

Green Briar got to his feet, shaking his head. "I think your grandfather told you too many stories as a child. Wolf-woman!" He laughed, reaching beneath his jerkin to extract a slim silver flask. "Drink." He pushed the flask into his friend's hand. "In a few days we will be home and you will be rid of your wolf-woman." He slapped him on the back. "Drink."

Katelyn watched through half-closed eyes as the Mohawks unrolled their sleeping mats and settled down for the night. The sentry propped himself up against a huge oak just inside the light of the fire and began to whittle at a stick with a huge jagged-edged hunting knife. He had tried to rouse the blonde-haired prisoner earlier by poking her with a sharpened stick, but had given up on the game when she had done nothing but emit a few weak groans.

At least she's alive, Katelyn thought as she moved a little, trying to find a comfortable spot. Turning her head, she stared through the darkness at Tipaakke's sleeping face. She had told him to rest after she had divided her share of the roasted squirrel with him. The other man, Joseph, had taken part of the dark-haired woman's share, after a little encouragement. The woman would only eat if he put the meat in her mouth; drink if he pushed the bag to her lips.

Katelyn studied Tipaakke's peaceful face. He had been so exhausted, yet now the harsh lines were gone from his face. A slight smile played on her lips. She would never understand how he could sleep so hard. No matter what happened during the day, whether it was an argument with her, or being captured by Mohawks, at the end of the day he still slept like a babe in a cradle.

Glancing to be sure the sentry wasn't looking, Katelyn reached out to brush her fingertips along the length

251

of his arm. She ached to touch his face, to run her hands over his smarting muscles, to ease the pain of the beatings. But, she dared not. Slipping her hand into one of his tied behind his back, she eased her eyelids shut, savoring the feel of Tipaakke's hand as his fingers tightened around hers. "I love you," he whispered so low that she wasn't sure he had spoken.

"I love you, too," she answered sleepily.

As the first streaks of dawn lighted the sky, the Mohawks roused themselves and began to break up camp.

At the first sound of movement, Tipaakke was awake and nudging Katelyn. "Wake up, love," he crooned.

Katelyn groaned, rolling her head back and forth. Her body was stiff from sleeping on the uneven ground and her wrists ached from being tied together the day before. "Ohhh, Fox . . . I don't feel so well." She rubbed her free hand over her stomach.

"Shhh," he warned. "Drink water. You'll be all right once you're up. We'll be moving soon. Have some dried berries."

Sitting up a little straighter, she pulled the water bag to her lips. "I thought you said I was done with this stomach sickness."

Tipaakke laughed. "I thought you were. Must be a son. My mother said her sons always gave her more trouble in the nest than her daughters."

Katelyn rolled her eyes. "Thanks, that's reassuring. I feel better already," she finished sarcastically. She glanced over at the other prisoners still sleeping. The blonde woman hadn't moved all night. "Beaver Hat said they were going to sell all of the women to some captain at a fort." She looked over at Fox. "No one is going to sell me as long as I've still got breath in my body."

Tipaakke shook his head, glad to see her spirits were still high. "I feel sorry for the man who tries."

Katelyn slowly got to her feet, resting one hand against the tree trunk to steady herself. The nausea came in waves as she took deep breaths, filling her lungs with sweet morning air.

"Today we will be crossing Lenni Lenape ground," Tipaakke mused. "Maybe we will come upon some of my people."

"Maybe." Katelyn let go of the tree, already beginning to feel steady on her feet. "But maybe not. Have you thought of a plan?"

"No. But today I will think. Now that I'm rested." He got to his feet, stretching as best he could with his arms tied behind his back. "Don't worry."

"Don't worry?" Katelyn ran her hands over her rounding belly. "This dress will not cover your son too much longer."

Tipaakke nodded. "We will be together, the three of us. I can feel it in my bones."

She ran her fingers through her snarled hair. "I wish your bones would tell us how to get away."

"We must wait until the time is right. Be patient, my love. The right time will come and we will make our move. But I will not risk the life of you and our child attempting to escape. When we go, we'll disappear into the forest, never to be seen by these men again." His bronze face tightened with concern. "Do not become too anxious. We're safe for now. We cannot make any mistakes. A mistake would cost us our lives."

"But how will we know when the time is right?" Katelyn glanced around to be sure no one was paying them any attention. "How will *I* know?"

"I will watch, I will wait, and I will listen. I will know when the time has come. I will tell you when to make ready. Don't worry Manito will protect us." He nodded his head with finality.

"I wish I was as confident as you."

"I have seen many things in my life Katie-girl. I have faced worse than these men. I am a survivor and so are you. It is not our time to go. Death has had many chances to take us, you and I." His dark eyes searched hers. "I told you. We're going to grow old together," he smiled.

"I know you've told me, and I almost believe you." She returned a smile of love, wishing she could touch him. "Don't worry about me, I'll be fine."

"I know you will. Someday we will sit around the fire with our grandchildren and tell them of the time we were captured by Mohawks."

"Grandchildren! I just think . . . Oh no, here they come." She straightened her back and stared boldly into Beaver Hat's eyes as he made his way to her. "I'm ready Mohawk brave. You are lazy. It is late. Let us move on."

Once the last embers of the campfire were buried and the prisoners were kicked awake, the Mohawk raiding party started heading north.

Katelyn was distressed to find that today she and Beaver Hat were walking up front with Green Coat and several other warriors. Tipaakke walked behind her with Pocket Watch, and Joseph and the two women walked behind them, each with their own guard. Several more armed warriors brought up the rear. Katelyn would much rather have walked behind Tipaakke, where she could keep an eye on him. But she couldn't think of a good excuse to give Beaver Hat for why she wanted to walk in the rear; so, she was forced to walk up front.

As the Mohawk party moved through the dense forest, following the narrow deer paths, Katelyn

254

glanced occasionally back at the other prisoners. Ti-paakke walked as if he were going for a stroll, despite his hands bound behind his back and the sapling stuck through them. Joseph and the dark-haired woman trudged on, as if in a trance. But the blonde woman could hardly walk. Again and again she fell and the warriors yanked and pulled on her until she was on her feet again. Several times, the leader, Green Coat, shouted an order to the man who was in charge of her. Katelyn couldn't understand the Mohawk tongue, but she could recognize threats in any language. If the blonde woman didn't pick up her pace, she wouldn't live to see another sunset.

As the sun climbed higher in the sky, the Mohawk warriors became restless. The woman prisoner was slowing them down.

Standing Snake dropped back to the rear where the woman prisoner walked. Katelyn didn't dare look back for fear of being cuffed by Beaver Hat again, but she listened intently as she walked, trying to figure out what was going on.

The leader spoke and then she heard another brave. When several men spoke in unison, Green Coat silenced them all. After a few more words, he moved to the front again. Katelyn wondered what was going on. What decision had he made.

Then she heard the scream . . . Katelyn spun around to catch a glimpse of the blonde-haired woman going down and one of the Mohawks yanking her to her feet. Only this time he didn't shove her forward.

"Did I tell you keep your eyes in front of your head, Wolf-woman?" Beaver Hat berated, knocking Katelyn in the back of the head with his fist. "You listen or be left for buzzards with her."

Katelyn was knocked to her knees by the blow, but she came to her feet in time to keep from being pulled over by the taut lead line. She shook her head to clear her rattled brain and tried to get her balance again. Another piercing scream came from behind as Katelyn scrambled to catch up with her captor. She had to keep up. She had to live . . . for Fox, for her baby. She closed her eyes, trying to block out the woman's pitiful pleas for help before her voice died in the distance. *There was no saving her now.*

The bile rose in her throat and Katelyn swallowed hard. They were going to kill her. But what were they going to do first? Why was she screaming like that? Like an animal caught in a trap . . .

"Don't listen," Tipaakke shouted before Pocket Watch elbowed him sharply in his broken ribs.

Behind Katelyn was a mass of confusion. Joseph was struggling, trying to break free. "Leave her alone, you stinking savages," he shouted. "Just let her die," he begged. A sob escaped his throat as the woman screamed again in the distance.

"Move on," Katelyn shouted to Joseph. "She's gone. Save yourself."

Beaver Hat stopped and turned around, grabbing Katelyn by the shoulders. The others began to pass, walking on as the Mohawk shook her until her teeth slammed together. "No English tongue, I tell you!" He slapped her soundly on the cheek and started forward again, giving her tether strap a hard snap.

With her shoulder, Katelyn hastily brushed away a tear that trickled down her cheek. She stared straight into the sky as she walked, trying to get a grip on herself. She couldn't help the blonde woman and she knew it. So why couldn't she just walk on? *Why did it have to hurt so much?*

Shortly, the raiding party came to a small running brook and the Mohawks allowed their prisoners to take their fill of water. Katelyn stepped into the water and bent to splash her face. After she'd quenched her thirst, she emptied her water bag and refilled it with fresh water. At least they weren't going to let them all die of thirst.

Once her bag was full, Katelyn perched herself on the bank as far from Beaver Hat as her line would allow her. Tipaakke did the same.

"We've got to get away," Katelyn whispered, pretending to be interested in a small brown toad basking in the sun. "Or I really am going to go crazy." She shifted the heavy wolf headdress she held in her arms. "I couldn't help her, Fox," she cried desperately. "There was nothing I could do." She choked down a sob, knowing she had to be quiet.

"No," Tipaakke answered softly. "There was nothing you could do. You are wise to know that." He longed to reach for her, to hold her, to guide her through her pain. *But all I can do is offer her meaningless words*, he thought with frustration. "Katie-girl, we'll find a way. You must be careful. You walk along a deadly cliff with the man who holds you. He fears you. I hear it in his voice. A man who fears is a dangerous man." Tipaakke looked skyward, guessing at the time of day and calculating how many more hours they would have to walk. He was worried about Katelyn. She could not walk indefinitely like his people.

"I don't know why he's afraid of me. All I do is smile like a fool and pretend I'm eager to stay with them. Why would that make anyone afraid?" Katelyn flexed her hands, trying to relieve the cramps. *Were the leather straps looser?* She flexed them again. Had she been able to move them like this earlier in the day? She didn't think so. "Fox . . ." she whispered. "I think the ties on my hands are looser."

Tipaakke forced himself not to turn his face towards her. "Are you sure?" He couldn't conceal the sound of joyous hope in his voice.

"Maybe it's just my imagination. But I think they are. I got them pretty wet in the water." She cast a sideways glance at Beaver Hat. He was still busy talking to another Mohawk brave.

"Keep trying to work them, dove. Work them!"

Katelyn watched as Pocket Watch snatched Tipaakke's line, forcing him to move on. She got to her feet and tugged at her own tether. The stolen moments of conversation with Tipaakke were never long enough . . . "Come, friend," Katelyn told her captor in Algonquian. "Time we moved north. You Mohawks are turtles."

Beaver Hat scowled, looking back at his friend Green Briar. "You see," he said in his own tongue. "This isn't right. A prisoner doesn't act like this." He got to his feet and quickened his stride to pass the wolf-woman. "Stay behind." He glared. "No speaking. You are not worth a few fire sticks to me."

Katelyn gave him her usual grin, but kept behind as he'd ordered. Fox was right. She would have to be careful. Beaver Hat seemed to be more nervous. But maybe that was because they were still passing through Lenni Lenape land.

Falling into stride with the others, Katelyn let her mind wander to ease the pain in her back and the ache in her arms from carrying the hefty headdress. She wanted to leave it behind this morning, but Tipaakke had insisted she keep it. It reminded the Mohawks of what they'd seen. Besides, she might need it. Her rabbit-hide cloak had burned in the cabin.

As the Mohawk raiding party moved through the forest at an unrelenting pace, Katelyn tried to figure out where they were. If only she'd paid more attention to what direction they had followed when Hawk had taken them to the cabin in the fall.

258

The sun began its slow westwardly descent as the hours ticked by, and still the Mohawks moved on. Without the burden of the weak white woman, they were making up for lost time.

Katelyn stared at Green Coat's back, trying to think about anything but the endless walking. How could the leader keep this pace up? They were practically running. How could *she* keep this pace up? How could a man ask his men to walk fifteen hours a day and then sit up part of the night on sentry duty? She watched curiously as Green Coat's head bobbed up and down with the rhythm of his step. At least he'd washed off the war paint from his face. Her eyes came to rest on the stick embedded in his ear. She remembered seeing it the day before, when she was still safe in the chimney. It seemed like years had passed since then. *What was that in his ear?*

A sickening feeling crept from Katelyn's stomach upward. That wasn't a stick. She swallowed hard, dropping her head and squeezing her eyes shut. *One foot in front of the other*, she told herself. *Keep up or he'll kill you. Don't look.* . . . It was a human finger bone that pierced his ear!

As the hours passed, Katelyn began to move more slowly. Somewhere among the needled pines and huge oaks, she lost all track of time. She was too tired to attempt loosening her bindings, too tired even to think. She moved mechanically, pushing one foot in front of the other. Nothing mattered at this point but survival. All she could do was walk on endlessly behind Beaver Hat, knowing she must keep up.

As the afternoon passed and the sun began its slow descent in the sky, the Mohawks began to talk among themselves, moving back and forth within the line. Katelyn didn't know what they were getting so excited about, and she was too exhausted to care. When several braves grouped together and disappeared into the forest to the east, she barely looked up. She didn't know where they were going—straight to hell, she hoped.

A little further down the worn deer path, Green Coat led the remaining Mohawks and their prisoners to the west, cutting through a thick hedge of thorned blackberries. The briars tore at Katelyn's hair and scratched her face unmercifully, but she trudged on. Once through the briars, she heard the sound of running water off in the distance. It wasn't the sound of the fast moving streams of the mountains, but just the trickle of a tiny fresh-water spring.

Finally, the group came to a halt in a narrow clearing just beyond the spring, and Katelyn turned to catch the first glimpse of Tipaakke she'd had in hours. Though his sun-bronzed skin was scratched and bleeding, he looked good. Even with his hands tied behind his back, he had kept up well today. He seemed to be barely winded.

Good, Katelyn thought wryly. *He seems to have had an easy day; maybe he's thought of a way to get us out of here.* Her eyes came to rest on Joseph and the remaining woman prisoner. They looked bad. Joseph was sporting a black eye and a swollen jaw—both results of this morning's tussel, she was sure. The woman looked much the same as she had earlier, only her eyes were a little glassier, her skin a little paler. Though she wore no evidence of physical abuse, Katelyn could see her pain ran deep. Could anyone ever recover from an ordeal like this? She suddenly realized how lucky she was to have been captured by the Delawares last summer and not by the Mohawks. A year ago she could not have come as far as the dark-haired woman. She would have been the other—lying dead in the middle of nowhere— tortured and left for the wild animals to devour.

Patiently, Katelyn waited until all of the Mohawk warriors had washed their hands and faces and had taken their fill of water. Only then, did Beaver Hat allow her to drink. Dropping her headdress, she drank and then refilled her water bag, keeping her wrists under the water. Though she hadn't had the energy to struggle with the ties for hours, she knew they were growing looser. When Beaver Hat pulled viciously on the line, she moved reluctantly from the water and followed him to a tree on the edge of the small clearing. For a moment Katelyn panicked, fearing he would untie her hands and retie one wrist to the tree. Then she would have to start all over again. But the Mohawk was in such a foul mood that he just shoved her to the ground and secured the tether strap to the tree. Without a word, he turned to join the group of Mohawks near the spring.

Katelyn slid to the ground, relieved that Beaver Hat had left her alone and thankful to be off her feet. Making herself as comfortable as possible on the hide of her headdress, she leaned back to rest her head against the ancient poplar. Through the low brush and patches of spring wildflowers she watched Tipaakke drink and then be led across the clearing in her direction.

"Put Lenni Lenape brave here," Katelyn called, smiling at Pocket Watch. ". . . Where I can keep eye on him." She narrowed her eyes, making them glisten.

"No." Tipaakke shook his head, drawing back at the sound of her voice. "No wolf-woman." He struggled to get away.

Pocket Watch laughed, giving Tipaakke's line a good snap. "I put prisoner where I want," he answered in broken Algonquian. He stopped, looking from the wolf-woman to the Delaware. "Here." Stepping up, he tied Tipaakke's line to Katelyn's tree. "I no believe story of wolf-woman." He glared at Katelyn. "But Lenni Lenape brave believe." He nodded his head in Tipaakke's direction, laughing at his own cleverness. Securing the lead line to the tree, he patted Tipaakke on the knee as he went by. "Maybe my friend no feed wolf-woman tonight. She say she like tender Delawares." He laughed again and disappeared into the forest.

Katelyn couldn't figure out what the Mohawks were up to. Why had they made camp so early? Where had the other braves gone? Somehow, the air seemed different among them tonight. It was an air of anxious anticipation.

Katelyn and Tipaakke sat side by side, his bare leg pressed against hers as they waited apprehensively. It was getting dark. The other Mohawks had been gone quite a while now.

Katelyn glanced up to be sure no one was watching them. "I can't figure it out, Fox." She shook her head, trying to chase away a buzzing mosquito. "I don't think that was a hunting party that was sent out earlier. They wouldn't be this excited over a deer."

Tipaakke shook his head. "They hunt, but not for animals. We're near a settlement." His brow was furrowed deep with concern. "They've gone raiding again."

Katelyn was silent for a moment, wondering who had fallen prey to them this time. Then she looked up. "I got my ties wet again."

"Good. Keep working it; keep them wet. It could be . . ." Suddenly, Tipaakke tensed. "Listen . . ." he told her, his voice hushed. "They're coming."

Katelyn listened to the faint sound of boisterous laughter and thrashing brush. "I hear them. Why are they so loud?" She stole a glance at Tipaakke's concerned face. *He's so handsome*, she thought.

"The raid was well rewarded." His voice was taut. "Whiskey. Take care. No telling what they will do now. Our people do not drink well. It makes them crazy."

Katelyn and Tipaakke sat in silence, both caught up in their own thoughts, as they waited for the marauders to emerge from the woods.

When the Mohawks entered the clearing, Katelyn recoiled in horror and disgust. The men were laden with guns, food and assorted loot, and reeked of whiskey and fresh blood. The braves' clothing was covered with splotches of deep red, and their movements were frenzied with the excitement of a fresh kill.

"It will be a long night, love." Fox rubbed his legs against hers, caressing her the only way he could. "You rest. Try to sleep. I'll keep watch."

"Sleep?" She laughed. "Who could sleep with that going on?" She motioned in the Mohawks direction with her chin. They were dancing now. Around and around the campfire they went, singing and hooting as they passed around the bottles of scotch. "I just hope we're not the entertainment." She glanced over at the other two prisoners who slept fitfully. "Maybe it would be better that way."

Tipaakke's head snapped around to face her. "Don't say that," he commanded in Algonquian through clenched teeth. "Do not ever say that. Life is a gift. The life that lives within you is a gift. You must fight for life." He stared through the darkness, his eyes caressing her heart-shaped face.

Katelyn's throat tightened and she fought back the tears that threatened to spill. A sob escaped her sunburned lips as she tried to gain control of her emotions. He was right. She was being silly. Why was she crying?

"I'm sorry." His voice came through the darkness to

envelope her weary body. "I don't mean to be harsh. I love you Katie-girl. You and the child are my life." The soft syllables of the Lenni Lenape tongue caressed Katelyn's senses. After not hearing his language for days, it filled her brain like the sweet song of the harpsichord. Or, was it just his voice . . . his vows of love that comforted her?

"I love you, too," she managed with another sob. "I just want this to be over. All I want is to be safe with you in your wigwam. You're the only one who's ever made me feel safe." She worked at the bindings on her wrists, wrenching them back and forth as the words spilled from her mouth. "I'm tired of being tough. I just want to be warm and safe. I just want you to love me." She spoke in Lenni Lenape, using English when she didn't know the words.

"Shhhhh . . ." Tipaakke crooned, as he flexed his fists in frustration. If only he could just hold her. Why had this happened to them? Why couldn't he protect his woman as he should?

"Fox . . ." Katelyn sniffed, twisting her wrists. "I've almost got it. . . . My hands are almost free!"

Tipaakke turned his head from her, watching the Mohawks as they moved about, laughing and dancing. "Take care that no one is looking."

"No, they're too busy with themselves." She raised her wrists to her mouth, tugging on the leather with her teeth. "As soon as I get them off I'll start on yours."

"No." He shook his head, keeping an ear out. "You must go swiftly. There is no time. It has taken you all day to loosen yours. Go back to my village. Get my brother. He will bring me home to you."

"No," she answered insistently, gnawing at the damp ties. I won't leave you." She raised her head. "If you're not going, I'm not."

"Listen to me. Don't be a child. It's the only way.

264

They've let me live this long. I'll be safe. You must get Mekollaan's help." He wanted to shout at her. To force her to her feet and to make her run. *Please*, he prayed silently, *grant me this wish. Let her live.* . . . He squeezed his eyes shut, sending his prayer heavenward.

"You wouldn't leave without me," Katelyn challenged, easing out a knot with her teeth.

"If it was the only way . . ." his voice stabbed her like a stone knife ". . . I would. You know I would."

Katelyn paused, raising her head to look at him through the darkness. "I can't."

"You can. You will," he whispered.

"What you doing? Why you talking?"

Katelyn looked up to see Beaver Hat standing in front of her. Where had he come from? Why hadn't she seen him?

"Speak Wolf-woman. Why you speak with Lenni Lenape brave?" His voice was lilted, evidence of the whiskey he held in his hand. Taking another sip, he reached out to kick her bound hands. "I say . . ."

Katelyn's eyes fell to her hands. Even in the darkness, Katelyn knew he must have seen the bindings fall. Slowly she raised her head to look at him. "Why do I speak to him?" Her voice was an enchanting whisper.

The whiskey gave the Mohawk the courage to look from the bindings on the ground to her face. His raven-black eyes pierced the moonlit darkness to stare at the ripe, pursed lips, the soft, haunting brown eyes.

Katelyn held her breath as an eternity passed. Her heart beat so hard beneath her breast that she felt sure he could hear it. Still, she kept her eyes fixed on his, knowing her life and the life of her child lay in this man's palm. Then she watched Beaver Hat turn slowly and walk back into the circle of firelight.

Katelyn's lip quivered as she slowly released her breath, her eyes boring holes in the Mohawk's back.

265

Was this some sick game? If she moved, would he put an axe through her chest? Out of the darkness came Tipaakke's voice.

"Run! Run, my love, before someone sees you!" Tipaakke's voice was on the verge of panic.

"No. I won't leave you." She leaned to tug at his bindings frantically. "I couldn't make it back without you. I'd die or they'd catch me." With her fingers she pulled at the knotted leather cord that bound his feet. If she could get his feet loose, he could run. Later they would remove the hand bindings.

"You could make it. You've learned more than you know." Tipaakke broke out into a cold sweat. "You must go. They will kill you if they catch you, my dove."

"They won't catch us." Katelyn successfully untied the first tight knot and started on the next. "We'll disappear into the night without a trace." She glanced up at Mohawks still dancing in a frenzied circle, cursing the darkness. If only she could see the ties easier! She knew that every moment she spent pulling at his bindings was a moment they lost getting away.

"Katelyn . . ." Tipaakke rolled back his head, not finishing his sentence. He could tell there would be no reasoning with her; he'd seen that look on her face before. "Hurry," he finally whispered. "It may be hours before someone notices we're gone, but it might be minutes. We must move quickly."

Letting out a gasp of breath, Katelyn struggled with the stone-hard leather. Finally, the binding came loose and she unwound the loops that entwined his feet. Giving him her hand, she helped him up.

"Run," he whispered through the darkness, nodding to the south. "Move."

Without another word, Katelyn slipped into the dense forest, refusing to look back. At first, they ran ducking and dodging as they made their frantic escape.

They didn't know how far behind the Mohawks would be, so they ran like the wind. Katelyn's moccasins barely touched the soft earth as they made their way back in the direction they'd come. Taking the lead, Tipaakke ran sure footed, refusing to stop long enough to let Katelyn untie his hands. "I'm fine," he reassured her. "We must keep moving until you can't run another step and then we must run a few more. Only then can we stop."

Finally, when her headdress became too heavy, Katelyn collapsed on the ground. "Must stop," she breathed. "Just for a minute, then we can go on." She was exhausted. Her stomach ached and her head pounded with pain. "I'm sorry."

"Shhhhh . . ." Tipaakke dropped onto the ground beside her, resting his cheek on her hair for a moment. He knew he was pushing her hard, but he had to. Her life depended on it. "Rest for a moment and then work on my ties," he soothed. "Then we'll go. They may not even realize we're gone until morning."

Katelyn raised her head from the ground. "But then they'll come looking for us, won't they?" She lifted her hands to his bindings.

"Maybe not." His eyes met hers in the darkness and then he nodded. "Yes, probably." He wished that he could comfort her with words of reassurance. He wished he could tell her that the Mohawks would just move on without them, but he couldn't lie. He couldn't give her false hope. She had to realize the severity of their situation if they were going to make it back to the village alive.

Loosening one knot and then the other, Katelyn worked in silence. She was too tired to talk. Too frightened to voice her thoughts. She knew their chances of getting away were slim, but at least they were together. She couldn't have left Fox behind, she'd sooner have stayed. "There," she whispered, rubbing his wrists where the leather ties had cut into his flesh. "You're free." She smiled weakly.

Tipaakke reached out with his arms, drawing her close to his body. He brushed his lips over her tangled hair, crooning sweet words. Katelyn relaxed against his hard chest, pulling her cloak closer to ward off the cool night air. Then, reluctantly, she raised her head. "It's time we moved on, Tipaakke Oopus."

He nodded, getting up off the bed of leaves, pulling her with him. "We won't go much further. Then we'll sleep a while."

"No." She shook her head adamantly. "I don't need to sleep. I'm fine." She started down the deer path they were following, but he grabbed her hand.

"No. We'll sleep while we have the chance. If the Mohawks follow us, there will be no more sleep." He started to run, guiding her with his hand. "You need the rest. You've not had a good meal or night's sleep in days. You must not grow too tired, you must be able to keep moving."

Accepting what Tipaakke said, Katelyn continued to run beside him, not speaking to conserve energy. She was six moons pregnant and exhausted. She didn't know how long she would be able to keep up this pace. But she'd run until she dropped. It was her only chance; it was their only chance.

For hours Katelyn and Tipaakke trudged on, running, then walking, then running again. They followed the narrow deer paths, the light of the moon showing them the way. They spoke little, stopping only when Katelyn was forced to.

Slowing his pace, Tipaakke turned to look behind him. She was still running, but her head hung low, her shoulders were slumped. She wouldn't make it much further. Her body was not used to taking this kind of

268

assault. She'd not been born to run with the wind as he had. Dropping to a walk, he wrapped his arm around her shoulder. "I'm thirsty," he told her, holding her tight, "I hear a stream that way." He motioned to the left. "We'll cut across and drink. Then we'll find a place to sleep. I think there's a cave nearby."

Katelyn leaned heavily on him, her voice barely a whisper. "How do you know where there's a cave? This area is too flat for mountains nearby." She ducked under the hanging branch he held for her.

"I recognize the trees. I've been here before hunting." He guided her in toward the stream. "I've told you before. I know this land for hundreds of miles. I was born here. My father was born here. Maybe I was born knowing the land." He knelt by the stream's edge, cupping water in his hand for her. "When a man's mind is not cluttered with the things the white man's mind is, there's room for much knowledge."

Katelyn drank water from his hand. "But how can there be a cave out here?" She leaned to drink with her own hands this time.

"I will show you."

Taking Katelyn's hand, Tipaakke led her downstream, following a winding course. In a few minutes he pointed to a steep bank on the opposite side where the soil had eroded and trees had fallen into the water, their roots still embedded in the bank. "There," he told her.

"There what?" She peered at the opposite bank curiously. "I don't see anything, Fox."

"Look beyond the roots. The bank is hollowed out where the water has washed away the dirt. We'll be safe there; you'll be able to get some rest."

"I don't suppose there's a bridge?" She smiled wearily.

He shook his head, glad to see she could still smile.

"No. We'll have to walk across. Give me your cloak and I'll keep it dry. We can wrap up in it until our clothes dry."

"Not safe to build a fire?" Katelyn searched his face in the dawning light.

He shook his head again. "Come." He took the cloak from her shoulders and stepped into the water. Katelyn followed behind, stopping in the middle, where it was waist deep, to wash her face and arms. Then she moved on, coming up on the opposite side beside Tipaakke.

Once on the bank, Katelyn began to slip her food and water bags off her head and pull off her dress. The cool early morning breeze made her shiver as she removed the damp things. "Brrrr!" She rubbed her bare arms briskly. "I hope the sun is hot today."

"It will be." Removing his linen shirt and loin cloth, Tipaakke slipped off his moccasins. "Give me your dress and moccasins. I will hang them in the trees to dry." He held out a hand.

"Is it safe to leave our things hanging in the trees? What if the Mohawks come?" She looped the dress over his arm. "They'll see our clothes and know we're here."

"If they get that close without us knowing, it would be too late anyway," he replied matter-of-factly. "Get inside with your cloak." He watched until her slim nude body disappeared through the brush that concealed the cave and then climbed the bank to hang the clothes.

Pushing her way through the dried roots and live brush, Katelyn entered the hollow in the bank. Once she ducked to clear the overhang, she was amazed to find how large the cave was. There, beneath the stream's bank, out of the wind, was a clean cozy place just big enough for her and Tipaakke to stretch out in. Wrapping her wolf-skin cloak and headdress around her for warmth, Katelyn sank to the hard dirt floor to wait for Tipaakke.

"Katie-girl?" Fox stuck his head in, the morning light streaming in through the hole in the brush he made.

"I'm in here."

Entering the cave, he rearranged the overhanging branches until they were in semidarkness again. "There isn't much food left. But I brought some dried berries and meat. We don't have time to snare anything this morning." He came to sit beside Katelyn.

"No. I'm not hungry. You eat it." She opened her cloak to him. "Get in here, I'm cold."

"We will both eat, whether we are hungry, or not. We need out strength." Moving over, he allowed her to drape the heavy cloak over his shoulders. "You are cold." Dropping the food bags at their feet, he wrapped an arm around her shoulder, pressing her body against his. "I'll have you warm in a minute. Want to lay down?"

"That would be nice." Katelyn waited until Tipaakke leaned back, his head resting on the dirt bank and then she laid down, her head resting on his chest. "I'm glad that wolf was so big," she told him snuggling against his warm body.

Tipaakke ran his hands through her hair, humming softly to himself. "Your hair is so beautiful. It feels differently than the hair of my people; it smells differently."

"It probably smells pretty badly right now." She laughed, scratching his bare thigh.

"I thought you were tired." Tipaakke's eyes met hers and he grinned. "You are never satisfied, are you, my vixen?" He ran an index finger over one peaked breast. "It is hard to believe that once you shunned my attention. Now you come looking for it."

"That was a very long time ago," Katelyn whispered, tickling his ear with her tongue. "I was young and foolish. I did not know the pleasures of a man and woman." Her finger traced a grapevine pattern over the curly patch at his groin, causing a stir.

Tipaakke groaned, his eyes resting on hers. "What a vixen you have become, my love. You tempt my very soul."

Katelyn lowered her eyelashes, pushing him onto his back until her wolf hide cradled them. "You are a most handsome man, do you know that?" She brushed her lips over his, drawn by his hot breath.

Tipaakke wove his fingers through her bright hair, forcing her mouth down hard on his. They kissed greedily, both fearing there would be no tomorrow.

Breathless, Katelyn pulled away, dropping her head onto his shoulder to inhale his mysterious masculine aroma. "Touch me," she murmured, running her fingers over his broad chest, lingering to tease his hard, male nipple.

Tipaakke joined in the rivalry, teasing her senses until his own soared. He watched her eyelid flutter as he brushed his fingertips over her budding nipple, coaxing her breast to a full peak. Sighing, he lowered his mouth to take the hardening bud, tugging at it with his teeth until she whimpered with pleasure. Arching her back, she ran her fingers through his long, sleek hair, guiding his head to the other breast. Running her hands over the wide expanse of his back, Katelyn explored each muscle, every tendon, massaging, kneading, sending shivers of delight down his spine.

"You are my heart," Tipaakke rasped, rolling her onto her back. He could feel her body hot and pliant beneath his as he lowered his head over her, drawing in her dark eyes. "You are my life." His lips met her softly. "How did I ever live these years without you?"

Katelyn pressed her lips to his fingertips, guiding his hand with hers. "You are my savior. I'll love you until the end of time for that."

"Hush. There will be no end of time for us. We live together in this world and then the next. Now love me, Katie. Love me."

Her eyes drifted shut as his kiss deepened, his hand spanning her stomach. Taking his sweet tongue in her mouth, she taunted it, sucking on it, tugging at it with her teeth. When his hand passed over her thighs she moaned softly thrusting her hips. "You are a tease," she murmured.

"It is what you like," he replied, slipping down. Planting soft, feathery kisses over her breasts and abdomen, he lowered his body until his chin rested in her patch of downy hair. With his tongue he made moist circles as she writhed beneath him, crying out his name. Twisting her fingers in his hair, she moved her hips to that ancient rhythm she'd come to know so well. Finally, when she could no longer stand the searing flames of desire that coursed through her aching body, she tugged at his arms. "Please," she begged, intoxicated by his love, "I need to feel you inside me. I need to feel a part of you."

Pressing his hard body to hers, he brushed aside the damp hair that clung to her face. "Shhh," he murmured, moving against her. "You have been a part of me since that first day. We are one."

Katelyn reached to run her palm over his cheek and then guided his mouth to hers. She moved her hips against his male hardness, fueling her own throbbing hunger. All conscious thought slipped from her mind as their legs twisted and their breath came faster.

Probing, Tipaakke guided his manhood to the hot, wet heart of her femininity and Katelyn arched her hips to welcome him, crying out with pleasure. At first, they moved slowly, letting the waves of building desire wash over them, but then she became more anxious and speeded up the rhythm. The two moved as one, and together they climbed higher, meeting at each crest of the building wave. Then, suddenly, a shudder coursed through Katelyn and she cried out, her fingers tightening on Tipaakke's shoulders until her knuckles turned white. When she relaxed, he picked up the rhythm again, pressing kisses to her damp face and shoulders. She threw back her arms, half laughing as she was caught up in the tide of love again.

Then, when Tipaakke could hold back no longer, he moved against her, hard and demanding, thrusting her towards another peak of ecstasy. Half sobbing, Katelyn clung to him, calling out with intense pleasure as her body convulsed again and again. With one more thrust and a euphoric shudder, Tipaakke collapsed on Katelyn, resting his head on her shoulder.

Together, the two rested in silence. Tipaakke shifted his weight to move beside her and layed his head on one rounded breast. Katelyn ran her hands over his back and buttocks, massaging his sleek muscles until she felt his wet tongue teasing her nipple.

"What do you think you're doing?" She scratched his head with her fingernails and he moved it with encouragement.

"I'm doing nothing." His voice was laced with amusement.

She giggled, pushing back his head. "Stop! That hurts." She tried to sound angry.

"It does not hurt." He stuck out his tongue to lick one hard, pink nipple. "You didn't mind a few moments ago."

She squirmed beneath him. "That was different."

"Oh, it was, was it." He caught her nipple with his teeth and tugged on it gently.

Katelyn arched her back, a faint flicker of desire running through her body again. She ran her hands through his black hair, a hum of pleasure coming from her lips. "You're insatiable," she murmured.

"I don't know this word, insatiable, but I know I never tire of you." He moved up until his face hung over hers, entwining his fingers in hers. "Come ride with me again, and this time we will take it slowly." He grinned devilishly.

Another hour passed as they satisfied each other's hungers, calming each other's fears, safe in their dark cave. And then they slept, content in one another's arms.

Chapter Twelve

It was nearly noon by the time Katelyn and Tipaakke dressed themselves and got back on the trail. As much as he hated to wake her, he knew that every moment counted if they were going to stay ahead of the Mohawks. Though he'd tried to convince himself the Indians might not even have come after them, he knew the chances of that would be slim. They were fierce warriors, and they didn't like being made fools of. If the Mohawks caught the Delaware brave and his wolf-woman, they would torture and kill them both.

With the sun beaming high overhead, Tipaakke headed south. Single file the two walked saying little. What was there to say? They were running for their lives and they knew it.

Desperately, Katelyn tried to keep up. She didn't want to slow Tipaakke down; she couldn't bear the thought of being responsible for his death. She wanted him to live, even if she couldn't.

"Keeping walking, Katie-girl. You are doing well." Tipaakke glanced over his shoulder, giving her encouragement.

"You, my love, are a liar." She tried to give him that saucy grin she knew he loved.

Tipaakke dropped back, draping his arm around her shoulders. The deer path they were following barely accommodated them side by side. "It is not wise to call a Lenni Lenape brave a liar. He might slit your throat for it."

"But only if he was not a liar." She smiled weakly, forcing herself to put one foot in front of the other. She was so tired; she could have slept for a week. She felt as if she'd barely closed her eyes this morning and Tipaakke was shaking her awake.

"I am sorry that this has happened. I wish that I could change what has passed." He fingered her hair.

"But you cannot." She shrugged her shoulders. "It's in the stars. Now will you please get back in front of me and keep the branches out of my face?" She tried to keep her voice light. She didn't want him to know how truly exhausted she was.

Into the afternoon they walked, cutting from one deer path to another, crossing streams, and climbing over fallen trees. Katelyn was amazed at how far she was able to walk when she didn't think she could take another step. But Tipaakke always coaxed her back on her feet, teasing, laughing, kissing her, giving her a reason to go on.

As the sun began its bright-orange descent over the horizon, Tipaakke began to search for a place to camp for the night. Had he been alone, he would have continued on until he reached his village another two days away. But Katelyn would never make it. She needed food and a place to rest. She needed a whole night's sleep.

Stopping near a stream, Tipaakke leaned to drink, motioning Katelyn to do the same. Flopping down, Katelyn took her fill.

"I think we will rest here for the night." Tipaakke stared into her tired brown eyes.

"No!" She grabbed his arm. "We can't stop. We've

277

got to keep going. They'll catch us! They'll kill us! They'll kill our baby," she sobbed.

"Shhhh," he hushed, taking her in his arms. "It's all right. I won't let them, Katie-girl." He kissed her tear-streaked cheeks. "I would kill you myself before I would let those animals touch you."

Katelyn sniffed, leaning her head on his solid chest. "Let's just rest a little and then move on. I just need a little sleep."

Rocking her in his lap, Tipaakke rested his chin on her head. "Yes," he soothed. "We'll just rest a little while and then we'll go. Now come and lay down here under the trees." He got to his feet and swung her into his arms.

"Put me down, Fox. I can walk." Her eyebrows furrowed.

"I know you can, you feisty vixen. But is there anything wrong with a man wanting to hold his woman?" He kneeled beneath a tall oak.

"No, I guess not," she answered sleepily.

"Now you wrap up here in your cloak and go to sleep." He tightened the closure on the wolf headdress. "I'm going to see if I can find us something to eat."

She stretched out a hand to him. "Please don't leave me. It'll be getting dark soon." She clasped his hand tightly, feeling like a small, lost child.

Tipaakke kissed her hand. "I won't, now hush. Go to sleep. I will wake you when the moon is bright and we will move on. Will that suit you?"

"Not too long." She held up a finger. "You come and rest too."

"I will, now go to sleep." He got to his feet and disappeared into the forest.

Snuggling down in the cloak, Katelyn drifted off into an exhausted, dreamless sleep.

"Katelyn." Tipaakke shook her shoulder vigorously. "Katelyn, wake up!"

Groggily, she opened her eyes, trying to focus. It was dark now, and only the light of the moon lit Tipaakke's face. "Is it time to go?" She yawned, stretching stiffly.

"Yes, hurry." He tugged insistently at her arm.

"Fox, what's the matter?" She got to her knees, peering into his hardened face. "They're coming." It was not a question, it was a statement. She could feel the chill that ran through his bones. Getting up, she pulled her cloak off the ground. "How far behind?"

"Very close. There's a scout party leading the way. The others are close behind." He took her face in his palms. "Listen to me, my love. We must do something."

Katelyn's eyes widened, but she said nothing. She was afraid to hear what was coming.

"We must separate."

"No," she breathed. The sound of the crickets and night birds filled her head. The trees rustled overhead. "I can't go on without you. I won't. They'd catch me." She shook her head frantically.

"Katelyn. We do not have time for this," he said sternly. He then regretted his tone when the tears welled in her eyes.

"You said you would care for me. You said you'd never leave me." Her voice was barely a whisper.

"I'm not leaving you and they won't get you. We're going to separate and meet back at the village." He shook her shoulders. "It's our only chance. I can lead them away from you."

"They'll catch you."

"They won't. I will lead them in the wrong direction and then I will disappear. I will take on the spirit of my

279

totem, the fox, and I will vanish before their eyes. Then I will double back. I will meet you at my village in less than two days."

Tipaakke's words numbed her. She didn't know how she could make it alone, but she knew this was the only way. "How do you know they will follow you and not me?" She dashed away her tears with the back of her hand.

"I will leave the trail of two. They will think we are together." He smoothed her hair with his hand, breathing in her scent. He wanted to remember every word, every touch. If he was killed, he would take the memory of her into the next life.

Katelyn nodded her head. "All right. I suppose you're right." She sniffed, holding back the tears. "Promise me you'll be there at the village when I get there." She wrapped her arms around his neck, laying her head on his shoulder. "Promise me you won't let them kill you."

"You find your way home, and I will be there, Katie-girl." He ran a hand over her rounded stomach. "Our child will have a father. Now you must go." The thought of letting her go alone tore at heart, making it difficult to breath. But it was the only way.

"Yes, I'll go. Which way?" She put up a hand helplessly. "I don't even know which way." She ran her hands over her meager supplies she carried in her bags, checking to be sure Tipaakke had filled the precious water bag.

"Go to the south half a day. Then into the morning sun. This is all Lenni Lenape land. You will come upon my people. They will know you are there before you do. Nothing happens on our land that we don't know about. Mekollaan may already be searching for us." His lips moved rapidly as he searched his brain, wishing he could give better directions. He had lived in these forests all his life. He just *knew* how to find his people.

"Here," Katelyn held out a small bag containing dried fish and berries. "Take this."

"No. I won't need it. I can find something in the forest to eat." He pushed the bag back at her.

Grasping his hand, Katelyn handed him the bag. "Take it. I have more than enough. I will be back in the village with Won in two days. How much can I eat? I will keep my water bag. You are better at finding water than I am." She tried to smile. *Will I ever see this face again*, she wondered.

"Now, go, Katie-girl. Don't worry about me. Be careful, and remember all I have taught you." He clasped her hand tightly, not wanting to let go.

"You've taught me much, Tipaakke Oopus. I will find your village. I will go home and wait for you." She brushed her thumb across his lips and pressed a kiss to it. "I will see you in a few days." She leaned until her lips met his and ran her fingers through his midnight hair, kissing him hungrily.

"I love you, wolf-woman." Tipaakke pulled away. He could have kissed those lips forever. "Go. Go swiftly."

A sob escaped Katelyn's lips as she pressed her mouth to his once more. And then she was gone, disappearing into the forest's cloak of darkness.

Once she was gone, Tipaakke turned his mind from her. She was in Manito's hands now. She would make it back, he knew it. Now he had to take care of the Mohawks. Quickly, he moved around the campsite, making it obvious that they'd been there. Then, he adjusted the brush where Katelyn had entered the forest. He was hoping that the Mohawks would be in such a hurry, they would pick up the obvious tracks

281

and follow him.

The hair rose on the back of Tipaakke's neck as he made his way down an old deer path, leading east. He knew the Mohawks had to be near. He could smell their evil, black hearts. Picking up his pace, he ran with his head thrown back. When he covered a good distance, he would leap off the path, into a tree and drop onto the ground in the forest. Then, he would return to the campsite, remove his moccasins and follow the deer path to the east again, walking beside his original tracks. Hopefully, the Mohawks would assume from the faint tracks that one of them had lost their moccasins. By the time they reached the end of the footprints and realized they'd been tricked, Tipaakke would be gone. He might even be able to catch up with Katelyn!

At first, after Katelyn left Tipaakke, she ran wildly, ducking and dodging the low-lying branches as she made her way south. But then, as her headdress became heavier, she realized that she would have to pace herself. She would never make it to the village if she pushed herself too hard. The forest was a dangerous place for a lone traveler — and even more dangerous at night. But she was going to make it. She knew it. She was going to reach the village and wait for Fox. He might even get there ahead of her!

With that thought in mind, Katelyn walked well through the night. She thought of all the good times she'd spent with Fox in the cabin and dreamed of the days to come with him. Looking up into the sky, Katelyn tried to figure the time. How long had she been walking? Was Fox safe? Had the plan worked? She stopped to drink from a small running brook.

Maybe at this very moment, she thought, Fox is drinking from another brook, safe and far from the Mohawks.

As the bright pinks of dawn began to peak above the woodsline, Katelyn began looking for a safe spot to rest. That all-too-brief nap she'd had earlier in evening had not been enough. She was near exhaustion again and she had to rest if she was going to make it to the village safely. Cutting off the deer path, she wandered through a thicket of ink berries and through a grove of ancient cedars. Just ahead, she spotted a huge fallen log. The tree, rotted by time and eaten by termites was the perfect place to hide. Fox would be proud of her when she told him about it!

Laying the headdress inside the hollow of the log, Katelyn crawled inside and tried to draw back the brush as best she could. Snuggling deep within the folds of the soft cloak, she slept dreamlessly.

Tipaakke steadied himself on the low branch, crouching to remain unseen. The Mohawks had been closer than he'd thought. He'd barely started on the second set of footprints when the scouts had reached their campsite. He reached down to retie his moccasins. There'd been no time to run after he'd finished the tracks, they would have heard or smelled him for sure. Besides, he wanted to be sure they didn't backtrack and go after Katelyn. Apprehensively, he waited in the tree, listening as the Mohawks drew closer. Good, Tipaakke thought. There are only two of them, if he had to, he could kill them both. He cursed silently for his lack of a knife. But the Mohawks had taken his and Katelyn's when they'd been captured. There'd been no way to steal one. He would have to kill them with his bare hands.

When the Mohawk scouts reached the point where the tracks mysteriously ended, there was a great hooting and hollering. They were burning mad. Though Tipaakke could only understand part of what they said, he could tell from his perch in the tree that they were mad enough to kill.

When the Indians turned back to retrace their steps, Tipaakke dropped silently to the ground and began to follow them. He hoped they were just going to return to the group and move north, but he had to be sure.

When the two Mohawks reached the campsite, they began to mill around. From the brush, Tipaakke watched, trying to make out their words. When they began to survey the bushes and got down on their knees to look at the grass, Tipaakke knew he was in trouble. They were searching for the true direction their captors had gone. They must have been sent by their leader to bring back him and Katelyn . . . dead or alive.

Without thought, Tipaakke rushed at the closest Mohawk, screeching as he knocked him to the ground from the rear and wrestled him over. Twisting the knife from the startled Mohawk's hand, he plunged it into his chest. Yanking the knife from the dying man's body, he tried to leap to his feet to take on the other Mohawk, but one foot was trapped beneath the dead man. He looked up just in time to see the war axe coming for his head. And then there was blackness . . .

Waking just before the sun was high in the sky, Katelyn drank from her bag, ate a few dried berries, and made her way back to the deer path. She knew she was taking her chances, traveling down the path, rather than through the open forest, but it was too difficult for her to make her way through the dense spring foliage. Until she reached the point where she thought she should head east, she would have to take the gamble and pray Tipaakke's trick worked.

As the late afternoon came, Katelyn's spirits began to drag. The novelty of the fear of being caught had worn off, the mosquitos were vicious, and she was afraid the path was leading her in the wrong direction. Squinting into the sun, she made a decision. It was time to turn east. It would be slower moving, but maybe she'd find another deer path leading in the right direction. Maybe she'd even find a road; she knew she had to be getting close to the white man's civilization. Tipaakke had told her that often roads were often made on the paths that the deer and Indians had traveled on for many years.

So, chewing on the last piece of dried venison she had, Katelyn stepped off the path and headed east. To her dismay, the sky was beginning to darken. The squirrels in the trees were chattering madly and the rabbits were scurrying everywhere. Heavy black clouds gathered and the wind picked up, making her thankful she still carried the burdensome wolf headdress. As she forced her way through a patch of green briars, she noted the change in the air, realizing that her ears were suddenly snapping and popping. That was how the animals had known a storm was brewing. Keeping her eye out for some sort of shelter, she quickened her pace, turning her face to catch the first light splashes of rain.

How am I going to get out of this? she asked herself miserably. The sky answered with a deafening rumble as a bright jag of lightening streaked across the sky. The rain began to pelt Katelyn's face in earnest as she

285

trudged on, doubting she would find any shelter here.

Up in the mountains there had been plenty of nooks and crevices in the rock to take shelter, but here, there was nothing but thousands of miles of great forest. Thinking of warm shelter, Katelyn smiled, remembering the night she'd spent with Tipaakke in an abandoned bear cave. They had tracked a deer for miles and when it had begun to rain, just as it was now, Tipaakke had taken her to a cave he had played in as a child. They spent the night together before the fire, telling stories and making love until dawn. Katelyn shivered, pulling the hide of the headdress closer. What she wouldn't have given to be safe in that cave with Fox right now.

As darkness overtook her, Katelyn continued to move on, soaked and miserable. After she'd tripped and fallen twice, she brushed the wet leaves from her hands and face and knelt to bend back the branches of a young sapling. She had to get some rest. Crawling under the make-shift roof of branches and leaves, she huddled under the meager protection and drifted into a fitful sleep.

When she woke at dawn, it was still raining. Soaked and stiff from sleeping on the wet ground, Katelyn felt worse than she had the night before. She was cold and tired and she couldn't stop shivering. But she knew she had to go on. She had to find the village.

It was mid-morning when James Carter spotted the Indian wearing the ceremonial headdress walking down the narrow dirt path. *That's odd*, he thought as he adjusted the brim of his leather hat to keep the rain off his face. *Why would an Indian be traveling one of our roads? They usually try to keep as far away from us as they can.* His hand slid to the flintlock on the wagon beside him. Maybe the Indian wasn't alone. He kept his eyes peeled, peering cautiously into the woods as he moved closer to the lone figure. He could see now that something was wrong. Was he sick? Hurt? Or was this some kind of Injun trick? James tightened his hand on his gun. But when he came up on him, he could see the man wearing the wolf's head could barely walk. He was swaying back and forth, his head rolling and his shoulders drooping. James wondered for a moment if he should stop or just move on. He didn't owe any Injun anything.

Katelyn never heard the wagon until it was right on top of her. She turned, startled by the sound to see the smooth haunches of a bay. Was she hallucinating? There weren't any horses in the forest . . . She blinked, confused by the fever that raged in her body and reached out to stroke the wet hair.

"Morning." James paused. He'd met plenty of Indians since he'd come to the Colonies, but he still didn't know quite how to handle them. They were an odd lot in his mind. He waited for the rain-drenched figure to answer.

Katelyn turned slowly to gaze at the man sitting on the wagon, dressed in oiled rain gear and wearing a wide-brimmed, leather hat. "Good morning," she answered, her voice distant. She felt as if her body was floating. She watched the man through a long tunnel of confusion. Was he real, or was he a dream?

"You speak English? Good." He nodded nervously. "Mighty poor day to be walkin'. Good for tobacco though." He watched the Indian closely, waiting for him to speak. But he said nothing, continuing to pat the horse. James cleared his throat. "Can I help you in some way?" He felt a little foolish addressing the wolf head. The Indian's face was completely masked by it.

Katelyn looked up. "Yes, I'm looking for a Lenni Lenape village near here. But I don't know where it is." She tugged at her cloak.

This is no Indian, James thought. *That's a woman's voice! A white woman!* He wrapped the reins around the brake and leaped to the ground. Why hadn't he noticed the dress beneath the cloak to begin with?

"You see, my husband . . . well, he's not really my husband . . . not yet." She lifted her hand to wipe her face. She was so confused. She wanted the man to help her find Fox, but she didn't know how to explain it. She couldn't remember the words.

"Your husband . . . Ma'am?" James reached out to steady the swaying woman. "You're not making sense, Ma'am." He stared at the dark brown eyes and heart-shaped face beneath the headdress. She didn't look much like a white woman, but she sure talked like one. "Are you sick, Ma'am?" He gripped her arm tightly.

"If you could just give me a ride. Just for a while." Spots of darkness flashed in front of her eyes as she tried to focus on the concerned face beside her. "Then I can walk again. I have to get back. The Mohawks, you see they . . ." Her voice trailed off into silence. He didn't seem to understand what she was saying.

"Ma'am, I think you'd better ride with me apiece." He turned her around and guided her to the side of the wagon. "Are you hurt anywhere?"

"No." She shook her head, smiling weakly. "Not hurt. Just tired. So tired. Cold . . . so cold in the forest today." She leaned heavily against him.

Steadying her, James jumped onto the wagon and reached down to help her up. "Don't worry, Ma'am. I got a place not too far from here. The wife will get you warmed right up. A little food and a fire will do

288

wonders for you. Then we'll talk." He settled her down on the seat beside him and picked up the reins. "Get up, Bess," he commanded. As the wagon lurched forward, the girl slumped over on the seat.

Katelyn woke slowly to the sound of a crackling fire and the smell of pork frying. As memory of the man in the wagon flashed in her mind, she shot straight up in bed. She had to keep moving. She couldn't be laying in bed! Bed? What bed?

"Good morning to you. Feeling better?"

Katelyn glanced quickly around the one-room cabin, her eyes coming to rest on a plump young girl. "Where am I?" She slid her feet to the floor noticing that she wore a simple white nightgown.

"I'm Pris Carter. My husband brought you here yesterday." She flipped the fat slice of pork over, and it crackled and spit in response. "We're beginning to think you'd never wake up." She wiped her hands on her apron and moved to the simple pine table in front of the huge fireplace.

"You mean I've been here since yesterday?" Katelyn stood up, clutching the frame of the rope-bed for support. Her knees were weak and her stomach was queasy. "Where are my clothes? I can't stay here. I've already wasted precious time." She moved to the table.

"That wolf thing is hanging in the barn drying, but the dress couldn't be saved. All torn up it was. How long were you out there in that woods?" She reached for a pitcher and poured a tankard of rich white milk. "Drink. It's good for the child." She motioned to Katelyn's round stomach, obvious beneath the thin nightgown.

Katelyn reached for the pewter cup and took a big

289

gulp of the sweet, warm stuff, licking the foam from her upper lip. "I thank you and your husband for caring for me, but I really must go. Could I have my dress and my moccasins?" She put the empty cup on the table hoping Pris would offer her another. How long had it been since she'd had a meal?

"We burned the Indian dress. It told you it was too torn up to wear. All of your possibles hanging out the way they were." Pris shook her head, crossing to the fireplace to check the frying meat again. "There's a dress there you can put on." She pointed to the end of the bed Katelyn had just gotten out of. "Better get it on. James and the boys'll be in shortly."

Katelyn stood for a moment in indecision and then threw up her hands in exasperation, going to get the dress. If she was getting out of here she'd have to wear something. She'd find her headdress in the barn on the way out. "Where're my bags? I've got to have the water bag." She slipped the nightgown over head, turning to speak as she did. Any modesty she'd once had was gone. It never even occurred to her that she should have asked for a more private place to change.

Pris turned to answer and swung back around, a faint blush creeping across her cheeks. How long had that poor girl been with the Indians, she wondered. "Don't worry about those, Katelyn. They're out in the barn with the wolf thing." She reached for the pewter plates on the mantel, taking care to keep her back to her.

"How do you know my name? I didn't tell your husband my name." Katelyn pulled the simple cotton dress over her head. She was glad Pris was larger than she was. The dress fit loosely and would be good for traveling. It would cover her growing stomach a little longer, too.

290

When James and his two sons walked in, Katelyn was still waiting for an answer. Why was Pris looking at her so strangely?

Katelyn walked to James and reached out to touch his arm. "How do you know who I am?" Like any Delaware, she came straight to the point. "What do you know about me?" Her soft brown eyes met uneasy blue ones.

"Sit." He extended an arm. "Eat. Then we'll talk." He took his hat off his head, put it on a wall peg and slipped past her. The twin boys of five or six did the same, staring with clear blue eyes as they took their seats on the bench at the table.

Katelyn stood with one hand on her hip watching the family pass the plates of steaming pork and biscuits. The aroma tantalized her senses as she considered her options. Something just wasn't right here. Should she make a run for it now? She watched one of the young boys take a bite of a biscuit, yellow butter running down his chin. Or, should she have her meal, get her things, and go? She took a step in the direction of the table. They certainly seemed harmless enough. After all, they had taken care of her since yesterday. She slid onto the bench beside the boys. Just one biscuit and a slice of pork and then she'd go . . . well, maybe two biscuits.

"Tell me what you know about me." Katelyn spoke to James with her mouth crammed with biscuit. It was so good!

James stabbed at a bit of pork with his knife and pushed it into his mouth. "I know you've been through a lot. People don't survive being captured by Indians very often."

"I was lucky." She took another biscuit from the plate and dipped into the butter crock with her knife. "There

291

were others who didn't get away. My husband and I outsmarted them." She saw no harm in the small lie, he would be her husband soon. She looked up at Pris. "Do you think I could take a few of these with me?" She held up her fourth biscuit. "I can't pay you for them now, but once I reach the village, I'll send something back in return. My husband will pay you handsomely for caring for me."

Pris glanced up at her husband, pushing a blond wisp of hair back off her face. The poor girl had been through so much, it was a wonder she had any sense at all.

"Don't worry, you're safe now. There's probably no helping those others." James pushed his plate back. "We don't have much luck getting captives back."

"No. I know where they're going. I *can* help." Katelyn got up from the bench, grabbing several biscuits and the last slice of pork. "If you could just give me my bags and robe, I'll go. I shouldn't have stayed this long." She watched as James' Adam's apple bobbed up and down. "Get my bags," she repeated.

"Why don't you just sit down and rest. In your condition, it's a wonder you've survived. You're safe here. Someone will be here to get you soon." The farmer brushed back his chestnut brown hair, wishing there was more he could do for the girl.

"Someone? Who?" She stuffed the biscuits and pork in the bodice of the dress and started for the door. "Who knows I'm here?"

James stepped between her and the door. He just had to keep her here a little longer. "Calm down. You'll be fine."

"Get out of my way," Katelyn ordered, glaring at him. "Move."

He shook his head. "Can't do that. I promised I'd

292

keep you here until he got here." James stood his ground.

"Who?" Katelyn tried to squelch the rising fear she felt in the pit of her stomach. She felt like a trapped animal.

Pris stepped in. "Your betrothed. Don't you remember him? Henry Bullman?"

His name sent a shock through her body as hard as if she'd been hit by summer lightning. "Henry . . . here?"

"Do you remember him? Poor, girl. They've had you almost a year." Pris reached out to comfort the girl.

Katelyn recoiled like a threatened animal. Ducking, she darted between James and the door, flinging it open and making her escape. Out into the barnyard she ran. She had to get her cloak and bags. Then she'd be gone. She knew she couldn't live in the forest without her water bag. Ducking into the wooden barn she searched frantically for her cloak. As her eyes adjusted to the dim light, she spotted her cloak and bags hanging from the rafters and reached for them. She could hear shouting and the sound of horses outside. Please, she begged, don't let him be here. Pulling the headdress on, she dropped the bags over her head and crept back to the door. It was the only way out of the small barn.

When she peeked around the corner, she spotted Henry immediately. No one could miss that flaxen hair. She couldn't let them capture her. She had to get back to the village. She was late already. When she realized she only had one choice, Katelyn made her move. If she could just get through the barnyard into the woods, she'd be safe. They wouldn't be able to catch her once she made it to the woods. Tipaakke's totem, the fox, would guide her deep into the forest where they could never find her.

293

The moment Katelyn sprang from the barn, James and Henry were on her. She'd miscalculated the distance to the wood's edge and only made it halfway across before they fanned out, reaching for her. Katelyn bit down hard on Henry's forearm. When he let go of her, howling in pain, she circled around James and dove for the underbrush in the pines. Just as she slipped under a tangle of honeysuckle the dog caught her leg. She'd never even saw the dog coming. Down on her hands and knees, she kicked at the hound with her free leg, ignoring the searing pain that ripped through her body as he sank his teeth into her calf.

When Henry and James pulled the dog off Katelyn and slid her body out from under the tangled brush at the woodsline, they thought she'd fainted. James pulled the linen shirt from his back to wrap her leg wound. Priscilla!" he shouted. "Get water and something to clean a wound with." Henry kneeled in the grass beside her, cradling her hand.

Katelyn stared at the two men through thick lashes as she remained perfectly still. Their voices seemed far in the distance as she wracked her brain to figure out how to get away. She relaxed her muscles and remained limp as they carried her back to the cabin.

"No. Bring her to the wagon," Henry ordered in a low voice. "It's just a flesh wound."

"But she needs the wound washed and dressed." Pris held a pot of water she'd been heating to wash the plates in. She wondered if she should tell him his betrothed was pregnant, even though she and James had agreed some things were left better unsaid.

"My uncle lives not more than an hour's ride from here. He's a doctor. He'll care for her. Please help me." He ran a hand through his blond hair, giving the farmer and his wife one of his best smiles. "She's been through enough. The wound isn't very deep. She'll be fine."

James moved slowly to help him, wondering if he just shouldn't insist they take her into the cabin. Still, the man had sailed all the way to England to bring her back for a wife. The two knew each other well, according to Bullman. Maybe he should just mind his business. After all, women fainted all the time.

Katelyn remained relaxed as they placed her in the rear of the wagon. She would wait until they were down the road, and then she'd just jump out of the wagon and run. She smiled to herself. Tipaakke would be proud of his woman.

Henry jumped up into the wagon and took the reins. "Thank you much for caring for Katelyn until I could get here." He reached into his coat. "I'm sure this will be more than enough to pay for your troubles." He handed James a small bag of coins and gave the reins a slap before another word could be said.

James held his wife's hand, watching as they disappeared down the narrow woods path. "I hope we did the right thing, Pris, he was in quite a hurry to get her away from here."

Pris shook her head. "Just wait 'till he finds out one of those Indians has gotten her with child. He's going to be in a real pickle then."

Henry was no sooner out of sight of the cabin when he pulled the wagon to a halt. "What kind of games are you playing, Katelyn Locke?" He turned to look down on her where she lay behind the wagon seat. "I know you haven't fainted. I could see you watching us. Why would you embarrass me like that?"

Katelyn sat up, and Henry's hand whipped out to catch her wrist. "Let me go . . ." she warned quietly.

"Let you go? I've gone to a lot of trouble to get here.

You've been saved, girl. What's wrong with you?" He tightened his grip on her wrist, wondering if she really had lost her senses.

"No want to be saved," she hissed, purposely speaking in broken English. She narrowed her eyes, boring vicious holes in his.

Henry stared at her, frightened by the look in her eyes. He reached beneath the wagon seat still holding her wrist and pulled out a length of rope.

"No!" Katelyn shouted, trying to twist away from him. "Let go. Leave me. I'm Lenni Lenape now." She placed her free hand on her heart.

Henry ignored her, tying her wrist to the side of the wagon. He had to get the girl to his uncle's as fast as possible. He'd know what to do with her. He'd know how to help her.

When the wagon pulled up in front of the large, red-brick farm house, Katelyn still hadn't been able to convince Henry to let her go. He thought her capture had somehow warped her mind.

Katelyn pulled at the rope that bound her wrist. "Don't do this, Henry. If I have to see this uncle of yours, at least untie me. You don't want to take your betrothed to meet your uncle tied to a wagon." She smiled, softening her brown eyes. "Please, Henry." If he would just untie her, she knew she could get away.

Henry ran his hand over his chin, considering her words. "No, you're right. It isn't very proper is it?" Picking up the reins, he clicked to the horse. "We'd better go around back."

"Henry! How could you do this to me, after all I've been through?" She kneeled behind the wagon seat, resting her hand on his shoulder. He smelled of whiskey and tobacco. There was no hint of the clean masculine smell Katelyn remembered of Tipaakke.

"Let me walk in."

"You tried to run from me. You've been pulling on the rope since we left the Carters'. Katelyn, I saw you chewing on that rope. You're not responsible for what you do." He patted her hand. "My uncle is a doctor. He'll be able to help."

Katelyn yanked back her hand, letting out an exasperated smile. *Maybe I'd better to play along*, she thought. *I need better clothing, food, a knife. And I need to get a better idea of where the village is.* Her first thought was to run the first chance she got, but the more she thought about it, the more she realized she'd be better to bide her time. She couldn't risk getting lost in the forest again. She was already late. Tipaakke would be waiting for her at the village.

Henry jumped down from the wagon and followed a brick path to the summer kitchen. "I'll be back with my aunt," he called over his shoulder.

Katelyn stepped over the wagon seat and sat down. She ran her hand over her round stomach, wondering where she'd be when the child was born. Thoughts of a young child running in and out of Tipaakke's wigwam flooded her mind. They could have such a good life, a happy life. Why was everything against them? She raised her head at the sound of a door. A tall, thin, matronly woman was walking in her direction with Henry in tow. *Here I go*, Katelyn thought. *If I can play a crazy wolf-woman, I can play a poor girl captured by wild Indians.* She laughed to herself . . . the only time she'd ever seen Tipaakke wild was on her mat . . . and she liked that.

"Good morning, dear." The woman put out her hand for Katelyn. "Untie her, Henry, this instant," she ordered.

Katelyn plastered on her best forlorn look and smiled down at the woman, taking her hand. "Good morning," she answered weakly.

"You poor child. Let me help you down. What you need is a good meal and rest. Let Aunt Minnie help you down."

Katelyn allowed the aunt to help her down, leaning on her broad shoulder. As they walked toward a door to the main house, Aunt Minnie turned back to Henry. "Take the wagon to the barn, Henry. Your uncle is waiting for you in the library." She nodded her head sternly. "I'm going to get little Katelyn tucked into bed."

Aunt Minnie took Katelyn up a back stairway and into a small but adequately furnished bedroom. "Jenny will be bringing up water for your bath immediately." She pointed at the big brass tub. "It's my pride and joy. When George said we were going to the Colonies, I said, George, I'll go, but not without my tub. He brought it all the way from England twenty years ago." She made herself busy folding and refolding a thin white nightgown that lay on the bed.

Katelyn nodded politely. "A bath would be wonderful. It's been days since I had one."

"They let you bathe?" Aunt Minnie's eyes grew wide. George had instructed her not to question the poor girl but she just couldn't resist.

"Of course. Tipaakke, the man who took care of me, . . ." Katelyn watched Aunt Minnie's eyes grow even wider. ". . . took a bath at least once a day in the creek. We were lucky if my stepmother bathed once a month." She leaned to look at the window, down on freshly plowed fields.

Minnie was at a loss for words when Jenny came to the door with the water.

"Boiling hot she is," Jenny told her Mistress, eyeing the red-haired girl that stood at the window.

"Well, stop standing there gawking. Pour it in with the cold." She pointed to the tub, already half full of water.

Jenny did as her Mistress bid, stealing another look at the girl as she went out the door. *Lordy*, Jenny thought. *She don't look crazy*. But from what she'd heard Master Henry saying in the library, she was plumb out of her tree. He said she was trying to get back to those savages! Jenny shuddered. The girl should have just killed herself when she got loose. It would have been the only proper thing to do.

Minnie waited until Jenny closed the door behind her and then spoke. "Come, Katelyn. Let me help you into the tub while it's still hot." She reached out her arms.

Katelyn's hand flew to her mouth in panic. No! She couldn't let her see her naked! The dress covered her belly, but without it, there was no doubt she was with child. She couldn't let them know. She was smart enough to know that while it might be acceptable to be rescued from savages, it would not be acceptable to carry one of their children. God only knew what they would do to her and her baby if they found out! Terrified, Katelyn shook her head. "No. Please. I'd rather be alone." She dropped her eyes demurely.

Aunt Minnie thought for a minute and then nodded. "All right, love. Take your bath and get into bed. Jenny will be up with a tray of tea and sweet biscuits shortly."

Katelyn listened to the door shut and to a bolt slide across the door. That's why she wasn't in the main part of the house! They were locking her in!

Henry paced the hardwood floor of his uncle's library. What was he going to do with her? He wished for the one hundredth time that his father was still alive to give him guidance. Things were such a mess at home. The tobacco had been planted late, one of the granaries had burned down, and now his fiancé had appeared from the dead, half crazed! Henry ran his fingers through his flaxen hair, his blue eyes coming to rest on his uncle's face. "What do you think, sir? What am I to do?" He threw up his arms helplessly.

George Bullman looked at the young man standing on the thick, woven rug. *Poor boy*, he thought. *He was ill-suited to life in the Colonies and he knew it. He had none of the hardworking adventurous spirit that his father had been loved dearly for. Henry belonged in England, or France. He would have done well at court.* George shifted his gaze, knowing he made the boy nervous. "She may come out of it, Henry. I've heard of cases where women were missing for years and returned to lead a healthy, normal life."

"Not many though . . ." Henry ran his boot along the edge of the rug dejectedly. "I don't know if I can help her."

"She's your responsibility, Henry. You certainly can't send her back to England." George moved from behind his chair. "Give her time. She may still be marriable, and if not, well . . . we'll think of something. There are places we could send her."

"But what do I do with her now? We can't keep her locked up there forever." He motioned above his head.

George shook his head. "No, we can't. I think it would be best if you took her home. That laudanum that I put in the tea should make it easy to transport her. You can take her home this evening. Once you've got her back at your place, treat her just as you would

300

have a year ago. Just don't let her out of your sight. She may be fine." He shrugged his broad shoulders.

"Are you sure we should have drugged her?" Henry looked to his uncle for reassurance, just as he had as a child.

George patted him on the back. "It's the best thing I know for a hysterical woman!" He laughed until Henry joined in.

Katelyn struggled to wake up. She felt as if she was drowning, only her breath came easily. Each time she thought she had almost reached the surface, another wave pushed her down again. She tried to stretch, to move her arms and legs, but her muscles refused to respond. She fought to raise her eyelids, as she listened to voices far in the distance.

". . . almost a year, she has. The master thought she was long gone . . . such a shock . . . to think, as big as she is . . . killed myself, I would have . . ."

The voices faded in and out as Katelyn pulled herself to the surface again. What was wrong with her? Where was she? Where was Fox? She needed Fox! Slowly her eyelids raised and she tried to focus. A woman . . . two women . . . servants.

"Pssst . . . she's movin'. Better get the master!" The woman giggled, nudging the other.

Katelyn wiggled her fingers and toes, thankful to have feeling in them again. By the time Henry came in the door, she was half sitting up.

"Katelyn!' Henry clasped her hand in his. "So glad to see you're feeling better."

Katelyn sat up a little straighter. "Henry . . ." She rubbed her eyes with her free hand. "Where are we, Henry? This isn't your aunt and uncle's."

"No. We came home yesterday. Uncle George gave you a little something to make you sleep." He patted her hand rapidly with his clammy one.

"Yesterday!" She jerked her hand away. "You drugged me!" Yesterday! Another day lost! "How could you do such a thing, Henry?"

He turned to motion the two maids out of the room. "Now, dear . . ."

"Don't dear me, Henry Bullman!" She spoke through clenched teeth.

Henry walked to the window. "I was hoping you would be feeling better." His voice was tense.

"I was feeling fine before you drugged me!" She swung her feet over the side of the bed and sat up.

"Uncle George is a doctor. He knows what's best for you." Henry leaned on the window sill, wishing he were anywhere but here.

"If *you* know what's good for *you*, you'll let me go. All I need is some food and water. Where are my things?" She slid her bare feet to the floor and stood up shakily. "Where are they?"

"You're not going anywhere. It's my job to protect you." He nodded his head, repeating his uncle's words.

"Protect me!" She spoke louder with each word. "I don't need any protection, except from you!"

Henry turned away to keep from looking at her in the thin white gown. "Get back in bed, you're not decent!"

"I'm perfectly decent. You're the only one around here who's not decent. And let me tell you something, Henry Bullman. If you don't let me go, you're going to wish you'd had someone here to protect you!" She pushed a finger into his back.

Henry turned slowly, keeping his back straight. His uncle was right. It was time he started acting like a

302

man. "You are my betrothed. You belong to me and you are staying here. I'm sorry that this has happened to you. I want to help you, but you have to let me." Now that he was warmed up, the words came more easily. "Now, once the . . . ," he cleared his throat, "um . . . child is born and sent away, we can proceed with our plans to marry. I've thought long and hard about this and I know it's my duty to marry you . . ."

"Marry you! Send my child away!" Her hands went instinctively to her belly. "I wouldn't marry you if you were the last man alive. And you're not sending my baby anywhere!" She grabbed two handfuls of his white linen shirt. "I have someone who wants to marry me. Someone who loves me. Now let me go!" Her last words practically deafened Henry.

"I don't want to hear about it . . . not any of it!" Henry curled up his lip, raising his voice to match hers. "And I don't want to hear anything about *him*." He started to back towards the door, ripping his shirt out of her hands. "You ruined everything, you know." He wiped at his damp eyes. "You weren't supposed to come back." He continued to back away from her, a step at a time. "You were supposed to be dead."

"Well, I'm not dead, no thanks to you," Katelyn shouted, stalking him.

"Hush. The servants will hear you."

"I don't care who hears me! You've already told them all that I'm crazy. Who would pay any attention to the rantings of a crazy woman?" Katelyn backed him against the door. "Who would listen to a crazy woman who said her betrothed left her to save his own skin!"

Henry shook his head violently, beginning to anger. "No one!" He lowered his voice. "No one would listen to such a thing." He smiled, staring her straight in the eye.

303

Katelyn suddenly realized the truth of his words. She took a step back, knowing she'd greatly underestimated Henry Bullman. He was dangerous, very dangerous. She wasn't with the Indians anymore. She had no rights. She was his property to do with as he pleased. The betrothal papers gave him that right. Katelyn tugged at her bottom lip with her teeth. What was she going to do now?

Henry straightened his shirt and reached for the door latch. "I will be back this evening to check on you. Perhaps by then you'll be feeling well enough to talk sensibly." He gave her a nod and slipped out the door.

Katelyn listened to the heavy bolt slide into place. Leaning against the door, she slid to the floor, her arms encircling her belly. A sob wracked her body. She didn't even know if Fox was safe! And now she was locked up in a bedroom. Wiping her tears with the hem of her nightgown, she sat up straighter, drawing up her knees. She couldn't feel sorry for herself like this. She didn't have time for such foolishness. She had to devise a plan to escape. When her eyes came to rest on the single window, she jumped to her feet. Maybe . . . but as soon as she reached it and pushed it open, she realized she'd been put in this room for a reason. She was two and a half stories off the ground; there was nothing to climb down—only the sheer brick exterior wall.

Taking a seat on the floor, Katelyn reached for a biscuit on the side table. If she was going to escape, she'd have to get Henry to let her out of the room.

When Henry returned to Katelyn's bedroom that evening, he found her looking much like she had the day he met her. She was wearing a dress of soft browns and wore her hair tied back with a narrow ribbon. The only evidence of the past year's events was her rich, dark suntan . . . and her protruding abdomen.

"Good evening, Henry." Katelyn held her hands clasped in her lap, smiling up at him sweetly.

Henry pushed the door behind him with one booted foot. "Evening. Feeling better?" He raised one eyebrow questioningly.

"Much." There was no hint of the raving woman he'd encountered earlier in the day. Her voice was soft and compliant.

Henry nodded, sliding his hands into the pockets of his ruby breeches. "Good." He nodded, walking to the window. "I think we should agree now what is to be done with you."

Katelyn nodded, getting to her feet to stand beside him. "As you wish." Standing beside Henry, Katelyn realized what a small man Fox was. Henry was a full two hands taller, though his build was slighter. The white man had none of the raw, solid strength of the Indian. His blond hair and blue eyes were pretty, but, they didn't hold a candle to Fox's dark masculinity. Katelyn laughed to herself. To think! She'd once thought Henry Bullman was the most handsome man she'd ever laid eyes on!

Henry cast a sideways glance, wondering what the girl was grinning about. He cleared his throat, ready to repeat the speech he'd rehearsed. He was glad to see that she was coming to her senses and that he could just ignore that earlier episode. "As I told you, I think we should still marry. I need a wife and you . . ." He cleared his throat again. ". . . and you need a husband. Now I want you to know that I don't hold you responsible for anything that happened to you during your captivity." He reached into his pocket and pulled out a perfumed handkerchief, wiping his brow. This was more difficult than he'd thought it would be. Why

305

was she looking at him with those cow eyes? "You did what you had to to survive. We will send the child away once it's born, as well as any servants who know of your condition."

Katelyn barely listened as he droned on. She wanted to scream! She wanted to knock him down and beat him with her fists! Instead, she remained silent, her eyes averted, nodding occasionally.

". . . see no need for this to go any further than it has to. Though many know you've returned, we'll simply say you're recovering and can't see anyone yet. Once the child is gone, you'll be introduced properly and we can be married by September. Do you understand what I'm saying?" He tucked his handkerchief back in his coat, brushing a stray piece of lint from the rich fabric.

She raised her eyes to meet his. "Yes. I understand, and I thank you." She lied as easily as she spoke. "You're very kind. I doubt that any other man would have the strength to go through what you have." She turned away, unable to watch him expanding his chest like a barnyard rooster. "And I apologize for all of the terrible things I've said." She pushed a wisp of hair off her forehead. "I don't know what would make me say such things . . . but with all that's happened and the medication . . ." She let her voice trail off until it was nothing.

Henry let out a great sigh of relief. Thank God Uncle George was right! She *was* coming around. All of this could be taken care of quietly, without too much fuss. In a few months they would be able to forget everything that had happened. And he would be able to keep his inheritance now that he'd found a wife.

"That's quite all right, dear." Henry moved to console his betrothed. "We'll speak nothing more of days past."

306

He took her hand, patting it lightly. "I know the shock has been great and you're not responsible for your words or actions." He smiled like a young boy whose bruises had been kissed by his nursemaid. He was so pleased to see that things were going to work out.

"Thank you, Henry . . . dear." Katelyn looked up at him. He was such a child. . . . but he always would be. She almost pitied him.

"Good. Now that that's settled." He released her hand carefully, trying to avoid looking at her stomach. He didn't know how he'd missed it that first day he found her at the Carters'. She'd been well covered beneath the ill-fitting dress, he supposed.

Katelyn's hand went self-consciously to her stomach, as if she might somehow protect her child from his gaze. "Henry," she approached him carefully. "Do you think I might come down and sup with you?" She lowered her eyelashes.

Henry eyed her carefully. She seemed sincere enough. Uncle George had said he should expect strange behavior. Captives did often side with their captors to begin with. Still, it was too early to give her a free hand. Besides, he didn't want her wandering about the plantation. The fewer servants who knew about this, the fewer he'd have to dismiss. "No. I think it's best you stay here and eat where it's quieter. I have a few friends stopping by to dine with me and I fear it would be too much upset for you."

"Mary brought me a larger dress." She turned to him anxiously. "You can't see a thing in it."

"No. You stay here." He moved to the door, reaching for his snuff tin in his breast pocket. "But if you're still awake when they leave, I'll bring you down for a walk through the gardens." He lifted the latch on the door.

Katelyn tried to conceal her angry disappointment.

"Well, all right. If you say so. But do come up for me later." She followed him to the door. "I'll wait up. It's so stuffy in here. I could use the air."

Katelyn listened to Henry drop the latch on the door and slide the bolt across. After the way she'd carried on that morning, she knew he'd keep a close eye on her for a few days. But at least he was going to take her out tonight. She would see the layout of the house and could begin plans for her escape. Luckily, Henry was very gullible. He believed what she said because he couldn't imagine a woman having a mind of her own. Katelyn flopped down on the soft goose-down tick, laughing. In three or four days time, she'd be on her way to the village.

Then another thought came to mind. If Tipaakke arrived at the village to find she had never made it, he would go looking for her! He would know to come to Henry's plantation. Even if she couldn't escape, he would come and get her. She knew he had outsmarted the Mohawks and wouldn't even take into consideration the thought that he might be dead. He had promised to be there for the child.

A warm wave of confidence came over Katelyn as she lay on the bed, thinking of Fox. By the time the baby came, she'd be safe in the village . . . safe in Tipaakke Oopus' arms.

Chapter Thirteen

"Good night, Katelyn," Henry called, rapping lightly on her bedchamber door.

Katelyn pulled the bedcovers up to her chin. "Good night, Henry," she replied in her sweetest voice. "I'll see you at breakfast." Tensely, she waited, listening for the sound of the sliding bolt on her door. Instead, she heard only the echo of Henry's footsteps as he padded down the carpeted hallway to his own room.

Katelyn smiled in the darkness, sitting up to prop her pillow against the carved cherry headboard. He had not locked her in; this made it two nights in a row. Her plan was working. Henry believed her act! He honestly thought she wanted to stay here with him; the fool thought she was going to give up her baby.

Resting her head on the plump pillow, Katelyn closed her eyes. If all went as planned, tomorrow night she would be on her way to the Lenni Lenape village, and by the next night, she would be with Fox again. With this thought, she peacefully drifted off the sleep.

Startled, Katelyn woke at the sound of the tall case clock's chimes. *Two o'clock?* She slid her bare feet to the floor. She hadn't meant to sleep this long; she'd only intended to take a short nap.

Reaching for her wrapper on the end of the bed, she slipped her arms into it and tied the cord. The hardwood floor was chilly beneath her feet. Tipaakke had told her that only in bare feet, could a man walk in perfect silence. She turned the brass doorknob slowly and held her breath, listening. All was silent in the household. The only sounds that could be heard were those of a sleeping house; Henry's light snoring, the scratching of branches brushing against glass windows, the haunting call of an owl. Her heart pounding, she made her way down the long hallway.

Taking care to keep her feet on the handwoven carpet, Katelyn hurried to the grand staircase. It would have been faster to go down the back staircase straight to the kitchen, but then she would have had to pass by the servants' rooms. That whole wing was uncarpeted and the floor boards squeaked unmercifully. Someone was bound to hear her.

Moonlight shone through the window at the top of the stairs, casting dark shadows on the steps. Taking them one at a time, Katelyn stared at the portraits that lined the wall. The eyes of Henry's ancestors followed her, staring accusingly. Their faces were cold and without feeling. Shuddering, she turned from them, knowing she could never have lived happily in this house. She doubted anyone could.

Stopping at the bottom of the stairs to listen again, she went through the great room, out the back door, and down the covered walkway to the summer kitchen. She was lucky it was late spring. If it were earlier in the year, she would have had to go to the cellar which housed the kitchen during the cold months.

Slipping through the hand-hewn door, Katelyn's heart caught in her throat. There, sleeping on the floor, was an old black man. Through the darkness she could see his white beard moving as he exhaled. Wheezing, he mumbled something and rolled over, presenting his back to her.

When it was obvious the servant hadn't heard her, Katelyn went about searching for the necessary items. In the pantry, she found a flour sack nearly empty. Dumping the flour onto the floor, she searched the shelves for food she could carry. Passing over the leftover slices of strawberry pie, she grabbed two handfuls of oatmeal cookies. In a jar she found some strips of dried meat and in a tin, a few hard biscuits. Stuffing her meager fare into the flour sack, she searched the floor-to-ceiling shelves for something to carry water in. Finding nothing, she cursed Henry silently for ordering her things burned. She needed her water bag. The hand-blown glass jars and pottery jug would be too heavy. Hearing the old servant grunt and roll over again, Katelyn slipped out of the pantry back into the main room of the kitchen. Picking up two sharpened knives from the work table in the center of the room, she dropped them into her flour sack. Now all she needed was some decent traveling clothes. She'd already been to the barn the day before to chose the most docile of the horses. She would ride the horse as far as she could and then, when the forest got too dense, she'd let him go. He was likely to find his way home on his own.

Eyeing the clean aprons that hung on pegs on the wall, Katelyn scratched her chin thoughtfully. Where could she find a sturdy pair of breeches and a shirt? Taking care not to disturb the sleeping man, she slipped out the door.

Staying close to the outbuildings, she made her way to the backyard. To her delight, there, hanging on a line strung between two trees, was a myriad of assorted clothing. One of the wash maids had forgotten to bring in her last bundle!

Dropping her flour sack onto the dewy grass, Katelyn pulled a man's homespun shirt off the line and tugged it over her wrapper. It fit! Then she reached for the nearest pair of woolen breeches. To her dismay, she couldn't get them closed over her thickening waist. Letting them slip to the ground, she stripped a large skirt down and tried that on. Pleased with the fit and heavy material, she removed a shawl and stuffed the items into her flour sack.

Swinging her sack over her shoulder, Katelyn started back across the moonlit yard. Then, after second thoughts, she ran back to the line and started randomly plucking clothes off the line and dropping them here and there on the grass. Pleased that it looked like a stray dog had gotten into the laundry, she made her way back to the house.

Wary of the night shadows that played off the walls of the great house, Katelyn slipped back into her bed-chamber and stowed away her provisions before climbing into the four-postered bed to sleep.

Night shadows played overhead distorting the shape of trees and branches. Wicked fingers of dark and light haunted Tipaakke as he struggled futilely to loosen his arms and legs. Captured days ago, the Mohawks had driven him like an animal north to their homeland, beating him until he feared he would lose honor and cry out with pain. Now he was tied, spread-eagled to the ground at the edge of the woods. And the forest that had once been his friend was now his foe. Night owls screeched deafeningly, wolves howled in the distance, incensed by the smell of human blood, and

312

insects crawled over his injured body biting and sucking the life from him.

Pain seared through Fox's limbs as he tried to clear his muddled brain. It was strange how once-familiar sounds could frighten a man so. Relaxing his strained, weary muscles, Tipaakke cursed himself for being so foolish as to allow himself to be captured. If he had been thinking clearly, he could easily have taken both of the Mohawk scouts, but instead, he had permitted his emotions to control him, and that was a near-fatal mistake.

Shuddering, Tipaakke watched a woodland snake slither over his leg. It was not a poisonous one, not this time, at least. Staring up at the moon, Tipaakke wondered where Katelyn was right now. He wondered if she was safe in his wigwam, waiting for his return, or if she still in the forest, lost and confused, traveling in useless circles.

Thoughts of Katelyn were what was keeping him alive now. If he chose to, he knew he could lay here and will himself to die. He had seen others do it. But he had promised Katelyn he would be there for her. He had promised he would be there for the child. Thoughts of his new son or daughter gave him the will to live, as well as thoughts of having Katelyn in his arms again.

For hours at a time he lay there daydreaming, only semiconscious. He envisioned what it would be like to come home after a successful hunt and find her cooking the evening meal outside his wigwam. He imagined what it would be like to watch her feed the baby, its tiny mouth nuzzled to her full breast. He conjured up thoughts of her warm, pliant body pressed against his until he thought he would go mad. He had to live! He had so much to live for!

313

A small dog yapped in the Mohawk village and Tipaakke cringed inwardly. Hadn't he had enough torture for one day? Who was coming now? Late into the evening, every woman and child in the village had passed by him, throwing sticks, heated stones, and pointed sticks. A dog had snapped and snarled at him, nipping viciously at his bare feet, and the onlookers had laughed with great amusement.

Trying to twist his head far enough to the side, Tipaakke watched one of the night sentries pass by the nearest fire. Something was not right. The air was tense, the crickets had taken on a deeper resonance. An unknown bird cackled in the trees, and Tipaakke shivered. He could hear odd movement in the village, sounds he should not have heard so late at night.

Suddenly, the village was ablaze with fire. Arrows shot from the trees and men shouted a haunting war cry. Mohawks ran from their lodges, unclothed, their weapons in hand. Women screamed, running from their burning homes, dragging their frightened children behind them.

Arrows dipped in pitch and lit on fire whizzed through the air and men ran to find cover. Tipaakke strained against his bindings trying to catch a glimpse of the men who attacked the village. Who would dare to enter Mohawk territory and attack a village? For years the Mohawks had reigned terror on other native Americans, ignoring old peace agreements and blood ties.

Watching women and children disappear into the forest, Tipaakke stared through the growing billows of smoke. A Huron? The attackers were Hurons! It was true that though they were cousins to the Mohawks, they had been at war with them for many years. But they were not a people who attacked unprovoked.

Suddenly, Tipaakke began to struggle furiously against the ties that bound him to the stakes in the ground. This was his chance! If he could just get loose, he could escape into the forest in the midst of the commotion! Glancing back to be sure no one watch, he spotted one of the Hurons running from one burning lodge to the other. What was he doing? Then he spotted the prisoner, staked to the ground just outside the boundaries of the village.

Tipaakke whispered words of prayer to the great Manito as the Huron neared him. He thanked his god for his life, regretting only that he would not live to witness the birth of his child. The Huron's face was hard and cold as he bent over the Fox, peering into jet-black eyes.

Tipaakke blinked once, and then again. Did the moonlight play tricks on a doomed man? "Mekollaan?" His voice was barely a whisper.

The Huron smiled. "Why do you not join in the attack, my cowardly brother?"

"Have you moved north to become a Huron, or are you just visiting with them?" He spoke in their native tongue, the words tasting good on the end of his tongue.

"Smart, no?" He tapped his temple with a finger. "Now our friends the Mohawks will not seek us out at our own village."

"No, but some innocent Hurons will hear from them, I'm sure. Now are you going to release me?"

Mekollaan laughed ignoring the pandemonium around him. He had found what he'd come looking for. "I don't know, foolish Fox," he knelt to cut the leather ties that bound his feet, "perhaps I should leave you here. At least then I would know where you are." He started on the other foot.

315

"I am in no mood for your jokes, Hawk." Tipaakke flexed his leg, wincing.

Mekollaan moved to cut his wrists free. "I was only supposed to come to the cabin for you. You lengthened my trip by many days. I have better things to do than to chase after my young brother."

Ignoring his last remark, Tipaakke sat up. He closed his eyes, willing the ground to cease spinning. "You didn't even notice that my sight has been regained."

"I noticed. How did it happen?" He held out one painted hand to help Tipaakke to his feet.

"It's a long story, meant only to be told around the evening fire." He shook his head. "It has been quite a winter, brother." He grasped his hand tightly. "As much as I hate to admit it, I missed you."

"I did not miss you. You cause too much trouble. Can you walk?" He steadied him. "Life was very peaceful in the village without you."

"I can walk. The bone in this leg is cracked," he tapped his left leg, "but it is not broken through."

"If it needs to be set, we will do it later." Mekollaan looked up at the burning Mohawk lodges. "We should start moving south. I will call off the others once we are safely in the forest." He stared at the burns and gashes on Tipaakke's near naked body. "If you cannot walk, Fox, we will make a litter and carry you."

"Gather our warriors. No more lives must be lost." He stared at his brother through the darkness. "I will not forget you came for me."

"You are my brother." Mekollaan dropped a hand to Tipaakke's shoulder and squeezed it. "Stay. I will be back. We meet the others south of here."

Tipaakke leaned heavily on a tree, watching Mekollaan disappear into the smoke. In a few moments he returned, his axe bloody in his hand.

316

"I almost had my head taken from my shoulders." He wiped his axe on the Huron leggings. "These Mohawks, they are not human; they have no honor. They fight like mindless animals." He tucked his axe in a band around his waist and reached for Tipaakke. "Come. Slow Turtle will lead the others out after us."

Tipaakke pushed his hand aside. "I'm no girl-child. I can walk, just lead the way." He hobbled behind him.

They rounded the burning village, and headed south into the forest. The brothers did not speak. It took all of Tipaakke's energy just to follow behind his brother. Now that he was on his feet again and his mind was functioning, he realized he had been injured worse than he thought. His leg ached sending shooting sparks of pain into his hip and his skin felt as if he'd been set on fire. Several times Mekollaan turned to offer assistance, hearing his brother struggle to keep one foot in front of the other, but the look in Fox's eyes made him silent. His brother's pride was injured, and he knew it was better just to leave him alone. If he fell, he could carry him. He'd done it before.

Finally, they reached the rendezvous point and Tipaakke collapsed beside the small waterfall. Drinking his fill from the stone reservoir, he leaned back against a leaning pine, catching his breath. "Is Katelyn all right? She made it back safely?"

Mekollaan leaned to drink, choosing his words wisely. "I thought she was with you." He looked up at the bright orange sun just peaking over the horizon.

"No." Tipaakke sat up. "She was not with me. You didn't see her with me did you?" His face was tense with fear and anger.

"I did not see her with you. I thought . . ." He looked Tipaakke straight in the eye. "I thought she was dead. I thought the Iroquois killed her."

317

"Why didn't you say anything sooner?" Fox got painfully to his feet.

Mekollaan clenched his fist. "Because I thought she was dead. I know you loved her. I didn't not want to open the wound."

"How many days ago did you leave the village?" He leaned against a tree, resting his forehead on his arm.

Mekollaan took off the Huron clothing, pulling his own from beneath a rock. "After I found the cabin, I returned to the village and got help. I had found a broken Mohawk spearhead near the cabin, so I knew who had you. I only guessed that you were still alive because I found no bodies. Once the other braves from the village joined me, we moved north. The trail was easy to follow because there were so many in the group. We found the dead woman on the deer path more than a week ago." He pulled his white man's woolen shirt over his head and tied his loin cloth.

"Seven days!" Tipaakke counted mentally. "Then she wouldn't have had time to get back by the time you left." His voice was hopeful.

"No. One of our scouts just joined us late last night. He was in our village two days ago. He brought a message from Father. When he left, the girl had not appeared." He shoved the Huron leggings beneath the rock.

Tipaakke's heart leaped to stick in his throat. What had happened to his Katelyn? He knew the Mohawks hadn't gotten her. They had him. And the chances of there being two raiding parties so far south was slim. Was she lost? Had she been injured? Why had he let her attempt to make it back on her own? Why hadn't he come up with a better plan?

"It isn't your fault, Fox." Mekollaan could see the pain on his brother's face plainly.

318

"It is my fault!" Tipaakke slammed his fist into the palm of his hand. "We were together. I had her safe in my arms and we separated." He looked up at the sun rising in the east. "Where are the others? We must go. I've got to get back to the village. Maybe she was just delayed." He turned to his brother. "I thought she would be safe, Hawk." He reached out pleadingly with one hand. "She learned so much this winter."

"Do not blame yourself. There is nothing to be done now but wait for the other men. Then we will start for home. Now sit down and stop moving like a frightened rabbit. Let me set your leg."

"No. I have to go now. I don't have time. I'll go on without you. Meet you back at the village in a few days." Tipaakke could not believe the stars that had crossed his path. How could a man fluctuate between having such bad and good luck.

"Don't be a fool. The wolves will have you for a meal, as slow as you will be on that leg." He pulled his knife from his moccasin. "Now sit. I will be back in a minute with wide bark to set the leg." He turned to go and then turned back. "Are you sure it would not be easier to just forget her?"

Tipaakke's black eyes grew stormy with anger. "No. She is mine. We were going to marry." He slid to the ground. "She carries my child."

Mekollaan nodded. "I will help you find her if you wish. But I do this for you. Not for her."

"Why do you dislike her so? She has done nothing to me. She made me very happy. She has given me a reason to live again." He pushed his long, dark hair off his shoulder.

"She is white isn't she?" Hawk's eyes grew steely cold.

Tipaakke laughed. "Wait until you see her. She is more Lenni Lenape than white now. She speaks our

319

tongue well. Only her hair and the color of her skin gives her away."

Mekollaan turned his head north, signaling Tipaakke to be silent. "There is Slow Turtle's call. The men are coming. Then we go." He shook a long bronze finger. "I will help you search for the white woman if that is what you wish. But we may not find her alive." With that, he disappeared into the woods.

By the time the other Delaware braves had appeared and changed from their Huron disguises, Tipaakke's leg was splinted and the brothers were ready to go. There had been only one casualty among the Delaware braves and two wounded. Mekollaan was proud of his men, and well pleased that the raid had been such a success.

For three days the Lenni Lenape braves traveled, reaching their home village late in the afternoon on the third day. Without stopping to speak to anyone, Tipaakke made his way to his wigwam. His hopes were high as he tugged back the door flap and peered inside. He had prayed all the way home that he would find his Katelyn safe within the walls of his wigwam. But upon looking inside, he saw that that was not to be. There was nothing inside but his sleeping platform, a few baskets hanging from the ceiling, two abandoned bowls and the accumulated dust of another season past.

Undaunted, Tipaakke made his way across the compound to Won's wigwam. He ignored the stares of his people, refusing to listen to their whispering. Woman and braves gathered in small bunches, discussing their brother's frenzied search. Some speculated that he'd lost his mind beneath the torturous hands of the Mohawks while others were sure the white woman had cast some sort of spell over him.

"Won, Won!" Tipaakke pushed through the door, not

waiting for her to respond. He found Won tucking her son into his sleeping platform. "Have you seen her?"

Won pressed a kiss to her son's forehead and turned to face Tipaakke. Her heart went out to her friend as she stared at his pained face. His shoulders were slumped, his body covered with gashes and burn marks. Reaching out, she stroked his arm. "No. She is not here, Night Fox." She tightened her grip on him. "Sit. Eat. I will find some ointmint for those burns. Your brother was foolish not to tend to them before."

"I can't." Tipaakke shook his head, his eyes distant. "I must find her. She's out there alone somewhere. I promised I would care for her." The Algonquian words slipped from his mouth, echoing in his ears. He was so tired. So confused. His body ached and his spirit cried out in agony. He wanted his Katelyn!

"Fox, listen to me." Won recognized his state of semilucidness and tried to reason with him in a way he would understand. "I know we must find her. I will help you."

"She isn't dead. Katelyn and I are going to have a child." He stared into Won's dark eyes. "She was my gift. I cared for her, I earned her respect. She loves me." He shook his head, beginning to sway on his feet. "She can't be taken from me now."

Won pushed Tipaakke gently to the floor of her wigwam. "If she is out there, we will find her." She brushed the damp hair off his forehead. "But first you must sleep and have your wounds tended to." He was burning with fever.

"No time. Must go now," he protested, making no attempt to get up.

"No. Tomorrow or the next day will be soon enough. You will have to trust the stars. If she is yours and it is meant to be, nothing will keep you apart," she soothed, stroking his hair.

Tipaakke's eyes began to drift shut. "You are right. I
must rest. But only for a little while." He allowed Won
to ease him down on a mat. "Then we will go . . . we
will find her . . . we will . . ." his voice drifted into a
jumble of words and then silence.

Won stood for a moment looking at the man she had
been raised with since childhood. He was a good man:
brave, honest, caring. It seemed unfair that he should
have such a difficult life. Sighing, she moved to search
through her medicine bags. She didn't know if Katelyn
was alive or not, but she did know the great Lenni
Lenape warrior, Tipaakke Oopus, loved her, so she
would do everything in her power to help him get her
back.

Finding the proper herbs, Won squatted to grind
them into dust. Right now she had to clean those
wounds and apply the healing powders. Once the
angry sores became calm again, and Tipaakke got
some sleep, he would be able to think logically again.
Only then could they make plans to search for his
white woman with the fox-colored hair.

Katelyn listened to the chiming of the tall-case clock
on the landing. Midnight. She chuckled to herself as
she pulled on the shirt she'd stolen from the line a few
nights before. Henry was such a fool! He believed her
lies; he believed she wanted to be his wife, to share his
bed with him! Tugging on the skirt, she sat down on
the cherry bed, reaching for the shoes on the floor. Her
moccasins had been burned with the rest of her things,
and the high-heeled things Henry had provided her
with were useless, so she'd had to steal a reasonable
pair of shoes. She hoped that the stable boy wouldn't be

too angry when he found his soft, deer-hide boots gone.

Slipping the boots over her feet, Katelyn ran her palm over her stomach. Beneath the dresses Henry had given her, her stomach wasn't evident, but in the stolen skirt and blouse, it couldn't be missed. She stroked the taut flesh, crooning soft words to her baby. "You will have a father, sweet one. Mama promises that." The baby stirred in response and Katelyn grinned. "You know what I'm talking about, don't you?" Getting to her feet, she crossed the floor to the door, grabbing the flour sack with her provisions off the bed.

Slipping noiselessly out of her bedchamber door, Katelyn made her way down the grand staircase and out the front hall door. A small brown dog yapped at her as she came around the corner of the house and pressed her body to the wall, disappearing into the shadows. "Shhhh!" she whispered at the dog who followed at her heels. The dog continued to bark, snarling and nipping at her ankles. Quickly, Katelyn fished an oatmeal cookie out of her flour sack and tossed it out onto the lawn. The brown mutt ran after the rolling cookie and Katelyn rounded the back corner of the house.

Following a red brick path, she made her way quickly to the barn fearing the little dog might return. Pushing through the stable door, she gave a sigh of relief. If she could just get the horse bridled and out of the barn without anyone noticing, she'd be on her way home to Fox!

Moving slowly through the pitch black stable Katelyn kept her hand on a wall to guide her. She counted the stalls as she went, keeping an eye out for any movement. The small bay she'd chosen two days before was in the sixth stall on the right. Up ahead, at the end of the long barn, she spotted light streaming from above. Standing still, she listened. She had known that two teenage stable hands slept above the barn in the hay loft, but she hadn't counted on one of them being awake!

What was that sound? Voices . . . laughter. Taking a step closer, she broke into a smile. One of those boys had a girl up there! That was what all the rolling and laughing was about. Hoping they would be too busy to hear her stealing the horse, she moved quickly to the sixth stall.

Speaking softly to the bay, she lifted the wooden bar that held her in and reached for its rope halter. Feeling to the left of the stall door, she found the mare's bridle, right where it had been yesterday. Luck was with her tonight! Continuing to murmur soft words of encouragement, as Tipaakke had taught her she should with all animals, she led her out of the barn.

Katelyn felt a pang of sorrow for her lost pony, Wooden Head, as she eased the bridle over the stolen mare's head. But there was no use thinking about that now. The Mohawks had her and it couldn't be helped. Still, she missed her. She had grown quite fond of the shaggy pony over the winter, and through her, had lost all fear of horses.

Catching the reins of the bridle, Katelyn led the horse to the fence, so she could get on. Standing in the barn, petting the horse yesterday, she had realized that with her growing belly, she'd never be able to get up on her own. Without a stirrup to aid her, she was too clumsy.

Throwing the flour sack over her shoulder, Katelyn started up the rail fence. Then, through the corner of her eyes, she spotted the lighted lantern moving across the dirt compound.

"And what do you think you're doing?" Henry's icy voice came out of the darkness.

Katelyn moved to swing her leg over the horse but he spoke again.

"Try it. Go ahead, go. But I'll send someone after you." He stepped up beside her, holding the lantern over his head. A young stable boy stood behind him, just outside the circle of light. "Better yet, I'll come after you myself." His eyes narrowed until he looked at her through mere slits. "And then there might be an accident." He shrugged his shoulders. "Wouldn't it be a pity if you slipped off your horse, hit your head on a tree . . . or maybe a rock?" He laughed deep in his throat.

Katelyn's hand tightened around the reins. "You wouldn't dare," she hissed.

"Oh, I would. Because if I can't have you," he shook his head slowly, "no one will."

She swallowed hard, fear tight in her throat. He might really kill me, she thought staring at his evil, twinkling eyes.

With one quick movement, Henry grabbed her arm and jerked her off the fence. "Now come with me," he said through clenched teeth.

"What were you doing in the barn?" She noted the straw clinging to his hair and clothes.

"Giving the stable boy some instructions on the hunt tomorrow. Not that it's any of your business." He snapped her arm hard, leading her towards the rear of the summer kitchen.

"Funny time to be giving servants instructions," she challenged, struggling to watch the stable boy disappear into the barn with the bay. His clothing was covered with straw, too.

Henry came to an abrupt half, spinning on his heels

to grab Katelyn by the shoulders and shake her violently. "Shut up! Do you understand me! Shut up!" He delivered a cold, stinging slap to her face. "Now if I were you, I'd behave myself, Missy, because around here, an accident could happen at any time."

Katelyn stared at Henry's pale face, her lips trembling. She had underestimated him again. He really might kill her. "I'm sorry." Her sense of self-preservation spoke out. She had too much to live for now. She wouldn't die at this man's hands. Life was just too precious. "I won't do it again."

"It's too late for sorries, bitch." He grabbed her shirt and propelled her forward, almost shoving her to the ground. "I think I'll let you spend some time alone, contemplating your situation."

"No." Katelyn shook her head. "Please Henry. I said I was sorry. I swear I won't try to get away again." She backed up. "I was just scared."

"Where did you think you were going? Back to your Papa?" He reached for the ice house door and swung it open. "Better yet, maybe you were looking for that red-skinned stud of yours!"

Katelyn spun around to run, closing her hands over her ears. The man was mad! She wasn't going to listen to him.

"Go. Run. I dare you." Henry stood by the light of the moon, his hands planted on his narrow hips, a smirk plastered on his face.

Slowly, she turned to face him. She had no choice. If she wanted to live, she had to do what he said. Her sense of Lenni Lenape logic told her so. This man was her only chance of getting back to Tipaakke.

"That's a good girl, Katelyn. Now get in there." He pointed into the dark abandoned ice house.

She clutched her hands. "Please don't do this to me,

Henry. I promise I'll be good. I won't go anywhere."

He pointed into the small brick building again. "I'm losing my patience, Katelyn dear." He smiled wickedly.

She started to back her way into the house holding her hands up in front of her. "Please, Henry. Don't do this." Tears threatened to splash down her cheeks. "Lock me in my room again if you must, but don't lock me up out here."

"I said get in there!" He shouted in a rage. "Now do as I say before I lose my temper!" He gave her a shove, pushing her into the ice house and knocking her to the ground.

For a long time Katelyn lay on her side in a ball, sobbing in the darkness. Why did nothing ever work out? Why hadn't she just been able to slip away into the darkness? It seemed so unfair! All she wanted was Fox. Tears ran unchecked down her face as she cried for what she wanted so desperately, but was seemingly unobtainable. *I don't even know where he is!* Frightened and alone, she spent the rest of the night huddled on the dirt floor, too fearful to even move.

Early the next morning, Henry returned with a blanket, some food and some water. At the flood of bright morning light, Katelyn cringed, shielding her eyes.

"Here is something to eat." Henry flung her the stolen flour sack and the old woolen horse blanket. "Though I don't much believe you deserve it."

She stared at him coldly, watching him put the water crock down inside the door. She said nothing.

"Today some friends are coming to hunt, so I won't be back until late tonight." He started to close the door and then opened it again. "Oh, don't look for the knives you stole from my kitchen. They've been returned. Also, don't bother to scream. I've given most of the servants the day off. And even if they did hear you, no one would dare let you out." He leaned on the doorway, brushing the velvet of his coat. "No one would blame me for locking you up, as crazy as you are. I have the right, you know. You're my property. I own you. That piece of paper your father signed sold you to me." Bowing grandly, he backed out the door and slid the heavy bolt home.

Katelyn let out a great sigh of relief as he banged the door shut. His anger had abated, so she was probably safe. He seemed dangerous only when he became angry and out of control. Now he was simply smug. Using the dim light that seeped through the cracks in the roof, Katelyn retrieved the jug of water and drank thirstily. The she found an oatmeal cookie in the bag and started to eat it. *If he's feeding me, he doesn't intend to kill me*, she surmised.

Munching on the cookie, Katelyn surveyed her surroundings. By the dim light, she could see that she'd been smart to stay where she was last night. She found that she was sitting on a platform. Only a few steps into the ice house there was a deep recess where the ice was stored below ground in the summer to keep it better insulated. Though the hole was only four to five feet deep, had she fallen into it in the dark, she might have broken her neck, or done injury to the baby. She could also guess that it would be very easy to fake an accident, if Henry wanted to.

With that thought in mind, Katelyn spent the rest of the day locked in the ice house, huddled in the corner with the horse blanket, praying Tipaakke was on his way to save her.

Tipaakke paced the hardened dirt floor of his father's wigwam, his face taut, his fists balled at his sides. His limp was only slight. "You do not understand, Father," he repeated in his native tongue. "I must look for her. I must find her, dead or alive."

The old white-haired Delaware brave nodded evenly, his pipe clenched in his teeth. "There will be time for that after the council meets."

"No, my Father. There isn't time. I've already lost so many days. I have a responsibility to her."

"You have a responsibility to your people as well, my son." Kukuus released a puff of smoke from his mouth and watched it curl above his head.

"I know I do, but . . ." Tipaakke didn't know how to make them understand. Why did the council have to meet tonight? How could he make his father understand how important Katelyn was to him. He looked at his father sitting cross-legged on the floor. "Father, don't you remember what it was like to love a woman?" He kneeled before him.

Kukuus threw back his head, laughing. "You think I am old, my son." He shook a bony, wrinkled finger. "But I am not that old. I still remember the first time I saw your mother as if it were this morning." He patted his own cheek. "She had a face the gods could be jealous of." He smiled, the memory of Silent Wind washing over him.

"Then you should remember why I must go now." Tipaakke gazed into his father's ebony eyes. "Call off the council meeting, just for a few days. I won't be gone long."

"No. Kukuus shook his head adamantly. "I cannot. We must meet immediately."

"What is so important that we can't wait a few days?" Tipaakke got to his feet. "Hawk, you talk to him. You explain why I must go."

Mekollaan got to his feet, crossing his arms over his bare chest. "I will not come between you and Father over this. You must settle it."

"But you said you would help me find Katelyn."
Tipaakke faced his brother.

"I have more than one loyalty, just as you do, Fox. I
love you, you are my brother. And I say I will help you
because you are my brother and you ask. But I also
love my people and I must do what they ask. They ask
that we meet for High Council at sunset." He ran his
hand over his black scalplock. "You must be there,
too."

Tipaakke looked from his father to Mekollaan and
then back again. His heart was torn between those of
his own blood and the one person that made life worth
living. How could he decide who was more important?

Kukuus watched his two sons, his heart swelling
beneath his breast. They were good men, both of them
playing off the other's strengths and weaknesses. They
would guide their people well, once he was gone.
Silently he sat, waiting for the younger son's decision.

Tipaakke stared off into space, his mind spinning in
a thousand different directions. He had to find Katelyn, but he needed his brother's help. He suddenly had
a feeling deep in the pit of his stomach. He thought he
knew where she was. He turned to face his brother, his
friend. "Yes, I will stay for the council meeting, and
then we will set out." He put out a hand to rap
Mekollaan in the chest. "You and I, we will find my
woman, and we will bring her home to my wigwam."

Kukuus, chief of his people, nodded his head in
agreement, proud that the Fox had been able to make
such a difficult decision.

The fires burned brightly and the women chanted
ancient songs of what had passed, and what was yet to

come. Single file, the council made their way to the Big House in silence. As they passed onto sacred ground, they cleansed their minds, preparing to listen and speak with their hearts. Only the chief of the Lenni Lenape knew what would be discussed this evening, but all knew a grave situation was at hand. Why else would the chief call the council so quickly?

The men and woman of the sacred council gathered in the circle their grandparents had gathered in. Each knew his place; they had been born knowing. Each man and each woman played a part in the delicate balance of nature. It was here in this circle that laws were created and all important decisions concerning the tribe were made.

Kukuus entered the Big House first, followed by his sons, Mekollaan and Tipaakke; behind them came the other members of the council. At the end of the long line, the Shaman danced, singing and waving his magical burning sticks. He called to the gods, praising their wisdom and requesting their guidance. Deep in a mystical trance, he sprinkled the seated council members with a dust of truth. Here, in the circle, all men and women spoke what they truly thought, what they felt in their hearts. There was no deceit, no concern for what should or should not be said. Here, the gods guided their words.

After a long silence, Kukuus raised his head, staring into the eyes of each member one by one. Then he spoke, his words echoing between the walls. "My people, tonight we gather for two reasons." He spoke in the Algonquian tongue, his voice strong and even. "We must decide on two separate matters." He took his time, taking a puff of his long-stemmed pipe. "The first is my concern for who will care for you when I leave this world. I have thought long of this and have decided that both of my sons should be chief when the time comes."

Tipaakke glanced behind his father's head, his eyes meeting his brother's. He could tell Mekollaan had already known of this, and was pleased by it.

The old man continued to speak, ignoring the whispers of the council members. "I now ask for your thoughts on this matter, brothers and sisters."

An older man stood. "There has never been such a thing. We have always had one chief." He held up a finger. "One tribe, one chief. It is the way it has always been."

Kukuus nodded. "This is true. But life changes. The land changes. And we must change if we are to survive. Together, I think my sons will serve you well. Both have good qualities, admirable qualities. Mix those qualities," he intertwined his fingers, "and you have a stronger chief."

Won came to her feet, waiting until Kukuus nodded, giving her permission to speak. "I think this is wise. Together, your sons will lead well." She nodded her head. "I am ready for change, Great Chief of the Lenni Lenape people."

Tipaakke listened as the council members each had their say. He was in shock. Never in the history of their people had two men ruled at the same time. He was the second son. He had never expected to be chief; he had never dreamed such a thing would be possible. As the members spoke, Tipaakke was amazed to find that most were in agreement with their chief. A final vote was taken, and he found himself chosen to be the next chief. Together, he and Mekollaan would lead their people.

"Good." Kukuus smiled. "My heart sings with happiness. I am pleased that you all see both of my sons worthy of such an important position." He reached to take each son's hand and squeezed them tight. Then he joined the brothers' hands in his lap. "I promise you, my people, that my sons will do you great honor as your next chiefs."

There was a great murmuring between the council members and then silence when Kukuus held up both hands.

"What we must speak of next, pains my heart greatly." The chief clutched his hands to his heart. "I have lived on this land all my life. My grandfather lived here and his grandfather before him. But I fear it is time we go, my friends."

Tipaakke turned to face his father. He couldn't believe the old man's words. Leave their home?

Kukuus continued. "We live too close to the white man. He is destroying us. His ways are not ours. He kills us with his firesticks and his diseases. He murders our spirits with his fire-water and heathen ways. Once we numbered more than we could count, now we are but a handful. I think we should move to the evening sun. We should pack our belongings and take our children to the land where our Shawnee cousins live. There, we are welcome. There, there are no white men. What say you, my friends?" Kukuus looked up, waiting for his people's response.

At first, no one said a word. Each man and woman had known deep in their hearts for a long time now that they could not stay here forever. Still, the thought of leaving was difficult. Here was their history. Here on this soil lay the bones of their ancestors. This was where life had begun for the Lenni Lenape people.

Mekollaan came to his feet. "My father is right, members of the council. We must go, before we are driven." He stood tall and erect, already looking the part of the next chief. "And I think we should begin preparing now. I would like to be in our new home before the snow flys again.

Tipaakke barely heard a word after that. Leave? The thought was frightening; but, deep in inside he knew the others were right. It was time they found a safer place to raise their children. But how could he leave? He had to find Katelyn! He couldn't go without her, not as long as there was a chance she might be alive. What if she returned to the village to find them gone? She could never find him on the Ohio river.

After the council had adjourned, their decisions made, Tipaakke followed his father and brother back to their wigwam. His voice was angry and accusing. "Why didn't you tell me of this, Father?" He closed the door flap behind him.

Kukuus took his time, seating himself on his worn leather mat. "I did not tell you because it was up to the council to decide."

"You know I can't leave now. I must find Katelyn." He ran his hands through his dark hair, catching the fox tail that dangled to the side. He fingered the soft fur.

"You do not want to be the chief of your people?" The old chief signaled to Mekollaan to light his pipe.

"Yes, of course I do. It is a great honor. I would be proud to share this with my brother. But I must make peace with myself before I can take responsibility for my people. Why must we become the chiefs now? You are healthy, you could live many years yet."

"You heard my reasons at the council, son. While I am still in this world I can advise you." He sucked on the long pipe between his teeth, exhaling a puff of sweet smelling smoke.

Mekollaan leaned on the frame of the wigwam. "I

knew Father was considering this, Fox. But the council's decisions were wise. As much as I hate to admit it, together we can guide our people better than I could alone. And it is true, we must move on before our people are destroyed." He stared at his brother with coal-black eyes. "I am sorry about your woman, but it would be better just to go now and forget her. You will be a great chief, you can have any maiden you desire."

Tipaakke spoke through clenched teeth. "What I desire is to have her back with me. You said you would help me find her." He crossed the wigwam to stand before him. "Do you go back on your word?"

"No. I do not. I said I would help you if you wish. I have already had contact with the half-Shawnee, half-white man, Red Coat. He thinks he has word on your Katelyn."

"Tell me, what did he say? She's alive isn't she?" Tipaakke's heart pounded wildly. "Why didn't you say something before?"

"You will not like what I have to say."

"Enough games, Hawk. Tell me!"

Mekollaan stroked his chin. "Red Coat tells me of a girl the white man say was captured almost a year ago. They say she is back with the white man that owned her. They say there will be a wedding in a few moons." He shrugged. "But these are tales carried by the wind. Who knows."

Tipaakke's eyes dropped to the ground. He refused to believe Katelyn would betray him. "Maybe it is not my Katelyn."

"Red Coat says she is a girl with hair of fire. Very beautiful for a white woman."

Tipaakke crossed his arms over his chest. "She was taken against her will. I must go to her." He turned to his father who had listened silently to his sons. "I will

335

return within two days. Then I will become chief. But first I must find her."

The old man nodded, his long white braids swaying. "Do what you must, but take care. We cannot wait for you, my son."

Starting for the door, Tipaakke faced Mekollaan again. "Are you with me, brother?"

"I am with you."

Chapter Fourteen

Katelyn ran through the tall meadow grass, leaping into the air and landing in Tipaakke's arms, her legs wrapped around his waist. Laughing, he spun her around and she leaned back, letting the wind whip through her long hair. Dropping her to her feet, he led her through the field of wild flowers, stopping to watch her pick a handful. Together they made their way to the stream where they both flopped to the ground, beneath a grandfather willow.

Giggling, Katelyn leaned to tuck flowers in the leather band Tipaakke wore around his head.

"What, you want me to be more like Won?" He yanked the wild daisies from his hair and sent them sailing into the air.

"Oh, no." She leaned back, letting her head rest in his lap. "I like you just the way you are." She traced intricate scroll patterns on his bare chest with a finger.

"What a vixen you are," he murmured, lowering his mouth to hers. "You are insatiable."

She snaked her arms around his neck, arching her back, her pink tongue darting out to taste his lips. "I only demand what is rightfully mine, my husband." She stroked his hard, lean chest as he untied the laces at her neckline.

"Demanding, you are." He slid his warm hand beneath her doeskin dress. "It's a wonder I have time for my duties at all, you keep me on your mat so much."

Katelyn breathed deeply, letting the waves of pleasure wash over her as he caressed one well-rounded breast. "This is your duty, she purred. Lacing one hand through his silky hair, she guided his head to hers, and their mouths met with great fury.

Suddenly, Katelyn felt herself being pulled from Fox's arms. The air grew stagnant and the sun began to fade, a darkness overtaking them. Something unknown held her in its grasp and was dragging her away. "No, no!," she screamed in terror, throwing her arms out to Fox. "Help me," she begged. But he couldn't. He called out her name over and over again as the distance between them grew. Then, there was total darkness . . .

Katelyn gasped for breath in the pitch blackness, tightening the horse blanket around her. Though her body was damp with perspiration, she shivered with cold. Shuddering, she wiped her face with her forearm. Her heart was pounding so hard, it echoed in her ears. *Only a dream*, she told herself, breathing deeply. *It was only a dream* . . .

But it had seemed so real! Her fingers went to her lips. She could still taste Tipaakke's mouth on hers; her breasts still tingled from his touch. Tears ran unchecked down her cheeks. She wanted him so badly! Why had all of these terrible things happened? All she wanted was to be safe in Tipaakke's arms. She wanted no part of this Tidewater life Henry was trying to force upon her.

338

Katelyn spent the rest of the night huddled in the corner of the ice house, too frightened to go to sleep. If she did, those dreams would return, as they had every night since Henry had locked her up. Again and again she had dreamt of being with Tipaakke, at the village, in the mountains, at the stream. And the dreams always ended the same. She was always pulled from his arms by some unknown force, and she always woke in a cold sweat. It was easier to remain awake then to go through that over and over again.

Sometime in the mid-morning, Katelyn heard the bolt on the ice house door. It had to be Henry. She had seen no one else since he'd locked her up. How many days had it been? She raised a hand to shield her eyes from the blaring sun. "Henry?"

"Good morning, love." Henry leaned on the door and ran a hand through his thick flaxen hair. "Sleep well last night?"

Katelyn rose slowly to her feet. "Just fine, thank you." She refused to let him get the best of her. He wanted her to cry, he wanted her to beg, but she wasn't going to do it. She would show no signs of weakness. Henry loved weakness in others.

"Sour grapes, this morning, are we? I came to have a civilized conversation with you, but if you're not up to it . . .," he began to close the door, ". . . I'll just come back tomorrow."

Katelyn didn't want to play his games, but if she didn't, she'd never get out of here. And she had to get out if she was ever going to make it back to Fox. "No, wait, Henry."

"Are you going to behave yourself?" He shook his finger at her like she was a naughty child.

"Yes." Katelyn lowered her head submissively. "I'll behave," she said quietly. She hated this! She hated having to grovel before him. But she had to do it.

"Good." He stared at her. "My, my, you're quite the mess this morning. You really must take better care of yourself." He shook his head, and then looked up, a sparkle in his clear blue eyes. "It's my birthday today, you know."

"Is it?" She tried to sound interested.

"Yes, indeed, and I'm going to have a party tonight." He clasped his hands together, tickled with himself. "A big one."

"A big party?" Katelyn's widened. If she could just get out of here, this might be her chance. She might be able to make her escape in the midst of the commotion. "Who's coming, Henry?"

"Oh, everyone! Everyone I like, that is. I'm just checking the guest list."

Katelyn's pulse quickened. "Am I on the guest list, Henry?" She held her breath.

"Well, you see, therein, lies my problem." He polished his fingernails on his coat. "I'd like to invite you." He looked up at her. "And so many have asked about you, but . . ." He shook his head. "You really haven't been a very good girl, Katelyn."

"I told you I was sorry. I told you I was confused. I won't do it again," she lied.

"Do you want to come to my party?"

"Yes, I'd like to come, Henry." She smiled prettily, flirting with him. He could be so gullible!

"Ask me."

"What?" Katelyn's eyes crinkled with confusion.

"Ask me if you can come to my birthday party."

She was so mad she could scream. How dare he do this to her! But she knew she had to go along with his nonsense. "Could I come to your birthday party, Henry?"

"You promise you'll be good?" He began to open the door a little further.

"Yes. I promise." Katelyn's heart pounded. He was going to let her out!

"You promise you won't try to escape and you won't mention a word about anything that's happened, either with the savages, or here?"

"Yes, yes I promise! I'll do just as you say." She took a step for the door, craving the warmth of the bright sunshine.

"Now I'm not kidding, Katelyn." His voice grew stern, the childish smirk disappearing from his face. "I'll not have you dishonor me in front of my friends."

"I won't. I swear it." She threw up a hand. "I won't say a word all night." She followed him, stepping out of the ice house. The bright sun pierced her eyes making her squint, but the fresh air felt glorious!

"Then you may come to the house and go to your room." He guided her with a hand on her back. "But I'm warning you. You make one more mistake and I'll not be held accountable for my actions. You really made me mad the other night." Up the walk they went, headed for the house.

"I'll do just as you say, Henry. I've learned my lesson."

"I thought that might do it." He held the door open for her. "Now you are to go to your room and stay there. I'll have someone bring you water for a bath and then I'll send up a seamstress. She'll have to alter one of those dresses I gave you, to disguise this disgusting condition of yours. She says she can do it. Says you're not too big." He led her up the main staircase and down the hall. "Our course once you can no longer hide yourself, you'll not be permitted out of your bedchamber."

"I understand." Katelyn hugged the wall, still a little uneasy on her feet.

"God sakes, girl! I should think you would!" He

opened her door. "Inside with you. I'll be up to talk to you later. I have to check with cook about the food for this evening. I'll be locking your door, of course."

"Of course." Katelyn still couldn't believe he was going to let her attend the party!

"Good day to you." Henry bowed stiffly.

"Good day." She waited until he shut the door and slid the bolt before she gave a squeal of delight. It felt so good to be out in the open air again. Even if she was still locked in. Running to push open a window, she stuck out her head, taking in great gulps of fresh air. Tonight she would escape. Somehow she would manage it. She was beginning to worry about Fox. He should have come for her by now. Had something gone wrong? She had to get to the Lenni Lenape village and find out.

Katelyn spent the rest of the day listening to the bustle of the house as they made preparations for the party, and making plans of her own.

Tipaakke and Mekollaan made their way cautiously through the forest. They had decided that first they must go to Henry Coward's and be sure Katelyn was not there. Then, they would begin looking elsewhere. The half-blood, Red Coat, had explained how to get to the coward's house and had warned them to be careful. It was no longer safe for an Indian to cross the land that the white men had stolen from them.

As the brothers moved silently through the trees, Tipaakke went over and over in his head what it would be like to have Katelyn in his arms again. He recalled the softness of her skin, the feel of her fingertips on his flesh, the smell of her freshly washed hair. He tasted her lips on his, he felt her breast in the palm of his hand.

342

But as they grew nearer to the white man's plantation, Tipaakke began to mull over the fact that she might not really be there. Mekollaan was right; she might be dead. So many things could have happened to her in the forest; she could have eaten poison berries, or wandered west into nothingness. She could have been eaten by a bear . . . or wolves. How would he deal with her death, he wondered, looking into the sun to mark his time. *I just won't think about that now. I will only think positive thoughts; I will go to this Henry Coward and I will take back what is mine. And then I will kill him for keeping my Katelyn against her will.*

Mekollaan glanced at his brother as he leaped over a fallen log. "What is this I see on your face, Tipaakke Oopus? A death wish?" He shook his head. "We are not warring," he told him in their native tongue. "We go in, we take her if she is there, and then we go." He gestured with a hand. "I want no bloodshed. I want no confrontations."

"Wouldn't you kill him if you were in my place?" Tipaakke plucked a berry from a bush and popped it into his mouth, continuing to walk.

"I don't know. We don't know what happened yet." He shrugged his muscular shoulders. "Maybe she went to him. We don't know."

"Don't even say such a thing, brother. She hates him! She would die in the forest before she would seek his help."

"She is not one of us. You don't know what she would do. She was alone, frightened. . . ."

"I said enough! Somehow he found her and he captured her and now he will die for it."

"You will be a chief soon, Tipaakke. You have responsibilities. You can no longer risk your life like a young buck. Our people depend of us."

"Don't you think I know that? Whatever happens,

after this, whether she is dead or alive, I will be ready to become a true member of the tribe again. I will accept my position and do my father the honor he deserves. Together, you and I will rule our people on the Ohio. But first," he balled up his fist, "first I must take care of this. If she is alive, I must have Katelyn. She is in my blood."

As darkness began to fall, the brothers crossed onto Bullman land and began to slow their pace. As they drew nearer to the big white farmhouse, to their dismay, they heard the sound of carriages and laughter. This was going to be more difficult than they'd anticipated. They hadn't planned on a house full of people.

Katelyn paced the hardwood floor of her bedchamber, her hands knotted in the folds of her dress. All day long party guests had been arriving by carriage and by boat. The house hummed with laughter, glasses clinked and children ran from their governesses. She could hear women passing by her room on their way to change from their travelling wear to their evening dresses. Soon, Henry would come for her, and she would be presented.

Crossing the room, her heeled slippers tapping on the floor, she pushed open a window. A warm breeze blew, ruffling the curtains, and the scent of plowed fields filled the air. Watching the sun slowly set, Katelyn wondered where Tipaakke was right now? Was he hurt or injured? Was he dead? Or was he somewhere right now, watching the sun set, agonizing over what had happened to her?

The baby stirred and she slid her hand down over her growing middle. The seamstress had done a superb job with the gown of green lawn Henry had brought her this afternoon. With the gathers loosened beneath the vee at the waist, she merely looked plump. Katelyn laughed at herself, thinking how only a year ago how pleased she would have been to have been given such a beautiful dress. She had never owned anything so fine. It would have been perfect for her with its wide three-quarter sleeves, delicate squared neckline, and narrow green-satin ribbons. But now, after knowing the comfort and freedom of soft doeskin, the green lawn was cumbersome and scratchy.

Turning back to the window, Katelyn stared out again wishfully. It was almost dark now. Back at the village she would just be cooking the evening meal over the fire in front of Fox's wigwam. Together they would eat, laughing and telling stories. Then, they would go to the stream and bathe. Fox would swim beneath the water and grab her feet, pulling her under. When she came up sputtering she would splash water in his face and threaten to dry off and go home. After that she might practice her swimming, and then, arm in arm they would retire to their wigwam and make love, nestled in the furs on the sleeping platform. Katelyn hugged her arms around her waist, her eyelids half closed. These fantasies were all that had kept her from going insane, locked in that dark, suffocating ice house.

Then she blinked. What was that she had just seen from her window? A flash of movement in the semi-darkness. There it was again! Someone racing across the yard. It looked like . . . it almost looked like . . . it couldn't be! Katelyn leaned further out the window, hanging onto the wide sill. Squinting, she stared into the yard. Whoever it was had disappeared behind the smokehouse.

Katelyn's pulse quickened as she spotted Mekollaan creeping from the shadows of the small out building. Where was Tipaakke? She had seen two figures!

Please, Heavenly Father, she prayed. Let it be him. . . . "Mekollaan! Here! Help me," she called in Algonquian. "Here." She waved her hands, her voice barely a whisper. It would be an end to them all.

Shading her eyes from the light of the lamp on the side table, she leaned further out the window, her round stomach resting on the sill. Then she saw him. Out of the shadows stepped Tipaakke Oopus, brave of the Delawares. He was breathtaking. Wearing only a loincloth, his body was painted in greens and browns to camouflage his movements. He wore his midnight black hair free and flowing, a fox tail intertwined and dangling at the side of his head. His face was sober, but it was a look of determination she saw. He had come to rescue her! She waved a hand, leaning to call to him and then she heard the rattle at the door.

"Katelyn, did I hear you speaking to someone?" Henry's voice came from the hallway.

She spun around just in time to see him coming through the door. Her hand flew to her breast, as if she might be able to slow her pounding heart. Her throat was constricted, she could barely breath. "Henry," she managed.

"What are you doing with the window open. I've told you about that before." He brushed passed her in his ruby-red velvet coat, closing the window with a slam. "The night air is not good for you." He looked her up and down. "The gown will do. Gads, what's wrong with you, girl? You look as if you've seen a ghost. You've mussed your hair." He reached out to smooth her elaborate coiffure, resting his other hand on the back of her neck, berating her as he worked.

At that instant, Tipaakke looked up to the second story of the great house to the place where the light spilled from a window. What he saw made his blood run cold. For a moment no words came, then he spoke

346

quietly in his own tongue. "There she is," he whispered. He could feeling his heart being wrenched from his chest.

"Where, brother, I do not see her." Mekollaan held his knife tight in his hand, his nerves on edge. He wanted to be done with this as quickly as possible.

Tipaakke's voice was barely a whisper as he raised his hand slowly, pointing to the window. "There."

What Mekollaan saw sickened him. His brother had cared for this woman, loved her, and in return, he got betrayal. "Come, we go. She is in the arms of another."

Tipaakke nodded his head slowly, his hand falling to his side. Tears welled in his eyes. He had never loved anyone like he loved his Katelyn. He loved her for her sweet voice, her laughter, her willingness to learn. He loved her for a million reasons, and now he hated her. "Yes. We go, my brother."

Together the two Lenni Lenape's crossed the white man's yard, slipping into the woods. "You have done wisely. She would never have fit in," Mekollaan told his brother. "She was never really yours. Manito had never meant us to mix with them."

Fox nodded in agreement as he forced one mocca-sinned foot in front of the other. *She never loved me,* he told himself. *She did the things she did, said the things she said to survive. I threatened to kill her so she did what she thought a wanted her to. She is not to blame, an animal would do as much. But she was not an animal! He was not an animal! He was a man with feelings. One did not toy with another's love. It was a sacred thing.*

Suddenly, Fox stopped dead. Without a word, he turned and headed back in the direction they'd just come.

"Tipaakke! What are you doing? Come brother, we go. The white woman has betrayed you! You cannot have a woman that has betrayed your love for her." He

347

reached out to his brother. He knew the pain he felt. It was the same pain that had ripped through his own body when that young Quaker girl had betrayed him so many years ago. "Please, come home. There is nothing here for you, only pain. You do not want her."

"No," Tipaakke's voice was icy cold. "I do not want her, but I will have my child."

Mekollaan leaped over a bush, following after him. "What do you mean? What do you speak of?"

"She carries my child. I will not have my son raised by her. I will not have a child brought up to hate and kill like a white man!" Tipaakke continued to walk, his stride long and purposeful.

"What is wrong with you? She still carries the child. You cannot take it." Mekollaan was beginning to wonder if the Iroquois torture had permanently damaged his brother's thinking.

"I will take her home and keep her until she has the child. Then she may go to her white man's hell if she wants." He spun around beating his chest with his fist. "But I will have my child."

"You can have another. Many if you like. You are a chief now; you do not have to limit your children to two." Mekollaan ran beside Tipaakke. "There will be many maidens to chose from when we get to the Ohio. You could marry a Shawnee cousin if you wish."

"I want no woman, only my child. I have lost one. I cannot control what happened then, but I will not have another."

"She won't come with you. She has her white man and her rich clothes. She has a big house and slaves to work for her. She will not leave this."

"I will take her. I will tie her and carry her. I will keep her tied to my wigwam until the child is born. Then I will push her out the door and tell her to go." Tipaakke entered the clearing where the Bullman

348

house stood and pulled his steel knife from the strap of his loincloth. He reached over his head to finger the arrows he carried on his back.

"You cannot do this, Fox. Is it worth risking your life to save a child that will be half white?"

He crept past a hedge of boxwoods, watching the white men and woman in their bright clothes enter the house through the front door. "You will understand someday when you have had a child of your own. It is a part of me. My blood flows as freely through its veins as hers."

Mekollaan followed his brother. This was madness! But his brother was not thinking clearly, so he must do it for him. In this state, there was no telling what he might do. He would just have to keep a sharp eye on Fox and trust Manito to watch over him.

Katelyn took the steps on the grand staircase one at a time, her arm linked through Henry's. Her legs shook beneath the green lawn gown, and her heart beat erratically, but she kept a smile plastered on her face. She had to play the game right to the very end, right until Fox rescued her, otherwise Henry might become suspicious.

At Henry's side Katelyn stood, putting out a hand to each guest as he or she was introduced, presenting her cheek to be kissed. As the minutes ticked by and the faces came and went, she began to feel dizzy. There were so many people, touching, laughing, apologizing, begging to hear of her capture. They all pushed and pulled at her, fingering her hair and gown, handing her one drink after another.

The heat of the room was oppressive. Katelyn wanted to rip off the foolish gown and run. The noise was unbearable as the party guests mingled, shouting to one another and joking. And Henry, he was the worst of it all. There the hypocrite stood, introducing his betrothed, in his bright red coat and red stockings and his high-heeled shoes. He ran his fingers over her neck and back, squeezing her waist for emphasis when he told this guest or that how happy he was to have her back.

Then, after the guests had been received, the music began and Katelyn was forced to dance with Henry in front of everyone. The feel of his arms around her made her sick to her stomach. The first stream she got to she would rip off the dress and dive in, scrubbing until his touch was washed from her skin. She would walk home to the village naked before she would wear Henry's gown.

But where was Fox? She was beginning to worry. Begging off the next dance, her voice lighthearted and playful, she stood beside Henry ignoring the planter he was speaking to. Her hand clutched the glass of cool water she'd asked for and her eyes scanned the windows. He should have spotted her by now. She was trying to stay as visible as possible, though she was forced to remain at Henry's side. Before they had left her bedchamber, he had threatened to retire her for the evening if she got more than a foot from him.

Tipaakke moved slowly beneath the windows, crushing young flower seedlings just transplanted by the gardener. Hugging the brick wall, he listened to the music and laughter, becoming angrier with each moment. How could he have been such a fool? How could he have been so wrong about her? Before this he had always considered himself a good judge of character. Fox tightened his grip on the handle of his knife, grabbed the edge of the sill and pulled himself up to look in the window.

"Tipaakke!" Mekollaan's urgent whisper came

through the darkness. "Get down. They will see you." He reached from behind to tug on his brother's bare leg. "Do you want to die at the white man's hand?"

"They cannot see me. Let go. It is light in there, dark out here. We can see into the light. They cannot see into the darkness." He scanned the room of guests looking for Katelyn. He had never seen so many people in one place at the same time. Just the thought of being in there with so many bodies, the noise, and the bright lights made his skin crawl. They were dressed brightly, laughing and talking, dancing round and round in circles. *So this is what my Katie-girl wants,* he thought sadly.

"Do you see her, Fox?" Mekollaan stood beside his brother listening for movement outside. If someone caught them here, they would likely both be killed.

"No. I do not. There are so many." He rested his feet on the edge of the cellar sill, a foot off the ground. "Wait." His heart fluttered against his will. There she was, beside Henry Coward. In her hand she held a glass. She was laughing, her cheeks rosy. Tipaakke's eyes drifted shut for an instant. The pain that tugged at his heart was almost too great to bear. They were going have such a good life together, he and Katelyn. Their life had just begun, there were still so many songs left to sing. His face grew taut. But she had betrayed him. Here she was smiling, standing so near the coward that had been willing to sacrifice her life for his own. Suddenly, Tipaakke was very glad his people were moving to the Ohio. He had no desire to live among these vile people. He wanted no memory of the fox-haired woman who had captured his love. Easing back onto the ground, he turned to Mekollaan.

"So you have found her. Now how do we get her out?" He was beginning to lose patience. The white woman was not worth losing his life over.

351

"Let me think. Something will come. Manito has guided my life in many directions, but I always feel his hand on my shoulder. He will show me a way."

Katelyn glanced out the windows over and over again, but she could see nothing since the lamps had been turned up. She was really beginning to get nervous. Tipaakke and Mekollaan should have done something by now. Perhaps someone had caught them! No, Henry would have been informed, and he certainly wouldn't have been able to keep such a thing from her. His pleasure in telling her he had captured her Indian lover would have been too great.

Then Katelyn spied the doors that led to the garden. Maybe he was waiting for the chance that she might step outside! That made sense. But Henry had insisted she must stay at his side. "Henry." She tugged at his sleeve.

"Just a moment, love." He patted her arm, continuing to speak with the older man who stood leaning on the carved-stair banister.

"Henry." She tightened her hand around his sleeve.

"What is it, dear?" His voice was sickeningly sweet. "I'm speaking with Roger right now."

"I hate to bother you, but it's rather warm in here." She fanned herself with her hand. "Do you think I might step outside for a moment?" She lowered her eyelashes coyly.

Henry wondered irritably what she was up to. "I'll go with you in just a few moments."

"No, no," Roger spoke up, laughing. "Go." He gave Henry a wink. "Your young lady calls. Don't stay on my account; I remember what it was like to be young and in love."

Henry nodded gracefully and steered Katelyn toward the door. "What do you think you're doing?" He spoke through clenched teeth, a smile still on his face.

"I told you. It's too hot in here and all of these people are making me dizzy." Her voice was equally sharp. "If I don't get some fresh air I'm either going to faint or be sick on one of your nice friends."

"You are a vulgar woman, and you will find I don't care for vulgarity." He nodded to an elderly woman, giving her a boyish grin. "Good evening, Sally. You will save a dance for me, won't you?" The old woman laughed, covering her mouth with her hand as he passed by.

Pushing the door to the garden open, Henry waited for Katelyn to pass by. "We'll go out only for a moment," he hissed in her ear. "I cannot play nurse-maid to you; I have guests to attend to. If you're going to be ill you will just have to retire early." He followed her down the brick walk.

"Go back to your guests if you like, I'll just get some air and then come back in." She tried to sound casual. Where was Fox? Could he see her?

"Oh, no, minx," Henry reached in his coat for his snuff box. "I told you. You won't be left alone until the child is born."

"Henry, someone will hear you."

"What do I care?" He stepped up in front of her. "I don't much like your games, Katelyn. I told you to keep your mouth shut."

She took a step back. The smell of whiskey was sour on his breath. She thought she had seen him drinking from a small silver flask. "I don't know what you mean."

He dropped a hand on her shoulder. "Suddenly you don't look faint to me." He toyed with a fat curl that dangled down the back of her neck. "Madame St. Claire did a superb job on your hair. You are the prettiest woman here . . . even in your deplorable state."

She tensed at the feel of his hand on her neck, but she didn't push him away. She wanted to be very careful. If he got mad he would take her back in and lock her in her room. Then how would Fox find her? Where was he? "I told you, Henry . . ." She stuttered a little. "It was hot. I felt faint. My condition."

"Well, you'd better get used to it, because once we've gotten rid of the little red bastard and we're properly married, I intend to keep you just this way." He wrapped his arm around her waist pulling her tight against him.

Katelyn turned her head away, but stood her ground. In a few minutes it would be over and she would be in Fox's arms again. Please, she prayed, please let him come soon.

Tipaakke crept slowly around the back of the house to where the light shone through the open door. Then he spotted them. He was tempted to put an arrow through the man's back, but he was an honorable man and honorable men did not shoot another man through the back, not even if he deserved it, not even if he was the enemy. Tipaakke waited for his brother to come up behind him. For a moment they both stood watching the coward caress Katelyn.

"Are you sure, you want to do this?" Mekollaan whispered.

The Fox nodded. "I will have my child."

"How do you want to do this? Do we kill him first and then take her?" He slid his knife from his moccasin. "He would be an easy shot with the bow from here."

"Wait." Tipaakke put up his hand. "I want him to see me. I want him to know who spills his blood. I want him to know why."

His brother's voice sent chills through his spine. "Fox, it will do no good. It will change nothing."

"But I will feel better." He nodded evenly. "You take Katelyn and get her out of here, no matter what happens." He turned and took Mekollaan's hand in his. "Promise me that no matter what, you will take her back to the village. Even if I die, I want my child to live among our people. Do what you will with her." He shrugged his shoulders. "Kill her if you like."

"I could not put her life before yours." Mekollaan held Tipaakke's hand tight in his own.

"Promise me."

Hawk stared into his brother's eyes. He could not deny him. "I promise."

Giving Mekollaan's hand a squeeze, he dropped it. "You go around to the rear. I will meet him head on."

"Someone might see you."

"We will be here and gone before anyone notices. Trust me." Tipaakke watched his brother disappear behind the monstrous boxwoods.

Katelyn caught sight of Tipaakke first. Her pulse quickened as she riveted her eyes to his. Over Henry's shoulder she saw the eyes of a man she didn't know. What was wrong? She wanted to cry out to him, but with one quick motion of his hand, he warned her to keep silent. She saw no love or warmth in his dark eyes, only the cold calculations of a killer.

Silently, Tipaakke walked through the garden, his head held high, his knife poised in his hand. Had she no shame? There she was, caught in her lover's arms, being caressed by him at this very moment, yet she did not hang her head.

Henry's breath caught in his throat at the feel of cold steel knife at his throat. "What the hell," he breathed, turning slowly to face the Indian. At the sight of the crazed red man, his bottom lip began to tremble. "You bitch," he hissed at Katelyn. "I'll kill you for this."

"Silence!" Tipaakke warned in his perfect sing-song English. "Speak again, white coward and I will spill your blood on the stone." He looked up at Katelyn, his eyes as cold as the knife he held. "Step back."

"Fox, what's wrong, I'm so glad to see you . . ." The words spilled from her mouth as she rushed to his side.

Before Tipaakke could think, his hand came up to strike her hard on the cheek. "I said get back!" he ordered.

Katelyn's hand flew to the mark on her cheek as she stumbled backwards from the force of his hand. Tears welled in her eyes and came spilling down her cheeks. "Tell me, my heart," she murmured in Algonquian."

"Mekollaan," Tipaakke snapped. "Keep her quiet!"

Katelyn turned to see Mekollaan coming up behind her. He grabbed her by the wrist, jerking her roughly to his side. "Silence, woman! You walk that narrow line between life and death."

Henry stretched his neck, craning to see Katelyn. "Is that all you want," he spit. "Take her! She's worthless."

"You were unwise to take what was mine." Tipaakke held his face only inches from Henry's. "I will take her. I do not need a coward's consent." He pressed the knife's blade to his neck, watching the thin line of red appear. "But first you will pay."

Henry flinched, squeezing his eyes shut as he felt the knife's bite. Petrified, he prayed for death to come quickly. He had no stomach for blood. He knew he would not be manly beneath the savage's torturous knife. "Then kill me!" he managed.

"No, Fox! Don't kill him! Please." A part of her wanted to see Henry die for all he had done to her, but it must not be by Fox's hands. She didn't want their love soiled by another man's death. She wanted no regrets. Besides, it was like Tipaakke had once said. Sometimes it was harder to live than to die. If Henry's life was spared, he would be haunted by memories for the rest of his life.

"You beg for your lover's life, do you?" Tipaakke's lip curled cynically. He felt as she had stabbed him with the knife and now held it in her hand, twisting and turning. But he would not let her see the pain.

"No!" Katelyn shook her head violently. She didn't know what was wrong with Fox. Why was he saying these horrible things? He knew she hated Henry. "Tell me what's wrong," Katelyn implored. "Speak to me, Tipaakke Oopus." She struggled to pull away from Mekollaan as he wrapped his arm around her waist and secured her against his body.

Tipaakke stared at Katelyn in indecision. His dark hair blew in the wind making a striking picture.

"Fox, sometimes it takes a greater man to let a man live than to kill him." Her voice wafted through the air, mingling with the sound of music and laughter coming from the big house.

Henry tried to speak but Tipaakke held him tighter, running the flat edge of the blade against his neck. "Speak and that will be the end of you." He uttered the words viciously.

Katelyn was frightened. She had never seen Tipaakke act like this. What had happened to make him so cold? She could tell by his eyes that he was still contemplating what she said. "Let him live. Whatever I have done wrong is between you and I." She didn't know what she'd done! If only he would speak to her rather than glare with those clouded obsidian eyes. "I am going with you. There is no need to kill him. He is not worth the effort it would take to wipe his blood from your knife." She spoke half in English, half in Algonquian, as she often did with him.

Tipaakke loosened his hold on Henry Coward slowly. The man could barely breath for fright. He would not admit it to Katelyn, but she was right. A man did not kill out of anger. *She* had betrayed him, not the white man. Henry had only accepted what had been his to begin with.

Katelyn wiped her tears with the back of her hand, watching Tipaakke's every move. She didn't know why Henry's life was suddenly so important to her. Maybe it was not so much Henry she was concerned with, but Fox. It was important to her that he be the kind of man that could walk away from something like this and go on with his life.

"It is not for you that I let him live," he told her. "I will soon be the chief of my people. A chief does not take lives unless he must." He stared at her. A part of him still wanted to take her in his arms . . . She had lost weight, but beneath the English trappings he could make out the faint outline of her thickening waist. "I release this man because I do not wish to carry his cowardly soul on my belt."

Mekollaan began to back his way through the trimmed boxwoods, pulling Katelyn with him.

Slowly releasing Henry, Tipaakke tucked his knife in his belt. "Go, coward," he whispered, then turned his back on him to follow his brother.

"No, Fox!" Katelyn screamed, an instant too late. Horrified she watched as Henry's fists came down on the back of Tipaakke's neck. It seemed that time suddenly stood still as Fox's body crumpled to the ground and Henry began to scream at the top of his lungs, calling to those in the house.

"Indians! Indian attack," Henry screamed. "Help me! Help me, someone!" He ran in circles, leaping up and down.

Then Katelyn felt herself being dragged away. She

struggled, beating Mekollaan on the back when he picked her up and threw her over his shoulder. "We can't leave him! They'll kill him!" She watched the people pour from the house, carrying pistols.

"Silence, woman." Mekollaan ordered in Algonquian. "You have done enough harm."

"But you can't leave him. Let me go, put me down. He is your brother, your blood. Help him!" She beat on Mekollaan's bare back, kicking her feet.

"Stop struggling. I will take you into the woods and then I will go back for him." He dropped into English so she would understand as he ran into the forest.

Katelyn watched Tipaakke's image disappear from sight. He still had not moved from where he lay. Running through the woods, Mekollaan carried her on his back. When he'd thought he'd gone far enough, he stopped, dumping her unceremoniously to the ground.

"Why did you leave him?" She demanded, watching, stunned, as he withdrew a piece of leather cord from his pouch and started to wrap it around her wrist.

"I promised. Now cease talking or I will knock your head from your shoulders." Mekollaan was furious. He should have known something like this would happen! Tipaakke had had nothing but poor luck since the day he had found the white girl! She was evil, bad magic. But he bound her tightly to the tree. "I will return. I must try to get my brother. Keep silent or I will put an arrow through your back."

"I don't understand what I've done!" Tears threatened to spill again. "Tell me what you are talking about, Hawk! I love Fox, we are going to be married. I would do nothing to harm him. I would give my life for him." She wiped her eyes with her hand, ashamed of her tears. "I would do anything to be lying in that garden now instead of him."

"I do not wish to hear your white man lies. You owe

me no excuses. I have always known what you were like, what all white women are like. How can you say you have done nothing when we caught you in the coward's arms." He checked to be sure the knots were secure. "He was taken by the Mohawks, tortured, and here you came, running back to your white dog." He spun around to go.

"No, you're wrong, you've got it all wrong!" she called after him. "They took me. I tried to get back. They forced me!" she sobbed.

"Silence, or you are dead," came Mekollaan's voice from a distance.

Katelyn sank to the ground, sobbing. Why had everything gone so wrong? How could Fox suspect her of caring for Henry? She despised him, he knew that! And now, because of her, they might kill him. Pulling off the heeled green-leather slippers, she threw them as hard as she could. She hated these clothes! She hated Henry! Yanking at the pale-green lawn, she gave up on the buttons at the back and began to tear the gown from her body. In a frenzy, she shredded the cloth, throwing it as if its touch might burn her skin. Once the gown was gone, she began to work at her hair, pulling the bone pins from her hair. She was not satisfied until every curl was unpinned, every bow was thrown to the ground and tromped on. Removing the useless underthings, she could finally breath again. The only thing she wore now was a wispy, thin shift, woven of the finest cotton.

Mekollaan moved through the forest like one of the Heavenly Father's other creatures of the woodland. He ran in silence, ducking and leaping so that he barely moved a branch or leaf, he barely left footprints in the soft earth. Fear raced through his veins driving him faster as he neared the Bullman plantation. He felt guilty for leaving his brother behind. But he had promised! And the word between two Lenni Lenapes was sacred.

By the time Mekollaan reached the garden and crawled on his hands and knees through the boxwoods, the white men had rolled Tipaakke over and were beginning to tie him up. There was a great confusion with men shouting and women squealing as they tried to get close enough to see the savage.

Mekollaan cursed Katelyn over and over again as he watched the white men pull Tipaakke to his feet and make him walk. With so many men it would be impossible for Mekollaan to get his brother out of there! At least he was alive. He was beginning to regain consciousness as the armed men poked and proded him along. What was that Henry Coward saying? It was difficult to hear through all of the commotion.

"He, he is the one," Henry shouted. "He kidnapped Katelyn and killed my servant." He was beside himself, shaking in his boots. "Look what he's done to me." He stretched his neck for everyone to see. "The red bastard tried to kill me."

"Hang the savage!" One of the party guests shouted from the crowd.

"Hang him! Hang him for murder!" Someone else joined in. The crowd of guests buzzed with frenzied excitement. "Kill the red bastard!" came another shout.

Mekollaan tensed his muscles. There beneath the trimmed hedges, he was so close he could have reached out and touched one of the shouting men. But he was no fool. With so many armed men gathered together, he knew any attempt to free Tipaakke now would be suicidal.

"Wait!" A large man spoke up, pushing back at the

361

crowd with a loaded rifle in his hand. "Stand back. We're civilized people, aren't we?" He stood between Tipaakke's drooping figure and the pressing crowd of angry men. "If this man has committed a crime, he will be punished. But first he will stand trial." The man turned to the two gentlemen who held Tipaakke between them. "Load the savage into my wagon and we will take him to Annapolis. There he will face his charges. If he killed the servant Jonathan last year, as Henry said, then he will be hung."

At that moment, several men came around the corner with a pack of dogs. "We got the scent, Henry. We'll find her!" a man in a green coat shouted. "Anyone up for an Injun hunt?" he called tugging on the lines of the baying hounds. "Saddle up!"

Mekollaan began to back out of the brush, slowly on his hands and knees. If he didn't get out of here fast, he would be surrounded. Men were swarming everywhere, saddling horses and carrying lanterns. Confident that Tipaakke was probably safe in the hands of the big man, he knew he had to get back to the village for help. If he was being taken to Annapolis, there would be a way to get him out of the white men's hands before they hung him for a crime he didn't commit.

Getting to his feet, Mekollaan ran as fast as his moccasins would carry him, across the great lawn and into the woods. "There goes another one!" he heard someone shout from behind. "He's getting away! Get the dogs!"

As Mekollaan made his way through the dark forest, he was tempted to leave Katelyn tied to the tree and just leave her behind, but he had promised Tipaakke he would take her back to the village alive.

"What's happened? Where's Fox?" Katelyn's eyes searched Mekollaan's as he cut her from the tree.

"We must hurry. The white men come with dogs."

He grabbed her arm roughly. "Fox is being taken to Annapolis. He's been accused of killing that servant your white coward murdered last spring."

Katelyn stumbled behind Mekollaan, trying to block out the eerie sound of the baying dogs. Over her shoulder, she could make out the faint lights of lanterns bobbing as the hunters made their way through the dense forest. "Go," she shouted. "Run, Mekollaan, I will keep up."

Chapter Fifteen

Through the dark forest Katelyn ran, the howl of the bloodhounds sending chills down her spine. "Mekollaan," she cried. "They're gaining on us." Her thin shift caught on a branch and she ripped it free. "I cannot outrun them." She cradled her round belly with her arms, leaping over a fallen log and sidestepping a thorn bush.

Mekollaan fell back, grasping her arm. Behind him he could see the swaying lights and hear the shouts of men as they encouraged the dogs. She was right, the men were moving closer. He could outrun them, but not with her on his arm. There had to be a way out of this! Steering her to the left, he decided to take a chance.

"Why are we changing direction?" Katelyn clung to Hawk's arm, grateful for his support.

"If we can cross the marsh safely, we can lose them." Mekollaan ran easily, trying to guide her through the dense forest.

"The marsh? Tipaakke said I must never go into the marsh; he said it was dangerous; he said . . ."

"Silence. We will lose them in the marsh and then we will back in the direction of the village." He ducked under a branch, forcing her to duck as well. "I must get more men."

"It's the only way?" Katelyn panted. Her side was beginning to ache and her feet smarted from the assault they were taking.

"It is."

"Then I go." She held his arm tightly, finding a strange comfort as they raced through the trees. Though they disliked each other immensely, they were both fighting for the same thing . . . their lives and Fox's.

As Mekollaan ran through the pines that skirted the marsh, he questioned Katelyn's behavior. Instead of running, she should have been fighting him. She should have been screaming and trying to go the other way. She should not have been at his side, forcing herself to move faster. Was there truth in what the white woman said? Could any white woman speak the truth? *Had* she been held against her will? He stared at her through the semidarkness. She had stripped off her fine dress, her stockings and her shoes. She ran barefoot, the thin gown clinging to her damp body, her unbound hair streaming down her back. What other white woman would have been willing to cross the swamps in the darkness to save the lives of two red men? Had he misjudged his brother's woman?

"Hawk, they're moving closer," Katelyn moaned, trying to catch her breath. "Don't let them catch us! I won't go back." She clung to his arm, her words frantic. "Don't let them take me. Don't let them take my baby."

Mekollaan found himself rubbing the white woman's arm to comfort her as they slowed to a walk. "They will not take you; I gave my brother my word. I will get you back to our village safely. He felt the earth grow soft beneath his feet. "Now stay beside me," he warned.

Katelyn held tightly to Mekollaan as they entered

the edge of the marsh. She could smell the salty tang of the bay as they made their way through the reeds. As they waded deeper into the mire, Katelyn began to feel water seeping between her toes. Her feet sank into the soft earth each time she stepped, the black mud rising up her leg with each step.

"Keep moving," Mekollaan ordered. "We will go a little deeper, then we will cut west again. No white man would be fool enough to enter the marsh in the dark of night."

Katelyn listened to the sound of the dogs dying away as the cattails grew taller. Far ahead strange lights blinked, here and there and eerie sounds began to fill her head. "What are those lights?" she murmured.

"The marsh is filled with spirits, good and bad. Do not look, just keep moving. This is a place of great magic, light and dark. It is not a place where we are welcome." His voice was haunting.

Katelyn shivered, clinging to Mekollaan as the light of the moon faded and a macabre whistling and moaning closed in around them. "What are the sounds?" The ill-smelling mud sucked at her feet with each step, threatening to pull her under.

"The old ones say it is spirits calling out, lost souls doomed to walk, caught between our world and the next. Others say it is the mud shifting, sinking." He brushed his hand over his scalplock. "I say it is both."

"How will we get Tipaakke away from them?" She spoke to drive the unnatural sounds from her thoughts.

"They are taking him to Annapolis to stand trial. They will lock them in their jail. My men and I will take him from there." He changed direction, moving toward the forest again. The sound of the white men and their dogs died off until they couldn't be heard.

"I will go, too. I can help." She ran her hands

through her hair, pushing it off her neck. She suddenly felt as if she was in a tub of steaming water. The air was thick and hot, hanging heavily over the marsh.

"You will not go. You will stay in Tipaakke's wigwam and wait for him." His face grew hard.

"I will not!" She struggled to pull her foot from the rich, black mud. "I will go with you. He is my life now. My child will have a father." She dropped into halting Algonquian. "He is my heart." She touched her hand to her breast. "I love him."

Mekollaan looked doubtfully at her. He wondered if any white man knew how to love. They were so full of hate and dishonesty. "I do not care. That is between the two of you. He thinks you have betrayed him."

"Betrayed him! Look at me! Does this look like betrayal?" She held out her hands, moisture pooling in her eyes. Her shift was plastered to her body, torn and covered with smudges of drying mud. "I would do this for no other."

Mekollaan nodded, but said nothing, taking her arm to guide her again. She was right. Her innocence was beginning to become apparent. He didn't know what had happened, but he knew that things were not always as it seemed. And he was a man who could admit when he was wrong. But this was not his concern; it was his brother's. Tipaakke would have to hear the facts and make his judgement.

Katelyn ignored Mekollaan's accusing silence. What did she care what he thought? Once she got to talk to Tipaakke, everything would be all right. He was a fair man; he would listen to her. He would know she hadn't betrayed him. But she would have to go to him, she would have to go to Annapolis. She couldn't stand to have this strife between them. Her heart ached for him; she knew how he must be suffering.

Unexpectedly, Mekollaan cried out. "Hurry girl, I'm sinking."

Katelyn turned, horrified, to see Mekollaan sinking in the silky, black mire. "No," she cried, feeling herself begin to sink. Scrambling, she released his hand. Falling onto her knees, she crawled forward, heaving herself onto more solid ground. Turning back to Mekollaan, she screamed, watching him sink like a stone tossed into a stream. The stinking mud had already reached his waist and was sucking him down as he struggled, trying to swim.

"Get back!" he shouted. "Keep moving. It's everywhere!" He thrashed to keep his head erect as he sunk deeper.

Terrified, Katelyn searched the ground on her hands and knees for a branch. Remembering when Tipaakke had fallen through the ice, she knew he needed something to hold onto, something he could use to pull himself out. Getting to her knees, she snapped several long cattails off at the ground and turned to see the mud oozing over Mekollaan's shoulders.

"Get back I told you!" he shouted in Algonquian.

Undaunted, Katelyn crawled back to the edge of the swallowing earth and held the stiff cattails out to him. "Grab on!"

His arms above his head, Mekollaan labored, stretching to grasp the reeds with his fingertips. Once he gained hold, Katelyn tried desperately to pull him out, but she didn't have the strength. Slowly, he was dragging her in.

"It won't work," he muttered. "Get back to the village. Tell my father what has happened. Send men for Fox." Mekollaan was now fighting to keep his mouth above ground.

Releasing the cattails, Katelyn crawled back and

skirted the quagmire until she was beside Hawk. Scrambling to her feet, she trampled on standing cattails until they lay flat in front of him.

With the cattails firmly in the harder soil, Mekollaan was able to pull himself gradually out of the mud. Panting, he lay at Katelyn's feet, unable to speak. Then, slowly, he raised his head and reached out with one muddy hand. "I owe my life to you." His words were solemn. "I will not forget."

Katelyn grasped his hand with her own, the mud that covered them mingling. She knew she had just made a friend.

Together, the two traveled through the night, and by mid-morning, reached the Lenni Lenape village. Exhausted, Katelyn allowed Mekollaan to lead her to Tipaakke's wigwam. Lifting the door flap, he motioned for her to go inside, ignoring his people, who crowded around them. "Go in. Lay down," he said in Algonquian. "I will send Won to care for you." Their eyes met for a moment as a silent thank you passed between them, and then he was gone.

Katelyn stumbled into the wigwam and dropped onto the bare sleeping platform. Though she had rinsed most of the black mud off her body, the smell of the mire clung to her. She wanted a bath desperately, but she didn't think she had the energy to make it to the stream and back. Pulling the tattered shift over her head, she flung it to the ground and stretched out nude on the platform. Tipaakke's scent enveloped her and she drifted off to sleep.

The scent of roasting meat woke Katelyn late in the afternoon. Sitting up, she looked around. Someone had been in to clean up the wigwam. The cobwebs were gone from the corners and it smelled of sweet, crushed herbs. Won, she thought, noticing the precious cotton blanket she was now covered with. Smiling, she got to her feet, wrapping the blanket loosely around her.

"Won?" Katelyn stuck her head out. "There you are." She grinned as her friend turned to fling her arms around her.

"I am glad to see you are safe." She ran her hands through Katelyn's tangled hair. "You look terrible."

"I am fine. At least I will be once we get Fox back."

"Hawk told us everything. I am glad that you and the Fox have found happiness, but it saddens me to know you have been through so many terrible things." She patted Katelyn's protruding stomach with one large hand. "What is this I see? A *daanus* baking in the oven? Or will it be a *giis*?"

Katelyn laughed. "We don't care. A healthy baby is all we want." She dipped her finger into the pot of stew that cooked on the open fire. "Mmm, I'm starved. I will bathe and then I must find Mekollaan. We will eat while we talk." Her eyebrows furrowed. "What?" She didn't like the look on Won's face. "What's wrong? Tell me."

Won shook her head. "He has gone."

"What? What are you talking about?" She clutched the blanket, her knuckles turning white. "What do you mean?"

Won opened and closed her hand in a flapping motion in the air. "The Hawk has flown."

"He's gone?" She erupted with anger. "He went without me? I told him I was going!" She balled up her fist, shaking it at Won. "I have to go. I have to set things right with him."

Won leaned to stir the stew. "Maybe Hawk is right. Maybe it would be better if you wait here, where you are safe from the white men."

"No. He would come for me. I must go to him." She left the hearth, heading for the stream, still wearing only the thin blanket. "Please find me a dress, Won. I will bathe, but then I must go."

Won followed behind her. "You do not know your way to 'Napolis."

"I'll find my way." Katelyn's chin was set with determination, her stride long and sure.

Won grabbed her arm. "Then I will go, too."

"Thank you. I will not forget your friendship." Katelyn squeezed her hand.

"But we do not leave until the sun rises again. Hawk did not leave that long ago. We would be foolish to start out tonight. We must gather what we need and sleep."

Katelyn hesitated. She really wasn't up to heading back the same way she'd just come tonight. "Are you sure it would be all right?" She searched her friend's dark eyes.

"Yes. I know Mekollaan. When he gets there he will sit, he will wait, he will watch. There is plenty of time to get to him." She turned to go. "Go to the stream, bathe and then you will eat. I will find you clothing for a journey."

Katelyn nodded. "Thank you," she whispered. "Tipaakke thanks you, too."

By nightfall the next evening, Katelyn and Won had reached the outskirts of Annapolis. They had made good time, and Katelyn was glad her good friend had come with her. She doubted she would have been able to find her way so quickly. As the two moved through the forest, Won told Katelyn of the decisions the Sacred Council had made and the importance of both brothers being made the next chiefs.

Katelyn's heart swelled with pride. The old chief Kukuus' decision was wise. Together, Hawk and Fox

371

would rule their people well. It was hard to believe her Tipaakke would be chief! She was sorry that the Lenni Lenapes were being forced to leave their home and move west, and she shed an invisible tear for Tipaakke's loss. But she was relieved to know that once they left the tidewater region, Henry and his men would never be able to find her. Won said there were no white men in the Ohio country.

"This way," Won called behind her. "I know where the Hawk lights. When he and Fox come to trade, they always camp in the same place." Won shifted the bag on her shoulder, lifting a branch for Katelyn to duck under.

Katelyn smiled up at her friend. Won had made the trip as easy as possible for her, insisting on carrying most of the supplies and going out of her way to take deer trails so they wouldn't have to fight undergrowth. With her rounded stomach, Katelyn found her balance was off and her movements were awkward. With each passing day she was getting bigger and she knew she was growing nearer to her time. She only hoped the child would be born before the Tipaakke's people began to move west.

As the sun began to set, Katelyn and Won reached Mekollaan's camp. After Won sounded the call and warned the other braves of their arrival, they entered the camp.

Mekollaan came striding across the small clearing, his displeasure clear on his face. "What are you doing here?" he barked in Algonquian. "Why have you come?" He pointed one bronze finger at Won accusingly.

"We have come to help." Won held up her chin as she swung her hide bag to the ground. She was dressed in a man's loincloth and moccasins and carried a knife on her side, just as the other braves did. She had explained to Katelyn that men's clothing was more appropriate in the forest.

"I told you to keep her there. You disobeyed me." He clenched his fist. "She was to stay where she was safe. Look at her." He held out his hand, motioning to her belly. "She is not fit to be out here. She should be home in the wigwam. The Fox will be furious."

Katelyn stepped between Won and Mekollaan. "Do not blame her." She spoke in Algonquian, inserting English words when she had to. "I would have come with or without her. He is mine." She touched her breast possessively with her palm. "I will help you."

"You will not! You will return to the village at once!" Mekollaan spoke through clenched teeth. "You must learn to obey Katelyn, I am the chief. If you are to be one of us, you must heed my words."

Katelyn looked up at him through a veil of lashes, a silly smile appearing on her lips. "You are not the chief yet, Hawk. Kukuus is my chief and he did not tell me I must stay."

Mekollaan let out an exasperated sigh. She was right, he was not yet the chief. She was smart. He fought not to return her grin. She should have stayed where she was safe; Tipaakke would be furious when he found she was there. But the truth was, any Lenni Lenape woman would have done the same. He was afraid he was beginning to like this white woman. He looked up at her determined face. Unless he picked her up and carried her back to the village, he could see she wasn't going anywhere. "Stay then," he told her gruffly. "But you must do as I say. Do you understand? I will not have my brother's precious white woman taken again."

Though Mekollaan's voice was rough and unyielding, and his words voiced disapproval, she knew she had won. And she knew she was gaining his respect. "I cannot promise I will do as you say; I must follow my heart. But I will try," she promised solemnly.

Mekollaan's eyes narrowed as he looked at Won. "You are to stay with her. If there is trouble, I want her far from here. Do you hear my words?"

Won tried to keep a straight face. Why did he think she had come? Of course she was going to remain at her side! "Yes, great chief-to-be," she responded. "I guard her with my life."

Mekollaan spun around without another word. He knew the two of them were laughing, but he ignored them and returned to the group of braves sitting cross-legged on the ground. How was a man to save face with a pair like that? He laughed to himself, shaking his head. Tipaakke was going to have his hands full with his white woman. He could see that coming. Of course things would have to be resolved between them first. The Fox would have to make his final decision, because once they left for the Ohio, they would never be returning. He would have to take her for his wife, or leave her behind.

Katelyn and Won laid aside their things and joined the circle of men. The plan was simple. Tonight, under the cover of darkness, the braves would go into Annapolis and locate where Fox was being held. Then they would find a place where someone could stand watch day and night. They would watch and listen, follow the jailors' routines and then figure out a way to get Tipaakke out of the jail before the white men held their trial.

Once darkness settled in on the tidewater settlement of Annapolis, Mekollaan and his Lenni Lenape braves set out to find their captured friend. Single file, the men moved through the inky blackness, down the main street of the town. Mekollaan had been in the white man's village many times, so he thought he knew where the jail was. In silence, the Delawares crept slowly towards the wharfs, ducking in and out of the shadows, listening to the voices of the white men gathered at the docks, or stumbling out of the local tavern.

Katelyn followed Won's lead, doing just as she did. When a door of a white brick house swung open, they leaped into a cultivated flower bed and listened to farewells. Katelyn couldn't believe the Delawares could stand so close to someone and not have anyone know they were near! Through a back yard and a small garden the braves went, and then down a side street near the Customs House. Slipping into the shadows of a large outbuilding, Katelyn and Won stood peering over a wooden fence. Across the brick-paved road stood the jail. Light streamed through two windows, illuminating the figures of two men sitting at a table. They were drinking from pewter mugs and playing at cards.

Mekollaan slipped beside Katelyn and squeezed her arm. He was surprised to see how beautiful she was, standing in the light of the full moon. She wore only a woman's undergarment, made much like his own loincloth, and a sleeveless leather jerkin that fell to her hips. Even with her protruding belly, she was hauntingly beautiful with her pale skin and fiery halo of waist-length curls. He was beginning to see why his brother had fallen in love with her. "This is where they hold their prisoners," he whispered. "The cells must be in the back, through the rooms where the men are sitting." He spoke in English so that she would understand everything he said. "Slow Turtle has just been to the rear of the building. He says there are two small windows very high. He thinks they lead to the cells."

375

Katelyn stared at the solid brick building; the thought that Fox was so near made her heart flutter. "Could he see in the window? Did he speak to Tipaakke?"

"No. I told Slow Turtle to keep silent. He could not see in the window. Too high. He could not climb the brick wall to look in. He said it would take three men standing stacked to see inside." He placed one hand over the other.

"What are we waiting for? Can you do that?" Her eyes met his questioningly. "We have to be sure he's there."

"We can. You stay here. The street that runs behind the jail is well traveled. I will take two others and leave the rest with you."

"Let me go," she tugged at his arm. "I want to see him."

Mekollaan laughed. "Look at you. You can barely keep your balance standing on a log. You cannot stand on a man's shoulders who is standing on another man's shoulders. Now stay here or I will throw you over my shoulder and carry you back to the village myself."

Katelyn nodded. She knew he was right. The thought of her standing on someone's shoulders was amusing. Pensively, she waited until Hawk and the two braves returned.

"He is there, Katelyn." Mekollaan made no attempt to hide his pleasure.

"You saw him? Is he all right?" She pulled at his muscular bronze arm.

"I did. I see cuts and bruises, but he is alive. They will keep him alive until his trial and then they will hang him in their town square until dead." His voice was laced with contempt.

"Hawk, did you speak to him?" Katelyn brushed her

hair off her shoulders.

"No. There was a guard there, and another prisoner in the cell. I could not take the chance."

She chewed on her bottom lip. "I guess there is nothing to do but wait now." It was hard to stand so close to Tipaakke, and not be able to see him, not be able to make him understand what had happened. She knew his heart must be aching.

"I will leave a man on watch here. By daylight he can hide inside this barn. It does not look like anyone has been inside in a long time." He pointed to the outbuilding behind them. From the inside you can see out through a crack in the boards. The men are finding a way to come in by daylight and not be seen."

Katelyn nodded, letting out a sigh. "Are you sure he was all right?"

Mekollaan considered his words, then spoke. "He will be when he learns that you have not betrayed him. Now come. We must go. It is not safe for so many of us to be so near the white men."

Tipaakke blinked, trying to get his swollen left eye open. One of the jailors had knocked him in the face with the butt of a pistol, practically putting out his eye. His whole face ached from shattered bones and shooting pains ran up the leg that had been fractured by the Mohawks. But the greatest pain he felt was in his heart. How could Katelyn have betrayed him like that? How could she have betrayed their love? He just couldn't understand it. He was so bitter. *Let the white men hang me*, he thought. *My soul is already dying. What was there to live for anymore?*

My child, that is what I must live for, he told himself. *And my people. Mekollaan will get me out of this, and then I will move to the Ohio with my people and my child. I will raise my son to be a true Lenni Lenape; and someday the white will wash from his blood and he will be a true red man. I will never tell my child how his mother betrayed him. She is dead. To me she's dead.* Tipaakke's body sagged to the floor and he drifted off to sleep again.

For the next two days, Mekollaan and his men watched over the Annapolis jail. They kept track of who went in and out of the building and at what times. But so far, Tipaakke had not been moved and they'd seen no way to get him out peacefully. Late on the second day, Won and Katelyn sat in the old barn on the corner of the old white woman's property and watched the jail. Like the others in the band of Delawares, they took their turn at the watch.

Katelyn sat in the dusty barn, leaning against the wall. She arched her back, trying to alleviate the ache in the small of her spine. The baby stirred and she ran her hands over her stomach.

"The child moves often." Won took a bite of a stolen biscuit and passed it to Katelyn. "It is a big one, a boy I am sure."

Katelyn bit into the biscuit. "It's a giant!" Slowly she got to her feet. "Sit, Won. I will watch." She rested her hand on her back.

"No. I will watch." Won peered through the crack in the barn.

"I'm tired of sitting. You've stood all afternoon. Mekollaan will be here soon. Let me watch." Her voice was insistent. She was so bored, her nerves jumpy from the long day of doing nothing.

Won slid to the ground.

"I'm sorry, Won. I didn't mean to snap at you. I just

378

can't stand this waiting. I'm so afraid for Fox. What if someone comes for him?" She leaned to peek out the wide crack.

"Mekollaan says the English white men are slow to punish. It will still be days before he stands before their council and then he will return to the jail before he is hung." She pulled another biscuit from her bag. "There is still many days. We must be patient."

Chewing on her biscuit, Katelyn stared at the jail-house door. A woman in sober garb was approaching the steps. "Won, come here. Look!"

Won moved to stare over Katelyn's head through the crack in the wall. "What is she? Does she mourn for someone's death?"

Katelyn laughed. "She is a religious woman. A Quaker. I knew of them in England. Look, she carries a basket. Is that bread sticking out?" Her voice was hushed and hopeful.

In silence they watched the woman disappear into the jail. A few moments later, she reappeared, the basket seemingly lighter, with no bread in sight.

"I think you are right, Kate-lyn. The woman takes food to the guards or to Tipaakke and the other man." She watched with curiosity as the woman wearing the black dress and white cap started down the hill and crossed the street. "Do you think she is warm in that?" Won wrinkled her nose. "She is covered from her chin to her toes. I would not wear such things. Not in the summer."

"The worst is the clothes underneath. I itch just thinking about it." She watched thoughtfully until the woman disappeared from sight.

When Mekollaan and another brave arrived to take the watch, Katelyn already had a plan sketched in her mind.

"No, Katelyn." Mekollaan shook his head.

"Yes, I can do it. I can get in and out without anyone thinking anything of it." She reached out beseechingly with one hand. "Don't be a fool, Hawk. Who else could do it? I'm the only white woman here. Neither you or Won could make yourselves look much like a Quaker woman."

Hawk continued to shake his head. He didn't like this at all; she didn't belong here in the first place. He should have made Katelyn stay at the camp. He should have known better than to let her stand watch. "No. It won't work."

"What do you mean it won't work. Of course it will work." Katelyn paced the hard dirt floor of the abandoned barn.

"Where are you going to get clothes? Food to take? What are you going to do when you get in there? What if a true Quaker comes and unmasks you?" Mekollaan wanted to be sure she was thinking. She was right, it was a good idea, though he wished Katelyn didn't have to be the one to go inside.

"If you see another Quaker coming, warn me with the whipoorwill's call. As for the clothes, I'll steal them. Won can cook some food, rabbit stew or something. We'll get bread out of the old woman's window. Biscuits have been left two days in a row." She motioned to the brick house the barn belonged to. "If I can get inside, I can get a good look around. I don't know how I'll get him out. Maybe he'll have a good idea."

"You will not get him out. You will take him the food and let him know we will get him out." He shook his long finger at her. "You will do nothing else."

Katelyn grasped Mekollaan's hands. "I know I can do it! Everything will be good between us again when I talk to him. Tomorrow . . ."

"No," Mekollaan interrupted. "You will not go to-morrow. Tomorrow you will get the food and clothing together. We will see if the woman comes again." He pulled his hands from Katelyn's, planting them on his hips.

Late the next afternoon, to Katelyn's delight, a Quaker woman appeared with food at the jail again. This time it was a different woman.

When the Quaker came out of the jail, Won slipped out the barn door. "I will try to follow her. You stay and watch."

"Come back for me; we should wait until nightfall to get the clothes." Katelyn squeezed Won's broad shoulder. "Take care, my friend."

Well after dark, Won returned to the barn where Katelyn waited with two other braves. Together, the two set out to steal the Quaker woman's clothes, leaving the braves to stand the night watch.

When Won reached a simple, two story, frame house on the outskirts of the town, she slipped through a back gate and crept past a sweet smelling herb garden. "Is it not beautiful?" she murmured to Katelyn who followed behind. "I think when we reach the Ohio, I will grow a garden like this outside my wigwam." She spoke in Algonquian.

Katelyn nodded. "*Ia*, so beautiful. Now how do we get inside?" she asked in English.

"Through the cooking room, here." She pointed to a heavy hand-hewn door. "Inside lives the woman, an old man and an old woman. We will slip in, then out, and no one will ever see us."

Katelyn took a deep breath, wishing the woman had just left clothes hanging on the line. That would have made things much simpler. "I see no light from the house."

Won nodded, starting for the door. "I saw the woman kneeling in prayer before I left, then she blew out the light." She pointed to a middle window on the second story. "The old ones sleep at the end of the house."

Moving silently, Katelyn and Won entered the Quaker house through the kitchen addition. The door was unbolted. Creeping through the airy room, Katelyn caught the smell of fresh baked bread. "Mmmm, do you smell it?"

Won ran her fingers over a long wooden table until she found the fresh baked loaves, lined neatly in two rows. "Take a loaf and put it in your bag," she told Katelyn. Slipping a strand of stone beads over her head, she laid them on the table. "Payment," she explained.

Katelyn tucked the loaf into the hide bag she wore around her neck; she was glad Won was leaving something in return for the bread and clothes. She was no thief.

"Come." Won whispered in Algonquian, laying a finger on her lips.

Through a doorway and up a narrow flight of steps they crept, their bare toes curling on the edge of each sand washed step. The house smelled so clean and fresh! Katelyn inhaled deeply, running her hands up the white-washed wall. This was so different from the cluttered, stale-smelling home Henry lived in.

Easing their way down the hall, Won ran her fingers along the chair rail that guided her to the woman's bedchamber door. "Here," she whispered in Algonquian. "You stay."

Sarah Hathaway's eyes flew open at the sound of the creaking floor boards. "Father?" She squinted in the darkness. What was he doing creeping through her bedroom naked!" She threw back the bedcovers and slipped out of bed.

Won's eyes grew large. In the darkness, the woman thought she was her father! *What am I going to do?* She could see the shadows of a dress hanging on a peg on the wall. Just another two steps, and she would have it!

"Father! I said what are you doing in . . ." Sarah's mouth dropped open and she froze in mid-sentence. That wasn't Father! It was a naked . . . she began to tremble violently . . . a naked savage in her bedchamber! She tried to scream, but no sound would come from her throat.

Won took a step forward, holding up her hands to prove she meant no harm. She spoke quiet, soothing words, trying to ease the girl's fright.

Katelyn stood silently in the hallway, watching the Quaker woman drop her head and clasp her hands in fevered prayer. *Poor thing*, she thought, *she's petrified!*

One more step and Won slipped the grey dress with the starched collar and a silk bonnet off the peg on the wall. She left the undergarments, knowing Katelyn would have no part of them. Then she began to back up slowly, watching the woman. The Quaker made no attempt to run, no attempt to cry out, she just stood there in her long white gown, looking like a frightened rabbit. Carefully, Won eased the bedchamber door shut and grabbed Katelyn's arm. "*Uishameela* . . . run!"

Down the stairs they flew, out the door and through the garden. It was not until they reached the woodsline outside the town that Katelyn threw herself onto the ground, laughing. "Did you see that poor woman's face?" She dissolved into a fit of giggles, rolling in the soft grass of the forest. "I don't think I've ever seen anyone look so scared, except maybe Henry!"

Won dropped down beside her, joining in the laughter. "I didn't mean to frighten the poor little rabbit. Do you think she will tell anyone?"

Katelyn shook her head, sitting up. "She wouldn't dare! Who would believe that a tall Indian wearing a loincloth and a red bow in his hair would come into her house and steal her dress and cap?"

Won's face grew serious. "Do you think I should have worn my skirt?"

Katelyn sniffed, running her hand down her friend's arm. "I'm not laughing at you! I love you. It's just that you're very confusing to people who don't know you." She reached for her skin water bag on her shoulder.

"Con-fusing? What is this word? I do not know it."

"It means people don't understand. You have a man's body, but you walk like a woman, you think like a woman, and you wear things in your hair like a woman." She touched her hair.

Won laughed. "Sometimes Won is confused, too. Come, we go back to the camp. Mekollaan will be waiting; he worries over you like a mother hen."

Chapter Sixteen

Katelyn leaned over the cooking pot, inhaling deeply. "It smells so good, Won. Are you sure we can't have just a little?"

Won shook her head, laughing. "I told you, I had only enough herbs in my bag to make this pot. When we get home, I will make you a whole pot of your own, but this," she tapped the precious metal bowl with her stirring stick, "this is for Tipaakke Oopus. He will know his friend Won sends it when he tastes."

Katelyn nodded. "So how do I look?" She spread out the sober skirts that had belonged to Quaker woman.

Won glanced up at her, standing there in the woods clearing. "Not like you belong here." She nodded approvingly. "You look very white. But cover your hair, those women, they did not wear their hair braided with crow feathers woven in the strands."

Katelyn picked the stolen silk bonnet off the ground and pulled it over her head, tucking her braids beneath. "Is this better?"

Mekollaan came up behind her. "Are you two ready? We must go soon." He faced Katelyn. "You must wipe the fire from your eyes if you want to look like the others."

Katelyn dropped her head and began to walk, shuffling her feet, murmuring a prayer. She knew how those Quaker woman behaved, she had seen them in England.

Mekollaan laughed. "That is good. You have convinced Hawk. But can you convince the white man jailors?"

Katelyn's head popped up, the drawn look on her face disappearing in an instant. "Of course I can. What am I going to carry the bread and stew in, Won?" She chewed her bottom lip nervously. "I hadn't thought about that."

"The stars are with you," Won replied. "Falling Rain found a basket yesterday on a step. It had little dogs in it, but he put them in the house." She crossed the clearing to search for the basket beneath a pile of leaves."

Katelyn began to giggle. "He didn't!" Her hands flew to her cheeks, rosy from nervousness.

Mekollaan refused to laugh. "The dogs must have belonged to the people who lived in the house."

"He just pushed them in the door?" She tried to suppress her laughter, knowing Mekollaan didn't like silliness. "How many were there?"

"Five, maybe six. Falling Rain did not count. He said they were brown dogs with white spots." He couldn't help, but grin. It was rather funny. Some poor white man would get up in the morning to find little brown dogs running around his house!

Won handed Katelyn a small, woven-reed basket. "I will put the stew and bread in the basket. Take care not to tip it or the Fox's stew will be in the bottom." She picked up two square pieces of hide and used them to remove the hot pot from the open fire. "Bring back Won's cooking bowl. It was my mother's."

Katelyn held out the basket for Won to pack. "Mekollaan, what if another Quaker comes while I am inside?" She was beginning to become uneasy. She was not so much concerned over getting into the jail and facing the jailors, as she was facing Tipaakke. What

386

was she going to say? What was he going to say? Would he believe her? I will make him believe, she told herself.

Mekollaan kicked at a pile of rotting leaves. "Two braves will watch from the end of the street, behind the drinking house. If one comes," he shrugged his shoulders, "my men will take her for a walk."

"You won't hurt her?" Katelyn tightened her grip on her basket.

"No, but we will have to keep her until the Fox is safe. We cannot let the white men know we are here or they will take my brother to another jail . . . or they will kill him now."

With that thought, Katelyn sobered. "I am ready, Hawk." She bowed her head, preparing herself to play the part of the Quaker woman.

"Do just as I have told you, Katelyn. Do not risk your life or Tipaakke's. You are only to get in, take him the food and get out. Do not try to get him out yourself." He stood in front of her, grasping her shoulders.

"I just want to talk to him. I will give him the food and find out how the jail is laid out." She stared up at him. His eyes were so like Tipaakke's, yet different. "I will do it right; you can depend on me."

When Katelyn and the Delaware braves reached the edge of the woods near Annapolis, they separated, as planned. The braves made their way to their designated spots on the street the jail stood on, and Katelyn entered town from the end where the Quakers lived.

Slipping from behind a red brick house, Katelyn made her way down the paved walk. Past the houses she walked, keeping her head down. The brick felt cool on her bare feet as she took care to keep them beneath the long, grey skirt of the dress. Around the corner she went and down the main street. The tangy smell of the bay filled her nostrils as she passed a gentleman on the street.

"Evening, Mistress," he called.

"Evening," Katelyn replied, keeping her head down so he couldn't see her face.

Turning to the right, she passed the Customs House. The jail was just a little further. Her heart pounded beneath her breast and she ran her hand over her round belly. It couldn't be hidden in the dress, but she and Won had decided it didn't matter. Even Quakers had babies.

Up to the door she stepped, whispering a prayer. Slowly, she lifted her hand to knock, just as she had seen the other two women do before. The door swung open.

"Evening to you, Mistress." A portly, red-faced gentleman in tight breeches stood in the doorway.

Katelyn swung the basket. "Nourishment for the heathen." She kept her eyes averted.

"Come in, careful of the step." He reached out to give her a hand.

Katelyn stepped into a parlor-like room, furnished neatly with a table and stools and several straight-backed chairs along the wall. A desk took up one corner. To her left was a closed door. "Thank thee, kind sir," she murmured.

The portly man stared at her. "I don't remember seeing you here before. He turned this way and that, trying to get a glimpse of her face.

"I . . . I stay with my aunt and uncle, just for a few days, then I meet my husband and go home." She glanced sideways at the two men sitting at the table, cards in their hands.

The man nodded his head. "Oh, who is your aunt and uncle?

Katelyn froze. What should she say? She had to say

388

something, he was waiting for an answer. "John and Sarah Goodgate." It was the only name she could think of; they were the Catholics that had lived near her father's church.

"Funny, don't know them." He shrugged his shoulders. "But then they keep mostly to themselves. Don't see them much in the Cock and Bull." He laughed and the others joined in.

Katelyn tried not to fidget. "I must take the food to the prisoner, then home for evening prayers." She tried to make her way past him, heading for the long hallway she assumed led to the cells.

"No, that's all right Mistress. Let me take it for you." He slipped the basket off her arm before she could protest. "I can take it for you. You don't want to see that beast," he glanced at her protruding stomach, clearing his throat, "not in your condition."

She tried not to panic. She had to see Fox. "No, I must take the bowl home to my aunt or she will be angry."

"We got pots here and bowls. Bruce, get one of those bowls for the lady. She brought food for the Injun." He turned back to Katelyn. "Sure smells good, Mistress. You cook it yourself?" He caught a peek of her face beneath the dark bonnet. Fetching thing she was with those brown eyes Was that a tendril of red hair he saw?

Katelyn's mind raced. They weren't going to let her see him! She had to do something. "If thou doesn't mind, sir, I would see the prisoner; give him some spiritual comfort." She took a step towards the hallway. She wouldn't come this close and not see him!

"Well, if you want." The jailor carried the basket to the table, lifting the lid. "But he doesn't speak any English."

She started for the cells. "The Lord speaks in all languages, sir," she called over her shoulder.

Trembling, Katelyn shuffled down the narrow hallway. When she stepped into the room that held the cells she was shocked. These were horse stalls! There were two cells, built of thick timber side by side. The outside walls were brick, with wooden bars on the front and separating them. Immediately she caught sight of Tipaakke's dark head in the cell to the left. The right held a blond haired man who slept in a bed of straw in a crate hanging from the wall.

"I have come to pray for you, sir," she said in her Quaker woman's voice. She moved to the front of his cell and grasped the wooden bars. His back was to her as he leaned on the back brick wall. Why didn't he turn around?

"*Maata! Maata Biindam!*" His voice was sharp.

"*Kihiila,*" she whispered. "Yes, listen to me; you must."

A chill ran down Tipaakke's spine, as he turned slowly to face her. His first reaction was to run to her, to press his body against the bars and wrap her in his arms. But he could not. He would not. She had betrayed him and his love for her. At first he said nothing; he just stared at her through half-closed eyelids. She was hauntingly beautiful in the dark garb, though he could see nothing but her pale, strained face. "Why do you come?" he asked coldly.

"To speak to you, to bring you food, to make sure you're all right." She clutched at the wooden bars until her knuckles turned a deadening white. "We're going to get you out of here."

"I want nothing from you." He eyed her round stomach. "Nothing but my child. Send my brother. I will take no help from you." He turned his back, unable to look at her.

"Fox, please," she pleaded. "I have only a few minutes." She reached out with one hand through the bars.

"You must listen to me, you must let me make you understand."

"I do not want to hear your lies." He felt as if his heart was being wrenched from his chest. "Just go."

"No, I won't go." Tears ran unchecked down her flushed cheeks. "I love you. You have to listen to me." She was beginning to grow angry with him. "You owe me that much!"

Tipaakke spun around in fury. "I owe you nothing!" He took three long strides across the straw-strewn floor. "I gave you all I had, and you gave me betrayal in return." He shook his head. "I owe you nothing white woman."

Tears stung Katelyn's eyes. She had to make him listen! She had to make him understand! When he turned to walk away she grabbed a hunk of his hair, without thinking. Snapping his head hard, she pulled her hand back through the bars, taking his hair with it.

"Ow!" he cried. "Let go of me!" He grabbed his hair with his own hand, trying to ease the tension.

Tipaakke's hair felt smooth and silky beneath her touch. "Now you listen to me," she ordered through clenched teeth. "What kind of man will not listen to another? Things are not always as they seem." She twisted his hair around her fingers, holding him tight against the bars. "Certainly a man who was about to become the High Chief of his people would not be a man who judged before he heard the facts."

Tipaakke swallowed hard. Suddenly he felt rather foolish. Why had he been so quick to jump to conclusions; that was so unlike him. She was right, he owed her a chance to explain. "*Gekiitte*. Speak. Fox will listen." His voice was soft.

Katelyn let go of his hair, but he remained pressed against the bars. "I'm sorry I hurt you," she whispered, this time reaching to stroke his head. "After we parted,

I became lost, it rained and I caught a chill. I was feverish and confused when a man picked me up on a dirt road. He figured out I was the missing girl and sent word to Henry." She hung her head for a moment, listening to Tipaakke's steady breathing. "He drugged me and locked me in his house. When I tried to get away he locked me in an ice house for days. I know it looked like he and I were close, but I had to pretend . . ." her voice cracked.

"Shhhhh . . ." Tipaakke soothed. "No tears, my love."

She went on. "I had to pretend because he said he would kill me. He said he was going to take away my baby . . ., he said . . ." She leaned against the bars, straining to brush her lips against his cheek. "I was so scared," she sobbed.

Tipaakke threaded his hands through the bars, smoothing the hair that tumbled from her bonnet. "Hush," he whispered, "or the jailors will hear you." He breathed deeply, inhaling her familiar, magical scent. She always smelled so sweet, so fresh. He knew she told the truth, and he knew he had been wrong to jump to such erratic conclusions. "Tell me why you begged for the coward's life, Katie-girl."

She covered his hands with hers as he held her face, tipping her chin until brown eyes met heavenly black. "I did not want his blood on your hands; you are too fine a warrior to waste your blade on such a man. I would not have you carry such a worthless soul on your belt." She blinked back the tears that flowed freely. "I will not have his dead body be the foundation for our love, our life together." Her lips trembled as she searched his eyes for understanding.

"I am sorry, my love," Tipaakke's voice was strained. "I am sorry I suspected you of betrayal. I think maybe I still feared our love. It was too beautiful to believe it was real, that it was solid. I was hurt so badly by the thought of your going to him, that I left no place in my heart to find you innocent."

"I would never hurt you on purpose, Fox. I love you." She pressed fleeting kisses to his rough palms and her tears mingled with his flesh.

For a moment they rested forehead against forehead, wishing desperately that they could be closer. But the wooden bars of the jail separated them just as Jentry's lies and the white man's prejuduce did.

"Know this, Katie-girl," Tipaakke murmured against her cheek. "I love you. I have always loved you. I love you today, I will love you tomorrow." He let the silence stretch between them for a moment and then, reluctantly, he lifted his head. "Where is my brother?"

"Outside, we found a place to hide across the street in an old man's barn." She sniffed, giving him her best smile. "We have watched you for days. I figured out how to get inside to see you."

"This is very clever." He nodded staring at the sober garb. "I am proud of you," he touched his bare chest, "here, in my heart. You will make a good Lenni Lenape wife."

"Mistress . . . mistress . . ." a voice came from down the long hallway. "Are you all right?" Footsteps sounded on the brick.

Katelyn slipped into the role of the Quaker woman, as easily as she had once slipped on a glove. She spoke, her voice true and clear. "And he did say, Repent ye: for the kingdom of heaven is at hand. For this is he that was spoken by the prophet Isaiah, saying the voice of one . . ."

The portly jailor came around the corner and stopped in front of the first cell. "Just checking to be sure you were all right." He sipped from a pewter mug.

Katelyn kept her head bowed, her hands clapsed in

front of her as she continued with the passage, ignoring the man. " . . . crying in the darkness, Prepare ye the way of the Lord, make his paths straight." She looked up at Tipaakke standing so close to the bars that she could feel his breath on her cheek. "Heed brother," she wagged a finger at him. "We are all sinners, and we must all struggle with Satan. Think brother, and I will return tomorrow." She glanced up one more time through veiled lashes to see his calm face. All was right again between them. She could read it in his eyes. She turned her head so that the jailor saw only bonnet, but no face, and mouthed the words, "I love you, Fox." Forcing herself to turn away, she faced the jailor. "Just quoting from the Good Book." She followed him back up the hallway. "I think this man's soul has a chance. I will return on the morrow, if it suits thee."

He shrugged his shoulders. "Doesn't make a difference to me, but I think you're wasting your time. I told you he doesn't know English."

"And I told thee that it makes no difference." She spied her rabbit stew on the table with bread, alongside sat her basket. "You will take the food to him . . . to them both." She didn't want to seem suspicious.

"Of course, of course!" He swept her basket off the table and handed it to her. "I'll take it right away myself. Don't want him to go hungry, do we? Want him to be nice and fat for the hanging, don't we boys?" The other men chuckled in reply.

Katelyn headed for the door, the basket on her arm. "Dost thou really think they will?"

"Hang him?" He opened the door for her. "Sure as living. The trial's to be at the end of the week. Going to swing the two of them together, him and the lady attacker."

Katelyn fluttered her eyelashes. "The Good Father knows there must be a better way." She stepped onto the brick walk outside the jailhouse door.

"No, not with these red devils, there's not. Good day to you, Mistress." He waved a hand as she headed back up the street.

It was all Katelyn could do to walk sedately up the brick path. She wanted to run and tell Won that all was right between her and Fox again; she wanted to assure Mekollaan that his brother was safe and well. But she knew she must follow the plan. She would have to walk back through the town and disappear into the woods on the other side. Mekollaan and Won would be waiting for her at the campsite.

Forcing herself not to smile, she kept to the role of the Quaker woman, placing one foot in front of the other. *He loves me*, her heart cried. *He still loves me!* She was so relieved. It had been so difficult to sit and wait when she knew Tipaakke was in such danger.

Suppressing the desire to skip up the hill, she walked past the houses that lined the busy street. Never again would she live in a house, or sleep in a bed, but she didn't care. Tipaakke's wigwam suited her just fine; she liked its coziness and warmth. As she passed the last dwelling on the street, she headed through the clearing to the woods.

Running her hand over her abdomen, she wondered what it would be like on the Ohio. "It doesn't matter," she murmured. "As long as we're all together, it will be beautiful."

Hurrying through the woods, she reached the camp ahead of schedule. By the time Won and Mekollaan arrived, she had already stripped off the stiffling dress and bathed in the nearby bay tributary. Slipping her sleeveless leather jerkin over her head, she tied the soft deerhide breechcloth on and sat down to eat a bowl of berries someone had picked.

"Look at you!" Won came strutting through the

trees, both arms out for Katelyn. "You get more like a Lenni Lenape each day. You risk your life, slip in and out under the enemies' nose and here you sit eating strawberries!"

Katelyn laughed, her cheeks turning pink. "I was hungry." She shrugged her shoulders, offering the reed bowl to Won. "I would rather have had the stew, but Tipaakke got all of that."

Won's face grew stoney. "No. He did not get my stew." She started to build a small fire, moving methodically.

"What do you mean?" Katelyn glanced up at Mekollaan. "I took him the stew . . . well, the jailor said he would give it to him."

Mekollaan picked up a stick and sent it flying through the air. "We saw you through the window. We also saw the jailors eat the stew and bread after you left."

Katelyn let out an exasperated huff of breath. No wonder Won was mad! She had spend all of that time preparing the stew for Tipaakke and those pigs had eaten it! "He didn't get anything?" She put down her bowl of berries, suddenly no longer hungery. How long had it been since Fox had eaten something?

Mekollaan squatted beside Katelyn. He has gone longer without eating. Do not worry. Now tell me everything that happened inside, Katelyn. Tell me where the cells are. Are there jailors with him? You must tell me everything." He stared into her doe eyes, well pleased. She had done well today, and he could tell by the serenity in her face that all was well between her and his brother. He was tempted to ask her about what had occurred between them, but he did not. That was personal, and he would not pry.

Sitting there in front of the fire, beside Mekollaan, Katelyn began to feel a new self rising from deep within. As she conversed with the great Delaware brave, she could feel his acceptance of her washing over her body like soft rain. His face had softened, his eyes twinkled, as he listened to her story, asking questions when he deemed it necessary, laughing with her as she told him how she had deceived the enemy.

The other braves and Won gathered around the fire as they took their evening meal, listening closely to all Katelyn said. A unique bond threaded between them as they discussed the possible ways of getting Tipaakke out of the white man's hand. They each knew that he would have to be rescued before the trial, because there would be no fairness in this trial. Only Henry would be permitted to give his story and only he would be believed. Tipaakke didn't stand a chance; he'd be hung at dawn the next day.

As Katelyn rested with the Lenni Lenape brothers she began to experience a closeness she'd never felt before. She had proved herself worthy of their respect and would hold it for a life time. Never before had she fit in with anyone like she fit in with these men, here, tonight. Even Mekollaan, who had hated her, now believed her worthy of his friendship. If only Tipaakke could have been here to share this with her.

Into the night the dozen braves, Katelyn, and Won, sat in a circle, smoking their pipes and mulling over Tipaakke's imprisonment. They knew there had to be a way to get him out; there was always a way. They simply had to come up with it.

After everyone had finally unrolled their sleeping mats and laid down to rest, Katelyn and Won lay next to each other staring into the burning embers. "I can't believe they ate his stew!" She tossed a piece of bark into the fire and watched the flames lick it up.

Won laughed, rolling onto her back. "We can never believe the things these white men do. I will be glad to move from here. This is no longer our home, it has been taken from us." She stared up at the starless sky.

"Wish I could poison the stinking dogs!" She threw another piece into the fire.

Won was silent for a moment, and then she sat straight up on her mat. "What did you say, Kate-lyn?"

Her eyebrows furrowed in confusion. "I said, I wish I could poison the dogs. It would serve them right, stealing Fox's food."

"You are very smart." Won wagged a finger, spinning around to face Katelyn. "That would work." Her eyes sparkled mischievously.

"What would work? What are you talking about?" She was beginning to get very sleepy. What was Won babbling about?

"That is how we can get the Fox out of his trap!" Won slapped her hands together, tickled with herself.

Katelyn turned her head. "Fox? A way to get him out? How? What are you talking about?" She rolled over on her side, propping her head up with her elbow.

"We will poison them!"

"Poison who? You're not making any sense, Won." Katelyn stared through the darkness at her friend, watching the firelight dance across her broad face.

"Poison the jailors." She held up her palms. "You take your basket of food to the jail, the jailors eat it . . ."

"You're going to kill all three of them? Mekollaan isn't going to like that; he said no unnecessary deaths." She shook her head, her eyes growing wide.

"No! I won't kill them, I just will make them very sick in their stomach." Won was beginning to chuckle, the beads around her neck clattering together as her body shook.

Katelyn got up and crawled over to Won, sitting up on her knees to face her friend. "I'm sorry, but I'm lost."

Her knees pressed against Won's. "How are we going to get Tipaakke out of a jail by poisoning the guards?" Her hand flew to her belly when the baby gave a hard kick. "He knows we speak of his father."

"It would be very easy. I will find the herbs to make up a medicine used to cleanse the body, only I will make it stronger, I will make another stew and put the mixture into it." She stirred an imaginary spoon with one large bronze hand. "Then, when the jailors eat the stew, they will have to run very quickly to the . . ." she searched for the right word. "The . . . what is your word . . . to the woods to . . . ?"

Katelyn was confused for a moment, but then she began to grin. "It's a purgative!" Her hand clamped over her mouth. "You mean they'd have to get to the necessary?" She giggled behind her hand.

"They would *run* to their little house in the back. And we would slip in the front, take our friend from the jail, and slip out again before a single white man saw us." Won crossed her arms in front of her chest, obviously pleased with herself. "It is simple, and no one must die. The jailors will also get a cleansing. Our people say it is good for the soul."

Katelyn and Won spent the remainder of the night making plans and discussing the safest way to get Tipaakke out. By dawn they were tired, but pleased with their ideas. It really would work. Mekollaan, however, was a little more skeptical.

"How do you know your potion will be strong enough?" He picked up a flat corn cake off the baking stone and took a bite. "They will know who poisoned them if they are given a chance to think. Katelyn will be trapped in the back of the jail."

Won mixed a sprinkle of herbs from her bag with hot

399

water and handed the bowl to Katelyn. "Drink," she ordered. Then she turned back to Mekollaan. "You think I do not know my plants? I will make them very clean." She nodded her head confidently.

Mekollaan licked the cake crumbs from his fingers. "Once these jailors run out of the jailhouse, how will Katelyn get him out? There would be no time to burn the wooden bars."

"That's the easy part." Katelyn took a sip of her steamy tea. "The keys to the big locks on the cell doors hang on a peg there in the back." She shrugged her shoulders. "I'll just unlock the door and let him out."

"The jailors will not eat the stew until after you are gone," Mekollaan said.

"You're right. We hadn't even thought of that." Katelyn sat down in the soft summer grass. "So, I'll just run back in and let him out after they've come out of the jailhouse and run around to the back."

"No, I will let my brother out. You will come back here and wait for us. We will have to flee quickly. They will know you let him out. They will be looking for you."

"No, Mekollaan." Katelyn's voice was clear and strong. "I must do this; it is important to me. He will soon be my husband; I must do this alone."

Mekollaan understood why she wanted to free him herself, but he hated taking the risk, especially with her so near to giving birth. But then a Lenni Lenape woman would have done no less for her brave. The Hawk knew he would have to let her do this, he had no right to stop her. He would just have to make sure nothing went wrong. "Yes, you are right. You must do it."

"And while she is getting the Fox out of his trap," Won explained, "you and your men will cause some trouble on the white man's streets. Burn some houses or something."

Katelyn swallowed a gulp of hot tea. "I don't think we need to set houses on fire, do we? Those are people's homes."

Won grimaced. "They do not need those big houses of their baked stone and grandfather trees. They should live in wigwams."

Mekollaan shook his head, laughing at Won. "I do not think it is wise to burn the Annapolis town, but there are other things that my men could do to get the white men's attentions."

Won tied her moccasins and slung a soft hide bag over her arm. "I do not know how long I will be gone looking for the plants I need. I may have to travel far. I have not seen the green-striped leaf bush so near to the great waters."

Katelyn finished off her tea and got to her feet. "How long do you think you'll be gone? We should do this tonight. You have to get back in time to cook the stew."

Won shook her head, raising her eyebrows. "I cannot say."

Mekollaan took a step nearer to Katelyn and reached out to touch her lightly on the shoulder. "I think we should wait until tomorrow night. It will give us time to prepare."

"No." Katelyn's face grew taut with concern. "Tomorrow is his trial. They will hang him."

Mekollaan's voice was gentle. "You said the jailor told you they would not hang him until the sun dawns the day after."

"That's what he said, but . . ." Her voice trailed off as her eyes met Mekollaan's. "Do you think he will be all right?" She was afraid to take any chances, afraid of losing him.

"I think this is best. Everything must go right, we can make no mistakes. One day will make no difference." Mekollaan planted his hands on his hips, watching Katelyn. The early morning light played off her hair, weaving sparks of firelight through her heavy tresses. He wished he could promise all would go right, but he could not. He, too, would be uneasy about Tipaakke facing the white man's council. But what else could be done? She could only take food just before darkness sets in, otherwise the jailors would grow suspicious. He thought for a moment and then spoke again. "If you can cook up something today while Won is gone, I think you can go back to the jail tonight. Fox will need to know of the plans we make.

Relief washed over Katelyn. If she couldn't get him out tonight, at least she could see him, touch his smooth cheeks, comfort him. She needed comforting of her own. The baby seemed to have shifted in the night and suddenly felt heavier, more burdensome. She knew her time was near and prayed they could get back to the village before it came. She needed to talk to Fox right now; she wanted reassurance of his love for her.

By dusk, Katelyn found herself traveling the same brick path to the jailhouse. On her arm, she carried the basket packed with crispy fried fish and more bread stolen from a summer kitchen. The fish had been her idea and she and Mekollaan had spent a pleasant afternoon fishing at the bay's edge. They had also dug clams, which would be steamed on the campfire for the Delaware braves' evening meal.

Humming softly to herself, Katelyn stepped up to the heavy hand-hewn door of the jailhouse and gave three knocks. Boldly, she turned to flash a smile in the direction of the barn where Mekollaan and two other braves stood watch. When the door opened, she stepped in.

"Good evening to thee, gentlemen." She kept her head down, hidden by the Quaker woman's black bonnet. "I bring food for the prisoners and words of salvation for the savage."

The red-faced, portly jailor reached to catch the basket on her arm. "Mmm hmm, sure smells good tonight, mistress. Let me take that for you." He swept the basket through the air and deposited it on the table where the other two were playing cards, just as they were the night before. "It's not quite time for them to eat, so I'll just keep the basket here for them." He grinned.

"As you wish." Katelyn bobbed her head and started down the hallway. "Good evening to you, brother," she called out to Tipaakke.

Tipaakke leaped out of his bed of straw and ran to the bars. He watched Katelyn come around the corner. Her face was like the first breath of spring air to him. Even in her dull, white woman's dress and foolish head-covering, she radiated beauty. He caught her attention and pressed his fingers to his lips. She would have to take care. The prisoner in the other cell was awake and would hear every word that passed between the Quaker woman and the Indian. They could not take the chance of letting him see any familiarity between them. Who knew what he might say to the jailors?

Katelyn smiled serenely, taking note of the blond prisoner who leaned against the wall, staring at nothing. "Are we ready for our evening lesson?" She continued with the charade, beginning to recite to him from the Bible. It just isn't fair, she thought, as she spoke from rote memory. She had wanted to talk to him! She had wanted to touch him. She wanted to tell him how near their baby was to coming into the world. Instead, she could only stand there in front of a cage, speaking in another woman's voice.

Tipaakke stood with his face pressed to the wooden

bars, his eyes resting on her bonneted face. As she recited from her people's law book, her eyes spoke words of a different nature. Those soft doe eyes spoke of the love between a man and a woman. They made promises of a life, together and sparkled with promises of the love flamed by a kiss, a soft-spoken word. There was no need for her to speak, he already knew what was in her heart.

As Katelyn droned on, speaking of salvation and repentance, her eyes searched Tipaakke's for the reassurance she needed, and she found that comfort. Now, if only she could tell him how they were going to get him out!

Suddenly, a thought came to her. She finished up with her last verse, and then spoke again. "Now in conclusion, heathen brother, let us dig deep within ourselves, and have a moment of silence so that we might contemplate our sins." She sneaked a glance at the blond prisoner. He was still standing there, staring, but paying no attention to them. Stepping closer to the bars, Katelyn whispered. "Tipaakke."

"It is good to see you, my love." His voice was smooth and comforting, so barely audible that she seemed to absorb his words, rather than hear them.

"You must stand trial tomorrow, we cannot get you out until the evening." She spoke quickly, keeping her head down to look as if she were in prayer.

"How?" he murmured. His hand ached to reach out and take her hand. Just one touch, that was all he wanted. He just wanted to feel her skin against his.

"There is no time. Just trust me, I will be here tomorrow night and I will get you out." Her voice quivered. "I must go." She inhaled deeply, inhaling his heavy masculine scent, pressing it to memory.

"Go."

"Amen," she spoke aloud, and then she reached out

404

her hand to his. "Good evening to you, sir."

Tipaakke smiled, taking her hand in his. It was only a brief, white man's handshake, but a streak of energy raced between them, sending shivers through their bodies. "Tomorrow," she whispered, and then she was gone.

When Katelyn entered the parlor of the jailhouse, the jailor had already emptied her basket. "Here you are, mistress. We thank you for your help." He handed her the basket and opened the outer door for her.

"Thou wilst take the food to the prisoners?" she asked shuffling out the door.

"Will, indeed, mistress. Good evening to you." He hurried her out the door, anxious to try the trout before it cooled.

"Sir?" Katelyn stuck her bonneted head back in the doorway.

"Yes?" The jailor leaned impatiently against the door frame.

"Thou says the savage's trial will be on the morrow?" She peered up at him through thick lashes.

"Yes, ma'am. Noon." He closed the door behind her.

Noon the next day, Katelyn found herself following the familiar brick walk through Annapolis. Dressed in the stolen Quaker garb, she headed for the court house on the main street in town. She and Mekollaan had gotten into a terrible fight over her going to Tipaakke's trial, but she had refused to take no for an answer. She had to be there when the jailors led him into the courtroom; she had to be there when Henry spun his lies committing Fox to death for a murder he'd done himself. Even if Fox couldn't see her there among the spectators, he would know in his heart that she was with him.

405

It seemed that everyone in the seafaring town was out today, dressed in their finest clothes, hurrying to get front seats in the court room. Venders stood on the sidewalks, calling out their wares and craftsmen set up booths in the streets displaying their metalworks and bolts of woven cloth. The air was filled with an electrical excitement as people called out to one another across the street, waving and laughing.

Katelyn kept her head down, shuffling down the busy street. *Bastards!* she thought bitterly. *They think they're going to a party. A man is going to be sentenced to hang for a crime he didn't commit today and they think its a day of celebration. These people, they were all so proud of their new way of life, their justice, their trials for all men. The truth is, this is all a farce. No one would care what Tipaakke said, no one would ask for his story. He had already been found guilty by the good citizens at Henry's birthday party, and all because his skin is red, rather than white.*

By the time Katelyn reached the courthouse, the room had already been filled to bursting and now people were spilling out into the street. Children sat on their father's shoulders, peering in the windows and men backed up wagons to stand on to get a better view.

Katelyn's stomach turned and twisted as she drew closer. Then the crowd began to part and she was pulled to the side by a young man in a gray coat.

"Best back up, they're bringing the savage." He pointed in the direction of the jailhouse around the corner.

Katelyn stood on her toes, craning her neck. What she saw made her blood run cold. Tipaakke was being led by the two jailors who had played cards. Links of heavy rusted chain tied his wrists and feet together so that he could barely walk. The portly jailor led the way, pushing the crowd back as he strutted like a rooster down the middle of the street.

Katelyn bit down on her lip until she tasted blood. How dare they shame him like this! But Tipaakke walked with his head held high, his long, midnight-black hair flowing over his shoulders. He resembled some pagan god, with his bare bronze chest and perfectly sculptured limbs. As he walked, pulling the long clanking chains behind him, his eyes pierced the souls of the men and women who stared at him.

A great hush settled over the spectators outside the courtroom as the prisoner passed, then they broke into a great buzz of whispers. "You think they could have clothed him, the poor creature," a woman commented, leaning to get a better look.

A man snorted behind Katelyn. "Heard they tried. My Uncle Morris knows the jailor's son and he says they tried to dress him in something decent. He says the beast ripped the coat into pieces with his teeth!"

Katelyn covered her hands over her ears to block out the horrible things these people said about Fox. *When we get away from here,* she vowed, *we will never ever come back. I don't ever want to see another white face again.* She squeezed her eyes shut to keep the tears from flowing. They thought he was some kind of animal.

As the sounds of the chains grew close, Katelyn forced her eyes open. Suddenly, she found herself pushing her way through the crowd to reach the street. "Excuse, excuse," she murmured. She reached the edge of the sidewalk just as Tipaakke passed. Their eyes met for one fleeting moment, and then he was gone, but he had seen her. He knew she was there!

As Tipaakke and the jailors entered the brick court house, the judge and jurors appeared. It was all Katelyn could do to remain silent as she caught a glimpse of Henry's face in the crowd. *Murderer*, her insides screamed. *You are the one who should be on trial!* But, she kept her head down, knowing he must not

407

recognize her.

The trial was all a blur to Katelyn as she stood at the window, listening to the judicial nonsense. Henry, dressed in a brilliant red coat and red shoes with green heels stood up and told of how he and his betrothed were attacked by the heathen and how the savage killed the servant Jonathan and kidnapped his beloved. As a matter of protocol, Tipaakke was asked to state his case. Surprising everyone, he stood, flashed a smile at all present and then spoke softly for the first time since his capture, in English. "I did not kill the dark-skinned boy."

"Then who did?" the bewigged judge demanded, startled that the red bastard spoke English.

Tipaakke tipped back his head, laughing until the sound of his voice reverberated. "That, you must ask Henry Coward." He pointed one long, bronze finger in Henry's direction, and the courtroom broke into frenzied conversation.

The rest was simple. Once the courtroom was in order again, the verdict returned swiftly. "Guilty as charged," the judge announced solemnly. "The Indian is sentenced to hang by his neck until dead. God rest his soul. God bless the King of England."

"God rest his soul," the crowd repeated. "God bless King George!"

For a brief moment, Katelyn thought she might faint. She had known this was coming, and she thought she'd prepared herself, but to actually hear the sentence was almost more than she could bear. I have to get out of here, she thought. The sun was beating unmercifully on her head, and her body was smothering beneath the Quaker woman's dress. Pushing through the crowd, she made her way to the sidewalk, and hurried back up the street. Her heart pounded beneath her breast and rivulets of perspiration ran down the sides of her face. *If I can just get back to the camp*, she told herself, *I will be all right*. The brick beneath her feet suddenly seemed uneven as she climbed the hill, stumbling around the corner of a building. The ground beneath her feet swirled and rolled as she ran across the meadow and into the woods. Racing blindly through the forest, she called to Won over and over again until she found herself in her friend's arms.

Words spilled from Katelyn's mouth as tears ran down her cheeks. "It was so horrible," she moaned. "I wanted to kill them. I wanted to kill them all. I'm so afraid."

Won led Katelyn through the trees to the camp and helped her to the ground, motioning to Mekollaan to stay back. "She will be fine, Hawk," she assured him in a whisper. "The baby could come soon. It is hard for a woman at this time." She pulled the black bonnet off her head. "She does not always have control over her mind and body." She brushed back the damp hair off Katelyn's head, and started to pull her dress over her head.

"Are you sure she is strong enough?" Mekollaan's voice was strained. He was concerned for Katelyn's health, but his brother's life depended on her right now. She had to be able to carry through with the plan.

"I said she would be fine. She needs sleep and peaceful time to think. Now leave us, take your men and go fishing. I will care for her and prepare all for tonight. We will be ready."

Mekollaan nodded, and turned to call his men. He would have to trust Won. What other choice did he have?

Chapter Seventeen

By the time Katelyn woke from her nap, the shadows of the trees were lengthening, and the air had grown cooler. For a few moments, she laid there on Won's mat, listening to the movement of the Lenni Lenape braves as they broke camp. Their voices were hushed and comforting, enveloping her like a babe's blanket. What ever had been in that tea Won had given her had certainly been strong! She had said it would calm her, relax her so that she could get some rest before evening. Katelyn remembered nothing after the first few sips! Slowly, she lifted her eyelids.

"I see you wake." Won smiled down at her. "Do you feel better?" She kneeled beside her.

"Much. Thank you." Katelyn sat up lazily. "I feel so foolish for carrying on so." She looked down to see that Won must have taken the Quaker gown off her and dressed her in her clean jerkin and breechcloth.

"Do not feel that way. We are your friends. There is no shame in what we feel in our hearts." Won turned to begin packing bundles of fresh flowers and herbs in her medicine bag. "I know it must have been hard to stand and listen to the white men say they will kill the man you love."

Katelyn ran her hands through her long hair, brushing it off her shoulders. The rest had done her good. All was in perspective again. She knew the plan and could recite it word for word, and she knew it was going to work. She would make it work! "How soon do we go, Won?"

Her friend got slowly to her feet. "Soon, Kate-lyn." She laid one hand on her shoulder. "You must get your things together. I will carry your bag until your part is done. We will not return to this site; Mekollaan says we head for home tonight."

Once Katelyn had packed her few belongings; her porcupine-quill hairbrush, her water bag, and her clean breechcloth and jerkin, she made ready to play the role of the Quaker missionary one last time.

Once Katelyn was dressed and bonneted, she sought out Mekollaan who was overseeing the cleanup of the campsite. The fire had to be buried, the leaves swept back over the bare spots they'd made, and all signs of human occupation removed. That was the way they found the small clearing, and that was the way they would leave it.

"Mekollaan," Katelyn spoke hesitantly, knowing what she wanted to say, but not knowing the words. She spoke in halting Algonquian, inserting English words when she had to. "I want to say I am sorry for misjudging you. I am sorry for the bad things I have said to you, and about you." She searched his ebony eyes for compassion. "I think I understand you now, and your ways. You disliked me because you were afraid I would hurt your brother."

Mekollaan stared at Katelyn standing there in front of him, dressed in a gown similar to the one the Quaker girl he had once loved had worn. Katelyn was nothing like she—who's name he would never speak again—but the dark bonnet with dangling strings brought back memories he had thought were long buried. It had taken a lot for his brother's woman to come to him like this, and he was touched. "And I am sorry for the same." He spoke in English, because it was her language, just as she had apologized in his. "I, too, misjudged. You are not the woman who betrayed me." He stroked his thick, dark scalplock. "I see why my brother, Fox, would love you."

"And I see why he would love you," she returned in broken Lenni Lenape, offering her hand to him. "Let us go to your brother with friendship in our hearts."

He took her pale hand, squeezing it tightly in his own. "And I am sorry for what I did to you the first day you came to the village. My manners were very bad."

Katelyn laughed, throwing back her head. "You are forgiven."

Their eyes met and held for a moment, then the Hawk broke the spell. "Let us go. It is time to find our brother and take him home."

Katelyn's palms were so damp as she walked down the familiar sidewalk, that she had to continually switch the basket from one side to the other and wipe her sweaty hands on her dress. It was almost dark by the time she reached the jailhouse door, just as planned. Whispering a silent prayer, and turning to give a wink in the direction of the barn across the street, she rapped on the door.

"Mistress?" The red-faced jailor wrinkled his face in confusion. "One of you already brought the prisoners a meal."

Katelyn forced herself to breath easily. "Oh, well, perhaps they might still be hungry." She lifted the lid on the basket to release the smell of fresh-baked muffins, clam soup, and raisin cookies. The muffins and cookies had been stolen from the tavern bakehouse, but Won had brewed the soup herself—special herbs and all.

The jailor sniffed, fluttering his eyelashes. "Yes,

ma'am, come to think of it, those prisoners might just still be hungry." His Adam's apple bobbed up and down as he wet his lips. "Won't you come in?"

Katelyn stepped into the parlor and nodded to the two playing cards. "Even', gentlemen." She dropped the basket on the table. "I know thee likes to take them their meals thyself." She nodded, smiling pleasantly. What did it matter if he saw her this time? He'd never see her again. "I'll just go and give the men some final prayers, and then be on my way. Does that suit?"

"Yes, ma'am. Just don't be long. I think those two will be wanting to get a taste of this chowder before it gets cool." He rubbed his hand absently over his drooping stomach.

Katelyn turned her bonneted head to keep him from catching her smile. "I will only be a moment." Then she disappeared down the hallway that led to the cells.

"Fox!" Katelyn ran to the wooden bars, pressing her face between the slats. Though the other prisoner was sleeping in his straw bed, her voice was hushed.

"Katie-girl!" Fox crossed his cell to reach for her. "You have come." He stroked her cheek with the palm of his hand.

"I told you I would be here." Suddenly the smile fell from her face. "What happened to you?" she crooned, running her fingers through his hair. His face was badly bruised again, his nose swollen, and his eye half closed.

"It is nothing. What is important to me is that you are here." He took her hands in his so that he could look at her sweet face.

"Tonight is the night, my love. Soon we will be in each other's arms again." She squeezed his hands. "Won will care for your wounds when we set you free."

"I am glad tonight is the night," he teased, "because tomorrow night I will be busy . . . busy hanging from

413

that grandfather oak in the square."

Katelyn's doe eyes grew wide. "Don't even say that, it's not funny."

"Look at you with your mouth puckered like a dried fish." He ran a finger over her lips, softening them. "Am I to escape from here only to spend the rest of my days married to such a shriveled, sharp-tongued vixen?"

"Do not tease me! We're not out of this yet. Kiss me Tipaakke Oopus, I must go."

"You haven't told me how you're going to get me out. Where is Mekollaan? Is he coming?" He tucked a stray curl beneath her black bonnet.

"He is outside. I will be back for you very soon. We have poisoned the food that I brought you with a purge. If the jailors eat it just as they did last night and the night before, Won says they should be running to the back of the building very soon after."

Tipaakke chuckled. "You must tell me everything later, now go, before the fat-bellied man comes."

"I hate to leave you, Fox." Her voice was soft and laced with emotion.

"I know, my wolf-woman," he told her huskily. "I dream of you day and night. I cannot wait to touch you again, to feel your naked body against mine."

Katelyn's cheeks grew flushed, not from embarrassment, but desire. "Soon, very soon. I promise." She tore herself away from him. "I must go. Be ready, I will be back very soon for you."

Entering the parlor, Katelyn gathered her basket and empty soup bowl, making a quick exit. She was as anxious to get out of there as they were to get rid of her.

"Good night, mistress," the jailor called behind her. "Please feel free to bring a meal to a prisoner any time."

Katelyn nodded her head and closed the door softly behind her. Glancing in the direction of the abandoned barn, she gave a quick nod and hurried up the street. Cutting across an alley and back tracking, she was in the barn within minutes.

"You did it!" Won squeezed her arm, a grin broad on her face.

"Of course I did it." Katelyn moved to peer through the crack in the wide boards. "Now all we have to do is wait." She looked anxiously to Won. "I sure hope those herbs of yours work."

"They will work. I put many times what was needed. Those men who lock people in cages will be clean for many days." Won handed Katelyn her hide bag. "There is food and water in there."

"Why will I need it? We'll all travel together." Katelyn kept her face pressed to the crack in the barn wall.

"You always need food and water." Won stood on her toes to try and see over Katelyn's head. "Can you see the white men?"

She gave an excited yelp. "I can! I can see them now. They're sitting down to eat!" Twisting her hands in the heavy cotton dress, she watched the men shovel spoon after spoon of Won's clam soup into their mouths. "How long ago did Mekollaan and the others go?"

"Just after you went inside. Cautious Wind will return soon. He will carry word when you go back into the jail."

Katelyn turned to her large friend. "Where will you be?"

"With you," Won answered evenly.

"Oh, no. I said I was doing this alone." She rested a hand on her hip.

"I will wait for you outside the jail place. Mekollaan says you must be protected." Won turned to nod at Cautious Wind who had just slipped in the back.

Katelyn nodded in agreement. "This is fair, I suppose." Then, without warning, she spotted frenzied movement through the window of the jailhouse. "Look! Quick!" she elbowed Won in the side. "Here they come." She giggled with glee.

When the jailhouse door swung open, Katelyn and Won were already out of the barn and coming around the corner. Slipping into the shadows, they covered their mouths to keep from laughing out loud. The first man was the tall thin one Katelyn had seen sitting at the card table. He leaped off the step, groaning and then raced around the back of the jailhouse, his knees knocking together. A few moments later, the other card player followed behind, heading for the necessary built in the back. Then finally came the red-faced jailor, and he was the most amusing of them all.

"My God! My God!" the man cried, running from the jailhouse, with one hand covering his mouth and the other holding his stomach. "Out of the way! Out of the way!" he moaned as he rounded the corner out of sight.

The moment he disappeared, Katelyn touched Cautious Wind on the back. "Run! Tell Hawk that all is well and he should light the fires." She gave him a push, waiting until he disappeared before she started across the street.

Stealthily, Katelyn and Won crossed the street in the darkness, keeping their eyes open for any movement. Won thought the jailors would be occupied for some time, but there was no telling how long it would be before someone else was sent to guard the prisoners. They were never, as a rule, left unattended. The head jailor actually lived in part of the jailhouse.

When they reached the door, Won gave Katelyn a quick squeeze on the shoulder and let her go. Katelyn bolted through the open door and raced down the hallway. Jerking the keys off the peg on the wall, she reached Tipaakke's cell.

"You've done it," he cheered, hanging on to the wooden bars that separated them.

Katelyn fumbled with the keys, trying to get one in the massive iron lock. It was so hot, she was suffocating! Why couldn't she get the key in the hole? Ripping the black, silk bonnet off her head, she sent it flying through the air. Freshly washed curls of deep red fell to her shoulders creating a curtain of fiery contrast against the gray, drab gown. "I can't get it! I can't get it!" she repeated over and over again, her hands shaking.

"Calm yourself, Katie-girl." Tipaakke's voice was warm, but insistent. "We have plenty of time."

"We don't have time," she moaned, shoving another key into the lock.

"Hey, what goes here?" The blond prisoner pressed his face to the bars that separated his cell from Tipaakke's. His eyes grew round when he saw the keys in Katelyn's hands. "You gettin' us out of here, preacher lady?"

"Not you, I'm not!" she spit, wrenching the key this way and that. Why wouldn't it open?

"What, you don't think I'm as good as that red bastard?" He gripped the wooden bars tightly, his face twisted in anger.

"Take the key out and put it in again," Tipaakke encouraged from behind the bars.

Katelyn pushed back her hair out of her face and inserted the key again. "Come on! Come on," she coaxed. This time the key began to ease right, click, clicking as she turned it. "It's coming," she murmured under her breath. "Just a little further . . ." Then with one final clank, the heavy lock fell open. For a moment Katelyn just stared at it, then she was ripping it out of the door and throwing up the wooden bar that kept the door shut.

Two steps and she was in Tipaakke's arms. Her chest heaved with terror as she clung to him. "I was so afraid I would never see you again," she cried. "They were going to kill you, Henry was going to have you hung."

"Shhhh," Tipaakke hushed, stroking the back of her head with his palm. It felt so strange to him to have her body pressed against him like this, with her protruding stomach rubbing against him. He dropped a hand to run it over the firm roundness, and she laughed, covering his hand with her own. "The child is so large," he murmured against her hair.

"Won says it will be a son." She peered up at him through a veil of damp, dark lashes. "My time is very near. Won says we will be lucky if we get back to the village in time." She smiled up at him.

"Hey you, preacher woman!" The blond prisoner moved to the front of his cell. "You're an Injun lover are you?" His eyes narrowed and his lip curled to one side. "You better let me out of here, bitch, because I've seen you, I've seen your face. I'll be tellin' the judge just who let the savage out."

Katelyn turned to look over Tipaakke's shoulder, her face hardening. "Why should I let you out?" she taunted.

"Cause you let him out," the prisoner snapped back.

She released Tipaakke, coming around to the cell. "Tell me something . . ." she raised an eyebrow, inquiring his name.

"Nathan, Nathan Michaels." His eyes gleamed at the thought of cheating the hangman.

"Tell me, Nathan." Katelyn step close to him. "Did you attack and rape that woman?"

"Hell, yeah," he replied, smiling wickedly. "But I reckon that ain't worth hangin' for."

Nonchalantly, Katelyn picked the ring of keys up off the floor, and returned them to the peg, casting a smug look at Nathan. "Guess we disagree."

Tipaakke grabbed Katelyn's hand and yanked her down the hall. "Enough, woman. Let's go!"

"Hey! Come back here!" the prisoner screamed after them. "Let me out of here, you Injun lovin' bitch!"

When Katelyn and Tipaakke appeared at the door of the jailhouse, Won waved them into the street. "Hurry!" she ordered in Algonquian. "The Hawk and his braves have lit haystacks on fire at the end of the main street. There are already white men running everywhere."

"Which way do we go?" Tipaakke questioned, holding tightly to Katelyn's hand.

"Up this hill, cross their main road by the water and between the great red houses. Katelyn knows the way, she will take you."

"What about you, Won, aren't you coming?" She reached out to grasp her friend's arm in the darkness.

"I stay here and watch for sick, fat jailor, then I come behind you when you are safely across the white man's road." Won waved a hand. "Now run, my friends. I can take care of this man with his loincloth down, if he comes."

Tipaakke tugged on Katelyn's arm. "Come love. Won will follow behind, we must hurry."

Katelyn's eyes searched his for a moment and then she nodded. "You're right." She looked back at Won who had flattened her body against the brick building and was creeping around the corner to get a look at the ill jailors. "We will wait for you at the edge of the woods."

Won nodded, motioning them to go and slipped around the corner of the jailhouse.

"Let's go," Katelyn whispered. "This way." Clutching Tipaakke's hand in hers, she headed up the side street.

Katelyn ran as fast as she could, up the brick

sidewalk, cradling her abdomen with one hand. Tipaakke ran beside her, guiding her with a hand, trying to help her keep her balance on the uneven bricks. In the distance they could see the smoke rising above houses and the light from a furious blaze. The sound of men shouting and wagons being pulled up the street with water barrels filled their ears. Then, just as they were reaching the end of the side street, someone stepped out of the Customs House.

At the sound of feet beating on the brick walk, Henry Bullman pulled a flintlock pistol from beneath his red coat. Tipaakke slowed to a walk, but continued up the path, holding tightly to Katelyn's hand. Katelyn swallowed hard, the pounding of her heart seeming audible. What were they going to do?

As Henry's eyes adjusted to the darkness of the street, he pulled back the hammer, chuckling deep in his throat. "So, we meet again, do we?"

Katelyn was turning deathly pale as they grew nearer to the smirking murderer. But calmly, as they walked, she slipped her hand down her leg, feeling for the knife she had strapped to her thigh before she left the campsite. From the look in Henry's eyes, she knew Fox was going to do it.

"Let us pass," Tipaakke ordered quietly. "I have what I wanted from you. And we know who killed the dark boy. There is no need for you to kill us. I will not speak of it again."

Henry laughed, walking towards them. "You think I care what you say, animal?" His face was contorted with power, as he waved the pistol this way and that. "We already saw what your word was worth, didn't we?"

"Henry, please, just walk away," Katelyn begged. "He's going to kill you. Do you want to die?" she screamed.

420

"He's not going to kill me, you stupid bitch! I've got the gun. I'm going to shoot him right in the middle of the forehead." He stopped only a few feet from where Tipaakke and Katelyn stood. "The question is, what am I going to do with you?"

"Just let us go, Henry," she pleaded. "If you take him on, you'll not survive." She could feel Tipaakke tensing his muscles beside her; she could hear his breathing becoming more shallow. He was preparing himself for battle, and he would not lose this one.

"Just shut your face, bitch. I'll deal with you in a minute."

"Do not speak to my wife in that manner," Tipaakke commanded, his voice deathly low. He released Katelyn's hand. "Get back," he whispered in Algonquian.

"Please, Fox. Don't do this, don't kill him." She pulled at his arm. "Please, let's just run."

"Your wife!" Henry shouted. "She isn't your wife." He pointed the pistol at her chest. "She was supposed to be my wife! My father got her for me. She was supposed to be mine!" His face was turning bright red, his chest heaving with rage. "And you took her and ruined her!"

Tipaakke could tell by look on the man's face and by the tone of his voice, that he was no longer in control of himself. Something strange and distorted was driving him mad. He hated to kill Henry if he was possessed by evil spirits, but he would have no choice if the man attacked them. "I said get back, Katelyn," he ordered sharply.

Katelyn released Tipaakke's arm, stepping to the side as she eased her knife from beneath her skirt. Anger was replacing her fear. How dare Henry speak of her like that, like she was some object that could just be passed from man to man. She could almost kill him herself. "What do you want me for?" she dared.

421

"Hush-Katie-girl," Tipaakke warned. "He is touched in the head. Do not anger him further."

Katelyn ignored Tipaakke, taking a step closer to Henry. "Well, can't you speak? Tell me! Tell the Fox and me what you would want with me." She got right up in his face, spitting fire.

"Shut up!" Henry urged in a strained voice, as he shook his head to and fro. "I told you to keep your mouth shut, you Indian lovin' whore!"

"Answer me, Henry Bullman," she taunted. "Tell me what you think you'd do with me if you had me." Her voice reached a threatening crescendo. "I don't look much like a young stable boy, do I?"

"I said shut up, bitchin' whore!" Henry screamed lunging forward to grab her around her neck, knocking her knife from her hand.

Katelyn screamed, struggling as Henry raised the pistol to her temple, holding her against his body. "Let go of me, Henry. This is so foolish."

"Yes," he told her, looking up to the Indian. "I think maybe this is a better idea." He tightened his hold on Katelyn, putting pressure on her throat until she struggled to breathe. "I think I'll kill her here in front of you," he told Fox. "And let them hang you tomorrow on schedule."

"Henry," Katelyn gasped, "that will make you a murderer as well. You'll hang beside him." She was beginning to get dizzy from lack of sufficient oxygen.

Tipaakke flexed his fingers, watching Henry Coward's every movement. The poor fool would make a mistake, and then the Fox would have him. He growled deep in his throat. He would have let the deranged man live; he would have let him walk away, but he had made his fatal mistake. He should never have laid a hand on Katelyn. Now, this confused, cowardly white man would pay for that mistake with his life.

"I won't hang for your death," Henry told Katelyn, laughing. "I'll just say he did it." He pointed to Tipaakke with the pistol before pressing the barrel to her head again.

"You have no wish to kill her," Tipaakke told him in a deadly voice. "She has done you no harm." As he spoke, he inched closer, easing into a crouching, attack position. The knife was too far away to reach.

"Stay back!" Henry screamed. "She's done nothing? She ruined my life! Everything was fine until she came here." Tears were beginning to run down his cheeks. "I was going to be a pillar of the community. The people were going to respect me, they, they . . ." His grasp on Katelyn's neck was loosening as fast as the grip he held on sanity. "Now get back! I see you creepin' closer, like some . . . some wild animal."

The moment Henry waved his pistol, Tipaakke was on him, knocking Katelyn safely to the ground and growling like one of the Heavenly Father's wild creatures. When Tipaakke's near-naked body hit Henry's, it drove him with such force that the pistol shot off, sending its single, lead ball uselessly into the night.

"Help me!" Henry cried as he went down. "Someone help me!" But no one heard his cries. Every able-bodied man in Annapolis was fighting the fire at the other end of town. Everyone who had been in the Customs House had gone to give a hand. Henry had remained behind, saying laughingly, that he wasn't dressed for the occasion.

Katelyn scrambled to her feet, unharmed to see Tipaakke and Henry rolling, entangled, into the street. "Fox! Let him go! He's crazy!" she shouted. "He can't hurt us now." She grabbed the knife off the cold brick, but made no attempt to get it into Tipaakke's hands. She didn't want him to kill Henry, she just wanted to run. "Please, Fox," she begged. "Let him go, someone will come!"

Suddenly, Katelyn spun around. She froze in terror at the sound of pounding feet. "Fox," she screamed, "someone's coming."

"Give me the knife," Tipaakke ordered, pinning Henry to the ground. "Give it to me," he ordered her in Algonquian.

"No! Come on!" She clutched the knife in her hand. "You can't kill him!" Then she heard the call of the whippoorwill and let out a sigh of relief. "Won?" she called into the darkness.

Won appeared from the darkness. "Run!" she warned in Algonquian. "*Uishameheela*, my friends!" She grabbed Katelyn by the arm. "Take your woman, Fox. The fat man comes with his gun breathing fire. I will take care of the coward-man!"

But it was too late, the red-faced jailor was already racing up the dark street, a flintlock rifle under each arm and a two pistols tucked in his drooping breeches. "Come on, Bruce," he shouted. "I see him! I see the red bastard."

Without thought, Won grabbed Katelyn by the back of the neck and started running. Katelyn screamed to Fox as her friend propelled her forward. "Come on. Let him be!"

Tipaakke let go of Henry and got to his feet. Katelyn was right, the coward was not worthy of death. But as the Fox started after Won and Katelyn, Henry got to his feet, throwing his body against Tipaakke's.

At that moment, a shot ran out and Katelyn spun around to see Henry and Tipaakke stumble under the impact of the lead ball and fall to the ground, rolling down a slight incline. "No!" she cried, wrenching herself free from Won to race back to Fox.

"I got him! I got the red bastard!" the jailor shouted over his shoulder as he tripped over the barrel of his flintlock and fell to the ground, spilling his guns all over the street.

The few seconds it took Katelyn to reach Tipaakke seemed to take centuries. "Fox!" she called, tears running down her face. She could hear Won behind her shouting for her to run, but she ignored her friend's pleas. She had no life if Fox was dead . . . let them kill her.

Just as Katelyn reached the tangle of blood-splattered bodies, Fox rose, separating himself from Henry's still body. Throwing his arms out to her, he caught her around the waist and spun her around. "Run," he told her.

Katelyn was laughing and crying at the same time. "What about Henry?" she cried out as they raced passed the Customs House, arm and arm.

"You can't help him," Tipaakke answered shaking his head. "The jailor sent him into the next world."

As they rounded the corner, Won spotted men running up the street, firing rifles. Someone must have finally heard all of the commotion. With the jailor on their heels and the white men coming down the street, Won saw no choice but to head for the wharfs. Signaling to Katelyn and Tipaakke behind her, she darted behind the Customs House and through another yard. "We must lose them," Won whispered as they pressed their bodies against a building, watching hollering, gun-wielding men run by.

Once the men had passed, Won, Katelyn and Tipaakke were able to cross another street and make it to the wharfs. All hell had broken loose by then in Annapolis; men with lanterns and dogs ran shouting in all directions. Guns were going off and the streets were being flooded by women and children. The three would never be able to get through the town. They were cornered at the bay's edge.

"A boat." Won told them. "We will go by boat." A smile crossed her face as she crouched in the shadows on the dock. "There, do you see that one?" She pointed. "They picked up their ropes, they are going."

Katelyn clutched Tipaakke's hand, as they crept down the dock, keeping to the shadows. Watching the two men that picked up line, they moved to the side of the *yawl*. Without a sound, Tipaakke landed on the deck and reached for Katelyn.

"Come on," Katelyn signaled to Won as she landed safely beside Fox on the boat.

But Won just shook her head, turning to speak to Tipaakke. "Here is my knife, Fox. take it." She tossed it to him. "Katelyn's is back in her bag. She has food and water."

Tipaakke nodded crouching in the shadows. Across the mound of covered crates, men moved about tending lines. "We will ride until we are safely away from these lawmen and then we will make the sailors put us on shore."

Won smiled. "On my own, I can lead these baying hounds on a chase and then I will vanish into the night." She put out her hand to Tipaakke. "I am glad to see you again, my friend."

Tipaakke squeezed her hand. "Thank you. We will not forget what you have done for us."

Won laughed, withdrawing her hand. "I had forgotten what it was to run naked through the night scaring the white men. I should not spend so much time in my wigwam baking cakes for my son." She kissed her palm and held it up to Katelyn. "I will see you in the village in a day or two. Do not be long or your child will be born in the forest with no one to attend to you but that worthless man of yours." Still chuckling to herself, she disappeared into the darkness.

Crawling on their hands and knees, Tipaakke and

426

Katelyn hid themselves on the *yawl* among the crates and parcels covered with oiled canvas. Moving silently, they crawled between the packing boxes until they found a roomy alcove near the center of the deck.

"Someone must have forgotten a crate," Katelyn whispered, having a seat on the deck and stretching out her feet. In a sitting position, the canvas cover just cleared their heads by a few inches. Here they would be safe and dry until Tipaakke deemed it safe to go ashore.

"It looks like it," Tipaakke replied, still on his hands and knees.

For a moment, a silent awkwardness stretched between them. So much had happened since they had last been in each other's arms. Yet as their eyes met, it suddenly seemed as if it had only been yesterday that they had clung to each other in the cave on the bank of the stream, making love until the sun shone high above. Had all of this really happened, Katelyn wondered. Had the Mohawks captured Tipaakke again? Had Henry really locked her up in that terrifying ice house? Had Tipaakke honestly believed she had betrayed his love? Or was it just a bad dream? Everything suddenly seemed jumbled in her mind. Slowly, she reached her arms out to him. "Tipaakke?" she murmured.

His heavenly black eyes never left hers as he crawled to her, taking her in his arms. "I never thought I would hold you again," he breathed against her hair.

Katelyn buried her face in his shoulder, clinging to him. "It's been so long, Fox . . . so long. I thought you were gone. I didn't think we could ever get you out of their hands."

"I knew you would do it, Katie-girl." He touched the end of her nose playfully with a finger. "With you, Won, and Mekollaan on my side, they didn't have a

427

chance."

Katelyn laced her fingers through his dark hair, reacquainting herself with his once familiar body. She ran her hand over his chin, giggling. "You have need of a clam shell, I would say, your face grows as hairy as a bear's." Actually, his beard was rather sparse, but she had grown use to the feel of his smooth cheek against her own.

Tipaakke examined his chin. "I am sorry, Madame Wolf-woman, but I have been busy trying to catch up with my wife. She will do anything to keep from sharing my mat; she will send the Mohawks to carry me off; she will even lock me in a jail and threaten to hang me."

"I am not your wife," Katelyn wagged a finger at him.

"Your are my wife in my heart." He pressed her hand on his chest. "And as soon as we get back to the village, you will be my wife by our laws as well." He kissed each of the tips of her fingers before he released her hand. "Now tell me about my child you carry here like a basket of squash." He stroked her tight stomach covered by the Quaker's gray dress.

"I will, but first you must help me get this thing off before I suffocate!" She got up on her knees, wiggling the dress up to her waist. "My own clothes are in my bag."

Tipaakke helped her get the dress over her head and then threw it in a heap on the boat's deck in the opposite corner of their little hideaway. "I think I like you better like this," he whispered huskily, cradling her in his arms. Even in the darkness, he could make out the faint outline of her sumptuous curves. "My child has made you blossom."

"Your child has made me fat," she teased, toying with a lock of his hair.

Tipaakke ran his hand over and over her stomach, marveling at what a miracle this truly was. "I have missed you, my son," he murmured, his lips pressed against her.

"How do you know it's a son?"

"Won said it was a son." He laid an ear on her round belly, listening. "He says he is a son."

"Won does not know everything." She laid back, resting her head on her skin bag. It felt so good to have him stroke the tight skin that itched day and night. "Maybe it is a daughter."

Tipaakke turned back to her, his face more serious. "You know it matters not. I would love a son or a daughter equally. There are advantages to having them both."

"I don't know what I want," she answered thoughtfully.

He crawled up, laying his head on one full breast. "Then we will just have to have one of each."

"Please. Let me have this one first. I have heard women's tales of childbirth before. I may not want any more if I live through the first."

Tipaakke propped himself up on an elbow. "Katie-girl, there's no need to fear bringing a child into the world among our people." He brushed her hair over her forehead, knowing she really was afraid. "There is no pain. Won will do magic with her teas. You will feel nothing but the joy of bringing another soul to our people. And after the child is born, you will be cared for by the other women of our tribe." He smiled down at her. You will not even have to make my evening meal. Others will bring for us for more than a moon so that we can be together."

Katelyn let out a sigh of relief. "My people think a woman must suffer in childbirth because of the sins she has committed." Then another thought crossed her

429

mind. "We will be moving soon! How can I have the baby if we are traveling?"

"I do not know when we are to leave. Soon I think; I will talk with Father and Mekollaan when I return. But, do not worry, you will be cared for. We will make a litter and carry you if we must, just like one of the old ones." He leaned to kiss the lips that were tempting him so. "You have heard that my brother and I will rule our people when my father has passed into the next world?"

"I have," she whispered, flicking out her tongue to taste his. "And I am so proud of my brave that my heart bursts with joy." She laced her hands through his hair, guiding him into a deeper kiss.

"Oh, Katie-girl, I thank Manito each day for you." He planted soft, fleeting kisses here and there on her face.

"I guess we really were meant to be together after all we've been through." She ran her hands over his bare back, noting the healing scars. She would not ask him about them now, but some night, as they lay telling stories before the firelight, she would have him tell her all that had happened after they separated in the woods that day.

"I told you, my heart;" her voice joined with his and in unison they spoke, laughing, "It was in the stars."

Just then, they heard the shout of a man on board the boat. "Cast off your lines," he ordered, "and tend your sheets!"

The merchant *yawl* gave a groan, and Katelyn and Fox felt it pull from the dock. Men shuffled back and forth on the deck as the mid-sized vessel began to rock and they eased away from land.

"How do we know where they're taking us?" Katelyn's eyes grew wide with concern and she sat up.

"We don't, but later we will sneak out of here and see what direction the wind takes us. Don't worry love, I could find my way home from anywhere on the great bay's shore."

"We can't go too far, Won says the baby will come any day." The boat rocked beneath them, making her uneasy.

"You worry too much, squaw," Tipaakke teased, hushing her protests with kisses. "Let me show you how to forget your silly worries."

"Show me," she answered, snaking her arms around his neck. "And let me show you how I love you."

Tipaakke laughed huskily as his mouth twisted hungrily against hers, pressing her to the deck. "So long I have dreamed of this . . ." he uttered against her flushed cheek. "I thought I would never feel you beneath me again."

She laughed, her voice throaty with desire. "Don't think I will be beneath you with this." She ran a hand over her protruding stomach, rolling onto her side. "But we're not going to let that stop us, are we?" She caressed his shoulders, playing lightly on his hard chest as she thrust her knee between his legs, bringing it up hard against his stiffening loins.

Tipaakke twisted his fingers in her hair, bruising her lips with his as she moved her knee against him, shooting hot flames of wanting through his starved body. "Ah, Katie-girl," he rasped as her head dropped to taunt one hard male nipple, "you are a vixen."

Katelyn ran her hands over his sleek, taunt muscles with a frenzied awakening. It had been so long since she had felt him within her! But first, she wanted to touch him, to feel his naked flesh against hers. She wanted to mold her body upon his until they melted into one.

Moving her knee rhythmically, she reached down to tug at the strings of Tipaakke's loincloth and he groaned, lifting his hips as her finger traced an intricate pattern over the soft leather. She taunted him with her fingers until he rolled his head to and fro, calling out to her in his ancient tongue.

Moans of pleasure filled Katelyn's ears, bringing a moistness between her thighs as she slowly removed the loincloth and lowered her head to the patch of crisp, dark hair that lay between his legs. Inhaling his haunting male scent, she pressed hot, wet kisses against his damp flesh, licking, taunting, nibbling until his breath came in short gasps and his hips rose and fell in a familiar dance of love.

"Come here, my heart," he groaned, holding out his arms, "or there will be nothing left of me for you."

She came to him, a hint of a smile on her face, and settled in the crook of his arm. She wrapped a hand around his flat stomach, holding her breath as his hand settled over one aching breast. She sighed, her eyelids drifting shut in anticipation as he caught one pink nipple between his finger and thumb and rolled it, coaxing it to a pert peak.

"*Ia- taakke, shiite-ia-min,*" he whispered huskily. "You are so beautiful, so hot beneath my touch." He lowered his head to touch a her hard, puckered nipple with the tip of his tongue, and all conscious thought slipped from her mind.

"Fox," she breathed, tangling her fingers in his ebony hair, guiding his mouth closer. "I've missed you so . . ." Her breath came faster and she arched her back, moving her thighs against his leg as he slipped it between hers. Tangled together, they writhed in pleasure, giving and taking until their movements grew frenzied with excitement.

Forcing his mouth hard on hers, Tipaakke slipped a hand to the core of her womanhood and she moved against him in encouragement. His tongue explored the hot, wet cavern of her mouth as his fingers parted her soft petals and stroked her steamy flesh until she whimpered with pleasure.

"Please, Tipaakke," she murmured against his ear. "You torture me, my love."

"Torture is pain, my heart," he answered dropping kisses on her round belly. "I do not give you pain, do I?" He brushed his fingers over her thighs, letting her catch her breath.

She laughed, digging her fingernails into his shoulders. "I don't know, I don't know anything anymore . . ." Her body jerked at the first touch of his mouth on the soft triangle of curls, but then she relaxed, letting the waves of pleasure wash over her as his darting tongue drove her higher and higher on each crest. "Fox, please." She tugged at his arms. "I need you." She could barely breath; her heart was pounding, her entire body aching with want.

"We have all night, my heart, let me love you," he whispered through the darkness, his voice hushed and caressing.

So Katelyn lay back, resting on the deck in their little alcove, and let him tease her higher and higher until her whole body throbbed with pleasure. Then with one great burst of firelight, she came floating back to earth, all thoughts, all feelings shattered into a million spiraling pieces.

When Katelyn finally lifted her heavy lashes, she found Tipaakke leaning over her, his hand playing lightly on her breast. "Have I killed you?" he teased.

She stared at him through the darkness, unable to resist his smile. "No, you didn't kill me, though you almost did." She lifted her chin to accept his lips. They tasted of both of them, of two loves that mingled together. "But you should have told me to keep quiet. It's a wonder one of those sailors hasn't stuck his head under here to see what all of the commotion was

433

about."

Tipaakke brushed her crimson cheeks with his fingertips. "Sounded like nothing but a kitten's mewing, my heart."

Katelyn rested her head on his chest, running her hand over his hard thighs. "I think you lie. I'm just glad the waves and the sails make so much noise."

For a few moments they lay in silence, listening to the sound of the waves beat and swoosh against the hull and to the sound of their own breathing.

Boldly, Katelyn reached down to caress Tipaakke's manhood, a twinkle in her eyes.

"I thought we were going to sleep now?" His eyes drifted shut and his tongue darted out to dampen his lips.

"Oh, we will," she cooed, leaning to take his hardening nipple in her mouth. "Soon."

Taunting and teasing, until Tipaakke's breath came fast again, Katelyn led him down the path of pleasure. Using his methods, and some of her own, she drove him to near madness before she finally crawled astride him. Accepting the full evidence of his love deep within her, Katelyn laced his fingers in her own, and began to move against him, sending hot sparks of fulfillment through her own trembling body.

Moving faster, she flattened against him as best she could, burying her face in his dark hair as she cried out his name. Guiding her movement with his hands on her hips, the two moved in perfect harmony, giving and taking until they drove madly towards their destiny.

Half sobbing, Katelyn sat up, moving with a final thrust as he spilled into her sending her to another shattering climax. Exhausted and panting, she collapsed on top of him, unsure whether to laugh or cry.

Tipaakke lay quietly, his arms encircling Katelyn's waist. Once her breathing became regular again, she lifted her head off his shoulder, and smiled down at him, moving off him to rest at his side. Both were still in awe of the joyous, throbbing pleasure that had coursed through their veins.

"Will it always be like this?" Katelyn whispered in the darkness, her voice lilted with sleepy satisfaction.

"Always," Tipaakke replied, brushing back dark-red strands of hair that stuck to her damp cheek. "We will never tire of each other. Each time we lay on the mat it will be new and beautiful." He propped himself up on an elbow to peer down at her. "You take my breath away . . . you rob my soul." He planted a whisper of a kiss on her love-bruised lips. "You have cast a magical spell over me, Wolf-woman; I am drugged by your love potion." He spoke in English to be sure she understood every word.

Katelyn smoothed his lips with her fingertips. "I love you," she told him, placing a hand over his heart. "I have always been yours, and always will be."

With those final words, she snuggled against Tipaakke's side and drifted off into a luxuriously peaceful sleep, the merchant ship rocking her, lulling her, like a babe in its cradle. She was safe in her lover's arms, safe at last.

With the coming of morning, Katelyn woke slowly, happy to drift in the memories of the previous night. Stretching like a wild cat, she eased her eyes open to find Tipaakke sitting at her feet.

"Why didn't you wake me?" Sunlight burst beneath the tarp through cracks in the canvas casting a heavenly light on Tipaakke's bronze skin. His hair framed his face with a sleek, black halo, emphasizing his chiseled face. He was the most beautifully masculine man Katelyn thought she'd ever seen in her life. *And he's all mine*, a voice whispered deep within her.

"You needed to sleep. I know it's been a long time

since you slept well." He laughed. "It's been a long time since I've slept so well." He got to his knees, his head brushing the tarp as he dug in her skin bag.

"Do you know where we are, Fox?" She really didn't want to ask, but she had to.

He nodded, handing her the water skin. "The great Manito's hand guides this boat. He has brought us a little closer to our village."

"How do you know?" Katelyn handed the skin back, wiping a dribble of water from her chin with the back of her hand.

"I was out on the deck just before the dawn's light. The shore is to our left, the sun rises at my right, we move north along the shore. The boat must be carrying this cloth to another port further up river." He pulled a handful of squashed berries from the bag, offering them to her. "When we reach shore, we will eat a better meal."

She took the berries without fuss; she didn't care what kind of shape they were in, she was starved. She was always starved! "They're carrying cloth?" She looked at the wooden crate to her side. "You opened one of their boxes?"

"Looking for food." He handed her a dry corncake. "How far do you think you can swim?"

"What?" Her eyes grew round as she reached for the water skin. "I'd probably sink like a stone in this condition." She motioned to her bare, round belly.

"I figure we are too far from shore." He took a sip of water from the skin and tucked it back in the bag. "We will make them take us closer. Here are your clothes." He tossed her the leather jerkin and woman's breech-cloth that had been in the bag.

"We'll what?" She pulled her jerkin over her head, slapping his hand away playfully, when he reached to stroke her bare breast.

"We will ask the sailors to take us ashore." He pulled Won's long gleaming knife from the bag. "I think they will do it."

Katelyn shook her head, kneeling to tie the soft doeskin breechcloth around middle. "I thought we were done with the adventures." She rolled her eyes.

"How did you think we were going to get off of here?" Tipaakke swung the bag over his shoulder, preparing to crawl out.

"I was kind of hoping they'd just pull into port and we'd get off." She gave him a silly little grin.

Laughing and shaking his head, he leaned to kiss her softly on the lips. "Come out when I call you." He slipped her his knife. "Try to act like a crazed Indian, it scares white men."

Letting out a sigh, Katelyn watched Tipaakke crawl down the narrow passageway between the crates and disappear into the sunlight.

When Tipaakke reached the sunlight, he crouched waiting for the proper moment. He had counted four men on board, with a possibility of a fifth. Odds were, one would pass by, and when he did, Fox would pounce. Sure enough, only a few moments later, a pair of skinny legs in cut-off breeches passed by.

"Holy Saints alive," Christopher Burtles breathed aloud as the savage wrapped his hands around Chris' neck and pressed the knife's blade to his jugular.

Tipaakke gave him the evil-snake eye, as Mekollaan called it, enjoying himself immensely. "Get captain," he ordered in his best savage voice.

"Marty! Marty, old boy, you best be gettin' yourself on deck!" the boy shouted, quivering in his ill-fitting boots.

A moment later a round, middle-aged man with a bald head appeared from the hold. He never even flinched at the sight of the loinclothed Delaware brave standing on his deck. "Need something, Chris?" He eased his hand to the left, hoping to make contact with the pistol on his belt.

"Do not touch the gun, or your man will die," Tipaakke ordered as three other men clambered from below. "I will hurt no one if you do as Tipaakke Oopus says." He narrowed his eyes. "Do you understand?"

Marty looked the Indian brave square in the face. He wasn't like most of the men in these parts, he had kind of an admiration for these red men. The brave was calm and collected. As long as he did as he was told, he surmised there would be no trouble. "Stand to come by port," he shouted to the men behind him. Watching them scramble, he chuckled. "Watch your heads lads, least your wives become widows. Handsomely," he bellowed to his helmsman. "Tend your boom-vangs." As the *yawl* came about, the Captain shouted one last command. "Steady her broad to starboard!" Then he moved lazily to lean one arm on a covered crate, looking back at the brave. "So tell me, how'd you get on here anyway?"

"Walked." Tipaakke gave him a crazy grin. He and Mekollaan had always enjoyed toying with the white men, playing the role of the savage could be so humorous. They had a great time acting the way the white men thought they should, but teasing with their minds at the same time. It had been a game since boyhood.

"Got on at Annapolis, did you?" Marty stroked his red beard. "You wouldn't possibly be the Indian they were supposed to be hanging this morning?"

"I did not kill the dark boy." Tipaakke replied, loosening his grip on the young mate's neck. There was going to be no trouble, he could tell by the look on the captain's face.

"No." Marty shook his head. "Don't believe you did.

438

Whole story sounded pretty damned strange to me." He turned to eye the nearing shore. "Can't take you much further or we'll hit bottom. Tides low though, you won't have to swim far."

Tipaakke nodded. "Thank you." Then he called in Algonquian, beckoning Katelyn.

When Katelyn appeared from beneath the cover tarp, dressed in a man's leather shirt with her stomach protruding, Marty blinked and then smiled. "Heard about her. If she was mine I'd be taking her back, too."

Katelyn walked slowly to stand beside Fox, her own knife clutched in her hand. All looked as if it were going well. Tipaakke seemed relaxed and the boat was heading toward shore.

A few moments passed and then the Captain spoke again. "Bring her into the wind, mates," he shouted. He turned back to Tipaakke. "You can let the lad go, you see we'll not harm you. This is close as I can bring you without riskin' my cargo."

Tipaakke loosened his hold on the boy's neck, releasing him. "Come," he told Katelyn in Algonquian, ushering her to the port side.

The Captain followed them, keeping a safe distance, "Good luck to you." He offered his hand. "If anyone asks in Annapolis, the boys and I saw nothing, heard nothing."

Tipaakke let go of Katelyn and grasped the Captain's hand. "Thank you. I have nothing with me to give to you in token of my gratitude, only words."

Marty tightened his hold on the red man's hand. "Thanks is enough. Good luck to you."

Taking Katelyn's hand, he turned to face the water. "It's not too deep," he told her just as they went over the side. "Just hang onto my hand."

Leaping away from the side of the boat, Katelyn surfaced, her fingers still laced in Tipaakke's. Floating on their backs, they turned to wave to the boat and then started for shore at an easy pace.

Early in the evening, Katelyn and Tipaakke wandered into the Lenni Lenape village, hand in hand. As they entered the compound friends and relatives swarmed around them, laughing and teasing, overjoyed to have their chiefs-to-be among them again.

As Katelyn was ushered to a fireside to eat and drink with the women, she couldn't help but remember how different this reception was from a year ago. Dogs still ran and barked, naked children still raced in circles around the wigwams, and the bare-breasted Lenni Lenape women still reached out to stroke her hair, even her round stomach. But it all seemed different now. Black eyes were more familiar than her own; their language more soothing to her ears.

Sitting cross-legged in front of a wigwam, Katelyn ate from a clam shell, talking with Won and the other women. Everyone was so kind to her; by becoming Tipaakke's chosen mate, she was instantly adopted into the tribe. Waving to Tipaakke as he made his way through the men to his father's wigwam, she flashed him a smile. "I'm all right," she mouthed, and threw him a kiss.

Late into the evening Tipaakke remained in his father's wigwam, in council with Mekollaan and the elders. By the time Fox's head appeared from beneath the leather doorflap, Katelyn was ready to go home. Home to their wigwam, to lie on the sleeping platform in her love's arms.

"You look sleepy," Tipaakke told her, accepting a slice of fried fish from one of the squaws. He squatted beside Katelyn, his knee brushing against her leg. "So how long do you think, Won?" He pointed to Katelyn's stomach.

Won nodded her head. "Soon, very soon, I say. So-

Falls-The-Water says the baby will come in a day or two." She moved around the small cooking fire, picking up dirty utensils.

Katelyn tried to get to her feet, moving awkwardly. "I'll sure be glad when I'm carrying this baby in my arms and not around my middle."

Tipaakke jumped up to take her hand and help her to her feet. "Come, love," he crooned in Algonquian. "Let us find our sleeping mats."

Thanking the woman for the hospitality, and giving Won a quick kiss on the cheek, Katelyn started across the compound leaning heavily against Tipaakke. "It's so beautiful here," she murmured, glancing at the neat circle of wigwams. "I know it is hard for you to leave." She stared into his dark eyes, mesmerized by their kindness. It was hard to believe that she had once been so afraid of him.

"It is hard," he told her in his own tongue. "It is hard because our children will not run across the same grass my grandfather ran on. They will not fish and drink from the same streams. But life is not always just as we want it. Our land changes, so we must change." He rubbed his cheek against hers, inhaling deeply. She smelled of the campfire, a clean, woodsy scent. She smelled like one of them.

"I think it will be better for you and I to go, though, don't you?" She ducked through the doorflap of his wigwam. "Away from the white men, I mean."

Tipaakke dropped the leather flap closed. The wigwam had been swept and dusted, the woven floor mats and blankets aired out. Someone had even taken the time to spread crumbled herbs on the floor, filling the air with a spicy fresh scent.

"Yes," Tipaakke whispered as he took her in his arms. The light of a three-quarters moon shone through the whole in the wigwam roof, casting dim, dancing shadows over them. "It will be better for us. We will go to the Ohio to live with our Shawnee cousins. There we will be safe, safe from their prying eyes. Once we cross the river we will set foot on land no white man has ever stood on. Among our cousins, our children will be able to grow up without fear of their village being burned and their parents being killed."

Katelyn tightened her arms around Tipaakke's neck. "When do we leave; I am ready to go." She stared at him through a veil of dark lashes.

"Now? You are ready to go now, tonight?" He tipped back his head to fill the wigwam with laughter. "Are you going alone? The rest of the tribe is not ready; they have just begun to pack for our journey. Besides, don't you think you'd better wait on this? He ran his hand over her stomach, smoothing her leather jerkin.

"Well," she teased. "Maybe a day or two." Threading her fingers through his heavenly black hair, she guided his mouth to hers.

"We should go to bed now, my heart," he murmured against her lips. "Tomorrow will be your wedding day."

Katelyn pressed her body close to his, running a finger down Tipaakke's bare thigh. "It *is* time to go to bed, my brave warrior . . . but not to sleep."

Epilogue

Ohio Country
1721

Katelyn raced through the flower-strewn meadow, clutching the cradleboard to her chest. Laughing, she ducked behind a grandfather pine to see Tipaakke coming across the field after her.

"Come back here," Fox shouted, as he leaped comically in the air, jolting his daughter he held balanced on his shoulders. "Come back here, Wolf-woman."

The little red-haired girl burst into giggles, beating her father on the head to make him move faster. "Catch her, Father!" she told him. "Run faster or she's going to win again!"

Rounding the tree, Katelyn broke into a run again, heading for the great river bank. "I'm the winner!" she shouted, jumping up and down. "Mama and little Kukuus win!"

Tipaakke swung Rain-Dropping-Softly to the ground, letting her run to her mother. The little girl hit her mother going full force and collapsed at her feet in another fit of giggles. "I think I will play on your side next time, Mama and let little brother race with Father. He's so turtle slow!" She looked up at her

443

mother with big black eyes, tugging at a fiery braid with her teeth.

"Slow? Slow am I?" Tipaakke tweaked her nose before reaching for the cradleboard Katelyn held out to him. "Next time you will run on your own, my little shiny stone."

Rain-Dropping-Softly tugged at her mother's short doeskin skirt. "May I go and skip stones, may I Mama?"

"You may, but no swimming without your father. The current runs too swiftly." She pulled the braid from her daughter's mouth and gave her a pat on the bottom. "Go with you." Turning back to Tipaakke, tears welled in Katelyn's eyes as she watched her husband smooth his young son's cheek with a finger. The Heavenly Father had been good to them, two healthy children in three years. But then children here on the Ohio were much healthier than those living nearer to the white men.

Tipaakke hung his sleeping son's cradleboard on the branch of a tree and reached his arms out for Katelyn. "Hurry, my wife. We have a moment alone."

She laughed, throwing herself into his arms, her full, bare breasts pressed against his chest. She had come to accept the Delaware custom of wearing only a skirt in the hot summer months, and was quite comfortable like this now. "Shhhhh . . ." She put a finger to her lips. "Your son will hear you and he will be awake wanting to eat again." Their lips mingled beneath the great pines, and Katelyn's pulse quickened at the feel of Tipaakke's hand on her breast. "You are worse than your son," she chided playfully. "Release me. I am a respectable Lenni Lenape woman now. I do not roll in the pine needles with strutting braves." Her tongue darted out to lick her moist lips.

"Not even if the brave is one of the chiefs of her

tribe?" He touched her tongue with his fingertip and she bit down on it gently.

"A chief, you say?" She raised a dark eyebrow quizzically. "Perhaps with a chief." This time their lips met more fiercely, and Katelyn strained against his body, pressing her hips to his in an ancient love dance.

Casting an eye in the direction of their playing daughter, Tipaakke eased Katelyn to the ground, cradled in his arms. He laced his fingers through her fox-colored hair and brushed a butterfly kiss over her lips. "Are you happy, my heart?" His voice sang of love, of contentment.

She looked up to see her son's cradleboard swinging over their heads. "I am happy, my heart," she answered in Algonquian.

"No regrets?"

Katelyn reached up to brush a shoulder length lock of black hair off his shoulder, enchanted by the heavenly black eyes that stared down at her. "Only that we did not meet long ago," she whispered.

Now you can get more of HEARTFIRE right at home and $ave.

Preview
Four Brand New
ZEBRA
Heartfire
Romance Novels...

FREE for 10 days.

No Obligation and No Strings Attached!

❤

Enjoy all of the passion and fiery romance as you soar back through history, right in the comfort of your own home.

Now that you have read a Zebra **HEARTFIRE** Romance novel, we're sure you'll agree that **HEARTFIRE** sets new standards of excellence for historical romantic fiction. Each Zebra **HEARTFIRE** novel is the ultimate blend of intimate romance and grand adventure and each takes place in the kinds of historical settings you want most...the American Revolution, the Old West, Civil War and more.

<u>FREE</u> Preview Each Month and $ave

Zebra has made arrangements for you to preview 4 brand new HEARTFIRE novels each month...FREE for 10 days. You'll get them as soon as they are published. If you are not delighted with any of them, just return them with no questions asked. But if you decide these are everything we said they are, you'll pay just $3.25 each—a total of $13.00 (a $15.00 value). **That's a $2.00 saving each month off the regular price.** Plus there is NO shipping or handling charge. These are delivered right to your door absolutely free! There is no obligation and there is no minimum number of books to buy.

TO GET YOUR FIRST MONTH'S PREVIEW... Mail the Coupon Below!

Mail to:

 HEARTFIRE Home Subscription Service, Inc.
120 Brighton Road
P.O. Box 5214
Clifton, NJ 07015-5214

YES! I want to subscribe to Zebra's HEARTFIRE Home Subscription Service. Please send me my first month's books to preview free for ten days. I understand that if I am not pleased I may return them and owe nothing, but if I keep them I will pay just $3.25 each; a total of $13.00. That is a savings of $2.00 each month off the cover price. There are no shipping, handling or other hidden charges and there is no minimum number of books I must buy. I can cancel this subscription at any time with no questions asked.

NAME

ADDRESS   APT. NO.

CITY   STATE   ZIP

SIGNATURE   (if under 18, parent or guardian must sign)   *2083*
Terms and prices are subject to change.

TANTALIZING HISTORICAL ROMANCE
From Zebra Books

CAPTIVE CARESS (1923, $3.95)
Sonya T. Pelton
Denied her freedom, despairing of rescue, the last thing on Willow's mind was desire. But before she could say no, she became her captor's prisoner of passion.

EMERALD ECSTASY (1908, $3.95)
by Emma Merritt
From the moment she arrived in Ireland, Marguerite LeFleur heard the stories of the notorious outlaw. And somehow she knew that it would be him who would teach her the heights of passion.

LOUISIANA LADY (1891, $3.95)
by Myra Rowe
Left an orphan, Leander Ondine was forced to live in a house of ill-repute. She was able to maintain her virtue until the night Justine stumbled upon her by mistake. Although she knew it was wrong, all she wanted was to be his hot-blooded *Louisiana Lady*.

SEA JEWEL (1888, $3.95)
by Penelope Neri
Hot-tempered Alaric had long planned the humiliation of his hated foe's daughter. But he never suspected she would become the mistress of his heart, his treasured, beloved *Sea Jewel*.

MIDNIGHT THUNDER (1873, $3.95)
by Casey Stuart
The last thing Gabrielle remembered before slipping into unconsciousness was a pair of the deepest blue eyes she'd ever seen. Instead of stopping her crime, Alexander wanted to imprison her in his arms and embrace her with the fury of *Midnight Thunder*.

Available wherever paperbacks are sold, or order direct from the Publisher. Send cover price plus 50¢ per copy for mailing and handling to Zebra Books, Dept. 2083, 475 Park Avenue South, New York, N.Y. 10016. Residents of New York, New Jersey and Pennsylvania must include sales tax. DO NOT SEND CASH.